MARVEL

THE TALES OF ASGARD TRILOGY

Also From Joe Books

Marvel Guardians of the Galaxy: Castaways

Marvel Captain America: Sub Rosa

Marvel Guardians of the Galaxy: Space Riot

Marvel Iron Man: Mutually Assured Destruction

Marvel Spider-Man: Enemies Closer

Marvel Avengers: The Serpent Society

MARVEL

THE TALES OF ASGARD TRILOGY

KEITH R.A. DeCANDIDO

JOE BOOKS LTD

Published simultaneously in the United States and Canada
by Joe Books Ltd, 489 College Street, Toronto, ON M6G 1A5

www.joebooks.com

ISBN 978-1-77275-486-5 (print)
ISBN 978-1-77275-542-8 (ebook)

First Joe Books edition: October 2017

MARVEL

Library and Archives Canada Cataloguing in Publication information
is available upon request

Printed and bound in Canada
1 3 5 7 9 10 8 6 4 2

MARVEL

THOR™

DUELING WITH GIANTS

BOOK I
OF THE
TALES OF
ASGARD
TRILOGY

BY
KEITH R.A.
DeCANDIDO

DUELING WITH GIANTS

BOOK 1 OF THE TALES OF ASGARD TRILOGY

KEITH R.A. DeCANDIDO

JOE BOOKS LTD

Dedicated to the memory of Scooter (1999-2015), the best dog in the history of the world. We really miss you, you big galoot . . .

PRELUDE

The skies are sometimes blue, sometimes black, sometimes gray.

When storms come and go on Midgard—which its natives generally call "Terra" or "Earth"—and are followed by sunlight, the sky goes from gray to blue, and the people, if they look up at the right time, are blessed with the sight of a rainbow.

Scientists and teachers will explain that a rainbow is a result of the refraction of the sun's light through the moisture still left in the air from the storm. And while they are right, there is more to it than that.

If humans see a rainbow, then they are getting the briefest look at a much greater tapestry, for they have seen a glimpse of the Bifrost—the rainbow bridge that leads to Asgard.

Asgard and Midgard are but two of the worlds that are linked by Yggdrasil, the great world tree that connects the Nine Worlds to each other.

The lives of the natives of Midgard are but brief, over in an instant. The denizens of Asgard are far longer-lived, and much stronger and more powerful, controlling forces far beyond those of most mortals.

Today, some Asgardians do cross the Bifrost to Midgard,

where they are viewed as "paranormals" or "super heroes"—or, in some cases, "super villains." In this modern age, they are far from the only beings of power who walk Midgard's lands.

A thousand years ago, Asgardians crossed the Bifrost in greater numbers. The peoples of one particular region—some mortals call it "Scandinavia"—did view the Asgardians as gods, and paid them tribute, worshipping them and telling tales of their adventures.

And a thousand years before that, many of those who would be worshipped as gods in adulthood were still children.

On one such day, a blond-haired youth named Thor—the son of Odin, the ruler of Asgard—did approach the Bifrost. A young man named Heimdall had recently been appointed to be the guardian of the rainbow bridge, for his senses were more acute than any other in Asgard. He could see an army gathering from many leagues away, hear their approach, even smell the ointments they used to clean their swords and polish their armor.

And so he had no trouble detecting the approach of young Thor. The boy was carrying a sword and shield and had an eager and happy expression on his face.

"Heimdall!" he cried. "I have heard that the forces of evil will soon attack Asgard!"

"Yes," Heimdall said. "Odin's noble ravens, Hugin and Munin, have reported that there are rumblings of an alliance among many of the foes of Asgard. The Norn Hag, the Rime Giants, the trolls, and the wolf gods are joining forces to do together what they could never accomplish while apart."

Holding up his sword, Thor spoke solemnly. "Then I must defend the Realm Eternal! I am Odin's eldest son, and it is my duty!" Then his face broke into a grin. "Besides, if I do enough good deeds I will earn Odin's uru hammer!"

Heimdall smiled indulgently at the boy. He knew that his younger sister, Sif, thought highly of the lad, and Sif was not one to give her affections to someone unworthy.

But after a moment, Heimdall let his smile fall away, for he had only recently been appointed to this sacred duty. He would not allow Thor to distract him. "Go away, Thor. Rest assured, if any do attack Asgard, I will know it and I will sound the Gjallarhorn."

"And I will be ready by your side when—"

"If you are by my side, you will distract me from my post—as, indeed, you already are." He put a friendly hand on the youth's shoulder. "Go, return to your home. The Gjallarhorn will be heard throughout Asgard, should the rumors be true. When that happens, you may answer the call to arms with everyone else."

Despondent, Thor returned to his home. Odin, of course, was not there—he was always busy in the throne room with affairs of state—but his mother, Frigga, was present.

As always, Thor's mother knew his mood instantly. "What distresses you, my son?" she asked upon his entry.

"I tried to stand by Heimdall at the Bifrost, but he sent me away! I will never earn possession of Father's hammer if I do not perform noble deeds in the service of Asgard!"

"And is that the reason for your desire to stand by the Bifrost, my son?"

Thor frowned. "What do you mean?"

"I simply question whether or not your eagerness to defend the realm comes from a desire to protect the people of Asgard, or because of the trinkets you will be rewarded with if you do."

That brought Thor up short. "But—" He hesitated. "If I am granted Mjolnir, then I will be able to perform my duties more properly!" He held up his sword and shield. "These weapons are strong and true, but compared to Mjolnir they are no better than the wooden training weapons I used as a boy!"

Refraining from pointing out that Thor was *still* a boy, Frigga called her son to her. He placed his sword and shield upon the end table, and then sat next to her on the couch in the grand sitting room of their home. "So you wish a more powerful weapon?"

"Only that I may protect the people better! I may be the ruler of Asgard sometime in the future—should, the fates forfend, something happen to Father . . ."

"Yes," Frigga said quickly, not wishing to dwell on such a possibility. "But in that instance you will rule, not fight."

"But I *must* know that I can protect the people of Asgard as best I can. So I *must* have the hammer!"

"What if you *don't* have the hammer?"

"If I am not considered worthy of Mjolnir, then I am not fit to be Asgard's protector!"

Frigga smiled. "You need not worry, my son. You do not wish

Mjolnir for its own sake, but for its ability to allow you to serve your function greater. *That* is why I am sure you will be granted it—and also why you need not worry about *when* you will be worthy. Your intentions are pure, and all else will derive from that."

Thor smiled at his mother and suddenly leaned over and gave her a huge hug. "Thank you, Mother."

"Now shoo, and leave me in peace."

After retrieving his sword and shield from the end table, Thor said, "Of course, Mother. Again, thank you!"

Thor went toward the rear entrance of the house with a spring in his step. He would use the time practicing with his sword while he waited for Heimdall to sound the Gjallarhorn to signal the coming battle.

As he worked on his parries and his thrusts, Loki suddenly appeared as if from nowhere, startling Thor.

"You would be wise, my brother, not to be so stealthy when approaching one carrying a blade. I would not wish to hurt you by accident—or, indeed, on purpose."

Thor spoke the words with a truly sincere smile, for though Loki was not his blood, he was still kin in all the ways that mattered. Thor had nothing but affection for his brother.

Loki returned the sentiment with a smile that was far from sincere, for he did not share the good feelings of his adoptive brother. He had his own designs on Mjolnir, knowing it would be a valuable tool in his growing ability with spellcraft. But he knew that Thor was going to be the one to get it, barring a catastrophe.

And Loki was definitely the person to provide that catastrophe.

"Mother said you were back here, Thor. I heard that you were trying to find a way to perform good deeds, that our dear father may deem you worthy of his bequeathing Mjolnir upon you."

"Indeed! Heimdall tells me that many of Asgard's greatest foes are gathering and will invade soon. But Heimdall stands true at the rainbow bridge, and he will alert all Asgard when the attack comes."

"Assuming it comes to a place Heimdall can see."

Thor frowned. "What do you mean?"

"I have discovered something. Come with me!" Without even waiting to see if Thor followed, Loki ran back toward the house.

Of course, Thor did follow him. He was compelled to learn what his brother had found.

Loki led him down the spiral stairs to the catacombs, the tunnels that connected this, Odin's home, with the throne room, allowing the All-Father to traverse between his home and his place of rule in relative peace and quiet. After all, if Odin were to stride through the streets of Asgard, he would be a figure of admiration and gawking, and after a long day of responsibility, he wished to be on his way to his dwelling with dispatch.

Thor and Loki had both made use of these tunnels as well, but now Loki was leading Thor down a route he had never gone before.

"I had no idea the catacombs extended so far," Thor said.

"Indeed," was all Loki would say in reply.

The tunnels twisted and turned so many times that soon Thor had completely lost his way. Loki, however, remained sure of foot as he traversed the halls, finally arriving upon a bend.

Thor was surprised to feel a breeze, and when they came 'round the bend, he understood why: there was a great hole in the wall, which led to a grassy plain outside the city walls of Asgard.

"What perfidy is this?" Thor asked, aghast.

Loki smiled. "A quite literal hole in Asgard's defenses. It was mere happenstance that I came upon it while exploring these tunnels. It is possible that Heimdall will still see the hordes coming, but he may not. And if Asgard's foes come through here . . ."

Thor nodded, raising his sword. "You were wise to bring me here, Loki. I will stand fast at this breach and defend Asgard against those who would destroy her."

"Excellent!" Loki clapped Thor on the back. "I knew I could count on you. I will go and fetch assistance."

Loki very carefully waited until he was well out of Thor's earshot before bursting into laughter. The truth was, of course, that he had not so much come upon the hole while exploring the tunnels; rather he was the one who created the hole during those explorations. What's more, he had sent a message to Skoll and Hati, the wolf gods who had brought several of Asgard's greatest foes together to plan an assault. Loki had learned of their secret covenant by his own means, and was determined to help them succeed in their plan to attack—so that Loki himself could drive them away and earn Mjolnir for himself!

But first, he'd need to be rid of his tiresome brother. Mother may have been equal in her affections to them both, but Odin very obviously preferred the blond idiot. Loki would need to make sure that the wolf gods and their allies did their part and took Thor out before Loki could make his own move.

Sure enough, Thor soon found himself face to face with a most impressive collection of foes: the Norn Hag astride Ulfrin the Dragon, accompanied by the wolf gods, and several trolls and Rime Giants.

Never before in his young life had Thor seen so many foes come at him at once. And Loki had not yet returned with the promised reinforcements.

Faced with no alternative, Thor charged forward. Knowing he could not overwhelm so great a force with his strength alone, he instead used his blade to smash a nearby rock that he knew covered a hot spring. The heated water burst forth and knocked the wolf gods aside.

However, those who felt the enchanted breath of Ulfrin the Dragon rarely lived long to speak of it. At the Norn Hag's command, Ulfrin breathed a sickly green smoke that caused Thor's very limbs to grow weak. He dropped his sword, unable to even muster the strength to hold it, much less lift the weapon.

And then he remembered what he had said to Frigga about his duty to Asgard, and how he longed to be worthy of Mjolnir so he could keep Asgard safe.

Shaking off the effects of the dragon's breath, he reached for his sword and struck the beast in the gullet with a mighty blow.

The dragon thrashed in pain, throwing the Norn Hag from its back.

That left only the Rime Giants and the trolls, and soon Thor was fighting them all for his life, as they came at him from all sides.

Just as he believed he would be overwhelmed, just as he was sure that he would die protecting Asgard and be brought to Valhalla far sooner than he'd hoped, he heard a very familiar voice cry out, "For Asgard!"

Looking back, Thor saw that Odin had arrived, with a dozen more warriors by his side.

Within moments, the foes had retreated, unwilling to face so great a foe as Odin, much less his warriors, pledged to die defending him. They had hoped for the element of surprise when Loki came to them with his plan, and now that was lost. The water-soaked wolf gods, the wounded dragon, the humiliated Norn Hag, and the defeated giants and trolls beat a hasty retreat.

Thor knelt down before Odin. "I am sorry, Father, I failed to defend the Realm Eternal."

"I say nay, my son, rise to your feet." Odin smiled beneath his thick white beard. "Heimdall heard the sounds of battle from your sword against the rock, the dragon, and the creatures' weapons and he had us come. You did well—had you not been here to defend this opening, these brigands would have been well within Asgard's borders before we were able to muster a defense."

"It is not just I who should be thanked, Father. 'Twas Loki who brought me to this opening and bade me defend it while he summoned help."

"Did he, now?" Odin shook his head. "I shall have to make sure that Loki receives *all* due credit for his actions this day, then."

Thor went home that night with a happy heart, for he knew he was that much closer to earning Mjolnir.

For his part, Loki's heart was far less happy. His plan had completely failed, and he was upbraided by Odin for not fulfilling his promise to Thor to send for help. Loki pleaded innocent, saying he got lost in the tunnels, but Odin did not appear to believe him.

Despondent, Loki returned home. Frigga was present.

As with Thor, Loki's mother knew his mood instantly. "What distresses you, my son?" she asked upon his entry.

"I had hoped to stop the vanguard of enemies that attacked Asgard today—after they defeated Thor. Then Odin would see that *I* am the one who should wield Mjolnir!"

"You wished Thor to be harmed?"

"Well, perhaps a little," Loki admitted. "I just wanted him defeated so I could show Father that *I* am just as worthy a son as Thor."

"You *are* just as worthy a son, Loki. Remember, Odin *chose* you as his son. He did not do that lightly."

"Perhaps." Loki sat next to Frigga on the couch and folded his arms. "But why does he not see what I can contribute?"

"Because you attempt to show him only through paltry schemes and misdirection! And by endangering your brother, his *other* son. That is *not* the way to Odin's favor."

"Of course, you are correct, Mother. My schemes must be *brilliant*!"

"Loki—"

Rising from the couch, Loki quickly ran from the room. "Thank you, Mother!"

Frigga sighed. No one had said that raising two boys to become heirs to the throne of Asgard would be easy . . .

CHAPTER ONE

When the troll's fist collided with Thor's head, the thunder god was at once surprised, exhilarated, and angered.

The surprise had been ongoing, commencing when the gaggle of trolls first appeared amongst Asgard's gleaming spires. Thor knew not how or why the creatures contrived to invade the home of the gods, but he had pledged long ago to protect the Realm Eternal at all costs. He did so two millennia ago when Loki led him to a hole in the tunnels beneath the city, and he did so now, and no doubt he would do so two millennia hence. Never would Thor shirk his duty to the Realm Eternal. And so from the very moment Heimdall sighted the trolls' invasion with his great vision, Thor took up Mjolnir and joined the fray. There would be time enough to learn the how and why of the incursion by the trolls after the battle was done. Indeed, such an investigation would need to take place, for Heimdall's all-seeing eyes should have detected the trolls' approach long before they got within Asgard's gates.

The exhilaration came from knowing he did not fight alone. His comrades-in-arms were right beside him: Balder the brave, Fandral the dashing, Hogun the grim, Volstagg the voluminous, and the mightiest of shield-maidens, the Lady

Sif. They were the doughtiest warriors a god could ask for to stand by his side, and Thor considered himself fortunate to number them among his friends as well as his battle-mates. Balder, Sif, and the Warriors Three had joined Thor in the square outside the Temple of Titans to face the thirteen trolls who had invaded the city.

The anger derived from the troll who had managed to sneak under Thor's guard and strike him. His winged helmet flew from atop his head, clanging to the ground beside him, and he also lost his grip on Mjolnir as he fell to the paving stones in a heap.

Thor looked up at the troll who had struck him, and smiled. "Well struck, but you will rue the day you challenged the son of Odin!"

Cackling in response, the troll said, "No such thing do I rue, thunderer, save that you still draw breath. I shall remedy that state of affairs now."

With that, the orange-skinned creature leapt at Thor's prone form. Thor raised his arms to defend himself from the troll's onslaught. Thor's foe was the biggest of the thirteen trolls who had invaded, standing head and shoulders above even Volstagg, the largest of the Asgardians. Doubtless that troll was the leader of the campaign, and Thor intended to defeat him directly. When he fell, the other dozen would soon follow.

The troll's meaty hands attempted to wrap around Thor's neck, and the thunder god countered by grabbing the creature's wrists. Though he could not break the troll's grip, Thor was able to keep his foe from impeding his ability to breathe.

Thor had once met an old god named Tiwaz, who nursed Thor back to health after a particularly nasty battle against the goddess of death, Hela. Part of the healing process had been that Thor had to wrestle Tiwaz each night in order to earn his supper. Wrestling had never been a significant component of the thunderer's combat arsenal in the past, but he learned a great deal from Tiwaz.

Today he put one of those lessons to good use. Though the troll was on top of him, Thor was able to use his hips to shift his weight back and forth, destabilizing the troll.

Soon, the pair was tumbling across the square, rolling toward the monument to Yggdrasil. The monument was a miniature re-creation of the ash that bound the Nine Worlds together, and Thor and the troll both crashed into it with a bone-jarring impact.

Their respective grips broken by their violent encounter with the monument, both Thor and the troll were momentarily dazed. Shaking it off, Thor clambered to his feet, pausing only for a breath to see how fared his comrades.

Balder was easily holding two of the trolls at bay with his sword, and a third lay at the shining one's feet.

Not to be outdone, Sif had left two troll corpses in her wake, and she was driving a third back toward the Temple of Titans with her blade.

Both Fandral and Hogun were holding their own with sword and mace, respectively, against two trolls each.

While trying to espy the last two trolls, Thor saw Volstagg sitting on the steps that led to the Temple of Titans, discoursing at great length. At first, Thor feared that the voluminous one had chosen to sit out the battle, but it soon became clear that sitting *was* the battle. The remaining pair of trolls were currently pinned to the temple stairs by Volstagg's rather large bottom. Said stairs were too distant for Thor to hear Volstagg's words, but no doubt the Lion of Asgard—who was one of the finest storytellers extant—was regaling the trolls with exaggerated tales of his exploits. Thor fully expected the trolls to admit defeat simply in a fruitless effort to get Volstagg to silence himself.

Satisfied that his friends were holding their own—and then some—Thor turned his attention back to the leader of the trolls. While they were all charged with the protection of Asgard, as the son of Odin and the heir to Asgard's golden throne, he had always felt the responsibility of keeping Asgard safe most keenly.

Which was why he had taken it upon himself to engage the trolls' leader. Cut off the head, and the body soon fell. Trolls in particular were a dim lot, and few had even a modicum of leadership skills. Thor knew that defeating this one would send the others into a tizzy.

And that was his responsibility as Asgard's protector. He would not allow these trolls to succeed where so many others had failed. Not while he drew breath, and not while he wielded Mjolnir.

"You are truly mighty, troll, and the thunder god salutes your effrontery. It is a true act of gall to invade the city of Asgard when all its defenders are near at hand. You risk much—but defeat will be your sole reward."

With that, Thor held up his hand and summoned Mjolnir to him.

Centuries ago, Odin approached Eitri, master of the dwarven smithies, and commissioned him to create a hammer from the enchanted metal uru that would become the mightiest weapon in the Nine Worlds. Molded from the core of an exploding star, tempered in the fires of the dwarves' forge, and infused with the enchantment of the All-Father himself, Odin named the resultant hammer Mjolnir, which means "that which smashes." Odin himself used it to defeat the giant Laufey. He had told his young son Thor that he would bequeath it to him if he were worthy, and Thor had spent considerable effort to make himself thus. The day Odin had at last gifted him with the hammer was the proudest of his long life.

Since that fateful day, Mjolnir had been as much a part of Thor as one of his limbs. Odin's enchantment meant that none but Thor could wield the hammer. Always when it flew from his grasp, it unerringly returned to him.

Until today. For Thor stood at the base of the monument to Yggdrasil, his hand outstretched—but Mjolnir remained on the ground of the square, unmoving.

The troll threw his massive head back and laughed. "Is the thunder god still truly that if he has not his great hammer? To mulch I'll pound you, Odinson, for without your hammer you're just another little god."

"I have heard such boasts from trolls since your kind first emerged from the caves whence you dwell, and never have I yielded."

"First time for everything," the troll muttered, and then again leapt at Thor.

The time for words was past, as Thor raised his arms to defend against the troll's punches. Their battle was hard-fought, no quarter asked nor given. First Thor struck the troll in its belly, but then the troll struck a blow on Thor's chest. Thor kicked his foe in the leg and heard the crack of bone, but even with a leg hobbled, the troll was able to backhand Thor so hard that he skidded across the square, coming to rest near where Sif fought her own troll.

"Need you aid, Thor?"

"Nay, fair Sif, tarry with your foe a while longer. I will show this knave that Thor is not one to be trifled with." Even as he spoke, Thor got to his feet and spied his hammer. Though still it would not return to him, he could clasp its haft in his hand.

But even as he lifted it, he knew something was amiss. Mjolnir was a tool of great power, and every time he held the hammer, Thor could feel its power almost as if it were a living thing.

What he held now was but dead weight.

So distressed was he over the seeming loss of his hammer that he failed to acknowledge the troll's speedy approach until it was almost too late. At the last second, Thor was able to roll with the troll's mighty punch, tumbling once again to the paving stones of the square. Had he not done so, surely the blow would have severed his head from his neck.

Again the troll laughed, raising his arms in premature triumph. "Is this the mighty thunder god of whom so many speak in fearful tones? For lo these many seasons I have heard Geirrodur and Grundor, Kryllik and Ulik speak in frightful whispers, cautioning us of Thor, for he is the mightiest of the Aesir and he will defeat you as he has defeated trolls for many ages."

Turning to scream at the heavens, the troll continued his rant. "I laugh at those pitiful fools who cringe in terror at Thor's might! I am Baugi! And today I will forevermore be known as Thorsbane, for I will have defeated the son of Odin!"

And then Thor belted Baugi in the jaw, sending the troll flying across the square and landing atop the Warrior's Walk.

"My thanks, Baugi, for your breathless rant," Thor said as he ran across the square toward the Walk, "for it gave me the opportunity to become less breathless myself and rejoin the battle properly."

He grabbed Baugi by the strap of his loincloth and threw him back toward the Yggdrasil monument. Though not as sturdy as the world tree itself, the monument was resilient enough to withstand the impact of a tossed troll.

"Be wary of boastful words, Baugi," Thor continued as he leapt down from the Walk toward the monument where the troll struggled to rise, "for it is actions by which one is judged, whether god, mortal, giant, dwarf—or troll."

Having holstered the now-powerless hammer in his belt,

Thor wielded it again as he landed at the foot of the monument, and swung it downward at Baugi's head.

Though seemingly no longer carrying Odin's enchantment, the hammer was solid enough. Mindful of its name, Thor used it to smash the head of the vain Baugi, backed by the immortal strength of the thunderer.

Baugi slumped to the grass at the base of the monument. He drew breath still, but he did not move.

"Rise, mighty Baugi. Face the god of thunder and defeat him as you boasted!"

When the insensate Baugi declined the invitation, Thor turned to see how fared his friends.

Sif had finished off her foe, and Hogun had done likewise for one of his. While Hogun swung his mace toward his remaining enemy, Sif had drawn off one of Fandral's sparring partners for herself. Meanwhile, Volstagg continued to regale the two prisoners of his expansive posterior with tales of bravery from his own youth.

Holding up his arms, Thor cried, "Minions of Baugi, behold your leader! He is defeated at the hands of the protector of Asgard! Yield now and you will be spared, or fight on and join foul Baugi in defeat!"

The trolls took very little time to mull. Hogun's foe held up his arms, and the two who faced Sif and Fandral did so but a moment later. As for Volstagg's audience, one of them cried, "Please, thunder god, either kill us or send us home to the Realm Below, but spare us further crushing by this crushing bore!"

"Hmph!" Volstagg said as he slowly and awkwardly rose to his feet. "So very like a troll to fail to appreciate the wisdom of their betters. Why I recall one time—"

Fandral held up a hand and said, "Enough, voluminous one! Thor promised to *spare* them if they yielded."

Volstagg let out a *harrumph* of annoyance, but spoke not further. Thor couldn't help but chuckle as he retrieved his helmet from the ground and replaced it on his head.

Thor then regarded each of the surviving trolls in succession. "Fandral, Hogun, and Volstagg shall escort you and your dead back to the Realm Below. Be sure to tell your fellows of Baugi's ignominious defeat, and that Asgard still stands."

The trolls said nothing, simply collecting their dead and then moving toward the outskirts of the city alongside the Warriors Three. Thor noted that the two on whom Volstagg had sat were walking gingerly.

Turning to his oldest friend as well as the woman who meant second-most to him among all the females of the gods of Asgard (behind only Frigga), Thor said, "Balder, Sif, I would beg that you bring Baugi to the dungeons that the troll may await my father's justice."

Sif said, "Of course."

"What of you, Thor?" Balder asked.

"I must go to the All-Father directly." He held up the hammer. "Something has happened to Mjolnir. Still do I sense its presence, yet what I hold here in my hand is but an ordinary tool. I doubt the trolls are responsible—if Baugi had such magicks as could neutralize my hammer, they would not have been so easily defeated this day."

A voice came from all around them in the square. "Ah, but where's the fun in an *easy* defeat, brother?"

Loki Laufeyson materialized in front of Thor. No doubt he had used his sorcerous abilities to shield himself from the battle until it was over. Ever the coward's route did Loki travel.

Odin's adopted son grinned widely and held out his arms, garbed in the green robes he preferred. "You did well, Thor, to defeat Baugi and his minions without your oh-so-precious hammer."

Reaching out with his empty hand, Thor clasped Loki's robes and pulled the trickster close. "Speak, Loki, what have you done to Mjolnir?"

His voice remaining calm despite the threat of violence from his brother—not to mention Balder and Sif, who had unsheathed their swords at Loki's appearance—the son of Laufey said, "I have done nothing to your hammer. I have, however, altered the air around it. If you don't mind. . . ?" To accentuate the point, Loki looked down at Thor's left hand.

Frowning, Thor let go of his adopted brother's raiment, and only then did Loki make a simple gesture.

Even as the false hammer crumbled to dust in Thor's right hand, the very air near the stairs to the Temple of Titans seemed to shimmer, revealing Mjolnir itself on the ground where Thor had earlier dropped it.

Clapping his hands to get rid of the remaining dust of the false hammer, Thor then held his own right hand out and Mjolnir flew to it, as ever.

Wrapping his fingers around the haft, Thor said, "What possible reason could you have for such a ploy, brother?"

"I did observe Baugi and his dozen thugs as they approached the halls of Asgard."

"Then why," Sif asked, "did you not aid us in defending the city against them?"

"I have always felt, fair Sif, that the defense of Asgard against such base foes is best left to those of greater physical strength and concomitant limitation of intellect. However, I did observe, in case Baugi's campaign threatened my own interests, and what I saw was a simple battle against a dull-witted fool." Again Loki grinned. "So I took the fool's hammer away."

Thor shook his head. "Were there two of you, Loki, you would comprise a single wit."

"And for how many decades have you been working on *that* bit of jocularity, thunder god? Nonetheless, my jest is complete, and so now I return to—"

"I say nay, Loki, you will come with me to see the All-Father." As Thor spoke, he placed the hammer in its strap upon his belt. The familiar weight was a tremendous comfort.

"For what purpose?" Now the trickster sounded nervous. "I did reveal myself precisely to avoid a confrontation with our father."

"You say you observed the trolls' approach, but even Heimdall himself did not spy Baugi and his legion until they were within the city gates. You will explain to Odin how you were able to discern what the guardian of the rainbow bridge could not."

Shaking his head, Loki started to make gestures to form the spell that would take him away to his keep. "I will do no such thing. The time of Loki is not to be wasted on such frivolities."

Again Thor reached out, grabbing Loki's arm before it could complete the sigil. "You will come at my urging—or at Odin's. Choose."

Loki did pretend to consider his options, but in truth he had no choice. Odin would, of course, do as Thor requested and summon Loki to speak before the All-Father. It was best if he not incur his adoptive father's wrath unnecessarily.

"Very well, brother, I will accompany you to Odin's throne room."

Leaving Balder and Sif to take care of Baugi, Thor and Loki proceeded to the palace, located at the very center of Asgard. Up the gleaming golden staircase they went, through the huge double doors guarded by two warriors—who, naturally, did not hesitate to allow ingress to the sons of Odin—and thence to the grand throne room.

They entered on the far side of the great space, which was large enough to hold hundreds of Asgardians, but which today was completely empty. Thor's footfalls echoed as they strode across the hall; Loki's own tread was light and silent.

Odin himself sat in the massive golden throne, his hands gripping the armrests, as his ravens, Hugin and Munin, flitted about his shoulders. The All-Father was receiving some manner of intelligence from the ravens, who served as Odin's eyes and ears throughout the Nine Worlds.

But as Thor and Loki approached the grand throne, Odin turned away from the ravens and fixed his one good eye on the pair of them. At the base of the stairs that led to the throne, both Thor and Loki removed their headgear and knelt before the ruler of Asgard. Thor did so quickly and eagerly, Loki slowly and reluctantly.

"Welcome, my sons. I assume you bring glad tidings of the troll invasion of our fair city?"

"Indeed, Father." Thor rose, as did Loki next to him. "With the aid of Balder, Sif, and the Warriors Three, the trolls were driven from Asgard's streets. Fandral, Hogun, and Volstagg are returning all to the Realm Below, save their leader Baugi, whom Balder and Sif are even now escorting to the dungeons, to await your judgment, All-Father."

"And judge him I shall, at a later time. But now I wonder why Loki's name is left out of the list of those who drove the trolls from our home."

Loki provided his most insincere grin. "I held myself in reserve, All-Father. A half-dozen gods seemed more than sufficient to deal with an arrogant, ambitious upstart such as Baugi."

Thor whirled to face his brother. "How now, brother? Why do you characterize Baugi thus?"

Loki blinked. "I beg your pardon?"

"Upstart, yes, Baugi was, but to name him as arrogant and ambitious indicates a knowledge of his character beyond what could be observed in battle."

"To you, perhaps," Loki said dismissively. "Some of us are keener observers of character than others."

Looking back at Odin, Thor added, "In addition, Loki did claim to observe Baugi's approach before Heimdall—and he hindered me in battle by keeping Mjolnir from my hand."

Up until this moment, Odin had been the picture of calm. He knew that matters were well in hand, for were they not, his sons' entry into the throne room would have been urgent and quick rather than calm and slow.

However, once Thor mentioned yet another example of treachery from Loki, Odin's face grew hard and he stared at his adopted son with his one good eye.

"Does Thor speak true, Loki?"

"Technically, yes, I—temporarily!—cloaked his hammer in a shroud of invisibility and covered it in an eldritch casing that physically restrained it from returning to Thor's hand. However, I did leave him a simulacrum of Mjolnir that served its purpose rather well. Indeed, his final defeat of Baugi was done with the ersatz hammer I provided him."

Fists clenched, Thor started to move menacingly toward his adopted brother. "All you 'provided,' dear brother, was a means by which Baugi could defeat me."

Loki did back up a step, but his expression remained one of amusement. "Ah, so the rumors are true, then? Without his hammer, Thor is as helpless as an old woman? Without the crutch of Mjolnir, he is truly crippled?"

"Enough!" Odin cried out, his voice echoing across the empty hall, cutting off any attempt by the thunder god to reply to the slander. "Your japes and jests are ill-timed, Loki, and foolish."

"Did the All-Father not receive notification that his second son is the god of mischief?"

"He did," Odin said slowly, "and I would ask in return if the god of mischief recalls that Odin is the All-Father, all-seeing and all-knowing. Whatever I do not see myself with my good eye is observed by Heimdall from his post or by my faithful ravens." Odin gestured behind him and to the right at the secondary throne, where Hugin and Munin had alighted. At times when Odin was unable to rule Asgard for whatever reason—lost in battle, say, or having succumbed to the Odinsleep—his proxy ruler would do so from that smaller throne, as none were willing to occupy the All-Father's seat. "Indeed, Hugin and Munin just informed me that they espied Loki Laufeyson travelling to the Realm Below himself not so long past. I wonder now if your observation of Baugi's personality traits came, not from seeing him in battle this day, but from a prior meeting? One in which you provided the troll with the means to enter Asgard's gates unnoticed by Heimdall or any other sentry?"

Loki said nothing in reply at first, finally speaking in a much less amused voice. "The All-Father's accusation is—"

"Completely in character for Loki," Thor interrupted, and his tone was, in turn, far more amused than it had been.

Odin rose and pointed an accusatory finger at his adopted son. "Loki, you have endangered the Realm Eternal, both by conspiring with Baugi and his minions and by interfering with Thor's ability to drive him back."

"Oh, *please*." Now Loki rolled his eyes. "The only thing Baugi endangered in the Realm Eternal was a few of the paving stones in the square outside the Temple of Titans. Surely Asgard's protectors are well able to handle thirteen trolls without straining themselves. I daresay even Volstagg could have defeated them by his lonesome." He snorted. "By boring them to death, no doubt. Still, no lasting harm was done."

Unimpressed by Loki's excuses, Odin asked, "And does Loki now number precognition among his talents? True, there are none braver than the six who faced the trolls, but *every* warrior has his end some day, and sometimes that end is ignominious indeed. Today might well have been that day, and it would have been Loki who was responsible. Therefore, it is my judgment—"

"Judgment?" Loki drew himself to his full height in outrage. "I did nothing that warrants—"

"Be *silent*!" For only the second time, Odin raised his voice, but this time the very walls did rattle from his bellow.

Wisely, Loki remained quiet.

"It is my judgment that you be confined to your keep for a period of one month. Hugin, Munin, *and* Heimdall will all observe your home with their keen eyes. Should you at any point remove yourself from your quarters, you will find the All-Father's punishment to be far more severe."

"Father, I—"

But Odin wished not to hear Loki's craven plea. "I have spoken! Begone from my presence! Thor, escort your brother to his punishment."

Thor once again knelt before his liege. "With pleasure, Father."

Grabbing Loki's left arm, Thor led the trickster forcibly from the hall. Loki kept looking back at the throne, which Odin had retaken, but Odin's visage remained hard and unyielding.

The two ravens flitted about the heads of both gods as they departed, making it clear that Loki would not have an unobserved moment for the next several weeks, and that his sentence commenced immediately.

As they left the hall, Loki shook his head, a miserable expression on his countenance. "Absurd. Simply absurd. I play a simple prank, and *this* is the All-Father's punishment?"

"I would say, *dear* brother," Thor said with a smile as wide as that used by Loki prior to Odin's judgment, "that you got off easy. Asgard itself was invaded by an enemy. For the All-Father to punish you merely by grounding you, as they say on Midgard, he is being far kinder than perhaps you deserve."

Loki fixed Thor with a withering look. "You'll forgive me, *dear* brother, if I put little stock in what *you* feel I deserve."

"What I feel matters little, for it is what the All-Father feels, and what he decrees, that all Asgardians must heed."

"So I am regularly reminded." Loki sighed heavily. "Ah, well. The joy of immortality is patience, and a month is but a blink of an eye. I shall occupy myself with some tasks about the keep, and the month will pass ere long. And rest assured, Thor, that my hands shall *not* be idle come the end of my sentence."

"And *you* may rest assured, Loki, that Thor will be ready for whatever foolish plan you might concoct."

"Speaking of himself in the third person the entire time, no doubt," Loki muttered as they proceeded to his keep, and the commencement of his exile.

He was sure that his house arrest would go by quickly.

CHAPTER TWO

Loki's house arrest did not go by quickly.

By the middle of the second day, he felt as if he'd been trapped within the walls of his keep for centuries.

It was all well and good to say to Thor that he had "tasks" about the keep, but in truth all that needed doing was drudge work. He had sprites and other magickal creatures to perform such menial duties for him. Indeed, they were under strict orders to perform them when he was away from the keep. Not only would the second son of Odin never lower himself to restock the pantry or dust the furniture or clean the privy or organize his scrolls, he refused to even be present when the magickal creatures indentured to him engaged in those tasks.

"So this is what it's come to, Father?" Loki cried out to the heavens. He doubted that Odin was listening, though no doubt his ridiculous birds were and would relay his ranting. "Have none of the Aesir even a spot of a sense of humor anymore? The trolls were nothing, a mere diversion for the gods of Asgard. I did Thor and the others a *favor* by giving them a foe to fight. My brother is never happier than when he's clumping creatures on the head, and I gave him the opportunity! And, yes, I hid Mjolnir, but let's face it, Thor has become far too reliant on that silly hammer. What if someday he loses it? Or breaks it? Or someone else becomes 'worthy' and takes it from him, as has already happened more than once? I was *helping* my brother—and yes, playing a bit of a joke, but shouldn't siblings have japes and jests between them?"

"Talking to yourself, my son?"

Whirling around, Loki saw that Frigga stood in his sitting room, a warm smile on her face.

"Yes, Mother, I am. It's my only guarantee of intelligent conversation."

After a moment, he sensed that it was in actuality an astral projection of his adoptive mother. Frigga only very occasionally employed the magickal gifts of her Vanir heritage, but Loki knew that she had plenty of sorcerous talents in her own right. Indeed, it was she who originally encouraged him, as a youth, to pursue such arts when he proved less interested in the art of combat than his adoptive brother.

"My apologies for the state of the keep, Mother, but I wasn't expecting guests. Odin's house arrest carried with it the implication that I am to bear it alone."

"His sentence only applied to you, my son. Any may come see you."

"Wonderful. I suppose I can expect Thor to come by and gloat at his earliest convenience."

"Unlikely—and I would not permit it if he wished to."

Loki blew out a breath. "Thank you, Mother. I don't suppose you could appeal to Father's better nature? Ask him for a less onerous sentence than being stuck batting about my home?"

"I'm afraid not, my son." Frigga's smile became more wry. "When Odin told me of his punishment, I told him that, if anything, he went too easy on you."

Drawing himself upright, Loki stared incredulously at her. "I *beg* your pardon?"

"Loki, you took Thor's hammer from him in the middle of battle against a troll. He could've been killed."

Snorting, Loki said, "I do not have that kind of luck. The fates would never favor me with so easy a death for him."

"He is your brother, Loki—and he is my son."

"And he has faced far worse than an out-of-his-depth troll with delusions of grandeur, and survived. I knew well that he would survive this." He chuckled. "Oh, Mother, the look on his face when he held out his hand and Mjolnir did not fly to his grasp—for that alone, the entire jest was worth it!"

"If it were truly worth it, my son, then you should bear your punishment without complaint."

Loki opened his mouth and then closed it, as he had no response to that. Damn his mother and her infernal logic . . .

Frigga moved closer to Loki. Instinctively, he reached out to her, but she, of course, had no substance.

"I do not understand why you must constantly play this game with your brother. The constant torment . . ."

"I am the god of mischief, Mother. Tormenting my fellows is my very purpose. I could no more cease to 'play this game,' as you put it, than Thor could stop producing thunder and lightning, or Heimdall could stop seeing over great distances, or Volstagg could stop eating."

Giving a mock-shudder, Frigga said, "Truly a black day in the Nine Worlds it would be if Volstagg were to stop eating. Why, our stores might actually overflow!"

Joining in the mocking, Loki added, "The chefs of Asgard might be permitted to sleep, as they will no longer need to work through the night and day to provide enough victuals for the endless stomach of the Lion of Asgard."

Both mother and son shared a laugh at that, and Loki found himself calm for the first time since Thor hauled him off to see Odin.

"Thank you, Mother."

"For what?"

"For caring."

"Oh, my dear, dear son." Frigga reached out as if to cup Loki's cheek in her hand, but stopped short, remembering that her presence was eldritch and not physical. "I have always cared. I have always loved you. Indeed, it is because I love you so much that I am so constantly disappointed when you engage in such petty and dangerous frivolity as this."

Loki had flinched at her insubstantial gesture, and then shook his head and moved away, the jocular moment now gone. His voice harder and more distant, he said, "There are those who would say that Loki is not capable of returning the love you espouse for him."

Frigga, however, refused to follow Loki into his suddenly more somber mood, the wry smile returning instead. "There are those who say that Loki's tendency to speak of himself in the third person shows an excess of pretension. Regardless, I have never cared for the gossip of others. I know both my sons, and know full well how they feel—regardless of whether or not they may express those feelings."

Turning to face his mother once more, Loki said, "Regardless, Mother, even as you express your disappointment, it is leavened with the expression of your love. That has not gone unnoticed." Again turning away, he added, "From the All-Father, all I perceive is the disappointment."

"His disappointment is only so great because his love is equally great. I know it is hard to see. Odin rules all of Asgard, and the weight of that responsibility is heavy indeed. But it makes it difficult to show his true feelings."

Loki turned and gave his mother a half-smile. "Somehow I suspect that the thunder god never doubts the affection Father has for him."

"Odin sentenced Thor to live life as a crippled mortal with no knowledge of his heritage. I believe that Thor may have wavered in his belief of Odin's love for him when the deception was revealed."

Shaking his head, Loki regarded Frigga with wonder. "You do have quite the gift, Mother."

"Thank you, my son." Frigga's image started to fade a bit. "I must leave you now, and tend to the throne room."

Loki frowned. That was Odin's domain solely. "Why the throne room?"

"Only to keep an eye on things. Asgard is quiet since the trolls were driven away, and Odin has grown restless and decided to go on one of his—excursions."

At that, Loki rolled his eyes. "Let me guess—he has disguised himself as an old man with one eye? It amazes me that he ever fools anyone when he goes on those—excursions, as you call them."

Frigga shrugged. "He enjoys pretending to be someone else. It is enough for him to remove his royal armor and his eye-patch and put on a battered old cloak. His disguises need not be as clever physically as your illusions, my son. Just by being an ordinary old man on horseback, people do not believe he is the All-Father. After all, would the ruler of Asgard travel alone on the road to Jotunheim?"

"That depends upon the horse. Is he riding Sleipnir?"

"Of course." Frigga chuckled. "The horse *looks* like an ordinary mount to the casual observer."

"Well, there you go—I have never *casually* observed anything. It is how I have thrived all these centuries."

"In any event, my son, I must go." Frigga gave Loki one last, loving look. "Be well, Loki."

Even as the astral image faded, Loki said, "That will be very difficult while I'm trapped in this house!"

Though he was glad of his mother's company for the brief time she was present, it served only to exacerbate his loneliness now that she was gone. With a sigh, he retired to the pantry. The talk of Volstagg's appetite had made him hungry, and his latest delivery of the golden apples of immortality had arrived that morning.

Idunn, the goddess in charge of the apples, took her duties seriously, including delivering a supply of the apples in her care to each of the Aesir every month. Every god of Asgard, regardless of his or her status within the realm, was given the same delivery. Idunn's neutrality was as strong as that of the fates, and even Loki did not dare challenge it, for that was the one way to risk being removed from her delivery list. He could anger Thor, Odin, Balder, Frigga, Sif, the Warriors Three, Heimdall, or anyone else in the Nine Worlds, and Idunn would care not. But if he dared anger her?

Of course, it might have been enjoyable for the trickster to do something to affect *all* of the apples. Loki's musing on this possible plan of action was cut short upon his entry into the pantry by a simply horrible smell. He'd not encountered a stench this awful since his visit to the Realm Below to convince Baugi to invade Asgard.

But trolls had yet to be introduced to the concept of bathing, while Loki prided himself on his fastidiousness.

So he was appalled to see that the pantry had gone to seed. Leftover foodstuffs from the first day of his house arrest had not yet been disposed of, dishes and cutlery had not yet been cleaned and put away, and flies buzzed about, one flying right in Loki's face.

Swatting away the insect, Loki immediately summoned the sprites who were tasked with the keeping of his keep.

Three tiny, winged, green-skinned creatures appeared before him, flitting about the pantry alongside the flies.

"Speak, speak, Loki Laufeyson!"

"Tell us how we may service the trickster god!"

"The god of mischief commands us!"

"Yes," Loki said impatiently, "I do. And have. Your job is to keep my home neat and clean, yet *look* at this place!"

The sprites flew around the pantry, noses wrinkled, and then all alighted before him side by side.

"We do as we are bid!"

"Clean the pantry we shall!"

"As soon as next you depart!"

Loki winced. He rarely was in his keep for more than a few days at a time, as there was always some new scheme to conceive, some campaign of mischief to enact. Therefore, the sprites had been under strict instruction to do their domestic chores only when Loki himself did not have to witness it. Under normal circumstances, Loki's comings and goings provided ample opportunity for the sprites to heed his directive.

But Odin's house arrest had changed things, and he needed to adjust his commands to the sprites accordingly.

Striding to the burlap sack containing this month's supply of apples, Loki said, "I have been forced to remain in the keep for the time being, so for now, you may perform your duties regardless of whether or not I am present."

The sprites all exchanged nervous glances with each other.

"If that is what the trickster desires . . ."

"If truly Loki is sure . . ."

"We will, of course, do as the second son of Odin demands . . ."

Loki shook his head as he pulled one of the golden apples from the sack. "Yes. Yes, you will. And do it quickly!" He took a huge bite out of the apple to emphasize his point, swatted another fly that flew in front of his face, and left the pantry in a huff.

At this point, Loki was fed up with everything. With Odin and his arbitrary punishments meted out against his son, who simply did what he was supposed to do as god of mischief. With Thor and his dull wits and insistence on dragging Loki to Odin in the first place. With Baugi and his minions, who couldn't even put up a decent fight against Thor and his idiot friends, even though Thor himself was relieved of his greatest weapon. With those friends, who insisted on joining Thor; had Balder, Sif, and the Warriors Three minded their own business, the trolls would have trounced Thor royally. With the sprites and their tiresome literal-mindedness, leading to a most filthy pantry. Even with his mother, who could have come in person and could have stayed longer.

Entering his bedroom, Loki fell more than sat on his bed and took a few more bites of his apple.

Once he consumed all but the core of the apple, he tossed it aside, hoping as he did so that the sprites would know to clean it up even though he remained. They might well have only followed his instruction with regard to the pantry and let the rest of the keep go to pot.

And then another fly came in and settled on his nose.

He swatted the fly, and then sighed, wondering if he should go back to the pantry and instruct the sprites to specifically get rid of the flies.

Then he wondered if he could cast a spell that would send all the flies to wherever Odin was disguised and riding Sleipnir.

And then, suddenly, it came to him.

Throwing his head back, Loki laughed long and hard.

It was perfect. Even Heimdall would be fooled.

First, Loki changed into his bedclothes. True, it was midday, but he would always be able to defend the notion of an afternoon nap as resulting from the boredom of house arrest.

Then he began composing a somewhat complicated spell that would create a simulacrum of himself. He also prepared to change his own shape, something Loki could do as naturally as breathe, though the transformation he planned would be of particular difficulty.

In order for his newly conceived plan to work, he would have to do three things at once, and two of those things could not be accomplished until the third was done, and that was out of Loki's control.

And then the third thing finally did happen, as he knew it would: another fly buzzed about his face.

At once, Loki performed the three actions required to enact his cunning plan.

He clapped his hands together to crush the fly between his palms.

He changed his own shape from his familiar dark-haired form to that of a fly.

He activated the simulacrum.

The eldritch doppelgänger occupied the exact space that Loki vacated when he made himself into a creature the size and shape of an insect, down to the clapped hands. Loki was confident that even Heimdall's keen vision would not be able to detect the switch.

Even as the fly he swatted fell to the floor, dead, Loki himself flew toward the keep's window in the form of that insect. He also instructed the simulacrum to yawn, lie down on the bed, and sleep.

Smiling to himself while shaped as a fly, Loki knew that Heimdall and Odin's ravens would see only that Loki had tried to kill a fly and then given up and gone to sleep.

And now he was once again free to move about the Nine Worlds as he pleased!

But as soon as he fled his keep, he realized that he wasn't sure where to go. So thoroughly had he accepted Odin's decree that he had given no thought to what he might do if freed, since that day had seemed so far away until his insect-related brainstorm.

As he flew upward, he caught a glimpse of Hugin and Munin, and upon seeing Odin's pet birds, he knew what he had to do.

Frigga had said that the All-Father was taking his horse on the road to Jotunheim. So Loki flew in that direction to see what Odin was up to and how he might interpolate himself into his adoptive father's adventure.

CHAPTER THREE

No one knew where Hrungnir got his golden horse.

The fearsome frost giant had obtained a large, gold-maned mount, whom he had named Goldfaxi. And since acquiring the horse, no one had been able to defeat Hrungnir.

Some say he won the steed in a game of chance with the dwarves. Others said it was a game of skill, but that seemed unlikely. Dwarves are too canny to be defeated by a giant by anything other than luck or strength, and no dwarf would enter a contest of strength with a giant, especially not one of Hrungnir's might.

Others say he stole the horse from the stables belonging to Karnilla, Queen of the Norns. At one time, such a notion would have been unthinkable, but Karnilla was kidnapped once by another giant, Utgard-Loki, and since then, the Norn Queen's reputation had suffered. Nonetheless, many of the giants who followed Hrungnir feared retribution from Karnilla.

Another story was told that Hrungnir purchased the mount from a stable on Midgard, where the mortals had used their science to breed a horse of great speed and power.

Regardless of where Hrungnir obtained the mount, Goldfaxi had proven to be a great boon. The horse was large enough to support the giant's girth, yet still fleet enough of hoof to outrun any mount in the Nine Worlds.

Or so Hrungnir claimed. In any event, the results spoke for themselves. Hrungnir and the other giants who had pledged loyalty to him had not yet lost a campaign since Goldfaxi became his steed.

On this day, Hrungnir led his followers to the outskirts of Nornheim. When he announced his plan, his trusted lieutenant, Thjasse, spoke to him in private.

"Is this wise, mighty Hrungnir? Karnilla is a vengeful queen, and if you approach her with the very horse that you stole from her—"

But Hrungnir only laughed boisterously. "Do not believe all the stories you hear, clever Thjasse. I have no reason to fear anything from the Norn Queen—though perhaps after today, I shall give her reason to fear me, eh?" Again, Hrungnir laughed, and he spurred Goldfaxi onward.

While Thjasse and the other giants struggled to keep up with their leader's golden-maned steed, Hrungnir rode ahead until he reached a farm located on the outskirts of Karnilla's lands.

A group of men and women who were tilling the fields saw Hrungnir, and put down their hoes and shovels and wheelbarrows and faced the giant.

One of the women stepped forward as Hrungnir brought Goldfaxi to a whinnying halt. "We know who you are."

"I should hope you are aware of Hrungnir the Mighty,

Hrungnir the Brawler, Hrungnir the conqueror of all he meets and conquers!"

The farmers exchanged a glance, and even Hrungnir realized that his phrasing was poor. But he was no Asgardian god with their flowery speech. He was a man of action.

"And what I meet today," he added quickly, "is you. My followers are hungry, and we will take some of your food."

"Without this food, we will starve," the woman said.

Hrungnir looked out at the fields, which were lengthy and full of plants in full bloom. "You are growing more food, far more than you shall need to feed yourselves."

"And what of winter?" the woman asked. "We must grow more than we need so we do not starve during the cold months, and so that we may be prepared in case of a bad harvest."

Hrungnir snorted. "Your future plans are of no interest to me, little farmers. I am Hrungnir, and I take what is mine."

"What if you are challenged?" the woman asked before Hrungnir could goad Goldfaxi onward.

Barking a cruel laugh, Hrungnir asked, "Who among you would challenge me?"

"Not you," the woman said. "Your horse. The reason *why* we know who you are is because of your steed. They say that Goldfaxi is faster than any horse in the Nine Worlds save Sleipnir, the steed of the All-Father himself."

"I would wager that even Odin's horse would be poorly matched against mine. So how would such as *you* challenge me?"

"Our horses are not fast, but they are strong. Goldfaxi may be fast, but can he pull a plow as well as our Alsvinnur?"

She pointed to the farm's large, brown horse, currently at rest but still tethered to the plow.

Again, Hrungnir laughed. "And what is your challenge, fair farmer?"

The woman bowed her head. "Alsvinnur was about to plow the north end of the field. Tomorrow, after he is rested, he is to plow the south end. Our challenge is thus: Alsvinnur will indeed plow the north end, and Goldfaxi the south. The two sections are of equal size. Should Alsvinnur finish first, you and your giants will leave us in peace."

Before the woman could continue, Hrungnir spoke. "And *when* Goldfaxi wins, you will not stand in our way as we take however much of your food we wish?"

"As you say. Do I have your word that you will keep to the bargain?"

Hrungnir's face grew serious. "On my word, fair farmer, Hrungnir the Mighty will abide by the terms of our wager."

"And I, Sveina, daughter of Herdis, subject of the Norn Queen, do also swear by Karnilla's crown that I too shall abide by the terms."

With that, Hrungnir dismounted Goldfaxi. By the time Thjasse and the others had caught up, some of the farmers had retrieved their spare plow and were in the process of hooking Goldfaxi up to it. Meanwhile, three others led Alsvinnur and his plow to the north end of the field.

Thjasse approached Hrungnir and asked, "What is happening, mighty Hrungnir? Why is Goldfaxi being tethered to a plow? That is the fate of old horses that no longer can be ridden. Surely that is not your valiant steed's destiny?"

"Not at all, Thjasse. The farmers have proposed a wager and I have accepted. Should Goldfaxi plow his half of the field faster than the plowhorse, we shall take what we wish without resistance."

Frowning, Thjasse said, "I assume you have found a way to guarantee victory?"

"Don't speak nonsense, Thjasse. 'Tis a wager, and a fine one at that. Besides, I have faith in my steed. Goldfaxi shall win, and then instead of being forced to kill and maim these farmers, they will tell tales to their fellows of Hrungnir's might without those tales being leavened by weeping for their dead and cries in pain from wounds."

"But what if Goldfaxi does not win?"

Hrungnir shrugged his mighty shoulders. "If Goldfaxi is *not* the strongest mount in the Nine Worlds, better to know it than not, wouldn't you say?"

Thjasse said nothing in response, thinking only that it was better to guarantee a tangible victory than hope for a moral one.

Sveina stood at the center of the field, holding up a handkerchief. "When I drop this cloth, the horses may start. Whoever reaches me first will win the wager."

Standing near Goldfaxi, Hrungnir waited for the cloth to

fall, while another farmer did likewise across the field, ready to goad Alsvinnur onward.

Amused by the whole thing, Hrungnir actually waited several seconds after Sveina dropped her kerchief before patting Goldfaxi on the rump. Even then, the gold-maned mount hesitated, unaccustomed to having to drag such a great weight.

But the giant's steed was made of sterner stuff, and he finally began his work—a full ten seconds after Alsvinnur commenced his.

Sure enough, by the time Alsvinnur was halfway through the north end of the field, Goldfaxi was fast approaching Sveina's position.

And when Goldfaxi arrived at the center of the field, while Alsvinnur still had a quarter of his land to toil through, all the giants gave a throaty cheer.

"Go, my loyal subjects!" Hrungnir cried out. "Take what food you wish from these farmers—but *only* food! Do not harm any of them, nor damage their things! Anyone who does so will answer to Hrungnir the Mighty!"

Thjasse and the other giants proceeded to the storehouse to raid it for food, while Hrungnir himself turned to untether his horse.

As he did so, he cast a glance at Sveina, whose visage spoke of a woman whose heart had broken. "You should be pleased, fair Sveina. Your bravery in the face of Hrungnir the Brawler was most impressive. That is why I spared your life and your things."

"And am I to fall to my knees in gratitude?" Sveina asked bitterly. "Without those stores, we will surely die this winter, only instead of the quick, violent death expected from an attack by your kind, it will be slow and painful."

"Be wary, Sveina, for Hrungnir's mercy is not unlimited. You still live, and where there is life, there is a chance. But you also defied the frost giants, and that never comes without a price to pay."

Within minutes, the giants had filled their burlap sacks with fruits and vegetables and herbs. In truth, they did not take as much as Sveina feared, for the giants preferred the meat of a beast that roamed the ground to the berries and roots that grew under it.

But food was food, and the giants still took more than their fill.

Hrungnir mounted Goldfaxi once again and rode away from Nornheim, having accomplished much for one day. They headed back in the direction of Jotunheim, Hrungnir leading his men in a song. They sang off-key, and Hrungnir was making up the words as he went along, making it hard for the others to keep up, but they all tried their best.

By the time the midday sun started its slow journey toward sunset, Hrungnir spied a lone traveler on the road from Asgard.

He was elderly, looking like one of the Aesir: large, by human standards, but still puny to one such as Hrungnir. His clothes were shabby and his white beard thick. Indeed, between the beard and the large floppy hat he wore, Hrungnir could scarce make out any of his face beyond his nose. A fly buzzed about the stranger's head, and he swatted at it absently, though the insect managed to avoid the old man's hand.

However, he rode a mount that was as impressive as any Hrungnir had seen outside of Goldfaxi himself.

"Ho, stranger!" Hrungnir cried out. "That is a fine steed you ride!"

The stranger bowed his head modestly, and spoke in a quiet tone. "My thanks, good sir. You, too, ride a most excellent horse."

"I had thought you to be of the Aesir, but perhaps not," Hrungnir said with a chortle. "None of those vain gods would ever speak with such respect to a frost giant. Indeed, were you not so old and infirm, I would expect you to unsheathe a sword at the very sight of me and mine."

Bowing his head, the old man said, "I am called Bolverk, and I wish no trouble, good sir. I am but a simple traveler who wishes to ride through these empty roads in peace."

And now Hrungnir let out a throaty laugh. "Truly you are not of Asgard, for all those who dwell in that thrice-cursed city know that peace is not the watchword of the frost giants—and certainly not that of Hrungnir the Mighty! But tell me of your mount, stranger. Rarely have I seen one with coat so bright and legs so strong. His gait is effortless even with the weight of both you and your supplies upon him. Whence comes this fine horse?"

"It is merely a family beast, good sir."

"What name has he?"

"None, good sir, for it is not the custom of my family to name those who cannot reply with voice to one's call."

Hrungnir laughed. "True enough."

"May I be on my way?" Bolverk asked humbly.

"Not as yet, Bolverk, for I must know which of our steeds would be fastest, my gold-maned mount, or your own unnamed beast."

The man who called himself Bolverk hesitated, for despite Hrungnir's beliefs, he was indeed of the Aesir, indeed the ruler of them all. Odin had changed into shabby clothing, mounted Sleipnir, the fastest horse in all the Nine Worlds, and hoped to take a lengthy ride alone in the lands between the realms. After the distasteful business with Loki and Thor and the trolls, he had hoped to have some time with only his own thoughts for company.

Word had reached him of Hrungnir and his horse Goldfaxi, and how they had been terrorizing the lands near Jotunheim. He had intended to address the issue before long, but after he had had a relaxing journey away from the burdens of his throne.

However, he was here now, facing Hrungnir, who was obviously confident in Goldfaxi's superiority. Had Odin truly been a simple traveler on an ordinary horse, that confidence would have been warranted.

"I challenge you, old man, to a race," Hrungnir said. "For I must know if Goldfaxi is truly the fastest in the land, and only through a race may it be determined."

"Do you not have faith in your mount, good sir?"

"In my own, yes, but in yours I can have neither faith nor surety, for they have not been tested against each other."

"And if I refuse this challenge?" It took all of Odin's will-power to keep his voice in the same humble tone he'd adopted for the role of Bolverk, for he found this giant's effrontery to be insulting.

"Then all the giants gathered here will take your steed from you and leave you for dead on this road. But," he added quickly, "the word of Hrungnir is his bond! You may ask the farmers who till the fields outside Karnilla's realm if you wish. They proposed a wager, and Hrungnir the Mighty did abide by it—and took only what was his by the terms of the arrangement, no more, no less."

"And what would the terms of *this* wager be?" Odin asked with Bolverk's quiet aspect, while again swatting at the fly that had harried him for half the trip from Asgard.

"Should you win the race, old man, you may continue on your way, unmolested by the frost giants. If you think this a poor reward, think of the alternative."

"And should you win?"

Hrungnir smiled. "Then I will claim your horse as my own, for the Brawler must also have the second-fastest horse in the realm."

Odin considered the giant's offer. It was best to accept the wager, for that provided the best outcome. He knew Goldfaxi had no hope of riding faster than Sleipnir, and once the All-Father won the race, he would go on his way, with none the wiser regarding his disguise.

If he lost—well, Hrungnir would learn that "Bolverk" was no mere elderly traveler to be trifled with. Odin would not give up noble Sleipnir without a fight, and the All-Father could fight very well.

Hrungnir pointed to the nearby Algarrbyr Hill. "We will ride from here to the top of that hill, then turn and come back down again. My lieutenant, Thjasse, will stand here and await our return. Whoever reaches Thjasse first shall be the winner." Hrungnir then stared at the old man. "Swear by the River Gjoll that you will abide by the terms of our wager."

Beneath his thick white beard, Odin did smile. The giant was cleverer than the All-Father had given him credit for. That oath was one that no Asgardian would ever break. "I swear by the River Gjoll that I will turn my mount over to you, should you win our race."

Only a fool wagered with a giant, but even Odin dared not go back on an oath sworn on the river of the dead. Breaking that oath would result in that river claiming the oath-breaker in question. And so now he needed to have the faith in Sleipnir that he accused Hrungnir of not having in Goldfaxi.

Thjasse stood between the two horses as they faced Algarrbyr. "Be on your marks! Set, and—*go!*"

Hrungnir kicked Goldfaxi hard with his heel, prompting the horse to gallop. For his part, Odin leaned forward, loosening the reins to give Sleipnir freedom to move his head and simply squeezed lightly with both knees.

At first, the two horses were neck and neck. Odin did nothing to goad Sleipnir on, simply allowing him to gallop at his own pace. Meanwhile, Hrungnir repeatedly kicked his own mount, urging Goldfaxi to gallop ever faster.

When they reached the top of Algarrbyr, Sleipnir was able to easily turn around, guided with only the slightest tug of the reins and a low whisper.

Goldfaxi proved more recalcitrant, as Hrungnir had to wrestle with the steed to stop him from continuing down to the other side of Algarrbyr, and to instead turn around. By the time Goldfaxi was convinced to turn all the way around, Sleipnir had already started on the downward slope.

From that point on, the race was decided. Hrungnir continued to goad and kick Goldfaxi, but moving downhill served only to make Sleipnir faster, and the giant's mount simply could not keep the pace.

Odin passed Thjasse on the ground half a minute before Hrungnir arrived. It might as well have been an eternity for the giant.

For a brief instant, Odin was tempted to reveal his true self. That temptation was at least partly borne of the murderous expression on Hrungnir's face.

"How *dare* you make a mockery of me?!" Hrungnir cried.

Deciding to maintain the fiction of Bolverk at least long enough to see if the giant would abide by his word, Odin said quietly, "No, good sir, I did not. You challenged my horse and I to a race, and I won it. You made me swear by the River Gjoll that I would abide by the wager. Will you do the same? Or is the word of Hrungnir worth less than that of a simple old traveler?"

Hrungnir stared at the old man for many seconds. Thjasse and the other giants regarded their leader, wondering what he would do next.

Odin stared back at Hrungnir, mentally preparing a spell that would reveal his true nature to these impetuous giants.

But then Hrungnir's face softened. "Very well, Bolverk. I gave my word, and I will not have it known that Hrungnir the Mighty was an oath-breaker. Bad enough it is that I must now be known as having the *second* fastest steed in the Nine Worlds."

Once again, the fly that had menaced Odin flew in front of his face. Waving it away with his hand, he gently squeezed Sleipnir twice with his knees, and the steed began to slowly canter back toward Asgard. This, Odin had decided, was a close enough call, and it would be best if he returned to the city and his duties as its ruler. Including, it would seem, musing on ways to deal with Hrungnir's aggressiveness.

The fly, however, remained behind even as Odin moved on. The All-Father's proximity forced Loki to remain in his insectoid disguise, but he knew that Hrungnir would not listen to the counsel of a fly. But as he hoped, the All-Father's silly ruse provided Loki with an opening. Throughout the entire encounter, Loki had feared that the All-Father would reveal himself. But he did not, and that gave Loki precisely the opportunity he needed.

Once Sleipnir was out of sight, Loki whispered an incantation. His form shifted from that of a tiny fly to that of a giant serpent.

The giants cried out in shock at the sudden appearance of a serpent in their midst. Hrungnir simply stared at the new arrival. "What sorcery is this?"

"Fairly simple sorcery, all things considered," Loki said, his voice low and hissing thanks to the reptilian mouth that he now had to wrap around his words. "I am Loki, and I would have words with Hrungnir the Mighty."

"It has been some time since our paths crossed, trickster," Hrungnir said dryly, "but I recall you having two legs, black hair, and fair skin, none of which are in evidence before me now."

"As I said, fairly simple sorcery—but necessary, as I must keep my true form disguised lest Heimdall know I am in your midst." Loki saw no reason to discuss the specifics of his house arrest with such as these. "But rest assured, I am Loki. If I recall the genealogy of Jotunheim correctly, you are a nephew of Laufey, which makes us cousins."

Hrungnir laughed. "It seems my cousin has fallen on hard times if he must lower himself to speak before me as a mere serpent."

"Be that as it may," Loki said loudly to be heard over the chortling of Hrungnir and his fellow giants, "I am here to inform you that you have been tricked. The traveler who just defeated you and your precious gold-maned mount was none other than Odin himself."

Hrungnir drew himself up to his considerable full height. "You lie!"

"Often, yes, but not in this instance."

"Why would Odin have lowered himself to appear as so mean a presence?"

"For his amusement." Loki tried to chuckle, but it came out as a hiss. "It would not be the first time the All-Father has done this. He does love his disguises, and you did observe that 'Bolverk' had but one eye?"

Hrungnir looked away, waving a dismissive hand. "That means nothing."

"Who but great Sleipnir could so easily defeat your own Goldfaxi in a contest of speed?"

Hrungnir turned and gazed back over his shoulder at the serpentine form of the trickster.

Loki pressed his advantage. "Use your intellect, Hrungnir, or is your appellation of 'the Brawler' an indication that you know aught else? I suppose it is possible that there is another old man with a thick white beard and only one eye who possesses a horse that is faster than yours . . ."

As Loki had hoped, Hrungnir's response was a mighty cry to the heavens. "How *dare* he?! He did this deliberately to make me look a fool!"

Silently, Loki mused that he himself would take over that particular role, but aloud he only said, "Hardly surprising. Your steed has gained a reputation, and no doubt Odin wished to teach you a lesson in humility. He is fond of such games. Why, he once did the same to my hated brother, Thor."

Hrungnir turned to face the serpent directly. "What?"

"Thor was getting a bit full of himself—even more so than usual—and so Odin sent him to Midgard and entrapped him in the form of a crippled mortal. For the powerful thunder god to be trapped in so frail a form was a cruel and dire punishment indeed. And that was how Odin treated his own flesh and blood! Can you imagine he would treat you any better?"

Shaking his head, Hrungnir started to pace. "I should have known. And of course, old One-Eye came in disguise. Had Odin publicly challenged me, I would never have accepted it. Only a fool would wager against Sleipnir, and Hrungnir is no fool."

"Indeed not." Loki faked sincerity with those two words, as had the giant, for in truth Hrungnir had believed Goldfaxi to be the match even of Sleipnir before the race proved him wrong once and for all. "The question is, mighty Hrungnir, what shall you do about it?"

"All Asgard must pay for this indignity. For too long the Aesir have toyed with us, but it ends now. Tomorrow we attack Asgard and show Odin and his foolish gods that Hrungnir is *not* to be trifled with!"

"And it would be Loki's pleasure to assist you in this endeavor."

Thjasse spoke, then. "And what would the trickster demand in return for this assistance?"

"Indeed," Hrungnir said with a nod to his lieutenant. "Loki aids no one but himself."

"Can even the god of mischief not do a favor for family?" Another chuckle that translated into a hiss from his serpentine mouth. "Besides, just the knowledge that you will invade Asgard is enough to warm the cockles of my heart. I've no love for the Aesir, nor Asgard, nor Odin, nor his oh-so-favored son. In fact, should you kill Thor, I would be in your debt."

Gazing skeptically at the snake, Thjasse asked, "You would forego the pleasure of killing your hated brother yourself?"

In truth, Loki would have preferred to do the deed himself, as Thjasse said, but he doubted any of these giants truly had the wherewithal to eliminate his brother. However, he also spoke the truth when he replied: "Though I would prefer that the thunder god perish by my hand, I have come to the conclusion over the years that it is best to be rid of him regardless of the manner in which that is accomplished."

Hrungnir regarded Loki for several seconds before saying, "Very well. The invasion will commence at dawn!"

"And I will show you a pathway that is hidden even from Heimdall's sharp eyes." It was the same passage he had granted the trolls, one of many ways in and out of Asgard that Loki had either created or discovered over the centuries. The first had been a hole in the catacombs underneath the city, through which Loki had led the wolf gods and their allies. He'd found and made many since, and they had proven very handy at times. Sadly, none of them led directly to his keep, thus preventing him from using them to escape his current predicament.

"You will show Thjasse and me this pathway today, trickster," Hrungnir said, "and then tomorrow we will attack, and the day after, Asgard will fall!"

CHAPTER FOUR

Loki's fatal flaw—well, in truth, he had several, but this was the one that mattered this day—was that he had a tendency to underestimate his rivals.

True, the passageways he'd provided for Baugi that enabled the trolls to penetrate the gates of Asgard were invisible to Heimdall—when Loki had so provided them. But Heimdall was not one to suffer a blind spot in his all-seeing expanse for long. From the moment the trolls arrived, he peered out amidst the gleaming spires of Asgard to locate the route the invaders took.

It was not long before he found it. And that discovery occurred before Loki's decision to assist Hrungnir in his intended attack on Asgard.

As a result, Hrungnir's invasion was not as much of a surprise as Loki had led the giant to believe.

From the outskirts of the city of Asgard—which he continued to flit about as a fly—Loki heard Heimdall's blaring of the Gjallarhorn, signaling that the city was under attack. Dawn had only just come, and Hrungnir couldn't have been within the city's gates yet. Based on the giant's plan, he would still be approaching the city from Loki's secret passageway beneath the Ida Plain.

Loki, however, did not concern himself. Just the fact that Asgard was invaded again gave him a warm and fuzzy feeling.

As for Heimdall, after sighting Hrungnir's invasion and blowing the Gjallarhorn, he was, as expected, visited by Hugin and Munin. After informing the ravens of what he saw, he remained steadfast at his post. Though he was, as ever, armed with Hofund, his enchanted sword, he did not join the battle, for his role as guardian of the Bifrost was too important. Indeed, it was at times such as this, when the city was in direct danger, that it became more imperative that Heimdall stand fast at the rainbow bridge, for it would not do for Asgard to be invaded from a second front even as they fought within the city walls.

Luckily, Heimdall's good sword arm was not necessary, for Asgard's defenders were well rested after their battle against Baugi and his trolls. Upon receiving Heimdall's message as relayed by his ravens, Odin immediately summoned Frigga, Thor, Sif, Balder, Fandral, Hogun, and not only Volstagg, but also Volstagg's wife Gudrun to his throne room.

Balder had been at his home, reading a letter from his former page, Agnar, who was visiting family in Vanaheim. Balder would have liked to have Agnar's good right arm by his side, but he would never arrive in time. Besides, the lad had earned the rest.

Sif, Fandral, and Hogun had been drinking in a tavern, wherein several foolish males had challenged Sif to arm wrestle. Not a single one was victorious over the "fair maiden," and each had to buy Sif a drink. Fandral had been encouraging people to bet, while Hogun kept his peace, as always. When the summons from Odin came, Sif defeated her last foe and instructed him to buy drinks for the house, since they were now being called away.

Volstagg had been home with Gudrun, putting their children to bed by telling them the story of how he singlehandedly drove Baugi and his trolls from the gates of Asgard. The children listened attentively and with bated breath, even though they knew full well that their father was but one of six who drove off the trolls. It didn't matter, though, because it was how their father told the story that delighted them.

As for Thor, he had been on his way to Midgard, for Thor was a protector with two mistresses. For all that the responsibility of protecting Asgard weighed upon him, protecting Midgard did the same. While the people of that world no longer worshipped him as a god—save for a few cultists, though Thor did not encourage such behavior—he still took his duties as the protector of mortals quite seriously.

For many centuries, he had vouchsafed the mortals against threats both terrestrial and otherwise, and never had he wavered in his loyalty to humans.

Still, Heimdall would not have blown the Gjallarhorn without reason. Just as Thor knew he could leave Asgard knowing that Sif and the others would protect the Realm Eternal, Thor also knew that Midgard would manage without him. That world was well-stocked with heroes—the mightiest of whom were Thor's comrades in the Avengers—and they would take up Thor's mantle of safeguarding the mortals until he could return.

Thor flew past Heimdall on the rainbow bridge, waving to the guardian as he headed back to the throne room. Alighting on the steps, he saw Volstagg and Gudrun approaching.

"Why have you brought your noble wife to this meeting, Volstagg? Not," he quickly added, "that her presence is anything but a benefit."

Gudrun inclined her head. "You flatter me, Thor, but all I may say for sure is that Odin's summons specified myself *and* my husband."

Volstagg indicated the door. "We shall never learn the truth of the matter if we stand out here."

"No indeed, my friend. Let us go to my father and learn what new foe threatens our home."

Upon arrival, they saw that Sif, Balder, and Volstagg's two boon companions were already present, as was Frigga.

"The Lion of Asgard has arrived, along with my lovely wife, and the noble Thor," Volstagg said.

Fandral grinned. "Aye, we knew of your arrival by the quaking of the ground."

Thor turned to the throne. "Speak, Father, and tell us why Heimdall has blown the Gjallarhorn and called us to battle."

Odin spoke plainly: "We are invaded by frost giants."

Fandral actually laughed. "Did we accidentally hang a sign on the city gates that reads, 'please invade'?"

Hogun, of course, did not laugh. "Regardless of the reason, the frost giants will not be allowed to succeed where the trolls failed."

Thor held his hammer aloft. "Hogun speaks true, Father. We shall again protect the city."

"Be off with you, then," Odin said. "As for my wife, you and Gudrun have an additional duty to perform."

Even as the men departed—Volstagg looking confusedly at Gudrun on his way out—Frigga said, "What would you request of us, husband?"

"The frost giants are dangerous, and I fear that my own arrogance is at least in part responsible for their current attack. I also would not put it past Hrungnir to try to get at the warriors of Asgard through our children. Therefore, Frigga, I must ask that you and Gudrun gather all the children of Asgard and bring them to safety within the Vale of Crystal."

"Will we be safe there?" Gudrun asked, skeptical that a crystal vale would serve as protection against giants.

Frigga put a reassuring hand on Gudrun's arm. "It is a place of magic, Gudrun, one that will protect any within its walls and keep out those who would invade it."

The wife of Volstagg nodded slowly. "Very well, Lady Frigga, if you say it is safe then I, of course, do not doubt you. But I must ask, All-Father, do you truly feel this to be necessary?"

"It has been some time since the frost giants came this close to Asgard. And Hrungnir has proven to be a deadly foe. I simply wish not to take the chance."

"Of course, my husband," Frigga said before Gudrun could object further.

Even as the two women departed Odin's presence in order to gather all the children of Asgard and bring them to safety, Thor did lead his dearest comrades to the Ida Plain to face off against another foe bent upon invading Asgard.

This time, though, they were able to engage Hrungnir and his subjects before they penetrated the heart of the city.

Astride Golfaxi, Hrungnir led the giants out of Loki's passageway and across the plain. He saw the half dozen warriors awaiting his arrival in the city and snarled. "Where is Odin? I would see him pay for making a fool of Hrungnir the Mighty!"

Whirling his hammer, Thor said, "Your foolishness is entirely of your own making if you believe that this day will end in aught but defeat for you and yours, Hrungnir."

Smiling, Hrungnir said, "If I must go through the thunder god to get to his father, then so be it! I will deposit your cooling corpse at Odin's feet like a dog at a funeral. And that funeral will be old One-Eye's!"

And then the time for words was past, as Hrungnir's giants stormed forward.

Thor tightened his grip on Mjolnir and instructed it to fly him toward the leader of the giants.

But Hrungnir expected such a frontal assault from the thunder god, and he raised his club and swung it like a player in the Midgard game of baseball. The impact sent Thor flying through the air into the heart of the Ida Plain.

The others attempted to take on Hrungnir in Thor's place, but all five were soon occupied by the mighty one's subjects.

Sif found the way to Hrungnir blocked by three giants.

"Ho," the largest one said, "'tis a maiden of Asgard!"

"She is comely for one so short," said the smallest one, who still stood head and shoulders taller than Sif.

The middle one chortled. "Perhaps she will massage our bodies to relax us when we have conquered this city."

"The only touch you will receive from me is that of my blade!" And with those words, Sif leapt at the largest, who was so confounded by the very notion of a woman warrior that he merely stood agape as Sif's blade met his throat.

Angered, the small one raised his axe. "You killed Kare!"

The medium one whirled his mace. "He was our brother! Let's get her, Pal!"

"You betcha, Gamni!"

Sif raised her own sword. "You will join your brother ere long."

Pal and Gamni both charged at Sif, a frontal attack she easily dodged by ducking under their high reach. She attempted to thrust her sword upward to strike one of the brothers in the gullet as she dodged, but she was unable to land the blow.

Rolling on her left shoulder, she got to her feet and readied herself for the next attack.

Gamni again whirled his mace and swung it toward Sif, and she again ducked under it. But then she thrust her sword arm upward and snagged the mace's chain, which wrapped around her armored limb. She then reached out with her other arm and yanked the chain farther up toward the spiked ball at its end, redirecting the ball toward Pal.

The ball crushed Pal's hideous face, and the small giant fell to the ground.

Gamni's face fell. "No! Pal! You killed him with my weapon!"

"You have a keen grasp of the obvious, Gamni," Sif said, extricating her arm from the chain. "Now yield, or join them with Hela in the realm of the dead!"

To Sif's complete lack of surprise, Gamni chose not to yield, instead lunging at her, arms outstretched.

He tackled her as she stood fast, sword outstretched, and they both fell to the ground in a heap. Gamni's massive form was like a dead weight atop Sif, and she feared he would crush her from that alone, never mind whatever further attack he might now commit to.

But that further attack did not come, and Sif soon realized that the dead weight atop her was well and truly dead. She assumed that Gamni had fallen on her sword.

Gathering up every inch, every muscle, Sif pushed as hard as she could, and managed to roll Gamni's body off her. Catching her breath, she looked over to see that the giant, now on his back, indeed had her blade protruding from his chest, as she had guessed.

Even as Sif fought the three giant brothers, the Warriors Three stood before Hrungnir himself, astride his gold-maned horse, surrounded by a phalanx of giants on foot who raised their weapons to prevent Fandral, Hogun, and Volstagg from such a frontal assault as Thor had attempted.

But the Warriors Three did not allow such trivial concerns as a dozen giants stand in the way of their desire to trounce Hrungnir.

His great longsword Fimbuldraugr upraised, Fandral led the charge, diving directly into the fray by leaping through the air. As he came down toward two of the giants, he slashed at them both before landing on the head of a third.

A grin forming underneath his thick blond mustache, Fandral cried out, "Hogun! A gift for you!" as he again leapt in the air, being sure to kick off the head of the giant he'd landed upon.

The force of his kick sent the giant sprawling toward the ground, but his progress was impeded by Hridgandr, the mace of Hogun. The grim one swung his great weapon into the giant's face, crushing the creature's outsized nose.

Fandral leapt to another giant's head and from that vantage point was able to smack another with the flat of his blade before again leaping and kicking to drive his temporary mount toward the ground.

"And one for you, voluminous one!" Fandral cried to Volstagg.

"Only one?" Volstagg asked as he reached back and then walloped the giant with a crushing right hook, which redirected the unfortunate giant to land atop the one whose face Hogun had pulverized. "You do insult the Lion of Asgard, Fandral, by only giving him *one* foe to vanquish!"

Hogun, typically, said nothing, instead sliding across the ground and using his mace to trip two of the giants, sending them both stumbling groundward.

However, they too found their journey to the dirt impeded by the fists of Volstagg. "See, Fandral? Hogun does appreciate Volstagg's prowess, for he gives me two giants to thrash!"

Normally, Fandral would reply to Volstagg's egotistical ramblings only by mocking them, but no appropriately cutting retort came to his lips. So he said nothing as he sheathed his sword and leapt to another giant, while Volstagg delivered a pair of uppercuts which sent both Hogun's giants flying to land atop the other two.

Fandral now hung onto the shoulders of one of the giants, dangling from the creature's back as if he were a cape. The giant struggled, trying to reach behind himself to grab the dashing one. For his part, Fandral took advantage of the giant's stumbling struggles to kick at his fellows. When the giant lumbered over to where the four giants lay atop each other, Fandral let go of the right shoulder. Reaching for his blade, he again unsheathed Fimbuldraugr from its scabbard and ran the giant through.

Even as the creature fell on top of his four insensate comrades, Fandral leapt to the head of another giant—but this one was ready for his assault and grabbed Fandral around the waist.

Fandral tried to gasp in pain, but even that was denied him as the giant's iron grip kept him from drawing breath.

Hogun had just tripped another giant for Volstagg to clout

when he saw that Fandral was snagged. Without hesitating, he twirled Hridgandr and threw the mace toward the giant's head.

Though the giant did not fall, the impact of the mace against his temple did cause him to loosen his grip on Fandral, enough so that he was able to push apart the giant's fingers enough so that he could leap away, landing on the ground right next to Volstagg.

"Ho, Fandral, have you decided to at last join in the fight instead of dancing about like a will-o'-the-wisp?"

Long accustomed to ignoring Volstagg's badinage for the good humor that it was, Fandral merely said, "I see no reason for you to have all the fun, voluminous one."

"Then let us thrash these unruly giants together!"

As the Warriors Three continued their battle against the giants protecting Hrungnir, Balder stood against a half dozen giants of his own.

"Be wary of Balder, my brothers," one of them said.

Another said, "He is alleged to be Asgard's greatest warrior, even greater than Thor!"

"Bah," said a third, "he's all talk and no action."

"Don't be so sure of that!" cried the fourth, who cringed a bit.

The fifth said, "'Twas he who singlehandedly gave Utgard-Loki his greatest defeat."

To Balder's surprise, the sixth said nothing, choosing instead to simply growl.

With a smile beneath his flat-horned helm, Balder said,

"'Twas not singlehanded, for I had aid from my friends in bringing Utgard-Loki to heel. Either way, you would think that the frost giants would give Asgard in general and me in particular a wide berth after that. But then, your kind has never been renowned for being quick of mind."

"Get him!"

Four of the giants ran toward Balder at once, and the brave one did almost pity their simplistic strategy. Even as the quartet of large creatures converged on a small target, Balder quickly dove away from his position, leaving the four giants to crash into each other, their massive heads colliding with those of their fellows.

As the foursome collapsed in a heap of cranial trauma, Balder turned his attention to the other two, which included the one who recalled his defeat of Utgard-Loki and the one who only growled.

The growler raised an axe and swung it directly at Balder's head with a speed that belied his massive form. Balder heard the whistle of the axe's blade as he barely managed to dodge it.

However, the other giant rather sensibly tackled Balder with a low dive when he was in his crouch. Balder and the giant rolled about on the ground for several seconds before Balder was able to extricate himself.

Now Balder stood between the two giants, the growler with his axe and the other one with his great sword.

For several seconds, Balder managed to keep both at bay. He ducked the growler's axe and parried the other's sword, then kicked the growler in the shin followed by a strike at the other's side, barely parried in time by the great sword. He rolled between the growler's legs, thus avoiding a swing of the great sword, and keeping the axe from cleaving his head in twain.

A much louder growl, now, as the giant turned and swung his axe at Balder, but this time Balder raised his sword to parry the blow, rather than dodge it. The giant's growl was cut off by an "Arooo?" of surprise, as the axe slammed into Balder's sword with a bone-shuddering impact of metal on metal. The giant stared, transfixed. Every other time some fool had tried to parry his great axe with a sword, the sword had been shattered by the giant's sheer strength.

Until now.

Balder took advantage of the giant's shock to rear back and punch the creature in the stomach with his full strength. The growling giant fell to the ground, having lost the ability to catch his breath.

That left just the one with the great sword, who regarded Balder angrily. "What did you mean that we are not renowned for being quick of mind?"

Rather than respond verbally, Balder simply pressed the attack with his own sword. The giant parried with surprising skill. Indeed, each time Balder pressed his attack, the giant responded with a parry that Balder recognized as a formal move from his own training as a youth.

"I am impressed," he said to his opponent. "Most giants rely on their brute strength to win the day, yet you possess skill with a blade that rivals even my own!"

"Say instead that my skill surpasses yours, for I am Bjarni, son of Thjasse, great-grandson of Ymir himself, and from this day forth I shall be known as the one who killed Balder the Bra—"

The rest of Bjarni's rant was cut off as Balder smacked Bjarni on the side of the head with the flat of his blade.

Bjarni fell to the ground, stunned, both from the blow to his head and at not being able to fulfill what he had expected to be his destiny.

Balder looked about and saw that Sif was now being harried by several giants, and the ones the Warriors Three had taken on were similarly ganging up on the trio. Hrungnir himself was hanging back away from the fighting, but unable to proceed forward to Asgard due to the melee he had inspired.

Now that he had a moment to himself, however, Balder had a tactic he could employ. But before he could begin to do so, he heard a distant rumbling.

And then the ground shook beneath everyone's feet as the sound of thunder filled the air.

And then the sky crackled with lightning that flashed in everyone's eyes.

And then a red-and-blue figure flew upward into the sky and started hurtling toward the giants.

Goldfaxi reared back on his hind legs and gave a pitiful whinny at the display. Hrungnir had to struggle to maintain his grip upon the horse, his legs tightening around the horse's middle while his hands clutched the reins for dear life.

Thor rocketed through the air and smashed into Hrungnir, knocking the giant from his mount.

The giants all ceased what they were doing, stunned at seeing their leader brought low.

Thor came around for another pass. "Yield, Hrungnir, or face the wrath of a storm as only the god of thunder can rain down upon you!"

"Make it rain all you wish, Thor," Hrungnir bellowed over the sound of the precipitation crashing down upon the plain, "but I shall not rest until I have had my revenge! I have already had indignity rained upon me from Asgard, so let your storm fly! Asgard will be mine, and Odin's broken body will be laid at my feet!"

"I say nay," Thor cried. "I say *never*! Asgard shall not be yours as long as I draw breath!"

"Time to end your breathing, then." Hrungnir grinned and leapt back upon Goldfaxi.

Thor whipped 'round his hammer. More thunder roared. More lightning flashed. And more giants cringed.

Balder knew that the giants' shock could only make his plan a better one. Balder had often been called "the shining one," and those words were no mere poetry.

"Everyone," he cried out, "shield your eyes!"

And then Balder used his unique ability to glow brightly.

* * *

Sif, Thor, and the Warriors Three all covered their eyes, while the frost giants felt the brightness even more than they were blinded by it. For Balder's brightness was that of the sun itself, and it was anathema to the frost giants, who preferred the chill of winter to the glow of summer that Balder's power provided.

Seeing what his dear friend had done, Thor immediately whirled his hammer as fast as he could over his head.

The thunder and lightning intensified more and began to strike the individual giants one by one.

Those frost giants who were not felled immediately ran out into the Ida Plain.

One of those was Hrungnir who, with a murderous look at the thunder god, kicked Goldfaxi into a gallop.

Again Thor whirled his hammer, but this time it was to have Mjolnir take him to the air again. Flying over the plain, he had a spectacular view of all the giants scattering to the winds, running toward the mountains at the far end of Ida. Ahead of all of them was Hrungnir atop Goldfaxi.

"Come storm!" Thor cried. "Obey your master, Thor, and strike at the varlets who would invade the glowing halls of Asgard! Strike! And do not cease until our enemies lie insensate at the feet of the god of thunder!"

Thor felt the power of the storm course through Mjolnir and through him. His birthright was to make the thunder and lightning obey him, and he gathered that power to him and let it loose through his hammer upon the Ida Plain.

Lightning cracked, thunder boomed, and rain fell from the

sky in sheets, pelting the giants and forcing them to their knees.

Sif, Balder, and the Warriors Three strode out into the plain, the rain rattling off their armor, and they gathered up the frost giants. Their foes whimpered, having been weakened by Balder's glow and frightened by Thor's might.

Thor landed alongside his friends and soon they had all the forlorn frost giants rounded up around the pile of more than half a dozen giants that had fallen as a result of Volstagg's fists.

And then he realized that one was missing.

"Where is Hrungnir?"

The others looked about, but the very storm that Thor had summoned had reduced visibility to almost nothing. The warriors of Asgard could barely even see the nearby mountains.

Thunder echoing behind her words, Sif said, "I do not see him, nor his gold-maned horse."

Thor shook his head. "Hrungnir's mount is second only to my father's own Sleipnir for speed. In truth he might easily have been able to outrun even this storm."

Fandral laughed, his well-kept blond hair now a dark brown and flat against his head from the rain. "What does it matter? We have taken Hrungnir's subjects!"

Volstagg added, "Hrungnir would be best to use his speedy horse to ride as far from Asgard as possible, lest he feel Volstagg's wrath as his fellows did."

"Yes," Sif said, "I doubt we will hear much from Hrungnir after this defeat."

Thor raised his hammer upright, and within moments the

storm dispersed, the rain slowed to nothing, and the sun started to shine again.

"Today is another victory, my friends! Let us bring these perfidious giants to Odin's dungeon. They shall enter the city gates, not as the invaders they had hoped, but as our prisoners. And then tonight—we feast!"

All five of Thor's fellow warriors cheered Thor as they led or carried the defeated giants to their fate.

CHAPTER FIVE

"Hilde! Flosi's touching me!"

"Am *not*! I wouldn't *ever* touch *you*, Alaric!"

"Would too!"

Gunnhild, daughter of Volstagg, hated being called Hildy—that was a stupid little girl's name—but was willing to be called Hilde, a subtle but important difference. She rolled her eyes at the behavior of her younger siblings.

Mother and Frigga were taking the children of Asgard to a place in the Vale of Crystal to be safe in case the frost giants invaded. They had charged Hilde with keeping an eye on Alaric and Flosi, one of her younger brothers and one of her younger sisters, who had been fighting for *weeks*.

Because she was the oldest girl, Hilde was always stuck taking care of the babies when Mother was too busy. This once, Hilde didn't mind so much, since she knew it was important for everyone to behave, and—even with Frigga's help—Mother had her hands full with all the other children of Asgard.

This wasn't the first time this had happened. When Surtur attacked Asgard, Frigga had taken the children into the mountains to hide. Odin had told Hilde that he wanted the children to protect his wife, and Hilde had believed him at the time, but now that she was older and smarter, Hilde knew better.

She wondered if these frost giants were as dangerous as Surtur. She guessed they had to be, if Odin sent them all away again.

"Flosi, *stop touching me*!"

"I'm *not*!"

Hilde sighed. She, Flosi, Alaric, and the rest of Volstagg's children were in the middle of the pack. Mother led the way through the mountain path, which was covered in snow; on one side was a huge drop to the ground that got even bigger the farther along they went. At least the path was wide, and everyone was staying on the side of the path that had the mountain.

Frigga took up the rear, making sure that the ones in back didn't stray off the snow-covered path. She was armed, which was different from the last time. When they ran from Surtur, the queen of Asgard had not been armed. That worried Hilde that the threat of the frost giants might even be worse.

Then again, Odin had been lost in the battle against Surtur, and not restored to Asgard for some time. Maybe Frigga just wanted to be prepared for the worst this time.

"Hilde, make her stop touching me!"

"*I'm not touching you!* I wouldn't touch you if I had to touch you to stop Ragnarok!"

Hilde cried out, "Enough! If you two don't stop talking, I'll throw both of you over the mountain!"

"You wouldn't dare." Alaric tried to sound tough, but Hilde could tell that he was scared that she'd actually do it.

Flosi was more defiant. "She *won't*. Mother would never forgive her if she killed us."

"Oh really?" Hilde asked, fists clenched. "*I* think that Mother will be grateful to have two fewer mouths to feed, and two less people making noise all the time. Wanna see who's right?"

Both Flosi and Alaric gulped audibly and then kept walking without saying a word.

Hilde smiled. It was just a question of reasoning with the little ones.

They trudged through the snow a bit farther in lovely silence.

So of course, it couldn't last. Out of nowhere, Alaric asked, "What's that noise?"

"*Will* you be quiet?" Hilde said

But then Flosi said, "I hear it, too!"

Those two wouldn't even agree that the sky was blue, so if they each heard something, there probably was a noise.

And then Hilde heard it, too. It almost sounded like a horse galloping.

She turned and called back to the end of their group. "Lady Frigga! Do you hear that?"

Frigga, though, had already unsheathed her sword and was turning to see what might be making the sound—which was growing louder.

Hilde looked at the mountain side of the path and noticed that the rock of the mountain face was faceted and had plenty of handholds. Without another word, she started climbing.

"What are you doing?" Flosi cried out.

Alaric also yelled, "Hilde, that's crazy!"

Frigga heard the commotion and turned around to see Hilde clambering up the side of the mountain. "Hilde!"

At this point, however, Hilde had gotten far enough up the rock face to see some distance down the mountain.

Calling out to Frigga, she said, "There's a giant riding up the path! He's on a yellow horse!"

Frigga felt her heart grow cold. "Are you sure, Hilde?"

In fact, Hilde was completely sure, but it didn't do to question the mother of all Asgard, so Hilde squinted and peered down the mountain again.

"Definitely a big giant and definitely a yellow horse. Moving fast, too."

"Not good," Frigga muttered. "How far up the mountain has he come?"

"He just passed that weird tree that Kevin and Mick tried to climb."

Frigga nodded. The two mortal children whom Volstagg and Gudrun had adopted at Thor's request after their parents died on Midgard had immediately tried to climb the twisted oak near the base of the mountain, and it had taken quite a stern admonition from Gudrun to get them to cease. It had taken them half a day to traverse from that tree to where they were now. Hrungnir's mount would close that distance in much less time.

"Come down from there, Hilde, and gather everyone!"

"Okay!"

While Frigga wasn't entirely sure why Hrungnir would be riding alone through these mountains—there were better paths from Asgard to Jotunheim—the best reason she could think of was that Thor and the others had routed the giants, and Hrungnir took advantage of his mount's famous speed to escape.

It also explained why the giant had come this way. Were he endeavoring to escape her son's wrath at all costs, he would not have paid close attention to direction.

Sadly, that put the children right in his path. The very fate Odin had sent them into the mountains to avoid was now dangerously close to coming to pass.

"What is going on?" Gudrun asked.

Turning, Frigga saw that Hilde had indeed gotten everyone to stop moving and gather in one place.

"You must all move quickly. Hrungnir is on his way, and he must be stopped. You will all need to move twice as fast and hie yourselves to the Vale of Crystal."

"I don't understand," Gudrun said with a frown. "Hrungnir rides the fastest mount in the Nine Worlds, save only Odin's horse. Are we to outrun such a beast?"

"You will if I delay him. Go, Gudrun!" she added, holding up a hand to cut off another objection. "The more you speak, the greater chance that the giant catches you. When you enter the Vale of Crystal, you will be protected. But you must get there—now go!"

Gudrun harrumphed, but she was used to not getting a word in edgewise, having been married to Volstagg all these years. "Come, children, let us move quickly!" While Gudrun was a woman of some size, she also could be quite swift afoot when the need called for it—usually chasing one of the little ones around the house when they got into mischief—and so she immediately strode forward up the mountain path.

While she tried to set the pace, several of the children outstripped her, with Hilde naturally in the lead. She was physically the strongest of her children, even more so than the boys, and also the fiercest. Gudrun knew her daughter would not go too far ahead, lest they be separated, but she also felt that they were all a little bit safer with Hilde in the lead.

Behind them, Frigga watched as the children and Gudrun fled. Up to this point, they had been walking at a leisurely pace, not wishing to tire the children out—particularly Kevin and Mick, who were less hardy than Asgardian children, even though they had been dining on the golden apples of immortality since joining the family. But now that there was danger, she doubted anything would stop them from moving at top speed to the Vale of Crystal. Frigga herself had placed the wards upon the Vale that would protect all those who entered from any harm. She also would know when those wards were triggered, no matter where in the Nine Worlds she might be.

Frigga then proceeded back the way they had come. Best to be as far from the children as possible when she confronted Hrungnir. Besides, there was a plateau less than an hour's walk down the path that would be the perfect place to confront him and delay the giant until her charges were safe.

As she'd hoped, she reached that plateau before encountering Hrungnir, though the hoofbeats of Goldfaxi now echoed loudly through the chill air, signaling that the giant's arrival was imminent.

When Hrungnir turned 'round the bend and arrived at the plateau, he found himself confronted with fifty women wielding swords.

And all of them looked just like Frigga.

Yanking on the reins, Hrungnir cried, "Whoa!" The action was wholly unnecessary, as the sudden sight of a phalanx of Friggas was enough to spook the horse, and he stopped all on his own.

"Is it not enough that I am tormented by the husband? Now the wife vexes me!"

One of the Friggas said, "You will not pass this plateau, Hrungnir."

Another added, "We stand before you united."

A third said, "And we will not allow you through."

"Ha! First Odin had to disguise himself, then Thor uses that stupid hammer of his, and now you use illusions! You Asgardians are all illusions and shadows and toys with no true power. I will destroy each and every one of you!"

With that, Hrungnir kicked Goldfaxi forward and swung his club at the closest of the Friggas.

The club's impact caused the simulacrum Frigga had created to dissolve in a puff of light.

Frigga had hidden herself behind a snowdrift. Unfortunately, the illusions required proximity and effort to maintain. All she needed to do was keep throwing images of herself at the giant until Gudrun and the children made it safely to the Vale.

Luckily, Hrungnir had a very direct and deliberate approach. He simply attacked each image of Frigga in turn. It took him some time to wade through all fifty, especially once Frigga had them move about and dodge the giant's club, making him believe that *this* was the real one because it put up resistance.

In truth, when there were fifty, Frigga could do little but make them stand in a particular pose and speak with her voice, but once he eliminated a dozen or so, it freed her to manipulate the images more aggressively.

For Hrungnir's part, he had hoped that fighting fifty versions of Odin's wife and killing all of them would bring him the satisfaction that his abortive invasion of Asgard had failed to provide. But all it served to do was frustrate him even further.

And so with each image of Frigga he clubbed into nothingness, he got angrier and angrier.

Seeing the giant's fury, Frigga sent two of her illusory selves toward the edge of the plateau.

One held up her sword. "Face me if you dare, giant."

"Assuming you are not a coward," the other said, her sword lowered. "My husband has already defeated you, and it seems my son has done the same—so you come to run and hide in the mountains only to be beaten by me."

"Your husband tricked me! And you will pay for his perfidy,

woman!" Hrungnir shrieked as he kicked Goldfaxi into a gallop, rushing headlong toward the two illusions.

But then the horse pulled up, showing more sense than Hrungnir, skidding to a halt before both mount and rider could go tumbling over the edge.

The snow kicked up by Goldfaxi's sudden stop was enough to penetrate the spell, and the two Friggas by the edge also disappeared.

Hrungnir patted his noble horse on the side of the head. "Well done, my faithful steed. We would surely both have perished had I assaulted these false images." He dismounted from the horse and again patted him, this time on the side. "Rest, Goldfaxi, for I have taxed you much this day. I will deal with Odin's trollop myself."

A dozen images remained, and Frigga was starting to feel the stress of casting so many illusions at once. Still, she persevered, for the wards in the Vale had not yet been activated. And so the twelve Friggas moved to surround the giant.

Hrungnir held up his club and smiled. "I know you are nearby, witch. Even Loki could not work such magicks from a distance, and you are far from your son's equal in sorcerous matters."

"Oh, you believe that, do you?" said one of the Friggas.

Another said, "I taught my son everything he knows."

"But," a third said, "that doesn't mean I taught him everything *I* know."

A fourth Frigga moved to attack Hrungnir with her sword,

an obvious frontal assault that the giant easily parried, sending another simulacrum to oblivion.

But even as Hrungnir swung his club through the insubstantial form of Odin's wife, two more illusions attacked him from behind, and while the swords they carried had no physical substance, Frigga had imbued these final eleven images with magickal force that could be transmitted through the blades.

Hrungnir screamed as the swords of the two illusions sliced through his belly, weakening him with eldritch force. Snarling due to the unexpected pain, Hrungnir swung his club blindly behind him to eliminate those two, and then he charged at three more of them, wiping them out before they could raise their swords.

Of the half-dozen remaining, several managed to strike Hrungnir, but none were enough to fell the giant, and soon enough they had all been dispatched, leaving the frost giant to stand, weakened, but alone save for his mount.

"I know you're nearby, witch!" Hrungnir bellowed. "Do not think you can hide from me! I may not have your gift for spellcraft, but the frost giants are as one with the snow and ice, and none may hide amidst the cold from such as I for long."

And then Hrungnir upraised his arms, commanding the snow on the ground to move away and blow off the very same cliff's edge that Frigga tried to trick Hrungnir into going over.

Within moments, Frigga's cover was blown away, and she was forced to stand and face the giant.

"Your pretty tricks are at an end, wife of the hated All-Father. And without your illusions, you are nothing."

Frigga raised her sword. "Do you imagine, Hrungnir, that I am helpless before you? After all, you know that the mother of Loki is proficient in the ways of spellcraft. Does it not follow that the mother of Thor is able to fight?"

"Ha!" Hrungnir followed his derisive laugh with a mighty swing of his club.

One that Frigga easily parried with her sword. For while it was hardly the Sword of Frey, the wielder of which could never know defeat, Frigga's sword was fashioned for her by Eitri, the master smith of the dwarves. And so when the giant's club—made from the mighty oaks that had grown in Jotunheim since the dawn of time—collided with Frigga's blade, it echoed throughout the mountains.

Hrungnir expected that the Mother of Asgard would have a powerful blade, but he did not expect her to have the physical strength to withstand even a parried blow from a giant.

Frigga took advantage of the giant's shock by pressing her attack. Hrungnir parried each of her strikes, but it grew more difficult with each one. The magickal blows from the illusory swords added to the brutal attacks by Thor to wear away at even the frost giant's mighty constitution.

Unfortunately, Frigga herself was also growing weaker. It had been a very long time since she had cast so many spells at once. But still the wards had not been triggered, and until Gudrun and the children were safe, she dared not let up on her assault.

Frigga swung her sword at Hrungnir's left side. He blocked it, of course, but she immediately swung the sword over her head and down at the frost giant's right ankle. Hrungnir was able to dodge the strike by lifting his foot, which prompted Frigga to thrust the hilt of her sword at the giant's chest. With one foot off the ground, Hrungnir lost his balance and toppled backward, but he managed to shove at Frigga before falling, and she too wound up on her back in the snow.

Both of them quickly got to their feet, one feinting, the other parrying, with neither gaining an advantage.

"You fight well, Frigga," Hrungnir said, respecting his foe enough to use her name rather than an epithet. "Odin chose his wife well."

"What makes you think *he* chose *me*?" Frigga asked with a sweet smile, and then kicked a pile of snow upward toward the giant's face.

It only distracted the giant for but a moment, but it was enough for Frigga to come at him with her sword—

—or, rather, attempt to. She slipped on the very snow pile she had just kicked and stumbled forward, right into the grip of the giant.

Hrungnir wrapped both his meaty hands around Frigga's waist. "You fought well, Frigga. Though I am the victor now, know that—unlike your husband with his tricks and your son with his foolish hammer—I truly believe that you could have beaten Hrungnir the Mighty in a fair fight. Alas, the Nine Worlds are many things, but fair is not among them."

Barely able to catch her breath from being crushed by the giant, Frigga asked, "Am I to be killed, then?"

"Oh no, my worthy foe. You are of far more use to me alive than dead. No, you are a prisoner of the frost giants."

Even as consciousness fled from Frigga, she at last felt the activation of the wards that surrounded the Vale of Crystal.

Gudrun and the children were safe.

And then Frigga's mind went dark.

CHAPTER SIX

The first thing Odin did when Thor returned to the throne room to announce that Hrungnir's forces were routed was to send his son to the Vale of Crystal to tell Frigga, Gudrun, and the children that they could return home.

"Perhaps I acted in haste to send them from the city," Odin said, "but I feared the wrath of Hrungnir might lead to the endangering of the innocents of Asgard. It is my sworn duty to protect them."

Thor smiled. "You need not explain, Father. Evil's strength is its lack of caring for the fate of those not involved in the conflict. While Hrungnir's animus is toward you, not the children, it would still be very much in his character to harm them to get to you. It was right that you sent them away." He knelt respectfully before the All-Father. "I will hie myself to the Vale of Crystal at once!"

After exiting the throne room, Thor whirled his hammer over his head, and then it shot into the air, pulling him along through the skies. He watched as the soldiers of Asgard brought the giants to the dungeon, joining Baugi the troll, who also dared to menace the great city. Then he flew leisurely toward the mountains.

Something caught his eye, and he cut short his flying to alight on a large plateau. The snow was heavily disturbed, and there were many scattered foot- and hoofprints, the former of two different sizes.

There had been a great battle on that spot, and it was recent. And this plateau was on the route Gudrun and Frigga would have taken to the Vale. It was unclear which of the two people walked away from the fight—the only prints that continued onward were those of the horse.

Again Thor twirled his hammer, but now he felt the need for haste. Urging Mjolnir to move at top speed, he flew to the Vale of Crystal. Located in the heart of the Asgard Mountains, the Vale was a dodecahedron made entirely of crystals. Mined millennia ago by the dwarves, the crystals were useful for the channeling of spells. The mages of Vanaheim traded the dwarves for the crystals and constructed this place. It had not had much use in a while, though Thor knew that his mother used to come here quite a bit, and also that she was capable of warding it against attack. No doubt, that was why the All-Father chose it as the place to hide the children of Asgard from the frost giants.

He alighted at the Vale's entrance—or, rather, where he was fairly certain the entrance was. Frigga had shown him the location of the hidden entrance once, and he recalled that all he needed to do was walk through.

Sure enough, he approached what appeared to be a solid wall of crystal and walked right through it to a large sitting room filled with chairs and tables and cushions.

The first words he heard upon entering were, "Frigga, you finally made it!"

Even as Gudrun said those words, Thor felt the impact of several small bodies on his legs.

"Thor!"

"Yay, it's Thor!"

"Is Asgard safe?"

"Are all the giants dead?"

Gudrun's words had given the thunder god pause, but he put on a smile for the benefit of the children. "Yes, Asgard is safe once more. Of the giants who attacked, only their leader Hrungnir got away. Rather than remain to face the consequences of his actions alongside his people, he turned and ran like the craven varlet he is."

Hilde—one of the few children not currently embracing Thor's calves—said, "We know, we saw him coming up the mountain. Frigga stayed behind to stop him."

"We thought you were her," Gudrun added. "She should have come here by now."

Anger boiled within Thor's heart. The mighty battle he saw the aftermath of on the plateau was almost certainly between Frigga and Hrungnir. Frigga, he knew, was on foot, and Hrungnir was riding the speedy Goldfaxi. Which meant that the fact that hoofprints were all that exited the battlefield bespoke a victory for the frost giant.

But he tamped down the anger, not wishing the children, or Gudrun, to worry. "I have come in Frigga's stead. The battle is won, and Asgard is safe once again. You may all return to your homes."

Gudrun let out a huge breath. "Thank the Fates. I feared we would be trapped in this crystalline labyrinth for weeks."

Thor chuckled despite himself. Gudrun hated being away from her own home. She often made excuses not to attend feasts in the great hall of Asgard, preferring to stay behind and keep an eye on the children too small to attend those feasts. While many teased Volstagg about how he went out on adventures with Fandral and Hogun to avoid being stuck at home with Gudrun, the truth, Thor knew, was that Gudrun herself was the one that preferred to remain alone, leaving the adventuring to her husband. A gentle home life was what she preferred.

Well, as gentle as possible with so many children underfoot.

Prying the children off his legs, Thor said, "I must return to Asgard immediately. The passage you came by is clear and safe—you may return at your leisure."

Gudrun favored him with a bright smile. "Thank you, Thor."

He bowed. "Of course, my lady Gudrun."

Only after he departed from the Vale and took to the air once more did he allow his concern to show on his countenance.

This battle with Hrungnir may have ended well for Asgard, but Thor now realized that the war with the giant had only just begun, and his foe had struck a brutal blow.

Upon returning to Asgard, he went straight to the throne room, where Odin was consulting with his vizier.

Odin saw his son enter, and dismissed the vizier, for they

were discussing minor matters of state that were of very little moment. He could postpone them to speak to his son, especially since he had returned so quickly from checking in on Frigga.

"I am afraid, Father, that I bring dire news." Quickly, Thor filled Odin in on what he had learned: that Gudrun and the children were safe, but Frigga was last seen going to engage Hrungnir.

"The children were well enough settled in that they had been at the Vale long enough for Mother to have joined them," Thor said, "*if* she had won her battle against Hrungnir. But the giant is a doughty warrior, whatever his flaws. Mother would be hard-pressed to be victorious against him."

For several seconds, Odin did not reply.

Then, without warning, he cried out with an incoherent scream as power flew forth from his fingertips, smashing several of the statues that dotted the throne room.

However, the outburst did little to assuage Odin's feelings on the subject. "I am a fool, Thor. I should have revealed myself to Hrungnir."

Thor shook his head. "That would have changed nothing, Father. Hrungnir's arrogance would have forced him to challenge Sleipnir even knowing that 'twas him and you rather than a stranger and an unknown horse."

"Perhaps, but I suspect the giant's attack was as much due to my deception as it was Sleipnir's victory over Goldfaxi. Had I but revealed myself—even after the race—then only I would have incurred Hrungnir's wrath. Instead, in my arrogance, I have caused the endangerment—possibly even the death—of the light of my very life."

The Warriors Three then came into the hall, accompanied by a strange creature that seemed to be dripping water.

Peering more closely, Thor saw that it was an ice elemental—a clump of ice given temporary form and substance. Such creatures were commonly employed as errand-makers in Jotunheim, but they did not survive for long outside the cold climes of the land of the giants.

"Forgive our intrusion," Fandral said, "but this messenger from Jotunheim was quite insistent upon an audience with Odin."

Odin sat down upon his throne, placing his hands firmly on the armrests. "You were correct to do so, Fandral. Bring him forward, ere he melts before speaking his piece!"

In the time it took for the creature to walk across the throne room, it became half a head smaller, its features less distinct, a trail of cold water left behind in its wake. Fandral, Volstagg, and Hogun walked alongside it, joining Thor at the foot of the throne.

The creature made a small bow to the throne before speaking. "Hail to Odin All-Father, king of the powerful gods of Asgard. I bring greetings from Hrungnir the Brawler."

"Arrive at the purpose of your journey quickly, messenger," Odin said in a grave, threatening tone.

Showing no signs of being so threatened, the creature continued. "The Lady Frigga is a guest of the mighty Hrungnir.

She is unharmed," the messenger added quickly, even as Odin leaned forward in his seat. "She will remain so, for Hrungnir has no quarrel with her. However, her release back to Asgard can be accomplished only one way: Thor Odinson must travel to Jotunheim *alone* and face Hrungnir in personal combat. It will be Hrungnir against Thor—neither may have assistance in any way from their fellows. If your son abides by these terms, then Frigga will be released back to you. If Thor does *not* abide by these terms—if, for example, another Asgardian comes with him or in his place—then Frigga's status as an unharmed guest of the frost giants will be rather negatively changed. If you accept, Thor must arrive in Jotunheim by nightfall. If Thor does not come alone, or does not come at all, then Frigga's life will come to a premature end."

And then the creature's entire body warped and melted; within seconds, there was but a puddle before the All-Father's throne.

"It would seem," Hogun said, "that the messenger was not instructed to wait for a reply."

Thor shook his head. "He will know his reply by whether or not I arrive alone in Jotunheim to face him."

Odin stared at his son with his one good eye. "Summon brave Balder and noble Sif to the throne room!"

Thor widened his eyes in surprise. It was unlike his father to consult with others on such a matter. His word was, after all, law.

Within moments, both had joined Thor and the Warriors

Three in the throne room. Thor quickly filled them in on the latest development.

When Thor finished, Odin said, "The decision before me is a difficult one, and while I typically would but *make* the decision and have done with it, I find now that concern for both my wife and my son do cloud my normally clear judgment. You are the finest Asgard has to offer, and so I ask of you: What do you recommend that Odin decide?"

Thor spoke before anyone else could. "You need not concern yourself with my own well-being, Father. Gladly will I face the giant in order to save Mother—or indeed even were her life not at stake. He has already escaped once."

"Thor is correct," Fandral said, "but he should not go alone. Even if the Lady Frigga were not his prisoner, it would behoove us to seek out Hrungnir and smite him for daring to invade."

"Agreed," Sif said. "One good invasion deserves another. We can have troops gathered within a day, and we will ride across the Ida Plain, through the mountains, and into Jotunheim. We will rout them, and take Frigga home after our triumph."

Volstagg nodded his round head. "Indeed! Why, simply allow the Lion of Asgard to march through Jotunheim, and the frost giants will be cowed by my magnificence!"

"Cowed with laughter, more like," Hogun muttered. "I respectfully disagree with my comrades, Lord Odin. Hrungnir does not strike me as one who goes back on his word. If any other than Thor approach, the Lady Frigga's life would be forfeit."

Balder nodded. "I agree with Hogun. Hrungnir is bold and fearless. And from what I hear, he has encroached quite heavily on Nornheim." Balder spoke obliquely, though it was hardly a secret that Karnilla, the Queen of the Norns, loved Balder, and that the brave one had taken to returning the favor. Still, Balder knew his friends disapproved of the liaison—they did not know the Norn Queen as he did—and so he spoke directly of it as little as possible.

Thor looked over his dearest friends. "My brave and noble comrades, I do appreciate your willingness to join me in Jotunheim, but Hogun and Balder are correct. For Mother's sake, I *dare* not do aught but go alone to face Hrungnir as he has requested."

Angrily, Sif asked, "And what proof have we that he will keep his word that he will fight you alone?"

"He will keep his word," Odin said. "Whatever else Hrungnir may be, he is no oath-breaker. He proved that to me when we raced, for he thought me a simple traveler and could easily have gone back on the wager. But he did not. And Balder is correct—I encountered him on the road that leads from Nornheim to Jotunheim. If he is bold enough to challenge both Karnilla and myself, then he is not one to be trifled with—particularly with Frigga's life at stake."

Sif, however, was not convinced. "He is still a frost giant. Perhaps he was willing to keep his word regarding a simple horse race, but now? He has been humiliated before his subjects—first by Sleipnir showing up his precious mount, and then by his failed invasion of Asgard. In order to win back their love and affection after so thorough a defeat as we handed him, he will need to do something bold. Obviously, he wishes to be the one to finally defeat Thor, but I'm sure he will settle for being the one to kill Frigga if he must."

"You speak wisely, Sif," Odin said, "and your words do give me pause—but no more than that." He rose to his feet once more. "Thor will go alone, and he will do battle with Hrungnir. So be it!"

Thor bowed. "As you command, Father."

"However," Odin added quickly, "Hrungnir requested only that Thor go to Jotunheim alone to face the giant in battle. He said nothing of what we might do here in Asgard. Balder, Sif, you and the Warriors Three will gather our forces on the Ida Plain. Summon Harokin and have him muster the Einherjar as well. Should Thor fall, or should Hrungnir become as poor at keeping his word as Sif fears, then the entire wrath of Asgard will be brought to bear on Jotunheim, and the frost giants will rue the day they ever left the cold confines of their land."

The five of them all bowed their heads. Balder said, "It will be done, Lord Odin."

Stepping down from the throne, Odin put his hands on Thor's shoulders. "I wish you well, my son. The life of your sweet mother—my noble wife—hangs in the balance. But I have ever relied upon your strong right arm and your ability to wield Mjolnir to defend all the Nine Worlds. I am sure you will do no less on this day."

"You may be assured, Father, that I would face Hela herself if it meant saving Mother's life." With that, Thor turned and left the throne room, his friends on his heels.

Balder patted Thor on the back. "Fight well, my friend. I wish I could go with you—but if Frigga is to be saved, I do believe that you have by far the best chance of doing so."

"Thank you, my old friend."

"Be wary, son of Odin," Hogun said. "Hrungnir did come upon Asgard more quickly than he should have before Heimdall's sharp eyes saw him. He may have aid in his campaign against us."

"You may well be correct, Hogun," Thor replied with a nod, "but it matters not. The life of my mother is all with which I am concerned this day. All I care for with regards to Hrungnir is how I may defeat him."

"And defeat him, you shall," Fandral said with his trademark grin. "I am sure of it!"

Volstagg added, "Indeed!" with a pat on Thor's back that, unlike the softer one from Balder, threatened to crack the thunder god's spine. Thor stumbled a bit forward as Volstagg added, "The only way you could be guaranteed victory is if I were to accompany you, of course, but failing that, I'm sure you'll do well on your own."

Thor couldn't help but laugh. Volstagg always knew how to disarm his foes and cheer his friends with his boasts. "Many thanks, my corpulent friend."

The Warriors Three and Balder went off to summon

Harokin, the leader of the Einherjar. The warriors of Valhalla were the greatest of the dead heroes of Asgard, gathered into a single fighting force, and there were few better to have at one's back in war.

However, Sif remained behind.

At first, they simply regarded each other. They had been through much, these two, as warriors, as friends, and as more than friends. Much was said with only an expression, and Thor knew just from Sif's eyes that she was concerned for the safety of both him and his mother.

"Be wary, Thor. I hope Odin is right—but I fear *I* am."

"It matters little, Sif, for I must fight either way. But if I am triumphant over Hrungnir, then it will matter even less, for the giant will be defeated once and for all and Frigga will be returned to us."

Sif smiled. "Be swift and brave, Thor—and if you should fall, be assured that all of Asgard will avenge you."

Thor gave her a small smile. "I'm sure that will comfort me on my way to Valhalla. Now stand you back."

As Sif moved backward, Thor again twirled his hammer, preparing himself for his journey.

To the skies, he cried, "Be you alert, Hrungnir, for the thunder god comes to face you for your final reckoning!"

And then, accompanied by the crash of thunder, he took to the skies and headed for Jotunheim.

CHAPTER SEVEN

Loki had observed the entirety of the battle on the Ida Plain with a combination of amusement and frustration.

The amusement was mostly at the expense of the frost giants themselves. While he had no great love for the denizens of Asgard, he had even less for those of Jotunheim. Laufey hid his son, ashamed of his tiny stature, and would have rather he died—though the giant could not bring himself to do the deed himself. Instead, after defeating Laufey, Odin took the giant-king's child in and raised him as his own.

Loki had, in truth, hoped for more from his blood relations. At the very least, he'd hoped they would get as far as the trolls did, but the trickster did underestimate Heimdall.

And perhaps he overestimated the giants in general and Hrungnir in particular. The Brawler had gained an outsized reputation as the latest of the gang leaders who had tried to rally the frost giants to his banner. Loki was beginning to think that Hrungnir's legend was entirely an artifact of the animal between his legs rather than the brain between his ears.

Obviously, Loki was going to have to help his cousin.

Hrungnir had retreated from the battle on that speedy horse of his, an act of cowardice that Loki had to admit to admiring, and Loki decided to follow him, to give him a piece of his mind, since the giant had so little a mind of his own.

Unfortunately, the journey proved more problematic than Loki had anticipated, as he had decided to do as Hrungnir did and take the most direct route to Jotunheim, through the mountains. Last time he'd taken the more circuitous route Odin had followed, via the Sea of Marmora, which was on level ground. But while the mountainous path was far more direct, it was also far colder, and Loki had reckoned without the nature of the shape he had assumed. Insects avoided winter climes for a reason, after all.

Struggling to stay aloft in the frigid air, Loki alighted in a crevasse that he hoped Heimdall wasn't keeping a close eye on. Once there, he transformed himself into a wolf.

However, while the lupine form with its greater mass and coat of fur provided more protection from the chill, even at a full gallop, a wolf could not progress through the mountains as quickly as an airborne creature like the fly.

For a brief moment, Loki toyed with the notion of simply teleporting, but that was an expenditure of magickal power he dared not indulge in. The simulacrum at his keep was complex and needed to be mentally maintained constantly in order to continue to fool Heimdall. And while the guardian of Asgard might not take notice of a crevasse in the mountains, he would surely discover if there was a hint that the sleeping figure in Loki's bed was anything other than Loki.

And so Loki took the time to lope through the mountains.

As he did so, he formulated the plan by which he would ensure that Hrungnir would, at least, put up a decent fight.

Eventually, the wolfen form of Loki arrived at Hrungnir's redoubt on the outskirts of the frigid lands. It was a massive stone structure that seemed hastily put together. It had none of the elegance of the stone castles that many other giants favored, but Hrungnir spent so much time away from it on his horse, Loki supposed he shouldn't have been surprised that he gave so little thought to the architecture of his headquarters.

Thjasse, Hrungnir's lieutenant—whom, Loki realized, had not gone on the campaign against Asgard—spied him as he approached the battlements and cried out, "Wolf!"

Through the wolf's snout, Loki said, "No wolf am I, but Loki, returned to speak to Hrungnir of his failure—and how it may be changed into a victory."

"Really?" Thjasse sounded dubious.

"Yes. I would speak with the mighty one."

Before Thjasse could say anything, Hrungnir stepped out through the giant doorway that provided ingress to the redoubt. "So, the trickster has returned. Good, because I would have words with Loki."

"And I you," Loki said with a snarl. "You made, if you'll pardon the expression, a gigantic mess of this."

"*I* have?" Hrungnir raised his arms as if to pound the wolf. "It was *Loki* who gave us a route that would take us *into* Asgard, not to an ambush on the Ida Plain!"

"It is true that Heimdall spotted you sooner than expected,

but still and all, you are frost giants! A gang of idiot trolls managed to do better against Thor and his comrades than you were able to accomplish. Had you not Goldfaxi to enable your retreat, you would be alongside your fellows in the dungeons below the Realm Eternal."

"And had I not Loki to 'aid' me—"

Loki interrupted, "You wouldn't have gotten as far as the Ida Plain. Do not be foolish, Hrungnir. You need me—apparently, even more than I believed." Loki then whispered the conclusion of the spell he had begun upon departing the mountains.

A mighty wind started to blow, gathering up the stones from the very ground around them. The wind whirled faster into a devastating funnel, but it swept up only the rock and earth around them. The snow and plants on the ground, even the hair on the heads of the giants, remained undisturbed by the currents.

With a mighty crack, the rock pieces slammed into each other, merging and forming a bipedal structure.

When the wind died down, the giants saw before them a giant-sized suit of stone armor. And beside it a massive club.

"Both the armor and the weapon are enchanted. No force may be brought against them that would cause them to be damaged. Even Thor's hammer would be unable to shatter the stone. So when next you invade Asgard—"

"There shall be no invasion of Asgard."

That brought Loki up short. "Whyever not? Has Odin's offense been eliminated? Has Hrungnir decided that being humiliated is *not* an affront that should be answered?"

"Oh, the affront will be answered, worry not. I have simply chosen a different path to achieve justice for Odin's insult. Even as we speak, Thor is wending his way to Jotunheim to do battle with Hrungnir in one-on-one combat."

Surprised, Loki asked, "And Thor agreed to this?"

"We will know soon enough. If he does not arrive by nightfall, then I will have to kill our guest."

"Guest?"

"A hostage from Asgard, whose life I am trading for battle with the thunder god. And now, thanks to you, I have the means to ensure victory!"

Thjasse then spoke. "Assuming Loki is amenable to your using his gifts to kill his adoptive brother."

"I believe I already addressed that particular concern, Thjasse. However, I will reiterate that I have no issue with Hrungnir being the cause of Thor's demise. My path to rule Asgard is blocked by both Odin and Thor. If Hrungnir removes Thor from the playing field, then my task is halved." He loped over to the stone armor in his lupine form. "So please, accept these gifts, and use them to win your battle with Thor."

"Excellent!" Hrungnir threw his head back and laughed. "This will be a battle for the ages! They will write of it in legend and song—and that song shall be 'The Death of Thor'!"

Loki was grateful that he was in wolfen form, as it meant the sigh of annoyance he let loose at Hrungnir's boast came out more like a snarl.

"Let me try this magickal armor you have provided, then."

Hrungnir walked over to the armor, and then hesitated, unsure of how to proceed.

"Merely touch it and it will encase you."

Hrungnir hesitated. "This is not a trick? Odin *is* still your father, and you *are* still the trickster. This may be a ploy to trap me within this statue you have magicked up."

"Technically, because he took me from your uncle, Odin can be considered my father, by default, I suppose. But do not believe that I have any filial regard. You may rest assured that there are no tricks here. If you are to fight Odin's other son, then I am here only to help. Touching that armor will place it around you, and you will be invulnerable."

With a chortle, Hrungnir said, "Excellent. My victory over Odin's favorite son is assured!"

Loki winced. It was certainly true that Thor was Odin's favorite. This never made any sense to Loki, as you would think a leader such as Odin would value brains and cunning over brute force. Not to mention that he was stuck with Thor as his son no matter what—he had *chosen* Loki. And yet he was still treated like this . . .

Yes, it would definitely be worthwhile to watch Hrungnir thrash Thor for the sins of their father.

Hrungnir stood by the stone armor that looked like a sculpture the giants had placed on their lawn. At first, he simply stared at it. It wasn't a solid piece of stone, he realized. The arms, legs, headpiece, and chestpiece were all separate, but linked together. The headpiece included a square gap for the giant's face.

Then the giant reached out to touch the armor, as instructed.

As Loki and the other giants watched, Hrungnir's body seemed to grow insubstantial, turned transparent, and then was sucked into the armor.

The other giants immediately tensed. Several of them raised their weapons.

Thjasse turned to face Loki. "What did you do?"

But then Hrungnir's face was visible in the gap in the helmet.

Cautiously, Thjasse turned again, this time to face his leader. "Hrungnir?"

Hrungnir raised an arm experimentally. Then he broke into a huge grin and reached down to pick up the enchanted club.

"Are you well, Hrungnir?" Thjasse asked, still sounding concerned.

"'Well?' Oh, Thjasse, I am far more than 'well.' With this armor surrounding me I am stronger than ever!"

Loki's wolfen snout curled back to bare his teeth, the closest he could come to a smile in this form. "You should test the armor's mettle."

Hrungnir tried to nod his head, though that was a difficult gesture in the armor. He turned to his fellow giants. "Attack me!"

The giants exchanged glances for a moment. True, giants sparred with each other all the time, and even Hrungnir engaged in those bouts from time to time, but those were mostly wrestling matches.

"I said, *attack*!"

Three of the giants raised their weapons and came at Hrungnir.

First, Arnborn swung at Hrungnir with his club. The weapon bounced off Hrungnir's side, and Arnborn was devastated to see a crack now running down the middle. "I've had this club since I was a boy!"

Next, Olav came at Hrungnir with his axe raised over his head. It came smashing down on the armor's helm, and splintered in twain, the axe head flying off into the snow, leaving Olav standing, stunned, with only the haft. "I stole this axe from a dwarf! It never even needed to be sharpened!"

And then Niels thrust his great sword right at Hrungnir's chest. The sword shattered upon impact. Niels then shrugged. "Never liked that sword, anyhow."

Hrungnir brayed a laugh to the very sky. "None shall be able to defeat me now!"

Thjasse, however, was more cautious. "We know that you cannot be harmed by even the finest weapons." He glanced at Niels. "Or the poorest. But fighting is offensive as well as defensive. Can you even move about in that thing?"

Hrungnir immediately strode across the snow to grab Arnborn. He moved remarkably swiftly for a person encased in stone, and he picked up a surprised Arnborn and tossed him aside.

"And your strength?" Thjasse asked.

Loki was starting to grow weary of Thjasse's skepticism. "The armor obviously does what I promised. Why must you—?"

"Because even Loki's truths are lies," Thjasse said.

Bridling at the interruption, Loki said, "That doesn't even make sense."

"No," Hrungnir said, "my lieutenant speaks true. Thjasse is clever and wise. I must know how strong I am now."

"The oak," Thjasse said immediately.

Hrungnir grinned. "Yes!"

The giants all moved to the rear of the redoubt. Loki followed on all fours, curious as to what oak they were speaking of.

Around back, they came upon a giant, grizzled oak tree. It had no leaves on it, and Loki soon realized that the tree was petrified.

Looking more closely, the trickster saw that the oak had scarring and markings all over it.

"This oak," Hrungnir said as he strode toward it, "has been the test of strength for my people for generations. Many giants have strengthened themselves against its unforgiving bark, but it has remained standing—it has remained unyielding." He pointed at one scar. "I remember my father making this very dent upon the tree. He said it was the mightiest blow he ever struck."

Hrungnir then reared back with a cocked fist and slammed it into the oak, shattering it into a million pieces.

The sundering of the petrified wood echoed throughout Jotunheim. Loki imagined that they heard the sound in all Nine Worlds, vibrating through the tendrils of Yggdrasil.

As the sound from the tree's destruction started to fade, a preternatural quiet spread throughout the area around Hrungnir's redoubt. Loki looked around and saw that the giants were all staring at the tree's remains in abject shock, their mouths hanging open. Flies could have entered their mouths unmolested, if it had not been too frigid for them.

Then, after several interminable seconds when Loki feared he was going to have to check to see if the giants were still alive, Hrungnir started to laugh.

Only then did the other giants join in, and soon the echoes of petrified wood being splintered were replaced by the echoes of braying laughter from a dozen or more frost giants.

"Oh, well done, Loki! This armor will ensure my victory over the thunderer! And after I have trounced him, then I will lead my forces back to Asgard! Armed as I am with this armor of yours, none shall be able to stop me. The broken bodies of Sif, Balder, the Warriors Three, Heimdall, and all the other puny gods will litter the path to Odin, where I will crush his one-eyed head on his very throne!" He faced his subjects and raised both hands in the air. "Victory!"

The giants all shouted, "Victory!"

Loki muttered, "You haven't won anything yet, fool," but his lupine voice could not be heard over the shouting.

Instead, he loped quietly toward the redoubt. Hrungnir mentioned a hostage, and Loki was curious as to whom the giant had kidnapped in order to bend Thor to his will.

CHAPTER EIGHT

Normally, when Thor was carried through the heavens by Mjolnir, the hammer's speed was more than sufficient.

But now, as he rocketed over the mountains toward Jotunheim, it felt agonizingly slow.

While he always felt heavily the responsibility of protecting both Asgard and Midgard, it was as nothing compared to the responsibility he felt toward Frigga.

Strictly speaking, Frigga was not Thor's mother, for Thor had been born of a union between Odin and Jord, whom some mortals called Gaea, the earth-goddess of Midgard. Thor had always assumed that his affinity for the world of mortals was at least in part due to that particular quirk of parentage.

But while Jord was the woman who bore him, it was Frigga who raised him. Odin could charitably be called a distant father, if for no other reason than his responsibilities as All-Father took up a great deal of his time. And often his love for his son had to be tempered by his need to be a fair and stern ruler of all Asgard.

So it was Frigga who took care of him. Frigga who fed him and clothed him.

Frigga who told him all those stories: of Odin and his

brothers Vili and Ve, of his father's battle against Laufey that cemented Asgard's dominance over the frost giants, of her own marriage to Odin that united the Aesir and the Vanir under Asgard's banner.

Frigga who tended the injuries of the rambunctious child who was constantly getting into mischief—both due to his own headstrong nature and due to encouragement by a most pernicious-minded adopted brother.

Frigga who comforted Thor when he was sad, laughed with him when he was happy, and helped him when he was confused.

Frigga who taught Thor to read, who taught Thor to think, and perhaps most importantly, taught Thor compassion. For while he learned about how to make the hard choices a ruler needed to make from Odin, it was from Frigga that he learned the need to leaven those decisions with kindness and thoughtfulness.

Frigga who accepted no credit for her own work in keeping Asgard safe and as peaceful as possible, given that they were surrounded by foes. Never did she allow herself to be considered one of the leaders of Asgard, though she performed a leadership role—including today. She accepted the responsibility, but shied away from the power.

Thor owed his physical strength and command over the storm to Odin. He owed his heroism to Frigga.

And now he felt as though he had failed her. True, Thor and the others were able to defeat the frost giants, but Hrungnir had gotten away, and that set in motion the events that led to Frigga being his prisoner.

Against the trolls, Thor had taken it upon himself to fight Baugi, for Baugi was the leader.

Against the frost giants, he had allowed others to get in the way, and Hrungnir escaped. He had focused on the entirety of the giants rather than Hrungnir himself. He should have left the other giants to his comrades and focused on the leader as he had with Baugi, but Hrungnir's mighty blow with his club had angered the thunder god.

When he was a youth, Thor regularly let his temper get the best of him. Young Loki often took advantage of that to provoke Thor for some prank or other. As he grew older, that temper combined with his strength and the power of Mjolnir to blossom into arrogance. It was what led Odin to change Thor's shape to that of a crippled mortal and leave him trapped, amnesiac, on Midgard to teach him humility.

While those lessons were well learned, there were times when Thor still let his arrogance get the better of him. He thought he could take on all the frost giants himself, rather than let his friends do so while he focused on Hrungnir.

And Frigga had paid the price for his allowing Hrungnir to escape.

Based on what Gudrun had said, Frigga had deliberately engaged Hrungnir so that Volstagg's wife and the children of Asgard would be safe. It was exactly that selflessness that Thor tried every day to emulate.

Today, he had failed. And he would not let it stand.

He soon arrived over Jotunheim, and quickly sighted Hrungnir's keep. It was a flimsy redoubt, and Thor had to admit to disappointment. He recalled the grand halls of Utgard-Loki and Ymir and even that of Laufey, the first victim of Mjolnir when Odin wielded the hammer before gifting it to his son. They were halls worthy of a leader.

This was not. Hrungnir's keep was barely a habitable structure. Thor realized that Hrungnir's reputation was built primarily on the speed of Goldfaxi. He was beginning to believe that the giant had come to resemble his mount, specifically its backside.

And then he saw the giants gathered around what appeared to be a statue.

As he alighted upon the ground, Thor saw the statue move, and realized that it was stone armor. Hrungnir's face was visible underneath the helm.

"Is this, then, how you face me, Hrungnir? Hiding behind stone raiments?"

"No more than you hide behind your own armor, thunder god. Do you not wear a helmet to protect your head? Mail to protect your chest?"

"Very well, Hrungnir, if you feel you must use armor to face me, then so be it! But first, I demand proof of life!"

The giant frowned. "I beg your pardon?"

Thor shook his head. "You *claim* to have my mother as your prisoner. I would have you back your claim with action and show me that the Lady Frigga is alive and well and in your care."

Hrungnir stared angrily at Thor for many seconds before finally saying, "Do you doubt my word, thunder god?"

"I do indeed. Odin claims that you are no breaker of oaths, but I have difficulty putting stock in the honor of one who bargains with the life of a wife and mother."

"Very well. Thjasse!"

Thjasse stepped forward. "Shall I bring the woman out?"

"Yes." Hrungnir was, as usual, pleased with Thjasse's cleverness.

Within moments, Thjasse had disappeared into the keep, and returned with Frigga. Her hands and mouth were bound, preventing her from weaving any spells that might aid in her escape. Thor cursed Hrungnir for his perspicacity.

"As you can see, Thor, your mother is unharmed. The bindings are necessary to ensure her remaining our guest."

"Hostage, you mean," Thor said.

"Take her away," Hrungnir said, and Thjasse quickly moved to obey his wishes, bringing Frigga back into the keep.

The leader of the frost giants then turned to face Thor. "Your father spoke the truth about me. As proof I offer the fact that I did *not* kill him where he stood after his mount defeated mine in a foot race. I promised him safe passage away from us if he won, and I granted him that. Indeed, when last I encountered the All-Father, it was *he* who lied, *he* who deceived! He gave his name as 'Bolverk,' and did not identify his horse as the great Sleipnir. So do not speak to me of honor, thunderer—the frost giants of Jotunheim know the meaning of that word far more than you Asgardians do."

"Your words do you more credit than your actions, Hrungnir."

"Then hear these words, Thor! We will fight—you against me. None of my subjects will aid me in battle against you, and none of your oafish comrades will aid you in battle against me. It shall be the god of thunder versus the mighty brawler. The only way you may win the Lady Frigga's freedom is by defeating me!"

"Then stand fast, Hrungnir, for defeat you, I shall! None may harm the personage of the mother of all Asgard without paying the price, and you may rest assured that the cost I exact will be most dear!" He twirled the hammer over his head and threw it at Hrungnir's armored form, grabbing hold of the strap as he did so. As he rocketed toward his foe, he cried, "For Asgard! For Odin! And most of all, for Frigga!"

And then Thor crashed into Hrungnir's stone armor with a bone-shaking impact that slammed through the thunder god and sent him sprawling to the ground.

Hrungnir himself had not budged. Thor felt a most unaccustomed pain all up and down his body, particularly in his arms, which were what hit Hrungnir's stone armor the hardest.

"What sorcery is this?" Thor asked.

"Does it matter? It is *my* sorcery because *I* use it." Hrungnir punctuated his reply with an uppercut at Thor's prone form.

The punch collided with Thor's jaw and sent the thunder god through the air toward the keep. So stunned was he by the impact that he let go of Mjolnir as he sailed over the cold ground and landed in the snow.

Propping himself upright, Thor said, "Not since last I fought the Hulk have I been struck by so great a blow!"

Hrungnir started running toward Thor, his footfalls shaking the very ground. "Allow me to surpass it, then!"

And again, Hrungnir bent low and threw an uppercut, one that sent Thor hurtling to the sky, along with a dusting of snow.

Ignoring the ache in his ribs, Thor reached out at the apex of his impromptu flight. Mjolnir flew into his hand, and he used it to stay aloft.

But Hrungnir was now reaching down to the ground to pick up his club, which he then threw right at Thor. The weapon was not usually one that would be thrown, but it flew like a missile through the air. Thor was barely able to dodge it by flying downward, back toward Hrungnir.

Since the giant used his club the way Thor used his hammer, he decided to return the favor, and he swung Mjolnir like a club, striking Hrungnir in the side of the head.

It had no effect.

Hrungnir reached out and grabbed Thor's arms and tossed him aside, sending the thunder god skidding through the snow.

The club fell back to the ground with a muted thud, and Hrungnir trudged over to retrieve it. "And so it ends, son of Odin." He walked over to Thor's prone form and upraised the club. "Now you die."

Hrungnir swung downward toward Thor's head, intending

to smash the thunderer's face in. He would be known throughout all history as the one who finally destroyed Thor.

But just as the club was about to strike, Thor reached up with his hands and caught it.

"I say nay!" Thor cried as he pushed back against the club's momentum.

Hrungnir's surprise at Thor's actions led the giant to relax his grip for but a second, yet it was enough for Thor to use all his strength to push the club away. Hrungnir stumbled backward a few steps, allowing Thor to clamber unsteadily to his feet.

The battle had only just begun, and Thor already felt as if he'd been fighting the Hulk for several hours. He'd had many brawls with the gamma-irradiated brute over the years, starting from the earliest days of the Avengers, and Hrungnir's blows were very much like those of the green monster.

But the primary difference between the jade giant and the frost giant he now faced was that the Hulk grew stronger as he grew angrier. The first time Thor and the Hulk clashed in the caves of Gibraltar, Thor had almost lost due to that particular quirk.

He knew, however, that Hrungnir operated with no such advantage. Indeed, anger would no doubt reduce Hrungnir's capabilities in battle.

And so Thor once again took to the skies as Hrungnir got his bearings.

"You speak of honor, foul Hrungnir, yet you use magic to bolster your prowess."

"How dare you!" Hrungnir bellowed. "I no more hide behind this armor than you do behind that absurd hammer of yours!"

"It is no secret that one who challenges Thor does also challenge Mjolnir. The two names are fair intertwined in the minds of all who know of me throughout the Nine Worlds. But when those same folk do speak of Hrungnir—if, indeed, they speak of you at all—their words ring out regarding Goldfaxi and his speed. A challenge against you is considered a challenge against *your* might, or the fleetness of your horse's hooves—*not* against magickal armor."

"It is also no secret that Thor wielded a sword before Odin granted him possession of Mjolnir. I'm sure the foes you faced in battle after being gifted that hammer were similarly caught unawares. Did it stop you from thrashing them?"

Thor smiled. "It did not. But then, they were also not foolish enough to give the god of thunder time to catch his breath after a pounding."

And then Thor raised up his arms and summoned the storm that was his to control. Lightning crackled through the sky overhead, one of the bolts striking the top of the giant's lowly keep.

Hrungnir laughed. "Do you truly believe that your puny lightning can hurt me where your fists could not?"

"Your assumption, foolish Hrungnir, is that the lightning will be brought to bear on you."

And then several bolts of lightning struck not Hrungnir, but rather the ground near the giant's feet.

The lightning turned the snow into gas instantly, even as it ripped through the dirt beneath, vaporizing it until Hrungnir no longer stood on steady earth.

Waving his arms in a futile attempt to maintain his balance, Hrungnir suddenly was painfully aware of how heavy his new armor was. He fell backward and landed flat on his back, momentarily helpless.

Thor pressed his advantage, knowing it would not last. He flew down to the ground and pounded on Hrungnir's armor with Mjolnir.

Many of the giants present thought they would never hear a sound as loud and horrible as that of the petrified oak shattering from Hrungnir's mighty blow, but they were now proven wrong. That was as a whisper in the wind compared to the noise that resulted from Thor's hammer striking Hrungnir's armor.

The very ground did shake like that of a rampaging beast. Stones loosened in the giants' redoubt, and a nearby evergreen tree almost uprooted from the violent impact. Many of the giants who were close to the battle doubled over from the pain in their ears, so great was the sound.

Inside the keep, Frigga was being held in a large room that had furnishings of great size, none of which she could actually reach. Thjasse had placed her near some oversized chairs, guarded by a single giant. That guard took up a position at the room's only window, which afforded him a lovely view of the battle. Said window was too high to be of any use to Frigga, though she could hear the sounds of the clash.

When Mjolnir struck the magic armor, the impact of uru

against enchanted stone was enough to cause Frigga to fall over, unable to maintain her footing, bound as she was. Her guard also lost his footing, but he recovered more readily, using the windowsill to steady himself. Upon noticing that Frigga had fallen, he made no move to help her, but simply chortled.

"So much for the heartiness of the Asgardians. Can't even keep your feet."

Were she not gagged, Frigga would have reminded the brute that her hands were bound, but even if she had been able to speak the words, it would likely have had little effect.

Then again, if she had been able to speak, she would have uttered a spell that would have removed her from this place. Her battle against Hrungnir had drained her considerably, and she was not yet at anywhere near her full strength, but she would, at least, have been able to send herself a league or two away from this keep, enough to give her a head start.

Although at this point, she suspected, it did not matter. Just the fact that Frigga had been taken had been enough to rile her son, she had been able to see that much during her brief sojourn out of doors. Even if Frigga were able to effect an escape, it would change nothing. She would not be able to make it all the way to Asgard to inform Odin that she was safe, which would enable him to send the entire forces of Asgard to take on Hrungnir and his minions.

Of course, if she were free, she could, at the very least, aid Thor, since the terms of the battle relied upon Frigga being Hrungnir's prisoner.

And Thor would need all the help he could get, for Frigga could sense the power emanating from Hrungnir's new armor. She wondered whence he received it, though she feared she could make a rather educated guess that was very close to her own home . . .

Falling down from the impact of Thor's strike had proffered one advantage upon her: The gag that the giants had placed on her was now directly between her head and the floor of the keep. Rubbing her head against the floor caused the gag to shift. With a bit of patience, she might be able to eventually slide it off.

Luckily for her, the guard evinced no interest in actually paying attention to her. He was back to watching the battle.

Thor's blow was sufficiently powerful that it affected its wielder as much as it did his surroundings. The very force of his strike sent the thunder god head over heels across the snow-covered ground.

For several precious seconds, Thor was dazed, but he forced his wits to focus, forced his limbs to pay attention to his wishes, and he got to his feet.

To his horror, Hrungnir was doing the same.

Initially, Thor feared that his blow had been for naught, if the frost giant could so easily regain his feet, but the armor allowed Hrungnir's face to be seen, and that betrayed the truth. His visage showed strain and fatigue, and Thor knew then that his blow was not in vain.

But it was also not likely to be repeated. Thor's very limbs felt as if they were made of rubber; his bones felt as fragile as they had once been made by a spell of Hela's. On that occasion, he had had to fashion special armor to protect himself very much like what Hrungnir had done. Thor had used the steel mills of the Midgard city of Pittsburgh to forge his protection, and he wondered where Hrungnir had obtained his.

But there was no time to speculate, for Hrungnir now ran toward Thor with his enchanted club ready to strike with his left hand. Barely able to stand, Thor found himself incapable of dodging the blow in time, so instead he raised his right arm and managed to catch the giant's arm in mid-swing just as he had caught the club earlier.

Angry, Hrungnir pushed with all his considerable, armor-enhanced strength. But Thor dropped his hammer and raised his left arm to join his right.

He would not yield. He thought of Frigga, trapped in that keep solely because she fought to protect the children of Asgard.

And so he gathered all his strength and pushed back.

For a time—neither Thor nor Hrungnir would later be able to say for sure how long it was—Thor pushed with both his strong hands against Hrungnir's enchanted left arm.

But then Hrungnir recalled that he had another arm.

The giant's fist struck Thor's chest with the impact of a thousand blows, and Thor stumbled into a crouch to try to catch his breath. Though it meant loosening his grip upon Hrungnir's arm, the crouch served also as a dodge, and the club flew harmlessly over his head. What's more, the suddenness of the action caused Hrungnir's arm to fly free faster than expected, and he lost his grip on the club. The weapon flew aside to land in the snow.

Thor knew he had to keep Hrungnir from retrieving the club, but that proved an unnecessary thought, as the giant evinced no interest in the weapon. Instead, Hrungnir grabbed Thor's arms at the wrists and pushed his arms downward into his chest, forcing him to stay in a crouching position.

With all his might, Thor tried to exert similar force, but it was for naught. He felt his arms start to crumple, his own body unable to straighten up from the sheer power attempting to crush him now.

"Do you feel it, Thor? The power that will ultimately destroy you? You may believe it to be the magick of my armor, but it is far more than that. It is my impatience with you Asgardians and your arrogance and your preening. It is my indignation at Odin's effrontery in making a fool of me in front of my own people. It is my anger at your belief that you are gods when you are nothing but tiny little humans with delusions of grandeur."

"Speak not of delusions, for I have done battle with much worthier foes than Hrungnir the Brawler and lived. I have faced many a frost giant, including those far more powerful than you, such as Ymir and Utgard-Loki. I have faced the god of mischief and the goddess of death. I have faced Surtur and the Midgard Serpent. I have faced the Hulk and the king of the vampires. I have faced the paramour of death and creatures who could destroy the universe with but a thought. I have faced the villains of legend and the tyrants of tomorrow." Thor gathered up every ounce of strength and straightened his knees, lifting Hrungnir from the ground. Hrungnir's face fell, his mouth agape as he felt his feet rise into the air, lofted by Thor's strength. "I have faced all manner of creatures great and small and triumphed, Hrungnir. And while I grant that one of those foes may someday be the one that brings me down, I say now that today is *not* that day! The one who defeats me will *never* be the likes of you!"

With that, Thor threw Hrungnir aside.

Even as the giant landed in the snow with a most resounding crash, Thor felt his own knees buckle once again. Every muscle in his body cried out to rest, but he could not heed their desires, for his foe still was able to rise.

And this time, Hrungnir was not happy. "The likes of *me*? Hah! Never have you faced the likes of me, Thor, for I will not be stopped. Not by your boasts, not by your hammer, not by your fists. Bring me down as many times as you may, I will *always* rise again to destroy you!"

Both combatants lumbered toward each other, now, each moving slowly as if hip-deep in tapioca. For though each dared not show it to his foe, both Thor and Hrungnir were overwhelmed by exhaustion and fatigue from their mighty battle.

But Thor knew that showing weakness would add strength to Hrungnir's desperation, and Hrungnir knew the same held true for Thor. And though Hrungnir had the magic of Loki's armor behind him, in truth he did not entirely rely on it sustaining itself against attack by Thor, for the giant knew that the source of the magic was not one he could trust. As for Thor, he knew not the source of the magic, only that it was damnably effective, as his aching muscles and weary bones could attest.

Yet still they clashed. Their chests collided, their arms reaching and grasping for purchase.

Thor pushed, and Hrungnir pushed back.

Thor struck, using all the might of his fists, but the armor would not yield.

Hrungnir struck, using all the might Loki's magic had granted his fists, but Thor's will would not yield, even as his mail splintered and his bones cracked.

After trading blows in this manner, Thor had a bit of luck. Their battle had disturbed a great deal of the snow on the ground, and what was normally packed and firm had become loose and slippery. Hrungnir was already unaccustomed to the extra weight of the armor. Keeping to his feet was difficult under the best of circumstances. The loose snow made the circumstances far from ideal, and once again Hrungnir found himself losing his balance and crashing to the ground on his back.

Thor took advantage of this respite to take flight once more. Again, he reached out to the power of the storm. "Winds blow, and rain fall! Thunder strike, and lightning roar! Thor Odinson commands you!"

A massive storm front appeared as if from nothing, the winds kicking the snow up off the ground, making it appear to the naked eye as if it were a blizzard. The low temperatures meant that the rain that would normally ensue instead came down as sleet and hail. Thunder echoed throughout all of Jotunheim, and a massive bolt of lightning came crashing down directly onto the prone form of Hrungnir.

The lightning coursed through the magickal armor, and the giant screamed, both in pain and outrage. He had been assured by Loki that Thor's power would be unable to affect his armor. But the thunder god's attack was considerably more powerful than his earlier thunder strike.

The winds howled louder, the lightning intensified, and the sleet and hail pounded the ground, forcing the other giants to take shelter within the keep for their own protection.

Brow furrowed with concentration, Thor threw more and more power into the storm. Lightning continued to crash into Hrungnir's armor, and the giant screamed louder in pain and shock.

Eventually, it became too much, even for Thor, and he had to stop. However, the storm had, at that point, gained a life of its own and dissipating it would take more effort than Thor had left. He had given the storm his all, and he shakily returned to the ground, the hail and sleet pinging off his helmet.

Still, he could easily withstand the ravages of a storm he had created—though such tumultuous weather was hardly a bother to the frost giants, either. Thor had brought it primarily for the lightning.

But even as his boots touched the snow, Hrungnir got to his feet.

He had a wide grin on his face.

"Is that all you have?"

And then he reared back and punched Thor in the stomach. Too exhausted from his labors, Thor was able only to relax his body and go limp to minimize the damage from the giant's blow.

As he skidded across the snow, Thor realized that the damage was minimized in other ways. He had taken many punches from Hrungnir this day, and this last one was by far the weakest.

Still, while that could be viewed as a victory for Thor, it had come at a high price. The thunder god's ears rang, his vision had gone blurry, his ribs were bruised at best, broken at worst, and he had trouble ordering his thoughts.

Hrungnir moved much more slowly toward his club. "You were wise to try to use the elements to stop me, Thor. Mere strength can no longer defeat me, and the only hope you had was to try to destroy me with your birthright." He picked up the club and laughed bitterly. "But you *failed*! And now it is my turn."

Thor managed to slowly clamber to his feet. He tried to force himself to speak normally, despite the difficulty he was now having simply drawing breath. "Have I failed, Hrungnir? You move more unsteadily. Your words come more slowly."

"But I still move! I still speak! You can barely stand!" He ambled toward Thor, rearing back to swing his club. "And you will not stand for much longer!" Hrungnir's club came careening toward Thor's head in the giant's massive right hand.

Unable to move with any dispatch, Thor instead raised his left arm to deflect the blow.

That proved both wise and unwise. The former because, had the blow struck the thunder god's head, it would likely have decapitated him.

The latter because it shattered his arm.

Again, Thor found himself reminded of Hela's curse. In revenge for defeating Hela in combat and earning the freedom of souls she had claimed as her own, the goddess of death had caused Thor's bones to become as brittle as kindling, something he had discovered the hard way on Midgard during a ferocious battle with the base villains known as the Marauders. Indeed, the pain that coursed through his arm at the splintering of bone now was the worst he'd felt since that day.

Hrungnir threw his head back and laughed. "This club destroyed an oak that has stood for millennia! You are an even bigger fool than I thought to trust that something as pathetic as your arm would stand against it!"

The winds from Thor's storm were still howling, and he focused past the pain that suffused his body in order to grab hold of them once again. Raising his hammer to focus the storm's power, he sent a vortex of wind to surround the giant.

Hrungnir felt the winds buffet him in short order. "What trickery is this?"

But Thor could not answer him, for all of his focus was devoted to increasing power to the mini-twister he was creating around Hrungnir and not collapsing from the agony of his broken bones.

The vortex increased its speed. Hrungnir tried to move forward, but found himself unable to—the force of the wind had become so intense in so short a time that he could not budge.

And then he started to rise.

Helplessly, Hrungnir found himself being raised up by the twister.

Sweat beading on Thor's brow despite the cold, the thunder god urged the vortex to even greater speeds, its force sucking Hrungnir ever upward.

When at last the frost giant was a full league in the air, Thor released the twister. It blew off, and Hrungnir plummeted to the ground.

Where Thor was waiting.

Just before the giant hit the ground he was met with Mjolnir, held by the strong right hand of Thor, who reared back and put everything he had into a swing with the hammer that sent Hrungnir flying across the snowy lands.

He then twirled Mjolnir overhead, gripping it tightly as it carried him to the far-off place where Hrungnir had landed. Falling more than landing, Thor was barely able to keep to his feet, and also barely able to avoid further aggravating his broken left arm.

His left arm now useless, his right arm still holding his hammer, Thor instead used his legs, kicking Hrungnir as hard as he might. Again, the giant flew through the air, and again Thor whirled his hammer and flew after him.

* * *

Back in Hrungnir's keep, all the giants had gathered in the large room where Frigga was held. Except for Thjasse, they all stood at the windows, watching the fight.

"Go Hrungnir!"

"Look at that punch he threw!"

"Thor ain't got a chance!"

"Hey, look, he's gettin' back up!"

"Hrungnir'll just take him down again, don't you worry."

Frigga was concerned that the greater number of giants who had fled to the castle to protect themselves from the storm Thor had called down on Jotunheim would make it harder for her to escape her bonds. But none of the newcomers paid her any mind. Indeed, the only one who even acknowledged her was Thjasse, and all he did was give a quick look to make sure that she was still there.

She had made some progress in getting her gag to slide off her face, but not enough to actually free her mouth sufficiently to cast spells.

"Ha! Lookit, he broke Thor's arm!"

"He's gonna feel *that* in the mornin'!"

"Nah, he ain't, 'cause in the mornin', he'll be dead."

"Yeah, him an' the rest'a Asgard."

"You bet, we'll be ridin' into Asgard and takin' *all* the gods! With Goldfaxi an' that armor, we can't be stopped!"

"Can he even ride the horse with that armor on?"

"If he can't, I wanna ride him!"

"Wait, what's Thor doing?"

Frigga kept rubbing her head against the floor on which she lay, trying to keep moving the gag farther down.

"Wow. I didn't think anybody could punch that hard."

"You obviously ain't never been punched by Thor before."

"I have, and I've never seen him punch anybody as hard as he just hit Hrungnir."

"Geez, I can't even see them anymore!"

Thjasse then left, to Frigga's relief. She had been observing Hrungnir and his band of giants for most of a day now, and Thjasse was the only one besides their leader who had even a modicum of cleverness. With only the imbecilic followers left, Frigga would have an easier time of things.

And then, at last, she managed to lower the gag enough to free her lips.

Slowly, quietly, she began to mutter an incantation. It was one her own mother had taught her millennia ago when she was a child in Vanaheim.

"Be wary, daughter," her mother had warned her. "This is spell only affects those who are already weak-minded. Those who are strong of character and self will not be swayed. In addition, this incantation should only be used sparingly and, most of all, wisely."

"But, Mother," young Frigga had said, "all spells should be used wisely."

That had prompted a happy smile from her mother. "Yes, my sweet girl, exactly. You have learned your lessons well."

Frigga had soon perfected the spell. It had been centuries

since she'd cast it, but she was certain she would be able to wield the incantation again.

She also mourned her inability to impart the same sense of wisdom into Loki with regard to spellcraft that Frigga's mother had imparted to her. Frigga had few regrets in her life. She was the wife of the greatest god who ever lived. She was respected by all of Asgard, and if that regard didn't necessarily extend to all the denizens of the other of the Nine Worlds, at the very least she knew she had the admiration of those whose opinion was worth considering. And she had nothing but pride in her heart and soul for Thor and all that he'd accomplished.

But she regretted deeply that she had been unable to do better with Loki.

She supposed that all mothers had their issues with their children. For all the influence mothers had, sons and daughters were still their own people.

Putting such self-indulgent thoughts aside, she finished the spell and saw that the giants were no longer gaping out the window, but instead staring straight ahead, waiting for Frigga to tell them what to do.

"Untie me," she said.

This, she realized, was a mistake, as all twenty or so of them immediately moved toward her, bumping into and stepping all over each other to try to follow her instruction.

"Stop!" she cried out, then pointed at one of them. "You, untie me."

Silently, the giant she pointed at shuffled over to her and undid her hands.

She shook her wrists out and then stretched her arms, trying to get feeling back into them. This was, she knew, only the first step.

Unfortunately for her next step, Thjasse chose that moment to reenter the room.

"What is going on here?"

Frigga was still too drained from her battle with Hrungnir on the mountain to do aught but maintain the spell on the giants, so she bellowed, "Attack him!"

All the giants started to amble toward Thjasse in a menacing manner, but Hrungnir's lieutenant quickly barked, "Stop, you fools! Do frost giants now take orders from puny Asgardians?"

Most of the giants stopped their forward motion and stood in confusion. Frigga's spell made the weak-minded open to the spellcaster's suggestion, but these giants were already used to taking orders from Hrungnir and Thjasse, and so this new instruction confused them.

And she didn't have the wherewithal to strengthen the spell.

One of the giants remained in her thrall completely, however, and attacked Thjasse.

Or, rather, he tried to. Thjasse countered the giant's clumsy attack, grabbed him, and threw him directly at Frigga.

She tried to run, but the giant was too large, her own legs too short by comparison, and her fatigue too great.

The weight of the now-insensate giant atop her was overwhelming, and Frigga found that she had to focus all her strength on keeping herself from being crushed.

A moment later, the weight was gone, and Frigga saw that Thjasse had removed his erstwhile attacker from atop her. While this was a laudable short-term result, the looks on the faces of the other giants that now all stood over her spoke ill of her long-term prospects.

"Bind her," Thjasse said. "And I would advise not making any further attempts to free yourself, my lady. The only reason I do not kill you is because Hrungnir gave explicit instructions that you were not to be harmed until the battle with Thor was ended. But if you give me reason, I will forego that instruction and kill you myself. Your value was in getting Thor to arrive in Jotunheim alone that he may be thrashed by Hrungnir, and that particular coin has been spent. Do not tempt the fates any further."

Even as one giant held her down, another bound her hands with the same ropes—more tightly this time—and then replaced the gag.

"Uh, Thjasse?" said Frigga's original guard, who was now back at the window.

"What is it?"

"I'm not sure Hrungnir's the one doin' the thrashing."

That got all the giants to return to the window, leaving Frigga once again bound and gagged on the cold floor.

What they saw was Thor continuing to kick Hrungnir's armored form about. They were farther and farther away from the keep, nearing Ymir's Ridge, named after a previous leader of the frost giants.

Thor had been treating Hrungnir as if he were a Midgard soccer ball, refusing to give the frost giant a chance to recover before Thor kicked him again.

But the pain in his left arm and chest was starting to grow roots, and he knew he could not continue on this course for much longer.

His latest kick had brought Hrungnir to the base of Ymir's Ridge, and Thor realized what he needed to do now.

Holding Mjolnir aloft, he commanded the lightning to strike at the ridge.

At his command, the lightning burst forth from the gray skies, shattering the ridge, and sending rock, dirt, and snow cascading downward onto Hrungnir's prone form.

The ground shook further, as the lightning's damage had a cascade effect, sending even more of the ridge collapsing atop Hrungnir. Realizing how bad it was getting, Thor quickly used his hammer to take to the air, letting the avalanche do its work.

But Thor was only able to go a short way before he had to land once again. The thunder god could take very little more, and if the frost giant was not defeated at last by this final blow, Thor was not at all confident that he could continue the fight.

Eventually, the avalanche ran its course. Ymir's Ridge was

broken and jagged, and below it, a massive pile of snow and dirt sat unevenly upon the ground.

The echoes of the ridge's agonized wounding faded from earshot, and soon all was quiet, save for Thor's labored attempts to breathe with his ribs so badly damaged.

Thor stood and waited in the quiet and the stillness. Cold air seared his lungs as he tried and failed to keep breathing without pain.

As the seconds passed, he hoped that victory was his, at last, and Hrungnir had been defeated.

But then the snow started to stir. The dirt began to shift.

And then snow and dirt exploded upward as Hrungnir, his magic armor chipped but intact, leapt to his feet.

Hrungnir himself was exhausted almost to the point of collapse, but he was physically unharmed beyond that. Besides, he had the stone armor to sustain him and keep him upright. And Thor was too far gone to be a worthy foe any longer.

"Look at you, Thor. You can barely stand. Surrender! There is no shame in giving in to your superior. You have given this fight your all, and truly I have never beheld a foe so worthy as you. If you surrender now, I promise that I will deliver you to Hela's embrace with speed and as little pain as possible."

Thor shook his head, an action that made his head swim. "Do you truly believe, Hrungnir, that I would accept so perfidious an offer as that?"

"Perfidious? I treat you as an honorable foe, and you—"

"Honorable? You threaten the very gates of Asgard over an

imagined slight, you kidnap the woman who raised me from a baby, you—"

"Imagined!? Odin made a fool of me!"

"Nay, mighty one, the fates did that. My father merely cast a light upon it. Odin was but travelling alone to be with his thoughts. 'Twas *you* who harassed him and dragooned him into your absurd contest. For that, you have brought havoc down upon Asgard, endangered the lives of dozens of gods and giants both, and for *what*? Vanity? Ego? And then to issue this challenge by toying with the life of the mother of all Asgard, and to change the expectations of battle with your eldritch armor. There is no honor in you, Hrungnir, nor in your actions. And you may rest assured that Thor will *never* surrender! Not even after I draw my last breath will I succumb to the likes of you!"

To punctuate his point, Thor threw his hammer with all the might he could muster—which, to be fair, was far less than usual—directly at Hrungnir.

The giant saw how weak the throw was, and opened his hands as if to catch Mjolnir.

Instead, the hammer slammed into the giant's hands, pushing them back into his chest. The momentum of Thor's throw sent the giant flying back, and while it didn't hurt Hrungnir, it did cause him to crash into the jagged remnants of Ymir's Ridge.

The hammer flew back to Thor, his right hand wrapping around the haft.

Hrungnir struggled to his feet, furious. "So be it, Thor! If you wish to fight until your dying breath, allow me to provide it!"

Thor said nothing. Instead, he twirled Mjolnir in front of him, which sent more and more snow and dirt churning up.

The giant was forced to raise his hands before his face to keep the dirt and snow out of his eyes and nose and mouth.

Every muscle in Thor's body cried out in suffering. Every bone felt as if it were either already shattered or about to be. Every pore felt as if it were on fire.

But still he moved forward, his hammer's twirling continuing to kick up more rocks and snow and dirt. He knew it was naught but an irritant to Hrungnir, yet it was hitting him in the one area in which he was vulnerable: his face, which the armor left exposed. And Thor needed the distraction of the detritus cutting into his face so he could get close.

Once he was near enough, he stopped twirling the hammer, dropped it, and then leapt into the air and punched Hrungnir directly in the nose.

Unprotected as it was, the nose was smashed, blood flying in all directions, even as Hrungnir stumbled backward into the ridge.

Teeth clenched, breaths hissing through them, Thor advanced on Hrungnir, unwilling to give the giant pause. He grabbed the armor at the seam between helm and chestpiece with his right hand, turned, and then threw the giant with all his waning strength back toward the keep.

Never was Thor more grateful for the fact that his power of flight came from Mjolnir rather than himself. That last throw took all Thor had, and he could barely stay upright. He had drawn on every last ounce of strength, and was still on his feet only by dint of the tattered remnants of his will power.

But Mjolnir's enchantment remained undimmed, and so with even the slightest throw, the hammer carried Thor to the ground outside Hrungnir's shabby castle. Thor landed clumsily in front of Hrungnir, even as the giant unsteadily rose to his feet.

To Thor's horror, he saw that Hrungnir's landing point was proximate to where his club had gone flying after Hrungnir had lost his grip on it. The giant now held the weapon in his hands once more.

Hrungnir was grinning. "Did I not tell you, thunder god? Bring me down as many times as you may, I will *always* rise again to destroy you!"

He held the club aloft.

Thor tried to raise his right arm, but he found he had not the strength even for that action.

It seemed that the battle had ended. Thor had nothing left to give, and he would soon be en route to Hela's waiting arms.

Hrungnir swung the club downward toward Thor's head.

And then the club shattered upon impact with Thor's helmet.

At first, both combatants merely stood in shock. Hrungnir and Thor both stared at the tiny, jagged bit of the club's handle that was all that remained in his stone-gauntleted hands.

Finally, Hrungnir spoke in a confused whisper. "How can this be? The club was indestructible!"

"Your use of the past tense serves you well," Thor said with a weak smile of his own. Again he reached out to the spot he had grabbed moments ago, right at the top of the chestpiece.

The stone crumbled in Thor's grip.

"No." The word escaped Hrungnir's lips with a gasp.

Buoyed by his foe's sudden vulnerability, Thor straightened. "It would seem, mighty Hrungnir, that the enchantment upon your armor had a time limit. 'Tis a pity for you that the same cannot be said for Mjolnir's magic. For while your armor's extraordinary gifts came from an inferior source, my hammer's comes from the All-Father himself!" Reaching back, Thor swung the hammer around right at the frost giant's chest. "Behold the eternal power of Mjolnir, hammer of Thor!"

Upon impact, the armor shattered into a thousand pieces.

Even though he dwarfed Thor in size by a considerable margin, Hrungnir now cowered so much that he seemed smaller. Again he whimpered a pathetic "no" as he backed away from the thunder god.

Placing his hammer in its belt loop, Thor advanced upon the giant, gathered what he could of his strength, and punched Hrungnir in the belly.

The giant fell to the snowy ground.

"I have brought you down, Hrungnir. Now, I believe, is when you rise again to destroy me."

Hrungnir did not move.

"I am waiting, Hrungnir! Surely your boast was not an empty one!"

The giant remained still upon the cold ground.

Behind him, Thor heard the sound of heavy footsteps crunching into the snow. Slowly, he turned around to see Thjasse and several other giants exiting the keep.

Thor looked up at Thjasse. "I believe the terms of our bargain were quite clear. I was to meet Hrungnir alone in combat, and the Lady Frigga would be freed. The god of thunder has met those terms, and I would now ask, Thjasse, that you meet yours."

Thjasse raised an eyebrow. "They are not *my* terms, Thor, but Hrungnir's."

"Are you not his lieutenant, sworn to uphold his rule?"

"For the moment, I am, yes."

Thjasse's face was inscrutable, and Thor feared that he would get not the rest and recovery he so desperately needed to mend his battered body, but instead yet more battle.

In an endeavor to forestall it, Thor said, "Consider your next move carefully, Thjasse. Asgard has played fair with Jotunheim. Hrungnir took Odin's wife, an action that would, in the usual course of events, lead to a far stronger response than this. But the All-Father did abide by the terms set out by the base villain who would besmirch the mother of all Asgard—as did I. Do not presume to try the patience of Odin, or me, or the other warriors of Asgard by taking back the word of your leader. Even now, Sif, Balder, and the Warriors Three stand ready with all the soldiers of the Realm Eternal and the Einherjar of Valhalla to storm the battlements of this land should any harm come to Frigga."

"Do they?" Thjasse asked with a smirk.

"Yes. They do."

Still looking at Thor, Thjasse called behind him. "Bring the woman!"

One of the giants dashed back inside.

Thor tried not to let the relief show in his face.

"You have done me a favor today, son of Odin, for Hrungnir's rule was far more predicated on his horse than his skills. Your victory is also a victory for me. That also gives me little reason to abide by any agreements Hrungnir may have made."

The giant returned, bearing a bound-and-gagged Frigga.

Thor tensed, prepared to fly through the air to remove his mother from the giant's grip by force if needed.

"However," Thjasse added quickly, "I also have little reason to begin my own rule with a war against Asgard. Therefore, you and your mother are free to depart Jotunheim in peace." The giant smiled. "After all, *I* currently have no quarrel with you or with Odin—or with the Lady Frigga."

With that, the giant inclined his head in a meager show of respect for Thor, and then backed away from the thunder god, never turning his back on him. "Release her!" he bellowed to the giant who had come out of the keep.

The giant removed the gag and undid the ropes that kept her hands behind her back. Immediately, Frigga ran to her son's side, putting a gentle hand to his right shoulder.

At her touch, Thor all but collapsed, no longer able to stand straight.

"Oh, Thor," she said.

Through clenched teeth, Thor said, "It is as if all the swords in the Nine Worlds are cutting through my left side. I do not believe that I am capable even of flying us home."

"I fear that I am unable to summon the power to bring us home by magickal means."

"Then we shall walk," Thor said.

Frigga shook her head. "You can barely stand, my son. Surely—"

Then they heard the muted clopping of hooves on snow-covered ground, and they both turned to see that Thjasse had brought Goldfaxi out.

"What is this?" Thor asked.

"Hrungnir has little need of his mount at present, and I wish you gone from our lands as quickly as possible. Save for Sleipnir, none may expedite that departure with as much dispatch as Goldfaxi here. Once you return to Asgard, merely pat him once on the rump, and he will return to us on his own."

Thor nodded. "My thanks, Thjasse."

"I do not do this for you, Thor, merely to be rid of you." With that, Thjasse turned and walked away, leaving Frigga to aid Thor in mounting the gold-maned horse. That was a lengthy and painful process, but once they were both astride Goldfaxi—as a horse bred to be ridden by giants, there was plenty of room for both on the steed's back—they began their trek back to Asgard.

CHAPTER NINE

Once again disguised as a fly, Loki happily flew back to his keep. All in all, it was a generally successful endeavor, and the memory of Hrungnir's righteous indignation and Thor being beaten to within an inch of his life would make the rest of his house arrest far more tolerable.

As a fly, he landed on the bed next to his still-sleeping simulacrum. He then disposed of the doppelgänger and restored his own shape at the same time. Then he "woke up" and stretched and yawned.

Still in his bedclothes, Loki wandered through his home. He noticed that the keep was now clean. The sprites, of course, knew that the eldritch being lying on the bed wasn't truly Loki. No doubt relieved that Loki was actually gone, the sprites had tidied up rather thoroughly. True, he'd told them to perform their function with him present, but he knew they would not be comfortable with it.

So it all worked out for the best. He expected that he would get bored ere long, but that would happen later. For now, he intended to enjoy himself.

He poured himself a flagon of the finest mead and sat in his favorite chair and instructed his scrying pool to show him the recent past—specifically, the beginning of Thor's conflict with Hrungnir.

It began with Thor blathering as he twirled his hammer and flew toward the giant: "*Then stand fast, Hrungnir, for defeat you, I shall! None may harm the personage of the mother of all Asgard without paying the price, and you may rest assured that the cost I exact will be most dear! For Asgard! For Odin! And most of all, for Frigga!*"

Loki almost giggled as he watched Thor crash into Hrungnir, falling violently to the cold ground, while Hrungnir himself had not budged.

Oh, the look on Thor's face! Even better than the look when Mjolnir didn't come back to his hand while fighting the trolls.

"*What sorcery is this?*" Thor cried, and Loki laughed heartily.

"It's *my* sorcery, dear brother! Mine that left you battered and bruised and hurting!"

Loki was about to view it a second time when the wards he kept around his keep signaled that someone was approaching.

And then he sensed the sheer power emanating from that someone, and realized that he was about to have a most unexpected visitor.

It was the work of but a quick spell to alter his bedclothes to that of his usual green raiment, and greet Odin as he entered.

"Well, well, well, I must say this is quite a surprise. Lucky for me, the sprites tidied up."

"Loki," Odin said in an unusually subdued voice. "I would speak with you."

"In my keep? This is—well, peculiar. I believe your usual mode is to summon people to your throne. A sensible method, I must say, as it puts everyone on your terms. After all, who would dare challenge Odin in his very place of power? Your raised throne gives you the high ground in your own territory."

Odin began to pace about the sitting room, not actually facing Loki. "I have come to you for two reasons. One is simply the letter of the law. You are forbidden from leaving your keep, and summoning you to my throne room would facilitate you breaking the terms of your punishment. I could hardly allow myself to be responsible for that."

Loki didn't see how that was much of a concern, since it was Odin's own punishment. What did it matter if he himself violated it? But he said only, "And the second reason?"

"I am not here as the ruler of the Realm Eternal, but as your father."

"And what does my *adoptive* father have to say to me?"

Odin ignored the dig and said, "I am concerned. Your house arrest cannot be pleasant for you. Loki is never happier than when he is out and about and engaging in his petty schemes."

"On the contrary, the petty schemes I miss not at all. It is the complex plots that I regret my inability to complete during this tiresome exile."

"Interesting, that you should mention complex plots. We were the victims of one just recently."

Loki folded his arms. "Oh?" His ignorance was feigned—not very well feigned, but still, he felt he should at least put up the appearance that he had no idea what Odin was talking about.

"After your punishment commenced, I rode out on Sleipnir in disguise. I wished—"

"Yes, I'm aware," Loki said with a dismissive wave.

That got Odin to finally look at Loki, shocked that the trickster would admit to any wrongdoing.

But then Loki smiled. "Mother told me."

Odin let out a sigh. "Of course." He turned away and again started to pace the sitting room, hands behind his back. "While riding, I encountered Hrungnir, the current ruler of the frost giants. He was astride Goldfaxi, his speedy golden-maned mount. He did not know who I was, but he recognized Sleipnir for the fine steed he is. And so Hrungnir did challenge me to a race between our horses."

"I assume Sleipnir won?"

"Naturally. But I did not reveal myself. I simply allowed Hrungnir to believe that he had been defeated by an ordinary old man."

Loki raised an eyebrow. "Oh, he must have been *livid* when he learned it was you."

Again, Odin looked at Loki. "He did learn it was me, yes. And how did you know *that*, my son?"

"Because you wouldn't be boring me to death with this incredibly uninteresting tale if he didn't."

For a second time, Odin was forced to concede to Loki's logic. "When Hrungnir learned I had defeated him, he viewed it as a personal insult—that I did not reveal my true self."

"Obviously," Loki said dryly, "he does not understand your obsessive need to pretend to be someone else. A trait Hrungnir shares with most sensible folk, if it comes to that, Father."

Odin chuckled. "Quoth the shapeshifter. Regardless, he attacked Asgard's very walls, but Thor and the others were able to stop him at the Ida Plain."

"Yes, I did hear the Gjallarhorn. Woke me out of a sound sleep, it did. What a pity I am under house arrest. I could easily have aided my brother."

"That was not necessary, for the frost giants were routed, their leader retreating on his golden steed. But on his way back, he did find Frigga in the mountains."

"And what, pray tell, was Mother doing *there*?" Loki asked angrily. It was a question that had been preying on his mind for quite some time.

"Protecting the children of Asgard at *my* instruction!" Odin snapped. "You covet the throne, Loki, so you would be well to know of *all* the responsibilities that such rule entails! That includes safeguarding *all* of Asgard's citizens! Frigga and Gudrun brought all the children of Asgard to the Vale of Crystal, where they would be safe from Hrungnir regardless of the outcome of his invasion." Odin looked away again, staring now at a bit of statuary on Loki's shelf. "Frigga did stay behind and do battle with Hrungnir to delay him so Gudrun and the children would be safe."

"Is Mother safe?" Loki asked blithely.

"She is now, yes. Hrungnir took her hostage, and bargained

with her life: He would do battle alone with Thor in exchange for Frigga's freedom."

Loki grinned. "Let me guess—my brother flew valiantly into the fray and did thrash the mighty Hrungnir?"

"He attempted to. Hrungnir had been gifted with stone armor that was proof against Thor's greatest blows."

"Impressive."

Odin turned to face his adopted son. "I am well familiar with the frost giants' magick. It is capable of many wonders, but *not* this armor."

Shrugging, Loki said, "Hrungnir has been raiding Nornheim—perhaps the armor is one of Karnilla's tricks, stolen by the giants."

"Perhaps. Its being stolen would explain why it suddenly failed in the midst of battle, allowing Thor his victory."

"That is certainly a good explanation." Loki clapped his hands. "Well, Father, I do appreciate you coming by to fill me in on the latest happenings in Asgard. Please do feel free to stop by any time."

"So you have nothing to say about Hrungnir's campaign against the Realm Eternal?"

"Why would I? I have been trapped here, as Heimdall is my witness."

Odin nodded. "Heimdall does indeed say that he did not spy your departure."

"Do you not trust me, Father?" Loki asked with a grin.

"Do I have reason to, my son?" Odin asked sadly.

They stared at each other for several seconds, and it was Loki this time who broke the gaze, looking away from his father's irritating visage.

"I notice that you have not asked Thor's condition?"

"He did battle and won. His condition does not matter, for he is still alive—were he not, you would have begun your oratory with that particular revelation. Thor is strong, and Asgard has the finest healers in the Nine Worlds. I have no doubt that he will be up and about and annoying me in no time at all."

"It does sadden me, Loki, to see the love that Thor always had for you spit back in his face."

Wandering back to his raised chair, Loki sat in it. Odin wasn't the only one who could claim the high ground in his territory with petitioners, after all.

"Do you recall, Father, the time shortly after Thor's exile on Midgard ended? He was no longer trapped in the body of the crippled healer on a permanent basis, though he did still share his existence. You were frustrated, because Thor had fallen in love with a mortal woman."

"Of course, I recall," Odin said gruffly.

"You kept summoning me to the throne room for advice on how to deal with it. And every time you asked, you referred to him as 'my favorite son.' Over and over, that was what you called him." He shook his head. "I had hoped that your little lesson in humility would last at least until the Blake persona died of old age, but I was not so fortunate. And then you rubbed salt in the wound by *constantly* reminding me that you had a favorite son, and that it was *not* me."

Odin shook his head sadly. "If Loki does doubt the love that the All-Father holds for him, he should think back on all the misery he has caused, all the havoc he has wreaked—and that, with all that, he still lives. And still thrives. Another ruler would *not* have been so considerate."

With that, Odin turned and left.

Loki simply stared at the now-empty sitting room. He grabbed for the flagon of mead, then angrily threw it across the room.

He sighed. The place had been so well cleaned, too.

In truth, he would have been more than happy to grant Hrungnir the stone armor indefinitely. While Loki's original intention was for Hrungnir to use the armor against Asgard's forces on his second attempt to invade, donning it to thrash Thor suited him just fine.

Until he saw *who* the hostage was that had secured Thor's solitary flight to Jotunheim.

Loki would have been more than happy to see Hrungnir make Odin's life miserable. If he thrashed Balder or Sif or the Warriors Three, all the better. If Heimdall was violently removed from the Bifrost by a blow from Hrungnir's club, Loki would shed not a tear. And he certainly had no issue with Thor being beaten within an inch of his life.

But Hrungnir saw fit to kidnap Loki's mother. That was not something Loki would easily forgive—or forget.

He could not help Frigga directly, for she would know of

it. While there were others in the Nine Worlds from whom Loki could disguise his spellcraft, he could not do so from the woman who taught him. And if he moved to aid his mother by magickal means, she would not only be aware of his efforts, but castigate him for it. She would, he knew, insist that he aid Thor rather than herself.

It was the selflessness that he loved about her, and that frustrated him no end.

And so he did as he knew Frigga would ask, and aided Thor by putting a limit on the enchantment. After a time, the armor and the club both would revert to simple stone, easily shattered by Thor's might.

Best of all, the time limit was such that there was still plenty of time for Hrungnir to put quite the beating on his *dear* brother.

Speaking of which . . .

Loki cast two quick spells, one of which restored his mead to its flagon and his side, the other of which started the scrying pool going again. With mead in his belly and a song in his heart, he watched again as Thor crashed into Hrungnir and fell insensate to the ground.

"*What sorcery is this?*"

Elsewhere within Asgard's fabled walls, Thor lay in bed.

Every single part of his body hurt, though it was as nothing compared to how he felt toward the end of the battle with Hrungnir.

Nonetheless, he had won the day. Goldfaxi returned him and Frigga to Asgard's borders and then galloped back to Jotunheim. Sif and the others had been waiting for him, and she and Balder brought him immediately to the healers, while the Warriors Three escorted the Lady Frigga back to her home to recover from her own ordeal. Harokin and the Einherjar returned to Valhalla, disappointed.

A knock at his door, and Thor looked up to see Sif entering with a pitcher of water.

"Ho, Sif! It is good to gaze upon your lovely visage!"

Smiling, Sif said, "Would that I could say the same, but your visage has seen better days."

His left arm immobilized in a sling, Thor moved his right hand to his face, which was covered in cuts and bruises. "Indeed. Your courage in facing me in this state speaks well of you."

Sif laughed, and Thor tried to, only to wince.

"I am sorry, Thor," Sif said quickly.

"Nay, apologize not, fair Sif. When I was a mortal healer, I did often say that laughter was the best medicine. And the pain does, at least, remind me that I still live."

"You have won a great victory today, Thor. Hrungnir's brutality will darken the land no more because of you." As she spoke, Sif poured some of the water into a mug. "The healers also say you need to drink many fluids."

"Another bit of advice I oft gave in my time as one." Thor smiled and took the mug, gulping the water heartily. "So what news is there from Jotunheim?"

"None of Hrungnir, that is for sure. It is said that Thjasse now rules the frost giants."

Thor nodded gravely. "They bear watching. Thjasse is clever, far more so than most giants—including Hrungnir, who was no fool."

Before Sif could say anything, Balder's voice came from the hall. "Ho, the house!"

"Balder!" Thor grinned with glee. To have not one, but two of his dearest friends visit filled his heart with unbridled joy.

The white-haired god entered, holding a burlap sack. "Idunn left these at your doorstep. It seems it's your time to receive the golden apples."

"They will be gratefully received," Thor said.

Balder dropped the sack by the bed and pulled out one of the golden apples of immortality and handed it to the thunder god.

As Thor did bite gingerly down on it—his jaw was quite sore, and his teeth ached—Balder said, "I have just come from Odin. The All-Father is consumed by affairs of state, but he promises to visit this even."

"Thank you, my friend."

Smiling conspiratorially, Balder said, "One of those duties is to talk down Harokin. He wanted to lead the Einherjar across the mountains to Jotunheim as soon as he saw you and Frigga ride home."

"Harokin is a good man," Thor said. "And I would feel as he, were our positions reversed."

"There is also a rumor," Balder added, "that the All-Father did visit Loki's keep."

Sif frowned. "Why would he do that?"

"I do not know."

"I do," Thor said quietly. "Hrungnir's route to invade Asgard was the same as that used by Baugi and his troll horde. More to the point, Hrungnir's armor did stink of Loki's magick."

Shaking her head, Sif said, "But Heimdall told me that Loki never left his keep."

"Even your sharp-eyed brother may be fooled if the trickster is determined enough."

"Perhaps." Sif did not seem convinced.

Balder shrugged. "Regardless, Odin will speak with him."

Thor nodded. "Would that I could be a fly on the wall for that discussion."

"Well," Balder said with a grin, "you *were* a frog once. Perhaps you can become one again."

Thor winced at the memory of one of Loki's more bizarre jests.

A booming voice came from the hall. "Frogs? Don't care much for 'em, though their legs can be quite tasty!"

Sif and Balder exchanged glances. "A voice that could shatter glass speaking of food," she said.

He nodded. "It must be Volstagg."

Sure enough, Volstagg squeezed his frame through the doorway, followed quickly by Fandral and Hogun. "Aye, 'tis the Lion of Asgard himself, bearing gifts!"

Volstagg was carrying a tray about half-filled with food. Behind him, Fandral said, "One of those gifts being a headache from the Lion's braying voice."

Thor chuckled and asked, "What bring you, my dear friends?"

"It is customary for a hero to return home from battle to a feast! Your injuries have delayed that, but Thor should wait for no feast—not when the feast can be brought to him!"

Peering at the collection of sweet meats and fruits, Thor said, "It seems more of a sampling than a feast."

Hogun glowered at his friend. "That is because Volstagg felt the need to test everything on the tray."

Volstagg harrumphed. "I could not allow my old friend Thor to eat subpar food. And while Gudrun is usually quite able in the kitchen, she was somewhat shaken by her ordeal in the mountains and the Vale of Crystal, and so I feared her culinary artisanship might have suffered. And so I did make the noble sacrifice of tasting the food, to ensure that Thor would only get Gudrun's best."

Everyone chuckled, and Volstagg set the tray down next to Thor, who gingerly reached for a bunch of grapes with his right hand. Gazing at Fandral, who sat on the bed next to Sif, Thor asked with a grin, "Could you not bring the tray yourselves and keep it from Volstagg's grubby paws?"

"We would sooner again beard the Fenris Wolf in his lair than attempt to separate the voluminous one from a tray containing victuals."

"Fie!" Volstagg went to stand near the window. "I was going to regale Thor with the story of how I singlehandedly slew Thrivaldi the Thrice Mighty, but since my efforts are not appreciated, I shall withhold the tale until I find myself amidst an audience who appreciates it."

Sif stared at Fandral. "Wasn't it *you* who slew Thrivaldi? I do seem to recall you boasting of blinding all six of his heads once."

"Actually, there were nine heads," Fandral said, "and I did only blind some of them."

Hogun stepped forward. "If I may interrupt the boasting for but a moment, I bring tidings of the Lady Frigga."

Thor straightened and swallowed a grape. "How fares my dear mother?"

"She is resting and regaining her strength. While her wounds at the hands of the giant were not as obvious as they were upon the thunder god, they still cut quite deep."

With a grateful nod, Thor said, "She will become strong again. It is a fool who underestimates my mother. Indeed, had she not needed to distract Hrungnir while Gudrun and the children got to safety, but instead fought Hrungnir outright, she might well have triumphed."

Fandral added, "Were it not for Hrungnir's enchanted armor, you would easily have triumphed."

"It matters not," Volstagg said. "True, Thor had a more difficult time of it, but of *course* he was triumphant! How could he not be?"

"I have lost battles before, old friend," Thor said gravely.

"Nonsense! I have told stories only of Thor's valiant triumphs over the foes of Asgard and Midgard. And we all know that Volstagg only tells truthful tales! Like the time I stood fast against Ulfrin the Dragon."

Thor grinned. "And how did the great Volstagg fare against Ulfrin's eldritch breath that saps one's very strength?"

Volstagg frowned. "Eldritch breath? Ulfrin had no such!"

"On the contrary, as a youth I faced Ulfrin, ridden by the Norn Hag herself."

"Hmph. Well, perhaps it was another dragon. What does it matter?"

Balder grinned. "When you are telling the story, friend Volstagg? Not a bit."

Throwing his head back and clutching his ample belly, Volstagg said, "Exactly! At least Balder understands! Now, then, where was I?"

Hogun actually came close to smiling. "Standing fast before Ulfrin the Dragon."

Sif grinned. "Or was it Fafnir the Dragon?"

"Perhaps," Thor added, "it was Fin Fang Foom?"

Dramatically, Volstagg sighed. "Will I never complete this legendary tale?"

"Not," Fandral said, "if at all possible."

Thor grabbed one of the sweetmeats and plunked it into his mouth, chewing carefully with his aching jaw. Though the pain of his wounds had not lessened, the pain in his heart had done so. Sitting here amidst his dearest friends, sharing their food—what little remained—and hearing their laughter rejuvenated Thor in ways that no healer's medicine nor godly stamina could.

And so he rested, and so he laughed, and so he ate and drank, knowing that Asgard was once again safe thanks to him. All he ever wanted was to protect all the peoples of the Nine Worlds. And once he was healed, he would do so again.

So be it . . .

THE END

ACKNOWLEDGMENTS

The number of people who deserve thanks for this book are legion, and I hope I manage to get all of them in. I will start with the folks at Joe Books and Readhead Books: Robert Simpson (who first approached me with this), Adam Fortier, Stephanie Alouche, Amy Weingartner, and especially my noble editor Rob Tokar.

Huge thanks, as always, to my amazing agent Lucienne Diver, who kept the paperwork mills grinding and more than earned her commission.

Of course, this trilogy owes a ton to the comic books featuring the various Asgardians that Marvel has published since 1962, and while I don't have the space to thank *all* the creators of those comics, I want to single out a few. First off, Stan Lee, Larry Lieber, Jack Kirby, and Joe Sinnott, who created this incarnation of Thor and his chums in *Journey Into Mystery* Volume 1 #83. Secondly, Lee, Kirby, and G. Bell, for producing "The Invasion of Asgard," a backup story in *JIM* #101, which inspired this novel's prelude. Thirdly, and most especially, the great Walt Simonson, whose run on *Thor* from 1983 to 1987 (as well as the *Balder the Brave* miniseries), aided and abetted by Sal Buscema and John Workman Jr., is pretty much the text, chapter, and verse of "definitive." In addition, I must give thanks and praise to the following excellent creators whose work was particularly influential on this trilogy: Pierce Askegren, Joe Barney, John Buscema, Kurt Busiek, Tom DeFalco, Ron Frenz, Michael Jan Friedman, Gary Friedrich, Mark Gruenwald, Kathryn Immonen, Pepe Larraz, John Lewandowski, Ralph Macchio, George Pérez, Keith Pollard, Valerio Schiti, Marie Severin, Roger Stern, Roy Thomas, Charles Vess, Len Wein, Bill Willingham, and Alan Zelenetz.

Also, while these novels are not part of the Marvel Cinematic Universe, I cannot deny the influence of the portrayals of the characters in the Marvel movies *Thor, Marvel's The Avengers, Thor: The Dark World,* and *Avengers: Age of Ultron* (nor would I wish to deny it, as they were all superb), and so I must thank actors Chris Hemsworth, Tom Hiddleston, Sir Anthony Hopkins, Rene Russo, Idris Elba, Ray Stevenson, Zachary Levi, Joshua Dallas, Tadanobu Asano, and especially Jaimie Alexander (who is the perfect Sif), as well as screenwriters Christopher Markus, Stephen McFeely, Ashley Edward Miller, Don Payne, Zak Penn, Mark Protosevich, Robert Rodat, Zack Stentz, J. Michael Straczynski, Joss Whedon, and Christopher Yost.

Also one can't write anything about the Norse gods without acknowledging the work of the great Snorri Sturluson, without whom we wouldn't know jack about the Aesir. In particular I made use of the *Skáldskaparmal,* which has the original story of Hrungnir's challenge of Odin and battle with Thor.

Thanks to my noble first reader, the mighty GraceAnne

Andreassi DeCandido (a.k.a. The Mom). And thanks to Wrenn Simms, Dale Mazur, Meredith Peruzzi, Tina Randleman, and especially Robert Greenberger for general wonderfulness, as well as the various furred folks in my life, Kaylee, Louie, Elsa, and the dearly departed Scooter.

MARVEL
SIF
Even Dragons Have Their Endings
BOOK 2 OF THE TALES OF ASGARD TRILOGY
KEITH R.A. DeCANDIDO

Even Dragons Have Their Endings

BOOK 2 OF THE TALES OF ASGARD TRILOGY

KEITH R.A. DeCANDIDO

JOE BOOKS LTD

For Meredith, whose heart is bigger than all the Nine Worlds combined.

"So comes snow after fire, and even dragons have their endings."

—J.R.R. Tolkien, *The Hobbit*

PRELUDE

The great world tree Yggdrasil sits at the center of the Nine Worlds, linking each world to the other eight.

The most populous of these worlds is Midgard, which its inhabitants refer to as Earth, but the most powerful denizens of the Nine Worlds reside in a different realm: Asgard. These immortals, ruled by the All-Father Odin, possess strength far beyond that of the mortal humans of Midgard.

Thousands of years ago, many Asgardians did cross the Bifrost—the rainbow bridge—to Midgard. The peoples of the region in which the Asgardians arrived saw the mighty immortals as gods, and so worshipped them. Today, some Asgardians still visit Midgard—particularly Thor the Thunderer, wielder of Mjolnir and master of the storms. In the modern age, he is viewed as one of many superheroes who protect humanity from chaos.

But as a youth, centuries before, Thor had been known as the protector of Asgard. The young god took his duties seriously, for he knew that such would continue to be his role as an adult when, as the son of Odin, he would take the throne of Asgard.

Odin knew of Thor's resolve, and so sent him to train

with his half brother, Tyr—the god of warfare. Also a son of Odin, Tyr was the greatest weapons master in all the Nine Worlds.

When young Thor left for his first lesson in swordplay with Tyr, however, he did not see that another followed—a girl in pigtails who stealthily tracked him to the Field of Sigurd.

Upon his arrival at the field, Thor was surprised to see not only the God of War, but also several other young men of Asgard. He recognized only one—a youth, blond like Thor, who went by the name of Fandral. All of the boys stood side by side, holding wooden swords.

"What deception is this?" the young god asked, confused. "I was told I would be taught by Tyr, yet I see a dozen others here."

Tyr laughed, tugging on his dark mustache. "Did you imagine, Thor, that you were the only boy in Asgard who wished to learn the craft of swordplay?"

"I suppose not." But Thor had hoped for private lessons from his half brother.

Tyr tossed Thor a wooden sword of his own. Thor caught it unerringly by the hilt and took his place in the line, right next to Fandral.

"Now then," Tyr said, "the first lesson is how to grip the weapon."

Over the next several weeks, Tyr taught the dozen boys how to hold a sword properly—how to wield it in such a way that it could defend as well as attack, how to assume the proper ready position, and how to grip the sword when striking or parrying.

He also paired up the students for practice drills and even had them spar a few times, giving points each time one struck the other with his wooden blade.

The sparring sessions were the only times that anyone was injured. Some of the students did not know their own strength—or their opponents had not taken Tyr's parrying lessons to heart. Of the two boys hurt, one was injured badly enough to no longer be able to fight; the other not badly at all, but his pride was sufficiently wounded that he refused to return.

And each day that Thor went to the field for his lesson, he was followed in secret by the girl in pigtails.

Finally, a month into Thor's training with the God of War, Tyr started the lesson with a lecture.

"Remember that the weapon you wield is only a tool. It is the heart of the one who wields it that will determine victory. All of you will grow up to be warriors of Asgard, and the women and children of the Realm Eternal will be relying upon you to protect them from our many enemies."

It was this statement that finally drove the girl to come out of hiding. She emerged from the other side of the large oak she had been taking refuge behind during the lessons and stood proudly before Tyr and his students, hands defiantly on her hips. "And what," she asked, "if the women prefer to defend themselves?"

Tyr smiled underneath his thick mustache. "At last you have revealed yourself."

Thor gaped. "Sif? Is that you?"

"Yes, Thor, it is I. And I find it strange that you and these other boys are deemed worthy of learning swordplay, but I am not."

Fandral laughed. "If so, girl, you're the only one who finds it so. Women are to be wooed and protected, after all."

Sif walked up to Fandral, and the latter was taken aback to realize that the girl was as tall as he was. "Boy, my name is 'Sif'—not 'girl.'"

"And I am Fandral, not 'boy.' You are Heimdall's sister, are you not?"

"I am."

Tyr interceded. "And she has been spying upon these lessons for quite some time. A true warrior, Sif, does not hide in the shadows. We are not dark elves or trolls who skulk about in darkness."

Turning to face Tyr, Sif said, "I might have asked to join the class, my lord, if I had believed for a moment that you would have consented."

"You know my mind that well, do you?" Tyr asked in an amused tone.

"When Thor first arrived, you asked if he was the only *boy* in Asgard who wished to master the sword." She indicated the dozen boys standing before her. "Your students are all boys."

"Boys who will one day become men who must fight for the Realm Eternal." Tyr shook his head. "I admire your spirit, Sif, but battle is important work—the work of men."

Sif stared up at Tyr's imposing presence. "Can only men do important work?"

"I did not—" Tyr started, but Sif would not let him interrupt her.

"Are the choosers of the slain not doing important work? The Valkyries were handpicked by Odin for their task—would you consider it unimportant? The Golden Apples of Immortality are kept by a woman, a task that is of sufficient import that we would lose our immortality were it not performed. Women bear the children that replace the warriors who fall in battle. Without them, Asgard would be empty. They who control our very destiny are women. I challenge you, Lord Tyr, to go to the Norns and tell them that the work they do is unimportant."

Tyr threw his head back and laughed. "Very well, little girl, you have made your point."

"Then I may join the class?"

"Of course not."

Thor stepped forward. "Why ever not, Lord Tyr?"

"Little Sif is a beautiful and wise girl—it would not do for her to injure herself."

Sif smiled. "I would worry more about my opponents."

"Nonetheless," Tyr said, "it is my class, and my rules."

"I have been observing your class since Thor joined it," Sif said, "and I have learned a great deal. I believe that I can defeat any of these boys in combat."

Fandral barked a laugh. "I sincerely doubt *that*, little girl. You may be able to make an argument, but that will do you little good in a battle of blades."

"More good than your boasting will, little boy," Sif said.

Tyr rubbed his chin. "Very well. Sif, you shall spar with Fandral. Best three touches out of five."

Fandral whirled on Tyr. "Why not first strike?"

Before Tyr could answer, Sif did so, quoting a past lesson: "Fortune may favor even the poorest warrior with a lucky shot."

"Indeed." Tyr spoke with respect, for the first time thinking that some of his words may well have been absorbed by the pigtailed girl.

Tyr grabbed one of the wooden swords and tossed it toward Sif, who caught it as unerringly as Thor had a month earlier.

Within a moment, the nine students and Tyr had formed a circle around Fandral and Sif, who faced each other. Each of them held their sword in a proper defensive position: blade pointed upward, ready to protect any part of the upper body.

Fandral moved around Sif, who moved only to stay facing Fandral at all times.

The boy grinned.

The girl did not.

Around them, most of the boys cheered Fandral on.

"Get her!"

"Hurry up and beat her, Fandral!"

"We'll never get back to classes at this rate! Thrash her!"

"Go, Fandral!"

"Beat the silly girl and get on with it!"

The one exception was Thor. Given his fellows' jeers, he decided to keep his peace. Though he bore Fandral no ill will, he was hoping for Sif's victory, for he did not share the belief held by his half brother and the other boys about a girl's place. Tyr, he felt, should welcome Sif into the class with open arms. After all, being a boy hadn't stopped two of the students from washing out of the class. Why not give a girl a chance? But then, Thor had been raised by Odin's wife, Frigga, and none would call *her* weak; if she presented a lesser aspect than Odin, it was only because everyone presented such an aspect when compared to the All-Father.

But Thor dared not say any of this aloud, knowing that it would only incur Tyr's wrath.

Eventually, Fandral's impatience cost him. After moving around Sif for the better part of a minute, he finally made the first move, an obvious swing that Sif parried easily.

They traded blows for several seconds—Fandral always attacking, Sif effortlessly parrying.

Realizing that Sif had been paying at least minimal attention to Tyr's lessons, Fandral redoubled his focus. He did several double and triple strikes, engaging in more complex maneuvers worthy of a proper opponent, which he belatedly realized that Sif most assuredly was.

Sif parried every strike.

Now Fandral grew frustrated and became more aggressive—so much so that he left his right side open with a two-handed left swing. Sif ducked that blow and simultaneously slid her blade sharply upward to touch the tip of her wooden sword to his ribs.

Tyr nodded. "One point for Sif."

Only then did Sif allow herself to smile.

As they returned to ready position, Fandral took a very deep breath through his nose and let it out through his mouth. It was a technique Tyr had taught them to keep control of themselves.

"Begin," Tyr said, and this time Fandral did not bother to circle, but attacked immediately.

Fandral's assault caught Sif off guard and she was unable to parry his second strike, his blade touching her hip.

"One point for each," Tyr said.

As they started their third round, Sif finally pressed an attack on Fandral. He had shown a tendency to raise his sword overhead far more often than was necessary, leaving himself vulnerable to low swings. So she waited for an opening, making sure to aim high in her initial attacks before switching to a low swing that caught Fandral completely unprepared.

"Two points for Sif, one point for Fandral."

To his credit, Fandral was more careful in the fourth round. Sif remained aggressive, but Fandral's defenses improved.

At one point, Sif slipped on some pebbles on the ground and barely managed to get her sword up in time as Fandral tried to take advantage. But as she tried to right herself, she fell again, and Fandral easily touched her leg with his sword.

"Two points each."

Thor stepped forward. "That was hardly fair, my lord! Sif slipped!"

"I wonder, half brother, if you did battle against a troll or a Frost Giant, and said to him, 'Wait! I slipped on a pebble and must right myself before we continue'—would it come to a good end for you?"

Sif said, "Thank you, Thor, but I accept the loss of the point. Life is seldom fair—if it were, I would not need to indulge in this charade to join the class."

Tyr nodded. "This shall be the final round. Whoever scores the point will win."

The opponents once again circled each other. Fandral had taken Sif's measure, and found her to be far more skilled than he would have imagined. Sif had taken Fandral's measure, and found him to be intelligent and adaptable. It was no wonder that Tyr had put him up against her—Fandral was clearly the finest of Tyr's students.

For several seconds, they dueled tentatively. Fandral struck; Sif parried. They circled again. Sif struck; Fandral parried. And again they circled.

As time went on, the fight grew more aggressive. The final round lasted twice as long as any of the others had, with neither combatant able to gain an edge.

And then it was Fandral's turn to slip on rough ground, and Sif wasted no time in pressing her advantage, slipping her blade under his to strike on his shin.

Tyr, though, said nothing.

"That wasn't fair!" one of the boys cried.

"He slipped!"

"She can't win on a stupid technicality."

Thor whirled on the last boy. "I wonder, Egil, if you did battle against a Frost Giant or a dragon, and said to it, 'Wait! I slipped on a pebble and must right myself before we continue,'—would such a battle end well for you?"

"That isn't funny, Thor."

Before Thor could reply, Tyr said, "No, it is not." He folded his arms. "But, he is correct. Were I to deny Sif her victory, I must also take away Fandral's second point. Therefore I must grant victory—and ingress into the sword class—to Sif."

"Huzzah!" Thor cried, and Fandral also cheered from his prone position.

"Thank you, Thor." Sif reached out a hand to help Fandral up; the blond boy accepted. "I am surprised to hear your approbation, Fandral."

"Do not be, fair Sif, for even had I been victorious, I would have argued for your inclusion in Lord Tyr's lessons. Asgard would be poorly defended indeed if it did not utilize your skill with the blade."

Thor put a hand on Sif's shoulder, next to one of her dangling pigtails. "As Fandral says, so say I. Welcome, Sif, to our sword class."

"Thank you both." Then she bowed to Tyr. "And thank *you*, Lord Tyr."

"Do not thank me yet, young Sif, for you will either become one of the finest swordsmen—or rather, swordswomen—in the Nine Worlds, or you will return to your home ashamed and without honor."

"I have never gone home ashamed, my lord," Sif said. "Pray you, begin today's lesson."

"I would say," Thor said with a smile, "that the first lesson has already begun. We have all learned that a girl may best a boy with a blade."

"Perhaps," Tyr said. "But it is yet to be determined if a woman may do the same to a man."

CHAPTER ONE

Not far outside Asgard, beyond the Ida Plain and the Asgard Mountains, lay the Field of Sigurd. Once, Tyr, the older son of Odin, did teach the youth of Asgard how to fight, but, over the centuries, Tyr had become jealous of his half brother Thor, and did become an enemy of Asgard.

Thor himself had many a fond memory of his training. Once, he had adopted a civilian identity on Midgard in order to live amongst the humans and better protect them—for the people of Midgard were as much Thor's charge as were the people of Asgard—and the name he had chosen was Sigurd, after the very field where he had been taught the ways of combat.

On this day—millennia after Thor, Sif, and Fandral had trained there—young Hildegard, called Hilde, daughter of Volstagg the Voluminous, moved silently through the underbrush. Hiding behind one of the great oaks of the forest, she gazed upon the ground, trying to find the path of the stag she was tracking, which, based on the way the leaves were disturbed, had been this way recently.

At least, that was what she thought that disturbance meant.

She moved silently, touching the ground only with the balls

of her feet, placing them carefully so they did not move the fallen leaves. The stag, unconcerned as it was with stealth, had not been as careful.

When she heard the sound of chewing, she realized she was close.

Not wishing to rush, Hilde moved behind a row of underbrush toward the sound, which grew louder as she approached. She took things slowly to ensure that she would perform her task properly.

Then she saw it.

No antlers, so it was a doe rather than a stag. The doe was stretching her long neck toward one of the trees, chewing on the leaves that jutted out from the ends of the lower branches.

Hilde noticed that most of the leaves in the doe's reach were gone. That meant Hilde now *did* have to rush, as the doe would be finished with her meal soon and would likely bound off, forcing Hilde to search again from scratch.

She walked up quietly behind the doe's rump, paused a moment to make sure the animal wouldn't move, and then touched the doe lightly. Surprised, the doe leapt an inch into the air and then bounded off.

From behind her, Hilde heard the sound of clapping, and a piercing alto voice rung out, echoing off the trees. "Well done, Hilde!"

Whirling around, Hilde saw the Lady Sif emerge from behind one of the trees. She had forgone her armor and was wearing simply a white tunic, black leggings, and boots, with her raven hair tied back. Her sword was sheathed at her side, and her hard face was softened by a bright smile.

"Were you following me the whole time?" Hilde asked.

"Of course. And you did very well, Hilde."

"Thank you, but—" Hilde shook her head, causing a few locks of red hair to fall into her eyes. "—how did you do it without me seeing you?"

Now Sif laughed. "Oh, Hilde, this past week I have taught *you* a great deal, but it is far from all that *I* know."

Lowering her head, Hilde said, "Of course."

"Still, you should be proud. None of the other students got as close to the target as you did."

"Really?" Hilde's face brightened, and visions of gloating over her siblings danced in her head.

"Come, let us rejoin the others."

Sif led Hilde to a large clearing—the very same clearing where Sif had won her way into Tyr's swordplay lessons as a child.

About a dozen children awaited them, all boys. Just as Sif had been the only girl in Tyr's charge, Hilde was the only girl in Sif's—though that was due to a dearth of volunteers, not by design. Indeed, Sif had hoped that more girls would ask to join the training, but only Hilde had done so.

The boys were seated around a campfire, and Sif was grateful to see that none of them had run away or done any damage to the camp. It helped that, each time she'd left to follow one of their peers who was testing their hunting skills, Sif had warned the group that if they misbehaved in any way, she would bring them before Odin himself, and they would be required to explain their behavior to the All-Father. That, it seemed, was enough to keep them in line.

They were loud, of course—asking a dozen boys to remain quiet was like asking a sun not to be hot—but at least they weren't shouting. Instead, they were telling each other stories, making fun of their peers, and speaking dismissively of adults—and discussing all of the other things boys talked about amongst themselves. Sif didn't care to know the specifics; she had had little patience with boys when she herself was a girl, and now she had even less.

Alaric, another of Volstagg's brood, saw Sif and Hilde approach, and got to his feet. "They're back! Hey, Lady Sif, how close did Hilde get? Not as close as me, I bet."

"No," Sif said, "she did not get as close as you."

That got a grin from Alaric. "Ha!"

Sif broke into a grin of her own, making Alaric's face fall. "She got closer."

"What?"

"In fact, Hilde is the only one of you to actually reach the target."

Shoulders now slumped, Alaric folded his arms angrily. "What do we need to know how to hunt for, anyway?"

"For food, obviously," said Bors, one of the grandchildren of Odin's aged Grand Vizier. He, and most of the other boys, had risen to his feet, excited about the news of Hilde's hunt.

Snorting, Alaric said, "If I want food, I'll ask Mother to cook something!"

Bors laughed right back. "I've seen your father—I doubt you need to ask your mother to cook."

Hilde strode forward. "Are you making fun of our parents?"

Stepping backward and holding up his hands, Bors quickly said, "Of course not, Hilde. I have nothing but respect for your parents, especially your father. Just please don't let him sit on me again!"

Sif held up her hands. "Enough! Everyone, be seated." The children returned to their places around the campfire, joined now by Sif and Hilde. Even seated, Sif towered over the children; while she did not have the height and breadth (and, in the case of Volstagg, the girth) of the male warriors she fought beside, she still was considerably larger than the youths of Asgard. "It is all well and good to know that you have hearth and home to rely upon for sustenance. But most of the battles of Asgard are not fought at home. On many occasions, I have found myself in need of provision while on a journey through the Nine Worlds to do battle on another plane.

"There was one occasion many centuries ago, when I was traveling to Niffleheim. I had brought jerky along to maintain my strength, but the journey proved longer than expected, and I had to ration my provisions. And then, when I came over a ridge, I was ambushed by a great beast."

One of the boys asked, "Was it Hilde's father?"

Bors shushed him.

"It was, in fact, a giant stag. I hadn't realized the creature was there, and it attacked as soon as it caught sight of me, attempting to gore me with its huge antlers."

"Did you beat it?" Bors asked.

Hilde rolled her eyes. "Of *course*, stupid, she's here telling the story, isn't she?"

"Oh, right."

"The *point*, little ones," Sif said in a menacing tone intended to forestall any more interruptions, "is that I was insufficiently aware of my surroundings. The stag outweighed me by one and a half times—"

"It *was* the size of Father, then," Alaric muttered with a grin.

"—and I was unable to defeat it. It unhorsed me and I was barely able to hold it off with my sword while on foot. Eventually, I managed to put enough distance between me and the beast to get back to my horse, which was unharmed, and I rode away. I had traveled quite some distance before I realized that, when the stag had knocked my horse aside, it was not just I who fell from the steed's back, but also my pack. I had no supplies—and no food. What I learned that day was that while it is commendable to know how to defend yourself against foes, there are times when you must fend for yourself against the harsh realities of nature. And that is why I have been teaching you how to be aware of the creatures of the wilderness, and also how to approach them in secret and on foot. Had I known how to do such things on the road to Niffleheim, I might not have lost my provisions, nor would I have struggled to survive without them."

Sif looked around at her charges, hoping that she was getting through to them. Children were not Sif's favorite people in the Nine Worlds, as she found them mostly to be obnoxious and tiresome. Enough so that Sif had asked Odin why he had given her this particular assignment.

"Once," Odin had said in response to Sif's query, "my son Tyr took charge of teaching the youth of Asgard the way of the warrior—as you well know, Sif, having been his first female student."

Sif had nodded, trying not to let her pride show.

"But Tyr has long since abandoned Asgard, and in the aftermath of Hrungnir's attack, I believe it would be beneficial for one of my trusted warriors to take up Tyr's mantle."

"I would be honored," Sif had lied. "But why me?"

"You trained under Tyr. And yes, so did Thor and Fandral, but Thor is still recovering from injuries suffered at Hrungnir's hands, and I do not believe that Fandral has the patience and discipline required to be a teacher of children."

"While I would agree with the All-Father regarding Fandral, would those sentiments not apply equally as well to me?" Sif had asked in a tone that made it clear that the answer to her question was yes.

Odin, however, had not taken the bait. "I believe, Sif, that you underestimate yourself. Besides, I recall you were not shy in your criticisms of Tyr's methods. Here is your chance to, as the mortals of Midgard say, put your money where your mouth is."

Over the millennia, Sif had seen Odin angry, haughty,

strong, righteous, and frightening. Which was why his rare forays into mischievousness always gave her pause, as it had on this occasion.

He was right, however, as she *had* had issues with Tyr's methods. That was why she had insisted on hunting being part of the children's training. There was far more to being a warrior than swordplay, something she learned only after Tyr's tutelage had ended—and despite it, not because of it. She would not allow the younger ones of Asgard to have to learn the hard way, as she had.

Looking at her pupils around the campfire, she continued with her lesson. "As you all know, the giant Hrungnir recently attacked Asgard."

"Why did he attack Asgard, anyhow?" Bors asked.

Sif sighed. They had just finished a long day of training, and the sun would be setting soon. It was, perhaps, the appropriate time to tell a story before they bedded down for the night; they would hike back to Asgard on the morrow.

"One day," she said, "a group of trolls attacked Asgard. Their way was paved by Loki, the Trickster, when he gave them a path that even my all-seeing brother, Heimdall, could not espy. And so they reached the very heart of the city before a defense could be mustered."

"That was you and Father, right?" Hilde asked. "The defense?"

"'Twas I, yes, along with Volstagg, as well as Thor and Balder, and your father's boon companions, the Warriors Three—Fandral and Hogun. The battle was—" Sif hesitated. "—*complicated* by more treachery from Loki. He hid Mjolnir from Thor, and left a false hammer in its place. But even denied Thor's greatest weapon, together we did rout the trolls and expose Loki's perfidy. The Trickster was brought before Odin and punished by being confined to his keep for a month—where still he sits."

"I don't understand," said Lars, another of the children. Sif suspected that the boy started many a sentence with those three words. "What does the trolls' attack have to do with Hrungnir?"

Sif recalled that Lars had never gotten within a league of his prey during his own hunting test, and she told him now what she had told him then: "Patience, Lars."

Lars sulked. "Okay."

"After having to punish his own son, Odin set out in disguise on his mighty steed, Sleipnir. While so doing, he encountered Hrungnir, who had a great steed of his own, Goldfaxi. From astride Goldfaxi, Hrungnir led his band of Frost Giants to menace the countryside in Jotunheim and Nornheim. Hrungnir did challenge Odin to a race of their steeds, though Hrungnir knew not that he was challenging the All-Father."

"Sleipnir won, right?" Hilde said urgently.

Sif smiled. "Of course. Odin's horse is the fastest in all the Nine Worlds, and there was no doubt that he would win the race against Goldfaxi. But at no point did Odin reveal himself, and Hrungnir did abide by the terms of their contest and let him go on his way. But somehow, the giant discovered that he had lost to the ruler of Asgard, and thought that Odin had played him for a fool. And so he brought his forces to bear on Asgard itself. Again, Thor, the Warriors Three, Balder the Brave, and I rallied to Asgard's defense, confronting the Frost Giants on the Ida Plain."

Alaric said, "That's when we went to the mountains!"

"Yes," said Sif with a nod to Volstagg's son. "Odin felt that the children of Asgard needed to be safeguarded, for Hrungnir had brought a larger contingent of combatants than the trolls had brought. And so he sent you all with his wife, Frigga, and your mother, Gudrun, into the mountains and to safety in the Vale of Crystal. But, as you recall, when Hrungnir made his cowardly retreat from the Ida Plain, he took the same route to Jotunheim that you children had taken through the mountains. Frigga confronted Hrungnir and kept you safe, but the giant did defeat her and take her hostage."

Hilde said, "I wish we could have helped her. Maybe then she wouldn't have been captured!"

"Indeed, young Hilde, and that is why Odin asked me to work with all of you. The children of Asgard may someday be called upon to aid in its defense. Plus, many of you will grow up to become warriors of Asgard. You must be prepared."

"Hey," Bors said, "what happened to Frigga? I mean, I know she got home safe, but how?"

"I heard the Warriors Three raided Jotunheim!"

"I heard Thor wiped out all the Frost Giants with his hammer!"

"I heard Odin smote them all!"

"In fact," Sif said loudly to cut off more speculation from the children, "the giants had a ransom for the Lady Frigga.

Hrungnir would free her if Thor faced him in one-on-one combat. However, the giant did not reveal that he wore enchanted stone armor until Thor arrived. But still, Thor was victorious, though he remains abed, recovering from the grievous wounds inflicted upon him by the Frost Giant."

"Wow," Bors said.

The sun was starting to set; Sif looked at the children. "And now night begins to fall, so it is time to see who has learned their lessons best, for we must have our evening repast."

"What's it gonna be?" Alaric asked, licking his lips.

"That depends entirely upon all of you. Now that you have learned huntcraft, you must go out and obtain our dinner using your new skills."

The faces of all the children fell—except, Sif noted, for Hilde's, which instead smiled with anticipation.

Sif had a feeling that she knew who would be providing tonight's meal. And of course, if they all failed, Sif herself would hunt. But what better way to test the children than to give them a task they were motivated by hunger to complete?

CHAPTER TWO

The first time Sif went to visit Thor after he was injured by Hrungnir, the thunder god was in relatively good spirits. He had rescued his mother, and Hrungnir had been utterly defeated. Not only had he been routed in the battle with Thor, but he had also lost the leadership of the Frost Giants.

With each subsequent visit, however, Thor's demeanor grew surlier.

"Good morrow, Thor!" Sif said upon entering his bedchamber, where he had lain for the better part of a fortnight.

"There is little I find to be good about it," Thor muttered.

Concerned, Sif asked, "Are your wounds not healing?"

"The healers do make their noises about progress, and I can indeed feel the slow process of bones mending."

"Then what is the issue?"

"It is taking so *long*!"

Sif could not help but laugh.

Bemused, Thor asked, "Does the thunder god's agony amuse the Lady Sif?"

"It does, actually." She sat at his bedside and put her hand on Thor's. "You have fought a great battle, Thor—one that will be spoken of at feasts and celebrations for millennia to come.

But all battles have a price, and you are paying it now. You were once a mortal physician—you should be aware of precisely how long it will take for such injuries as you sustained to right themselves."

At that, Thor did allow himself a smile. "It is a saying on Midgard that doctors are the worst patients. It would seem that I am proving that maxim, even if I am no longer truly a human healer."

Shaking her head, Sif said, "If Tyr could see you now . . ."

Thor barked a laugh. "Ah, my half brother would not have a kind word for me under any circumstances."

Remembering an incident not long ago when Tyr did battle with Thor in an attempt to win her affections, Sif shuddered. Tyr's unwillingness to consider Sif's wishes had remained a theme throughout their interactions, from his initial refusal to allow her into his sword-fighting class to his mistaken belief that defeating Thor would cause her to fall into Tyr's arms.

"But enough of my own unseemly complaints." Thor sat up straighter in the bed. "You have obviously returned from training the children. How fared them?"

"Some better than others." Sif told Thor of their adventures—including the success of Hilde and some of the others, and the failures of the remainder.

"Be watchful, Sif, or Hildegard shall eclipse you as the finest shield-maiden in Asgard."

Sif chuckled. "If it were to be so, I would be honored—for as children go, Hilde is almost tolerable."

Before the conversation could continue, a knock came at the front door to Thor's home.

"Are you expecting anyone?" Sif asked.

"None who would feel the need to knock. Only the healers or my boon companions come, and they may enter freely."

Sif rose from the bed. "I will determine who this strange visitor might be, then."

She approached the front door and opened it to a small, young man with a very thin beard, who was drenched in sweat and who breathlessly asked, "Is Thor at home? I was told that he'd be here!"

"Be calm, my friend. Thor is indeed at home, but in poor condition to receive visitors whom he does not know."

"Forgive me, lady, but I *must* see the thunder god! I am Frode from the village of Flodbjerge. Thor is the only hope to save us!"

Sif smiled wryly. "Then Flodbjerge may well be doomed, for Thor is badly injured. He is not to leave his bed for another fortnight, at least."

Frode's face fell. "Oh, no! All is lost! Please, may I at least see him, so I may tell my doomed fellow villagers that I did at least witness that Thor was unable to come to us in our hour of need?"

"Of course." Sif led the nervous young man in. As they moved through Thor's home to the bedroom, she added, "You are aware, are you not, that there are other warriors in Asgard who might serve to defend your village?"

"I cannot speak to that, milady, only that I was charged with contacting Thor as soon as possible!"

"And so you have," said Thor, for that last phrase was said as Frode entered the thunder god's bedchamber. "What message is it that you bring to Thor Odinson?"

Bowing before the foot of Thor's bed, Frode said, "I am Frode of the village of Flodbjerge. For a fortnight now, we have been attacked regularly by a dragon! We have attempted to defend ourselves, but the dragon is far too mighty for those such as us to do battle with, and several of our townsfolk have lost their lives. We require the God of Thunder's strong right arm and mighty hammer, Mjolnir!"

Thor sighed. "Would that I could help you—but as you can see, I am in no condition to answer my own door, much less fly to your aid. But you may take heart, noble Frode, for there is another in this very room whose strong right arm is the equal of mine own."

Frode leapt to his feet and gaped at Sif. "Your maid?"

Sif glowered at Thor for a moment, and then turned her attention to Frode. "I am the Lady Sif, young Frode. I serve at the pleasure of no one, save for Odin himself."

Frode once again fell to his knees, but this time was fully prostrate. "My lady! Please accept the deepest apologies of your humble servant, for I did not know 'twas you."

Shaking her head, Sif said, "Rise, Frode, for the fault is not your own. One would not expect a warrior of Asgard to be answering doors—your mistake is understandable and easily forgiven."

Getting slowly and cautiously to his feet, Frode said, "Thank you, my lady. You are too kind."

"As for your problem, I have just spent a week performing a task that has been, shall we say, far from my first choice in activity. I believe that doing battle with a dragon will be far more palatable. Besides, it has been centuries since last I fought such a creature."

Thor smiled, recalling Sif's fight against a dragon on Midgard a millennium ago. "You may rest assured, Frode, that there are few in the Nine Worlds better suited to save your town from this foul beast. I'm sure the Lindworm of Denmark would attest to that, were it able to speak from Hel."

"We are honored. The Lady Sif is renowned in song and story as one of Asgard's finest warriors. I would be privileged to bring you back with me, milady."

Sif nodded to Frode, and then went to Thor's bedside. "Be well, Thor."

"I shall. Your company shall again be missed, but I have no doubt that Volstagg will be present ere long to bring me food and then eat it all himself while he regales me with exaggerated tales of his exploits."

"Of course he will. You are a captive audience—Volstagg's favorite kind." Sif smiled and kissed Thor on the forehead.

"I expect that you will return known once again as Sif Dragonslayer," Thor said.

"Perhaps." She turned to the man from Flodbjerge. "Come, Frode, let us be away!"

CHAPTER THREE

Flodbjerge, not too far from Asgard, was located at the base of the Valhalla Mountains. To get there, Sif and Frode had to traverse along the Gopul River on foot. Sif had taken the time to change into her red armor and white headpiece, which served to keep her dark hair out of her face. She had considered and rejected the notion of taking along the cloak—Flodbjerge was warm this time of year, and she suspected that the cloak would merely get in the way.

"Many of our horses have been wounded or killed by the dragon," Frode had explained with regard to his coming to Asgard without a mount. "The few able-bodied ones that remain were deemed too valuable to risk on a journey to Asgard."

As Sif clambered over a large rock that blocked their path, she said, "I understand why. The passage to your village is not suitable for any but the heartiest of steeds."

Even as they continued on foot along the Gopul, Sif noticed that they were not alone. Someone had followed them from Asgard, but Sif decided that the trail was difficult enough that eventually their pursuer would have no choice but to reveal herself. She kept her counsel for the time being, not wishing to worry Frode. While the young man was abject in his insistence that Sif was a perfectly adequate substitute for Thor, Sif also knew that the rest of the villagers might not think the same.

She had dealt with such idiotic disappointment more times than she was able to count. “But you’re just a *woman*!” “You’re not Thor.” “But there are *three* of the Warriors Three!” “You seem rather, well, *small* for a warrior.” “They call you a shield-maiden—shouldn’t you be carrying a shield instead of that heavy sword?” And so on.

When the western bank of the Gopul was no longer passable, Sif and Frode looked to cross to the eastern bank, which opened up to a wide plain that Frode said would lead directly to Flodbjerge. Looking up, Sif could see the Valhalla Mountains, at the base of which was located the village.

They chose a crossing where the river was at its narrowest, and where several rocks that were larger than the river was deep allowed easy passage across.

“It shouldn’t be long now,” Frode said as he leapt onto one of the rocks. “Be wary, milady, as the first rock is slippery.”

“Thank you.” Sif followed him, making sure to keep herself sure footed as her boot landed on the wet stone.

A minute later, when she and Frode were most of the way across the river, Sif heard a small scream and a splash.

Turning, Sif looked down with amusement at the tiny form of Volstagg’s daughter Hilde, flailing her arms and legs in the river, her red hair plastered damply to her head. The girl had slipped on the first rock.

Leaping back a few rocks, Sif smiled down at Hilde. "And you were doing so well up to that point."

"You knew I was following you?" Hilde asked, treading water.

"As I said, Hilde, I have not come close to teaching you all that *I* know." Sif reached out her hand.

Hilde grabbed Sif's hand and allowed herself to be pulled out of the water. Sif guided her to the eastern bank, where Frode was waiting.

"Who is this?" Frode asked, confused.

"Hildegard, daughter of Volstagg the Voluminous. Hilde, this is Frode of Flodbjerge."

To her credit, Hilde attempted to curtsy, though it was difficult, as her bulky brown tunic and black leggings were quite waterlogged.

Introductions finished, Sif looked down at Hilde. "Why have you followed us?"

"Um . . ." Hilde looked away. "I've never seen a dragon before."

"I should send you back to Asgard."

"Please don't!" Hilde grabbed Sif's armor and looked up at her with a pleading expression. "I want to see the dragon! And I want to help! You spent all that time teaching us—I want to put what I've learned to good use!"

Sif shook her head. "You realize that if anything happens to you, your father will likely sit on me until I expire."

"He won't! I promise! Besides, I can take care of myself!"

Frode spoke up. "Milady, we must hurry."

Shaking her head, Sif pulled Hilde's wet hands off her armor. "Oh, very well. It's probably more dangerous for you to find your way back across the Gopul without me keeping an eye on you."

Hilde grinned. "I thought I was keeping an eye on *you*."

"Ha!" Sif chuckled. "However, you're not going anywhere near the dragon. Come, let us tarry no longer."

"We will be there within the hour," Frode said. "I fear that Oter will attack again soon."

"Oter is the dragon?" Sif asked. Frode had been parsimonious with details up to this point, so focused was he on his mission to return to his village with a warrior. Sif knew she would get the details soon enough, and regardless, it wasn't as if she would refuse to help the town.

"Yes, milady. He named himself the first time he attacked. 'I am Oter,' he cried, and then exhaled his unholy, flaming breath upon us. However, those three words are the only ones he has spoken aloud."

"How often does he attack?" Sif asked.

"There has been no pattern to it, but what is most passing strange is that he turns his attention to a different portion of the village on each occasion." Frode shook his head sadly. "Our village will be naught but a cinder soon, unless you stop him, milady."

Sif had no response to that, and so instead asked the next obvious question. "Where does the dragon come from?"

"The mountains, milady—but a more specific location, I

could not say. Fast is Oter, and wily. He comes from a different spot within the Valhalla Mountains on each occasion, and we cannot see his destination when he departs because of all the smoke caused by his foul breath."

Hilde spoke, having spent much of her time since they had crossed the river trying and failing to wring the water from her soaked clothes. "We should try to track the dragon. Perhaps we can beard Oter in his lair!"

Regarding Hilde dubiously, Sif said, "'We' shall do no such thing, young Hilde."

"But you said my tracking skills were excellent!"

"Of a deer, which does walk through the forest upon hooves that leave distinct marks upon the ground. How, pray, shall you track a dragon through the air?"

Hilde looked down, abashed. "I hadn't thought of that."

"In any case, child, it is I who shall do any bearding."

Frode pointed and said, "There it is!"

Turning, Sif followed his finger and spied the village. Several small structures lined the river, with larger ones a bit farther inland. Sif also saw many boats in the river, all close to a natural port at the water's widest point.

As they drew closer, Sif observed that many of the structures were burnt and pitted; there were also many piles of wood, ash, and stone that had likely once been buildings.

"We have been fortunate thus far," Frode said, "in only one way—the dragon has yet to turn his attention on our fishing boats."

Hilde smiled. "My father has often spoken very highly of the fish from Flodbjerge."

For the first time since Sif met him, she saw a smile on Frode's visage. "High praise indeed from Asgard's finest epicure."

Sif noticed a boathouse that seemed abandoned—but also not burnt. "What of this structure?"

"The Gopul overflowed last spring and caused water damage to the boathouse. It was always too small for the purpose in any case, and so we built a new one farther north. This boathouse is no longer used."

Two women and one man ran toward them as they passed the abandoned boathouse. "Is he coming?" the man asked breathlessly.

"The God of Thunder is unavailable," Frode said.

One of the women said, "You were told to bring Thor."

Sif stepped forward. "Thor was badly injured in battle with the Frost Giants. I am the Lady Sif, and I promise I shall defend your village from this scourge."

Both women looked up at Sif with awe. "We are honored, milady."

"Thank you for agreeing to defend our village."

The man, though, frowned at her. "I thought you'd be taller."

"When did Oter last attack?" Sif asked, pointedly ignoring the man.

Before anyone could answer her question, a voice cried out from the direction of the port. "The dragon is back!"

Amid the screams, wails, and curses that followed, Sif turned back toward the river and saw in the distance a green-scaled form winging its way toward the village. In the small amount of time it took her to register the dragon's presence, it was almost on top of the port.

Quickly, Sif brandished her sword and sprinted toward the river. She ran as fast as she could, but the dragon had already reached the port and was breathing fire upon the fishing boats, the occupants leaping into the water in order to save themselves from the flames.

The dragon flew up into the air and circled around to take another pass at the port.

Sif kept running, but slowed her pace so she would reach the water's edge at just the right moment, and, as Oter made a low pass near the river, again breathing fire at the fishing boats, leapt onto the creature's left wing.

The wing was about twice as long as Sif's height, and her extra weight caused Oter to list to the left, nearly plummeting into the river. Sif plunged her sword into the creature's wing and Oter screamed, fire blasting from his maw.

The dragon flailed. Sif yanked out her sword and struggled to gain purchase on the wing. Green blood oozed from the wound and dripped down the wing, making it slick to the touch. Sif felt herself slipping.

"You will trouble this village no longer, dragon!" she cried as she attempted to clamber along the wing toward Oter's body.

The dragon craned its head toward Sif, staring at her with huge, yellow eyes underneath two large horns protruding from his forehead. He replied in a deep, resonant voice that sounded as though it came from Hela's domain. "If I cease, it shan't be thanks to your pitiful doing!"

With that, Oter dove straight for the river, breaking through the water's surface.

Water smashed into Sif's body and she struggled to both breathe and hold on to both the dragon and her sword.

She maintained her grip on her sword, but when the dragon broke through the river's surface to once again take to the sky, Sif was left behind in the water, along with the many fishermen who had abandoned their boats.

She swam to the surface, and upon breaking through, found that fewer of the boats were on fire than had been before Oter dove underwater. No doubt the creature's displacement of the river had soaked many of them, thus negating the dragon's work.

Of the creature himself, she saw no sign. His speed was as great as Frode had indicated, and the dragon was already long out of sight.

"Next time, Oter," Sif muttered under her breath.

As Sif started to swim toward the port, she heard a familiar voice cry out, "Don't just *stand* there, get those rafts moving!"

It was Hilde, directing the villagers, who Sif saw were standing stunned at the devastation wrought by Oter.

Frode was the first to act on Hilde's words, saying, "She's right—we must retrieve those people before they drown!"

"Help!" a voice cried from behind Sif. She whirled around

to see two people, a man and a woman, struggling to stay afloat.

Quickly, Sif swam toward them and grabbed both of them, one in each arm. "Hold on," she said, and used her powerful legs to kick toward the shore. It was much slower going without the use of her arms, but she managed to get them all safely to the port.

Frode and two other men were waiting for her, and they pulled the two people out of the water. Once they were safely on dry land, Sif hauled herself up—her armor now even more soaked than Hilde's clothes had been after she had fallen into the river earlier.

Over the next hour, Sif helped retrieve those who remained in the water. At one point, she noticed Hilde helping people off a boat that had been docked during the dragon's raid. Sif walked over to Volstagg's daughter, who was giving a blanket to a soaking-wet child, and asked, "Was this boat attacked, as well?"

Hilde nodded. "It's the only one that was in dock that was hit. Bad luck."

As night fell over Flodbjerge, a boy ran up to Sif. "Excuse me, milady?"

"Yes?" Sif knelt down so she was eye to eye with him.

"I bear a message from the village council. They're ready to see you, as requested."

"Excellent." Sif stood. "Where?"

The boy pointed.

Sif followed the boy's finger to the town's meeting hall. Or rather, what was left of it. The walls were made of stone, but there was still considerable fire damage, and the roof had been destroyed.

"Can I come with you?" Hilde asked as they approached the hall.

Shaking her head, Sif said, "No, Hilde, I wish you to aid the healers. Many were injured."

Hilde rolled her eyes. "Anyone can do that."

"Perhaps." Sif stopped and looked down at Hilde, putting a hand on her shoulder. "But look at these people, Hilde. Their homes have been destroyed, and they've spent the past several weeks cleaning up after repeated vicious attacks. They're exhausted. I believe that the sight of a strong, young woman of Asgard who does *not* walk around as if she's already been defeated will do wonders to help the injured get well."

"All right," Hilde said. "I want to help."

"This task will help immensely."

Nodding, Hilde ran off.

Sif entered the hall. Without a roof, the inside was just as cool as the outside now that the sun had set. Stools had been brought over from the tavern—also a burnt, pitted wreck—as the hall's furniture had been destroyed by the dragon.

The council included Frode, two other men—Bjorn and Olaf—and one woman, Helena. Olaf and Helena were two of the trio who had greeted Sif on her arrival—Olaf was the one who'd expected her to be taller. The third person she'd met was

Bjorn's wife, who was the town healer, and was well occupied elsewhere in the wake of Oter's carnage.

Helena spoke first. "To begin, Lady Sif, may I express the gratitude of all of Flodbjerge for your assistance today. Several of our people would have died had you not driven off the dragon so soon, and then aided in the rescue efforts."

"Of course," Sif said with a bow of her head. "Although I am not entirely convinced that I was the cause of the dragon's departure. But, of course, I am pleased to aid you in whatever way possible."

"Again, thank you."

"To that end," Sif continued, "I would like to know the full story of how the dragon came to beset you. Frode began to tell me, but the dragon's attack curtailed his account."

"Of course," Helena said, and turned to Bjorn.

Bjorn leaned forward on the stool. "We have always been a quiet, peaceful village, and have relied these many centuries on the protection of Asgard and Lord Odin. We sustain ourselves through trade, as the fish in our waters are considered delicacies by most of the Nine Worlds. While oftentimes our citizens have been conscripted to do battle against Asgard's foes—for example, many citizens of Flodbjerge fought against Surtur's minions—for the most part, we have lived our lives in peace. That changed a fortnight ago, when Oter first attacked."

Frode shuddered. "It was horrible."

Nodding, Bjorn continued. "That first time was a bright, sunny day, much like any other. Midday here is our most active time—the boats have come in from the river, and the daily catches are being sorted and stored. It was, in fact, *right* at mid-day when the dragon first appeared."

Bjorn closed his eyes and exhaled slowly. This was clearly difficult for him to remember, and Sif felt a pang of regret for asking, but she needed the information. Tyr may have taught her how to wield a sword, but it was through her own millennia of experience in battle that she had learned the best weapon in warfare was intelligence. It wasn't enough to know that a dragon attacked the village. She needed details of how, which might lead to why. And why might lead to another how—to wit, how to stop Oter.

Finally, Bjorn went on. "He seemed to come from nowhere. One moment, we were sorting the fish, the next he was upon us, his girth blocking out the sun as he descended."

Helena shuddered. "He destroyed an entire section of the village."

Leaning forward, Sif asked, "Which section?"

"Does it matter?" Helena was confused at the query.

"It might."

Olaf said, "The northeast corner of Flodbjerge. Four houses near each other. It was only those four, and then he departed."

"And after that?" Sif asked.

Olaf looked helplessly at Sif. "After that, what?"

"I must know where Oter attacked each time."

The council exchanged glances with each other.

Urgently, Sif asked, "Can you show me on a map?"

"Of course." Helena rose from her stool and walked to a table that held several scrolls, a few codex books, and a large map.

Sif joined her.

Helena pointed at the map's northeastern section. "That is where the first attack occurred." She pointed at a place a bit farther west, but still on the town's northern edge. "Then here." Then the northwestern corner. "Then here."

The pattern Helena described indicated that the dragon was moving methodically through the village—almost in a grid.

Almost, because it had skipped two sections. One was near the center of town, which should have come after the attack that damaged the meeting hall and the tavern. The other, on the town's northern outskirts, should have been the third place raided. "He didn't attack either of these two spots. What are they?"

Pointing to the northernmost section, Helena said, "There are four houses there that were destroyed in an avalanche last winter—the same has happened five times in the last decade and the families who lived there chose to rebuild their homes elsewhere. We have all agreed to leave that area free from construction.

Frode indicated the section nearer to where they now sat. "This is our storehouse. It is kept cold by spells we acquired from Niffleheim, and our winter stores are kept there so that we may eat even when the Gopul River freezes over."

"So there are no people in either place?"

Olaf shook his head. "No one uses the storehouse in these warm months, no. Why?"

Sif nodded. "It makes sense. I believe that Oter is not attempting to destroy your village."

"That's absurd!" Bjorn said. "How else do you explain what has happened?"

"If he wished to destroy Flodbjerge, he could have done so the first day he blotted out the sun and ravaged the northeast corner of your village. But he did not. Instead, he has been moving methodically, predictably. Indeed, I can say most assuredly that he will next set his sights upon this collection of structures along the riverbank." She placed a finger on the grid, showing where the next attack would occur.

"The repair shop." Frode shook his head. "That is the facility where our seacraft are taken for repair when they are damaged. Much of the equipment stored there is unique and would be difficult to replace."

"Then I suggest you remove those items, and quickly," Sif said sternly.

"But wait," Bjorn said, "he *hasn't* been moving predictably. Like you said, he skipped the three homes and the storehouse."

"Yes. Because I believe that he is not out to destroy—he is searching for someone. Oter is in the mountains, and therefore has an excellent vantage point from which to observe your comings and goings. But he must be searching for a specific person, and so he is checking each of the populated areas. He is skipping those parts of Flodbjerge that are uninhabited because they do not serve his purpose."

"But for whom does the dragon search?" Olaf asked.

Sif shook her head, sadly. “I do not know. But if we are to learn that person’s identity, we would be well to do so with dispatch.”

CHAPTER FOUR

When she had woken up that morning, Hilde had had no intention of following Sif in an attempt to assist her. In fact, after spending a week in training with her, she'd had no intention of seeing Sif again for a very long while.

But then Alaric had been an idiot.

Years ago, when she was very small, Hilde had seen her father's collection of hunting knives for the first time. One in particular caught her eye because of the intricately carved dragon design on the hilt. Volstagg had told her that it was his second-best hunting knife, the one he had used when he, Fandral, and Hogun had gone after the Fenris Wolf. His best hunting knife was the one Gudrun had given him as a wedding gift—and Volstagg would never part with it—but he did that day promise to gift Hilde the dragon-hilt knife when she was old enough to use it properly.

Upon returning home from her week with Sif, Hilde had been hoping that now would be the time for that gift. And then she had checked her father's collection, and had seen that the dragon-hilt knife was gone.

Hilde had been devastated, so she had gone to her mother.

"Oh," Gudrun had said, "your father is hoping it can be

repaired, I think. Something about Alaric using it on a hardwood tree."

"What!?"

Livid, Hilde had sought out her brother. "Did you use my hunting knife?"

Alaric had stared at her, confused. "You have a hunting knife?"

"The one with the dragon carved on the handle! Father promised it to me!"

"Why would he do *that*? Anyhow, I needed it to cut down that hardwood tree on the lawn."

Hilde had been unsure which appalled her more, that he was dumb enough to think a hunting knife was the right tool for cutting down a tree, or that he had used *her* hunting knife.

So she jumped him.

They'd scuffled for a few minutes before Mother broke up the fight. "What in the name of all the Nine Worlds are you two *doing*?"

Alaric—doubled over and clutching his stomach, as Hilde had gotten in a good punch to his solar plexus—had said, "She just hit me for no reason!"

"Is that true, Hilde?" Gudrun had asked her.

"No, it's not." Then Hilde had looked away. "I had a very *good* reason. He ruined my hunting knife!"

"How is it *yours*?" Alaric had asked yet again.

"Father promised it to me!"

"Well, don't worry—the smith'll probably fix it."

"*Probably*?" Hilde had almost jumped him again, but a look from her mother stopped her.

Gudrun had stared down angrily at both of them. "Go to your rooms, both of you. And don't come out until supper."

Hilde had no idea whether Alaric had acceded to Mother's request to stay in his room, but Hilde hadn't lasted more than five minutes before climbing out the window to seek out the Lady Sif.

Mother didn't understand. That was *Hilde's* knife! Father had *promised* it to her!

She quickly found out that Sif had gone to visit Thor, and Hilde had arrived just as Frode was explaining about the dragon.

Since returning home would have incurred Mother's wrath, she decided to go with Sif. But Sif wouldn't have given Hilde permission to come along if Hilde had asked. She instead followed a dictum that she'd learned from two of her adopted brothers, Kevin and Mick, who, although born and raised on Midgard, had been taken in by Volstagg and Gudrun upon being orphaned: "It's easier to obtain forgiveness than permission."

Besides, Sif would be so much more impressed if Hilde used her hunting skills to track Sif and her companion!

Hilde hadn't expected Sif to know she was there all along, but she should have guessed Sif would know. Either way, she was grateful that the lady had let her stay.

Now, Hilde was helping gather the debris from one of the destroyed boats that had been brought to shore. She couldn't carry much—Hilde was small, and most of the others were bigger and stronger than she was—but she was fast and agile, so she made up in speed what she lacked in strength.

When she brought the last pile of debris to the shed, where it would be sorted through to see what was still useful and what would only be good as kindling, a man approached her.

"Excuse me—you're the girl who came with the Lady Sif, yes?"

Hilde looked up to see a tall, gaunt man wearing only black—tunic, pants, boots, belt—all entirely black. Hilde found it to be rather depressing. Most of the occupants of Flodbjerge wore muted earth-and-jewel tones—probably because these didn't look as bad when they got wet. The man had a very thin beard and short dark hair.

"Yes, I'm Hildegard." She used her full name, figuring it would make her sound more like a woman of Asgard than a child of it, never mind how small she was.

"Good. I need to speak with the Lady Sif immediately. Do you know where I can find her?"

At first, Hilde opened her mouth to tell the man where to find Sif, but then she stopped. "Why do you need to know?"

"I *must* see her."

She stared at the man's hands and clothes. They were all clean and pristine, except for his boots, but even they had only mild scuffing on them. "Have you been helping with the cleanup?"

The man hesitated. "I'm sorry?"

"This town was just attacked by a *dragon*. Maybe you saw it?"

"Of course I did! Look, Hildegard—"

"Your clothes and hands are clean. You haven't been helping, have you?"

Again, the man hesitated. "If someone had asked—"

"You needed to be *asked*? Nobody asked *me* to help—I don't even live here—but I volunteered, because I thought it was *important*."

"Then you're a very good girl. Your parents must be proud."

Hilde didn't respond to that, as her parents were probably wondering where she was and worried sick about her at this point. But in general, the man was right—she knew that both Volstagg and Gudrun were proud of her. And so was Sif—she had all but said so after Hilde had touched the doe's rump.

Aloud, though, Hilde said only, "Why should I take you to see Sif?"

The man took a breath. "My name is Regin. I only recently moved to this village."

"Okay. Is that why you think you're exempt from helping out? I know if *I* had just moved somewhere, I'd want everyone to like me and want me to stay because I pitched in whenever something went badly."

Regin let out a long breath. "Perhaps. But I prefer to keep a low profile. You see, I came to this village because it's quiet and out of the way, and I like to keep to myself."

"They've been under attack by a dragon for *weeks*. I really think—"

"Look, *little* girl," Regin said in a tone of great impatience, "are you going to take me to Sif or not?"

"I'm still waiting for you to answer my question."

Regin frowned. "What question?"

"Why should I take you to see her?"

A third hesitation, then he finally said, "I have information she will need to combat the dragon."

Hilde blinked. "What?"

"I said—"

"I heard what you said. If you know about the dragon, why haven't you told anyone else?"

"I told you, I like to keep to myself. I very rarely leave the rooms I rent. And at first, I didn't see the dragon. I just heard—and sometimes felt—the attacks, and later listened to the stories people told about them. But until today, I never actually *saw* it." Regin closed his eyes for a moment, then reopened them. "My bedchamber window looks out on the docks, and today I saw the dragon quite clearly. And I recognized it as Oter."

"We *know* his name is Oter."

That surprised Regin. "I'm sorry?"

"According to the town council, he called himself Oter the first time he attacked."

"Hm." Regin rubbed his bearded chin. "Well, in any case, I need to inform Sif of what I know. Trust me, she will want to hear this."

"Fine." Hilde started toward the town hall. Maybe Sif and the council were done with their meeting, in any case.

Sure enough, as Hilde and Regin approached the town hall, Sif and another woman were exiting the building. Hilde recalled that this was Helena, the head of the town council.

"Sif!" Hilde cried out. "This man wants to talk to you!"

Helena seemed to recognize the man. "You're that new arrival—Regin, isn't it?"

"Yes, ma'am. I rent rooms from Mala and her husband."

"And what business do you have with the Lady Sif?"

"It is with you, as well, ma'am," Regin said, "and with the rest of the council. You see, I know who the dragon is and where he comes from."

Sif had barely acknowledged the man up to this point, but now she turned to face him. "Then speak, and be quick about it! The more knowledge we have of this dragon, the easier it shall be to slay him."

"No!" Regin said a little too forcefully. Then he took a breath and got himself under control. "Apologies, milady, but I do not provide you with this intelligence to aid you in slaying Oter—but rather to save him."

Angrily, Helena said, "What possible reason could you have for wishing such a creature to be saved?"

"Because he is my brother."

CHAPTER FIVE

Night had fallen over Flodbjerge, and torches had been lit in the meeting hall. Sif and the members of the council had returned to their seats, and two more stools were brought in from the tavern—one for Regin and one for Hilde.

Bjorn and Olaf had both objected to Hilde's presence, as she was just a little girl, but before Sif could speak up to defend the honor of Volstagg's daughter, Frode had said, "Young Hilde is a bright and talented young woman. I believe she should be allowed to be part of this as much as Sif is."

Helena nodded. "Very well."

Hilde folded her arms and muttered, "Hmph."

Sif smiled. "Hilde did also find Regin here."

"Yes." Helena turned upon the gaunt man. "You said this dragon is your brother, and I must ask how this is even possible."

At that, Sif stared at Helena. "Two of Loki's sons are the Midgard Serpent and the Fenris Wolf. It is not as bizarre as you might think."

"And in fact," Regin said, "Oter once looked as you or I. But I get ahead of myself."

"Please do tell us of yourself and Oter," Sif said.

Helena added, "And explain why we should consider showing him mercy."

"Is not the fact that he is brother to one of your citizens enough?" Regin asked.

Olaf snorted. "You are barely a citizen of this town. In fact, had Helena not recognized you, I would have assumed you to be a stranger to us."

"It is true that I arrived comparatively recently, and it is also true that I keep to myself. But I would hope that the good people of Flodbjerge would not be cruel to a family member of one of its citizens."

"Several *other* of its citizens are now dead or injured because of said family member," Bjorn said, "so I would say you hope in vain."

"Nonetheless," Sif said quickly, "we know nothing of the dragon's motives and origins. Knowledge of such may affect how we approach the beast." Turning to Regin, she said, "Speak, Regin, and tell us of your brother."

"Oter and I were born in Nastrond, under the rule of the evil Fafnir. Our mother died when our younger brother was born—our brother, too, died soon thereafter."

"That's *awful*," Hilde said.

"It is, but I never knew either my mother or my brother, as Oter and I were both still very young when they died, so neither of us truly felt the sting of grief. Our father, however, was not so fortunate. He loved our mother dearly, and felt the pain of her loss every day." Regin shook his head. "However, we still needed to survive. Father was an expert hunter, and he trained Oter and I to hunt as well. In truth, however, his greatest skill was properly skinning the animals we captured to preserve their pelts. We would skin the animals, sell the meat to one of the butchers in Nastrond, and then sell the pelts. Our family gained a reputation as the purveyors of the finest pelts in the Nine Worlds."

Sif regarded Regin with renewed respect. "Tell me, Regin, is Hreidmar your father?"

Regin nodded. "Yes. You knew him?"

"By reputation only. The merchants from whom I have purchased furs for long winter journeys have always recommended the furs of Hreidmar because they are the finest."

"That pleases me greatly, milady. My father was truly an artist with a skinning knife."

"Yet you speak of him in the past tense."

"I am afraid so." Regin lowered his head. "As I am sure you are all aware, Nastrond was a most lawless place under Fafnir's rule. Bandits roamed the countryside, and one day, when we were on our way to the market in Gundersheim, we were beset by one."

"Only one?" Sif asked with surprise.

Bjorn turned to Sif. "Why does that surprise you?"

"In my experience, such roadside bandits travel in numbers—it is difficult strategically for a single bandit to ambush a group. After all, if you wish to steal items from travelers, it is risky for one to remove valuables without having at least one other accomplice to hold weapons upon the victims."

"As it happens," Regin said, "the bandit who set upon us learned that lesson on this particular day. He attempted to make off with our pelts, but without that second person you mention, Lady Sif, he was unable to stop my father from attacking him in retaliation. But the bandit was armed as well, and his sword proved a more efficacious weapon than my father's skinning knife. So overcome with grief were we that we allowed the bandit to escape, as we were concerned only with being by our father's side for his final breath."

Helena pursed her lips. "I am so sorry."

Sif, though, said nothing, steeling herself instead for the next part of Regin's tale. Far too many stories of people transformed into creatures began with grief over a lost loved one.

Regin continued. "We brought our father back to Nastrond and performed a funeral for him. From that day forward, Oter and I swore we would track down that bandit and wreak revenge upon him for what he had done. For many months, we searched throughout Nastrond, Varinheim, and Gundersheim for the brigand who had taken our father from us."

Hilde, now literally sitting on the edge of her stool, was enraptured by Regin's story. "Did you find him?"

"Eventually, yes, Hilde, we did—but by the time we did so, we had spent all our coin. Our business was robust enough to keep us alive and fed when all three of us were active in its work, but after our father's death, my brother and I renounced the task of securing and selling pelts in favor of our quest for vengeance. By the time we were able to trace the brigand—to a cabin buried deep in the Norn Forest—all of our savings were gone. We were living off the land—cold, starving, miserable, with thoughts only of revenge."

"You must have loved your father a great deal," Hilde said.

"Yes," Regin said, "but it was more than that. We always aided our father and did what he told us. Without him, we had no guidance, no wisdom to lead us—we were the sons of Hreidmar and always did we do as he ordered. Vengeance was all we had left. And so it was a pair of thin, reedy, desperate, hungry men who approached that cabin in the Norn Forest."

"Was the brigand alone?" Sif asked.

Regin nodded. "And it was when we confronted him that we learned why—the cabin had only a pallet and no other furniture, for there was no room for it. All the rest of the space was filled with gold and jewels. Never had we seen the like. Oter and I were transfixed upon entering the cabin, and we lowered our swords and gaped.

"The bandit did stare at us. 'Who are you?' he asked.

"'I am Oter,' my brother said, 'and this is my brother, Regin. We have come to claim vengeance upon you, for you have slain our father, Hreidmar.'

"'I did?' The bandit seemed surprised.

"Angrily, I said, 'You set upon us on the road to Gundersheim and attempted to rob us. When our father tried to stop you, you did stab him!'

"The bandit shrugged. 'If that is what you do recall as occurring, I will not gainsay you. I have set upon many travelers on the road of which you speak, and I am sure that I have slain many such.'"

Sif frowned. "Did he not even put up a fight?"

"No, my lady, he did not. I hesitated, but Oter did not. He raised his sword and ran the man through without another thought."

Hilde shuddered.

Now Sif raised an eyebrow. "However, it would seem that your financial difficulties had come to an abrupt end."

Regin looked away. "After a fashion."

"Explain."

"We put as much of the gold and jewels as we could in our packs—including an emerald on a chain that the bandit wore around his neck. Our plan was to return to Nastrond and begin anew. The journey home was slow and arduous. Our plunder was quite heavy, and our horses were weak and feeble, for we were no more able to feed them than we were ourselves. As soon as we reached the village of Midluna, we immediately did purchase food and fresh mounts with our newly obtained gains.

"But soon, my brother and I did squabble. I wished only to return to our previous life, using enough of the bandit's gold to get our business started again, and putting the rest aside for use in our respective old ages. We were still young men, and the possibility of family was a real one.

"Oter, however, wanted none of that. 'We now have wealth beyond our wildest dreams, brother. Why put *any* of it aside? Why should we work and scrape and bow? What purpose is there in long days and nights in the forests and lakes in an attempt to capture game? What reason is there for us to travel throughout the Nine Worlds to marketplaces only to haggle with imbeciles who do not appreciate the value of our work? And why put money aside when the money is there for the taking?'"

"I take it he did not convince you?" Sif asked wryly.

"He did not. And so he stole away in the night—with the treasure and both our horses. He left only the emerald necklace, along with a note saying not to try to find him.

"Left with no recourse, and no coin save for an emerald that I doubted would feed me for more than a month, I returned to the bandit's cabin. I hoped that it was well provisioned, and at least I would have a place to sleep and eat while I determined what next to do, since my future plans had relied on the notion that I would have half the plunder.

"The day after my arrival, a dwarf smashed down the door. He had an axe raised over his head, but hesitated upon spying me in the sitting room. 'Who are you, and what have you done with Siegfried?'"

"I assume," Sif said, "that Siegfried was the bandit?"

Regin nodded. "I said to the dwarf, 'He is dead, his gold and jewels taken by a man named Oter.'

"The dwarf stared at the necklace around my neck. 'From whence did you obtain that necklace?'

"My sword was in another room, and the menace in the dwarf's tone made it clear that I should not prevaricate. 'From

Siegfried. Oter is my brother, and he and I both sought revenge on him for our father's murder. But while I wished only for vengeance, Oter determined also to gain the wealth and prosperity of Siegfried's riches. And so he abandoned me, leaving only this emerald.'

"'Then your brother is a fool. That emerald is a charm that protects the wearer from all curses.'

"This surprised me, but also pleased me, obviously—for being immune to curses was a state of affairs I found to be advantageous. 'No doubt,' I said, 'Siegfried used it to protect himself from anything he might have stolen that was cursed.'

"'You speak true, stranger,' the dwarf said, 'for the gold he stole from the dwarves was so cursed.'"

Sif shook her head. "The dwarf also spoke true when he named your brother a fool. Those who steal from the dwarves quickly learn to regret it."

"Indeed." Regin sighed. "The dwarf did, at least, spare my life, satisfied as he was that Siegfried was dead—though he did take the emerald from me."

"A pity," Bjorn said.

With a glower at Bjorn, Sif said, "Hardly. Charms to fend off curses are but stopgaps, and tend only to cause the curse to seek its foulness elsewhere." She turned to Regin. "I assume the dwarf explained that the curse of this particular gold was to turn any who hoarded it into a dragon?"

"Yes, milady."

Olaf asked, "How came you here to Flodbjerge?"

"By the time I returned to Nastrond, there was nothing of it left. Even the river was fused to a faceted crystal."

Quietly, Sif said, "The wrath of Odin. Fafnir did rule in Nastrond, and so vile was he that all who had goodness in their hearts were driven from the land. Those who remained were amongst the foulest beings who ever populated the Nine Worlds, and Odin did destroy them all."

"I know not of that, milady," Regin said, "but I do know that I had no home to return to. So I did wander the Realm Eternal, finding what work I could with my skills as a hunter. Eventually, I amassed enough coin to settle in a new place, far from my old life."

"And you happened to come here?" Sif asked. "To the very place where your brother has hoarded his cursed gold?"

"I know not how Oter found himself in the Valhalla Mountains, Lady Sif, but I do know that it is the first time I have encountered my brother since he left me in Midluna. And I wish to save him from this awful fate. He has suffered enough, trapped by the gold and the desire to hoard the treasure but never spend it. That, you see, is the true curse of the dwarves. A dragon may only protect his hoard, and perhaps add to it, but the protection of it becomes all."

Sif rubbed her chin thoughtfully. "No doubt he believes you to be a threat to his hoard, as you claimed it together, and so he has been attacking Flodbjerge to eliminate that threat."

"No doubt." Regin nodded.

"It also explains why he attacks in the manner he does."

"How so?" Olaf asked, confused.

Sif stared intently at Olaf. "Curses are extremely powerful. If Oter is compelled to protect the hoard, he cannot be away from it for very long. So his attacks last only as long as he may stay away from his treasure."

Helena hopped off the tavern stool. "Revealing though all this may be, it is of no relevance."

Regin's eyes grew wide. "How can you say that?"

"I am truly heartbroken over what has happened to you and your brother, Regin. To lose a father is a terrible burden. But the responsibility of this council is to safeguard the village. In order to do so, Oter *must* be killed—and quickly, before more of Flodbjerge is leveled, and more of its citizenry killed or injured."

Bjorn shook his head. "If Oter is looking for his brother, why not simply give him what he seeks?"

Regin blanched.

Helena turned upon Bjorn. "No. I will not sacrifice any more of Flodbjerge's denizens to this dragon."

"He's barely one of us!" Bjorn cried.

Shaking her head, Helena said, "That matters not. Besides, there is no guarantee that giving Regin to Oter would even stop the dragon."

"However," Sif said in a hard voice, "there *is* a guarantee that if you commit so craven an act as to give Regin over, you will divest yourself of my protection—and that of any of Asgard's warriors henceforth."

Quickly, Bjorn said, "I meant no disrespect, Lady Sif; I simply wished to consider all the options."

"Then let me provide you with another option," Regin said urgently. "The curse may be removed."

That got Sif's attention. "You might have stated that earlier, Regin. Tell us how, quickly!"

"Oter must be defeated in combat at his lair, and then physically removed from his hoard. Only then may the curse be lifted."

Olaf nodded. "There is only one thing for it. Milady, you must send your girl here to Asgard to fetch Thor."

Sif whirled on Olaf with fury behind her eyes. "I beg your pardon?"

Hilde jumped off her stool. "I don't have to go to Asgard for anything, because Sif can win in *any* fight—even with a big, stupid dragon!"

After throwing a small smile at Hilde, Sif turned back to Olaf. "For millennia, the greatest foes I have faced are fools such as you, who would use gender as a criterion for determining a warrior's heart. Be assured, Olaf, that I have fought many foes for many decades, and none have yet earned the title of 'Killer of Sif.'"

Holding up both hands, Olaf said, "Please, milady, do not misunderstand me. I hold you in the highest regard."

"Save, perhaps, with regard to my height," Sif said wryly.

"Indeed, Lady Sif, I expected greater height from you precisely because the tales of your prowess are so impressive. But it is not your gender that I find lacking. Were Balder the Brave present in your place, or any of the Warriors Three, or Harokin, of the Einherjar, my response would be the same. Thor is the God of Thunder, the son of Odin. Save for the All-Father himself, there is none mightier in the Nine Worlds. And he has slain dragons before."

Sif smiled. "And you think I have not?" The smile fell. "Regardless, Olaf, even if I acceded to your request, it would not be possible for Hilde or me to fulfill it. The God of Thunder is abed, and the healers have urged him to remain so for many more weeks. Thor did do battle against Hrungnir of the Frost Giants, and while the giant was defeated, Thor's victory came at a great price. As Helena said, time is of the essence, and we cannot wait for Thor's recovery to ask him to take on the dragon—nor is such a query required."

"As I said, milady, I meant no disrespect to your abilities as a warrior." Olaf sounded nervous now. "I merely point out that you are not Thor."

"And Thor is not Sif. Remember that, Olaf, and remember that the path of my life is littered with the corpses of those who thought me weaker or lesser than the men around me."

Before Olaf could even consider formulating a response, a man ran into the hall.

"The dragon returns!"

Helena's eyes grew wide. "Never has the interval between attacks been so short."

Frode frowned. "The last attack was shorter than the others—perhaps that is why?"

Shaking her head, Sif said, "The reasons matter not. Oter will find Flodbjerge to be far better defended than it was in the past!" She pointed at Regin. "Hide him in the most secure location you have in this village. Do all that is possible to deny Oter his prize."

"And what will you do?" Regin asked.

Sif unsheathed her sword. "End this madness once and for all!"

CHAPTER SIX

Sif ran out into the thoroughfares of Flodbjerge, sword at the ready. Looking up into the sky, she saw Oter heading for the houses alongside the river in the southwestern portion of the village—exactly where she had expected him to strike next.

Angry that they had not had a chance to remove the items from the repair shop, Sif revised her opinion of Frode's earlier remarks. Perhaps Sif's resistance *had* caused Oter to leave Flodbjerge sooner than he had planned. She had wounded him, after all, which was more than had happened to him on any of his other attacks.

The dragon was swooping downward, toward the large structure that had to be the repair shop. But he was still quite distant, having just come out of the mountains. Gritting her teeth, Sif ran toward the shop, hoping that she would be able to reach it before the dragon's arrival.

Her feet carried her well, for she did indeed arrive ahead of the dragon. She held her sword aloft and said, "Ho, dragon! Be gone from this place! You will not find your brother here, and if you do any more harm to the good people of this village, you will face the wrath of Sif!"

The creature swooped over the repair shop, then flew up and

around, making a loop in the air. He stopped, hovering over the shop, and Sif was able to get a better look at the dragon than she had before, lit as he was by the torches along the Gopul River and by the dragon's own maw, which smoldered and glowed. While Oter's wingspan was impressive, Sif realized that it created the illusion that the dragon was larger than he truly was. In fact, his body was only about twice the size of that of Sif herself, though his wings unfurled to twice *that* length again.

The dragon spoke, and Oter's voice rumbled as though shuddering forward from the very earth itself. "The wrath of Sif? Am I to be impressed by this declaration? Who are you, little girl, whose wrath claims to be sufficient to challenge Oter the dragon?"

"I am Sif! I am she who has done battle against the Frost Giants of Jotunheim and the minions of Surtur! I have fought alongside Thor the Thunderer and Beta Ray Bill! I have faced gods and villains! I am a warrior and a goddess, and you are a failed peddler of pelts who has been granted delusions of menace by a dwarf's curse!"

"And are only words to defeat me this day? You claim to be a goddess, and claim also to know the man I was. But all I see is a little girl who speaks words that mean nothing. No man has ever defeated me in battle, and I highly doubt that a woman will do so now."

"Flodbjerge is under my protection, dragon. Return to your hoard and cease your search for your sibling."

"And if I refuse, little girl?"

Now Sif grinned. "Oh, I sincerely hope that you do, Oter, for I will take great pleasure in ending your reign in a much bloodier manner."

The dragon chuckled, smoke bursting forth from his maw. "You risk much, little girl."

Raising her sword, Sif cried, "Choose, dragon! Return to your hoard and live your life in peace, or stay and end your life in battle!"

Oter did not answer with words, but instead dove straight for Sif.

Sif also dove, rolling away from the dragon's attack. Oter arced back upward.

To Sif's relief, the dragon didn't actually attack the repair shop. Whatever else Sif calling him out had accomplished, it served well the purpose of focusing Oter's wrath on her rather than on his devastating search for his brother.

Getting to her feet, Sif sheathed her sword, then ran toward another nearby structure and leapt to its roof, her powerful legs easily propelling her upward. As soon as her feet gained purchase, she ran to the far edge of the roof.

Oter was flying back down toward the same building onto which she'd leapt, making Sif's plan that much easier to enact.

The dragon opened his maw, preparing to use his fiery exhalation on Sif, but she leapt into the air, a running start giving her even greater distance than her jump from the ground had.

Flying through the air, she reached out to gain purchase upon one of the dragon's talons. In addition to his wings, the creature had four short legs on the underside of his body that ended in three sharp talons each, and Sif managed to snag a talon on one of the forelegs.

Screaming, Oter flew upward, then quickly bucked left and right in an attempt to dislodge Sif.

Any hope she had to stab the dragon was dashed, as Oter's movements made it incredibly difficult for Sif to maintain her hold upon the creature's talons with even two hands. A one-handed grip would be insufficient, and she would plummet to the ground or the river.

The dragon continued to change directions in ever-more chaotic maneuvers, trying to dislodge Sif, but she would not let go.

So Oter altered his strategy. He flew straight upward into the dark night sky, as fast as his lengthy wings would carry him.

One of the things that made Thor stand out from his fellow Asgardians was the gift of flight granted him by his Uru hammer, Mjolnir; even Odin had not the ability to carry himself through the air.

On Midgard, Sif had encountered many of Thor's colleagues, dubbed "superheroes" by the mortals, who could fly through the air unaided. Sif had even fought alongside some of them.

On those occasions when someone had carried her while using their power of flight, Sif had always found it exhilarating. She thrilled at how the wind moving past her could be experienced by all five of her senses at once—the feel of it pressing against her body and running through her hair, the sight of it filtering through the tears it caused in her eyes, the sound of it as it roared in her ears, the smell of her sweat, instantly evaporated by it, and the taste of it on her tongue even as it dried her mouth.

None of that exhilaration was present now as Oter streaked ever upward, rising nearly to the peaks of the Valhalla Mountains.

But still she held on.

The wind didn't just press against her body as she clung to the dragon's talon, it pounded her. Her eyes were forced shut by the intensity of the flight, and the roar of the wind nearly deafened her. The only smell her nose could detect was the fetid stench of Oter's fiery breath, and her throat had gone so dry, she could taste nothing.

But still she held on.

Then Oter ceased his upward motion. The dragon hung in the air for but a second, yet to Sif it seemed much longer; they were poised so high that when she briefly opened her eyes, the village of Flodbjerge was but a speck on the ground beneath her.

Oter craned his neck downward, and suddenly, both dragon and his unexpected passenger plummeted. With each second they went faster, accelerating toward the Gopul River.

But still she held on.

She had to use both arms and both legs, but Sif did still clutch to the dragon's talon, refusing to give in. He could not harm her directly, as it was impossible for him to crane his head to his underside in such a way for his breath to be effective—even were he willing to immolate his own limb. And his talons were stunted and far apart, each unable to reach any of the others.

Left without those two options, Oter was forced to try to shake Sif off.

As he descended toward the Gopul, he angled himself so that he would not enter the water directly, but would instead skim its surface with his belly.

The dragon's underside, including his talons and the Lady Sif, hit the water with sufficient force that it was akin to striking a stone wall.

But still she held on.

Battered, bruised, bloody, soaked to her very bones, Sif refused to loosen her grip even as Oter once again flew up into the air.

The dragon hovered for a moment. "Still you vex me, little girl!"

That hesitation, and expression of annoyance, was all Sif required to let go of the talon with one hand, unsheathe her sword, and run it into the dragon's underside.

Oter's scream filled the heavens with fire as he reared back his head, crying and thrashing about in agony.

With only one hand gripped upon the talon, Oter's thrashing managed what could not be done before, and Sif lost her hold.

The dragon still hovered over the Gopul, so Sif straightened her body and dove into the river.

This plunge into the cold waters of the Gopul was far kinder than the previous one had been, and she surfaced after only a moment.

Oter stopped his cries of pain long enough to peer down at Sif. "You will rue the day you challenged me, little girl!"

Sheathing her sword while treading water, Sif said, "You will rue the day you called me 'little girl.'"

The dragon dove downward at Sif, so she submerged herself once again, swimming underwater toward the shore.

Even as she swam below the water—her strong legs propelling her, her capacious lungs allowing her to hold her breath—Oter breathed fire at the river. But while Sif could feel the heat of the flames, and they no doubt turned the water's surface to steam, she was deep enough to remain unharmed.

Upon reaching the shore, she clambered out of the water and unsheathed her sword.

Oter hovered over the river, glowering at her with his watery, yellow eyes. His voice rumbled even louder now. "You vex me, little girl, and you will die at my hand!"

"Unlikely." Sif ran downriver, away from the town, hoping that Oter would follow.

That hope was fulfilled, as the dragon flew after her, catching up to her as she reached the southernmost part of the town and the abandoned boathouse she had noticed on their way in.

Sif ran into the boathouse, then immediately ran out the other side, out of sight of the dragon.

As she'd hoped, Oter headed straight for the boathouse itself, coming to a halt just outside it, and exhaling heavily upon it.

The dilapidated wooden structure immediately caught fire,

but Sif was already far enough away from it to be unharmed, having run outside and doubled around.

Oter raised his head and cackled—a low, rumbling sound that seemed to shake the very sky.

"Burn, little girl, burn! None may challenge Oter and live! Not that fool Siegfried, not my idiot brother, not the dwarves, and not our f—AAAARRRRRGGGGGGHHH!"

That last cry came as Sif leapt onto the dragon's back and plunged her sword into his scaly hide.

Oter flew back and forth, writhing in agony. Sif, with no talons to grip, fell to the ground, but managed to roll onto her right shoulder as she landed, dulling the impact.

As she got to her feet, Sif paused a moment to catch her breath. She ignored the fact that her entire body felt like one big bruise.

Oter thrashed about in the air. Sif's sword still protruded from his back, and the dragon was helpless to remove it. His tail hit the river hard, violently splashing water all about, including onto the engulfed boathouse.

Looking down at Sif, his yellow eyes now murderous, Oter screamed in a voice that shook the very foundations of Flodbjerge.

"You *will* die for this, little girl!"

"Many have made that claim, including other dragons far fiercer than you, Oter, yet Sif remains—and they are all dust."

"As will you be shortly."

But before the dragon could make good on his threat, he was

pelted by debris—tools, rotten food, and other detritus flew threw the air, striking the dragon's hide.

Both Sif and her foe turned toward the source of the impromptu missiles.

A group of villagers had gathered nearby, and at the forefront of them was Hilde.

"Get away from here, dragon!" cried the daughter of Volstagg. "We're sick of you, and we don't want you here!" She punctuated her outburst by heaving a rock the size of her hand.

The rock flew through the air and slammed into the dragon's neck. It was followed quickly by a broken rake, a few more stones, and rotten fish (the stench of which, after a moment, reached Sif's nose).

Oter screamed, flames bursting from his mouth and into the night air.

And then the dragon turned and flew toward the mountains, Sif's sword still jutting from his back.

Sif watched in fury as the creature flew away, and then turned in surprise at the sudden sound of the villagers cheering.

Slowly, she walked over to the villagers, the water from her two trips into the Gopul making her armor squeak as she moved. Several of the villagers had already broken off, led by Frode, and were moving to put out the boathouse fire before it could spread. At least the dragon's splashing tail had made that job easier.

"Wasn't that great?" Hilde asked, a big grin on her face.

But Sif only glared at the girl. “Hardly. The fight was not yet finished!”

“It is now,” Helena said.

Sif turned on the leader of the council. “Twice did I strike a blow against the dragon, but before I could even consider a third, you drove him off! And he still has my sword! You interfered in a battle that was not yet complete!”

Helena merely stood with her arms folded. “Milady, every time the dragon has attacked, there have been deaths and the destruction of valuable property. Until tonight. Tonight, no one died, and the only damage was to a boathouse that was already half fallen to ruin.”

“Besides,” Hilde said, “Regin said you had to defeat the dragon and take him away from his hoard to turn him back into a person again. Can’t do that if you defeat him *here*. You have to find his hoard.”

Helena added, “Which is preferable to another pitched battle against a creature who breathes fire within the confines of Flodbjerge. Or would you have the dragon destroy what few structures are still left standing before you defeat him?”

Sif’s retort died on her lips. She could argue with neither of them. Well, in truth, she *could*—but the arguments all boiled down to her desire to continue the fight regardless of the consequences.

Turning to look at Frode and the others using buckets to scoop water from the Gopul to extinguish the boathouse fire,

Sif was reminded that the consequences of continued battle could be dire indeed.

"Very well. I will track the dragon to his lair."

With that, Sif moved off, determined to end this.

CHAPTER SEVEN

Volstagg was late arriving home.

He had intended to come straight back to the house after visiting with Thor, but he had been sidetracked by the fruit merchant, who had had some wonderful pears and persimmons for Volstagg to sample. And then, he had been distracted by the stew being cooked inside one of the inns on the main road, which he of course needed to taste to make sure it was up to the cook's usual standards. And then, he had been waylaid by some young people who wanted to hear tales of Volstagg's bravery, and who was he to deny his public?

When Volstagg did arrive home, he saw several of his children playing. He observed that the very youngest were nowhere to be found—which was well, as they were supposed to be in bed by now.

The older children were playing games together, or reading books from the library, or munching on some dessert or other that Volstagg intended to sample to make sure it was of adequate quality for his offspring to consume.

As he did the latter, he noticed that Alaric and Hilde were conspicuous by their absences. They were not of a temperament to go to bed early—indeed, there were some nights when

Volstagg feared he would need to strap them to their beds to get them there by the witching hour.

After sampling the desserts, and leaving at least a little bit for the children, Volstagg regarded his wife Gudrun, asleep on the couch.

For a moment he smiled, enjoying the peaceful sight of his lovely wife, lying on her side, arms wrapped around a throw pillow. Times like these reminded Volstagg why he had married her.

Then one eye opened. Gudrun spied Volstagg, and shot upward. "Where have you *been*?" she said in a scratchy, scolding tone—made worse by the dryness of her mouth upon waking.

"I—"

"*Don't* give me excuses! The children have been simply *awful* most of the day, and where were you? Hm?"

"Well, I—"

"And the worst part is that Hilde and Alaric got into a fight!"

That brought Volstagg up short. "What about?"

"I have absolutely no idea. It was something about one of your hunting knives—the one you're having repaired."

"Why were they—"

"And another thing—dinner was absolutely ruined because you were supposed to be home for it, and I had to waste all the extra food I cooked because I thought you were to be here."

"I—"

"So what do you have to say for yourself? Well? Answer me! Why will you not speak?"

Conversations like this reminded Volstagg why he so often went on adventures.

"I assume," he finally said, "that you confined Alaric and Hilde to their rooms?"

"Of course! They know the punishment for roughhousing. I do not approve of such behavior in this house from *anyone*."

Volstagg nodded. "I will speak to them."

As he moved toward the back of the house, which contained all of the children's bedrooms, Gudrun called out, "We are not finished discussing dinner!"

"Of that I have no doubt," Volstagg muttered.

Vaguely, he remembered that Alaric had used the dragon-hilt hunting knife in a ridiculous attempt to cut down the hardwood tree on the lawn.

As he approached Alaric's room, Volstagg recalled that he had long ago promised that knife to Hilde. In truth, he offered many items to his children, not expecting them to recall the conversation the next day, much less years later. Hilde had been just a small child when she'd taken an interest in the dragon-hilt knife, and Volstagg had not yet learned what a special girl his daughter was to become. He had promised her the knife, thinking nothing would come of it.

The fight that had ensued this day indicated that something had come of it, and far sooner than Volstagg would have expected, even if he had intended to gift the knife to Hilde.

Opening the door, he saw Alaric lying on his bed—he shared the room with several of his brothers, but the other boys were playing games or eating dessert elsewhere in the house—in very much the same position Gudrun had been in on the couch.

However, Volstagg's mien was not melted by Alaric's angelic visage, as it had been by Gudrun's—partly because he was upset at his son, and partly because the boy himself had a frown on his face as he clutched his pillow to him.

As soon as Volstagg entered, Alaric sat up. "It's not my fault!" he cried out without preamble.

With a smile, Volstagg said, "You do not even know the purpose of my entering."

"Yes, I do. Mother told you to yell at me for getting into a fight with Hilde, but *she* started it!"

"Tell me precisely what transpired, my son." Volstagg took a seat at the foot of Alaric's bed. The springs groaned from the weight of the Lion of Asgard's corpulent form.

"I was just *sitting* in the living room! All of a sudden, Hilde comes out of *nowhere* and asks about *her* knife. I didn't think she *had* a knife, and I *said* so! She said the dragon-hilt knife, which I thought was *your* knife that you used against the Fenris Wolf. And then she *hit* me!"

"Did you explain to Hilde why the knife in question was not on the shelf?"

Alaric squirmed a bit. "Well, yeah."

"Hilde spoke the truth," Volstagg said, patting his son on the knee. "I did promise that knife to her when she became old enough to wield it properly. Be grateful that today is not that day, for she might have used it on you."

Frowning, Alaric asked, "How could she if it's being repaired?"

"Never mind that," Volstagg said quickly. "The point is, you took something that wasn't yours."

"But you already punished me for that! That's not fair!"

Volstagg shook his head. "Ah, my son, it is important that you know that, despite the best efforts of parents to protect their children from this awful truth, the fact of the matter is that life is almost never fair. And a life as long as we Aesir live means that such unfairness comes in even greater quantity." Again, he patted his son on the knee, and then said, "Now then, go to sleep. Tomorrow, I expect three apologies from you, and they are to be heartfelt."

"Three?" Alaric's voice squeaked. "Why three?"

"One to your mother for putting up with your nonsense, one to Hilde for taking her knife, and one to me for using that knife in a manner that is, quite frankly, appalling. A hardwood tree, really, son?"

"I'm sorry, Fath—"

Volstagg held up one finger. "No! The apologies must be proffered publicly to the entire household come morning."

"Do I have to?"

"Rest assured that you will receive one apology in exchange from Hilde, also in front of the entire household."

Alaric grinned at that. "Good."

After tucking his son into bed, Volstagg left the room and went to the room shared by the girls. To his consternation, however, he saw only the youngest girl, Flosi, asleep in her bed.

Hilde's bed was neatly made and completely unslept in.

To be sure, he checked the wardrobe—Hilde would sometimes hide therein, though that had been mostly when she was much younger.

But it only had the girls' clothes in it.

"Father?" came Flosi's bleary voice from her bed.

"Have you seen your sister, Flosi?"

"You mean Hilde? Nuh-uh, she wasn't here when I came to bed."

With a heavy sigh, Volstagg patted his little girl on the head. "Thank you, Flosi. Go back to sleep now."

"Okay," she said through a yawn, and fell back to sleep almost instantly.

Quickly, Volstagg returned to the front of the house.

"Hilde is not in her room."

Gudrun had gotten up from the couch and was now in the kitchen cleaning up the dishes, one of which, at her husband's words, she dropped. "What!?"

"My dear, I am sorry, but Hilde is not in her room, and Flosi says that Hilde wasn't there when she went to bed."

Letting out a moan of anguish, Gudrun dropped another plate onto the floor.

Volstagg quickly led Gudrun out of the kitchen and back to the living room, lest she destroy all their crockery. "Hrolf!" he called out to one of his sons. "Clean up the mess in the kitchen, please!"

"Yes, Father!"

Volstagg sat Gudrun down on the couch and said, "Worry not, my dear love, for the Lion of Asgard will not allow any harm to befall our daughter. I will go immediately to Heimdall and ask if his all-seeing vision has spied Hilde. If he has, I will follow his directions as to where to fetch her. If he has not, then I will leave no stone in any of the Nine Worlds unturned until I have found her! So speaks Volstagg!"

CHAPTER EIGHT

Having spent the remainder of the evening before going over maps of the area that had been provided by the Flodbjerge council, Sif waited until morning to begin her journey up the mountain. While no one was sure precisely where in the mountains Oter was keeping his hoard, Sif did poll the villagers to get at least a general idea of the vicinity where it was likely to be.

"The difficulty," Frode had said to her after they had discussed the matter, "is that when the dragon departs, we are far more concerned with assessing the damage to both people and property to pay significant attention to his destination. As well, that damage, as we said, is accompanied by a great deal of smoke. Oter seldom approaches from the same direction, and we rarely see him until he is almost upon us."

However, they had been able to narrow down Oter's destination to at least a section of the mountains—one that Bjorn had assured her had plenty of caves in which the dragon could hide himself and his pile of gold and jewels.

At first light, Sif provisioned herself with jerky provided by Olaf and his wife, and took her leave.

"I still think," Olaf said, "that Frode should've brought Thor."

His wife smacked his arm. "Hush, Olaf. Sif drove off the dragon single handedly last night and hardly broke anything in the process. Remember when we were visiting your mother in Varinheim while those Storm Giants were trying to invade, and Thor stopped them? He made a total mess! Throwing that hammer all around, knocking things over, all that lightning. Just awful. This lady knows how to fight in a civilized manner."

Sif smiled and bowed her head to Olaf's wife. "Thank you, my lady. I will endeavor to minimize the collateral damage to your fine village."

Bjorn came up to her, holding out a longsword in a scabbard. "It's not much, milady, but I thought you might prefer not to engage the creature unarmed. It belonged to my father, and he used it in battle on Midgard alongside Thor, defending the mortals there."

On the one hand, Sif was grateful, as it was always better to do battle with a good sword in your hand than without. On the other hand, she had no idea whether this was a good sword—especially if it hadn't been used in a millennium.

But then Bjorn unsheathed the sword, and Sif saw that it was sharp and gleaming. He said, "I have cared for it well. Every morning when I awaken, I sharpen it. Every evening before I sleep, I polish it."

Bjorn handed Sif the sword, and upon wrapping her hand around the hilt, she knew immediately that it was a well-balanced weapon—heavy enough to be strong, but light enough to be swung.

"My father named the sword Gunnvarr," Bjorn added.

Sif held it upraised in a salute. "I thank you for the loan of Gunnvarr, and pray that it tastes Oter's blood ere long."

Bjorn bowed. "You're very welcome, milady."

Sif's next stop was to fill her canteen from the Gopul River. It would be at least a day's walk up the mountain, and she hoped that the dragon would be compelled to remain by his hoard for at least that duration, wounded as he had been by Sif's sword.

As the river water flowed into her canteen, she heard the light tread of a child approaching. Without turning around, Sif asked, "What is it, Hilde?"

"How—?" Hilde sighed loudly. "Never mind. I want to come with you."

Sif rose and turned to face the girl. "Hilde . . ."

Volstagg's daughter held up both hands. "Look, I don't want to *face* the dragon again—I don't think throwing things at him will work a second time—but I want to at least help *track* him. Once we get into the mountains, he'll need to be tracked, right? You taught me all those skills, and I want to use them!"

"Hilde, it will be a difficult path to traverse."

"It's just mountains. When Mother and Frigga took us through the Asgard Mountains when the giants attacked, we were fine. And these mountains aren't as high, or as snowy!"

Sif sighed. The desire to keep the daughter of the Voluminous One safe warred with Sif's lack of desire to leave Hilde alone in the village to cause mischief unsupervised. The people of Flodbjerge had enough to worry about.

"Unless you don't think I'm good enough," Hilde added.

Sif winced. Not long after her lessons with Tyr had ceased, she, Thor, and Fandral had learned of an imminent attack upon Vanaheim by a contingent of trolls. Odin had asked Thor and Fandral to come along, along with two others who'd been part of Tyr's lessons—but not Sif.

Sif's response to the All-Father then had been, "Am I not good enough?"

Odin had relented then, and Sif felt compelled to do so now. Besides, if nothing else, the company would be pleasant. Slowly, she said, "It might be useful to see how much you truly learned during the week we spent together. It is far easier to enact lessons learned the same day—the true test is if those lessons are retained after time."

Hilde jumped up and down and raised her arms. "Yay!"

They walked back into town, Sif placing her canteen in her pack.

Regin approached them from the council hall. "Helena informs me that you wish to speak with me, milady."

"Yes, Regin. It is possible that Oter will come down from the mountain while I—" Sif looked down at Hilde. "While *we* are searching for him. Therefore, it is imperative that you hide yourself. I recommend that you hide in the storehouse. Your brother already knows it is a place you are not likely to be."

"That is very sensible, milady, thank you."

"Be warned," she added quickly, "that the place is kept cold by magic that preserves its piscine stores."

Regin smiled. “Our family’s hunts took us to the northern regions of Nastrond, and often into Niffleheim itself. Many is the night I spent in tents during the fiercest blizzards that the northern realms could offer. Cold and sleep are old friends of mine.”

Sif put an encouraging hand on his shoulder. “Excellent. I will do what I can to save your brother from his curse—but know that I will put the safety of these good people over that of a man who leaves his brother abandoned and penniless.”

“I do understand, milady. I ask only that if the opportunity for mercy presents itself, you do take it. I would very much like my brother back—but I also fear that he has been lost to me ever since he left with the cursed gold.”

Sif nodded, and then set off, Hilde right behind her.

The initial travel proved difficult. The Valhalla Mountains, though shorter than Asgard’s mountains, were much steeper at the base.

After spending the better part of the morning clambering up a sheer rock face, Sif and Hilde found a natural pathway up and around one of the mountains that took them on a more pleasant, if still difficult, path.

At one point, Hilde muttered, “The Asgard Mountains had far more straight passages than this.”

Sif chuckled. “The Asgard Mountains have had many more travelers upon them, situated between Asgard and Jotunheim; they are a much-trod-upon path. By contrast, these mountains see far less foot traffic. No doubt that is part of why Oter chose them as the place to hoard his ill-gotten wealth."

Eventually, they paused to eat the jerky and drink the water, to regain their strength after the first part of their journey.

"Tell a story, Sif?" Hilde asked.

In truth, Sif would have preferred to eat in peace, but Hilde seemed so insistent and enthusiastic at the notion. "Be warned, I am not the storyteller your father is."

"It's okay—nobody tells stories like *he* does. But I want to hear about one of *your* adventures."

"Shall I tell you of the time Thor and I fought the Midgard vampire known as Dracula? Or when brave Balder and I faced the Enchanters? Or when Beta Ray Bill and I fought the demons who menaced his home world? Or when I joined the Avengers in battle against mutants in the Savage Land? Or when your father, Fandral, Hogun, and I did—"

"No, I want to hear about an adventure that's *just you*. Not when you're helping out one of the other warriors of Asgard—an adventure of *Sif*."

"Very well." Sif leaned back against a rock. "Balder and I faced the Enchanters in the realm of Ringsfjord. Foul sorcerers, were they—three who possessed the Living Talismans, and therefore power to rival that of the All-Father himself. Originally, Odin did instruct only Balder to go to Ringsfjord to gain intelligence regarding the Enchanters and their plan to attack Asgard, but I spoke of my own time spent in Ringsfjord, and so Odin did grant me leave to accompany Balder on his journey."

"I thought you weren't going to tell that story."

"I am not; I merely mention our mission as a prelude to the story I *am* to tell." Sif took a bite of her jerky, washing it down with the water from her canteen before continuing. "My previous trip to Ringsfjord that gained me that familiarity came during the time of Thor's exile on Midgard, when he was trapped in the body of a lame mortal healer named Donald Blake. But the blink of an eye in Asgard, it *seemed* an eternity to those of us who love Thor—for to be without the thunder god's companionship for so long was difficult."

Hilde grinned. "Companionship? Is that what you grownups call that?"

Sif glowered at the girl. "My relationship with Thor is *not* the subject of this story, Hildegard."

"Father says that—"

"We shall not discuss Volstagg's gossip, either," Sif said sternly. "You wished to hear the story of my first journey to Ringsfjord, and Thor is only a part of it, insofar as his absence prompted the journey." She shook her head ruefully. "After a fashion."

"What do you mean?"

"There was a couple of my acquaintance who lived in Asgard. The boy was the son of the stable master, and the girl was the daughter of the seamstress royal. They grew up together, and the stable master and the seamstress did promise the two of them to each other."

Hilde wrinkled her nose. "Okay."

"You do not approve?"

"I don't want to marry *anyone*! And if I do, it'll be someone *I* want, not someone chosen by my parents."

Grinning, Sif said, "I doubt Hogun will ever wish to marry, Hilde."

Hilde turned away and blushed. Her crush on Hogun was the worst-kept secret in the Realm Eternal.

"In any event, Hilde, not all are so fortunate as to indulge their own wishes. Look at the All-Father and Frigga."

"What about them? They're the best couple in Asgard!"

"And theirs was an arranged marriage, just as that of these two children was to be. Odin and Frigga did marry to unite Asgard and Vanaheim."

Hilde blinked. "I didn't know that."

"The daughter of the seamstress felt much as you do. She was fond of the boy, but had no wish to spend the rest of her life with him. However, she couldn't bear to disappoint her mother, and so she concocted a plan. In Ringsfjord there is a great stone known as the Eye of Gerda. It is one of the finest jewels in all the Nine Worlds, and it is guarded by two trolls, who take turns watching it. One guards while the other sleeps. The troll on guard holds a weapon known as Sigivald—a club that guarantees victory to its wielder.

"The girl told the boy that her most fervent desire was for him to give her the Eye of Gerda as a wedding present. She believed that he would go on his own to obtain the jewel, and then be defeated by the troll. Since the troll's weapon was only a club, she believed that the boy would not be unduly harmed, and that he would return to Asgard injured but alive—and unwilling to marry her for the shame of his failure."

"And instead, he sent you?" Hilde guessed.

Sif nodded. "I did owe the boy, for he had nursed my mare back to health after she was injured during a battle against the Storm Giants. I had thought the mount to be lost forever, and she was the finest horse that ever I did ride. When he presented my mare to me, ready to charge into battle once again, I did tell him that I would perform any favor he asked."

"It was mean of him to ask you."

Sif shrugged. "It was practical. For while the girl had only simple sisterly affection for the boy, he was utterly devoted to her. Neither he nor I knew of Sigivald, only that the Eye of Gerda was guarded by a troll armed only with a club. The boy was no fighter—he barely knew which end of the sword to hold, much less how to wield one."

"That's not really even, is it? I mean, he just nursed a horse. You had to fight a troll!"

"It is not a question, Hilde, of scale, but of ability. It is not within my power to return a horse to a healthy state after an injury, but it is within his. It is not within his power to do battle with a troll, but it is within mine.

"And so I set forth on the very mare that the boy had healed. This was not long after Odin had exiled Thor to Midgard—to teach him humility, or so the All-Father said—and I was feeling his loss keenly. The distraction of a quest was very welcome, and so I did ride into Ringsfjord.

"The terrain there is difficult, as the ground is subject to quakes and tremors. It is made almost entirely of rock, and I have been told by others that it is a great source of magic—which is why the Enchanters did later use it as their base of operations. However, I was able to work my way through, dodging falling rocks and navigating uneven stone passages before finding my way to the troll.

"The troll did not speak, but stared mutely ahead. I did challenge him verbally, but he said not a word.

"'I wish to take the Eye of Gerda!' I cried, but the troll still simply stared.

"Until, that is, I came within a hand's length of him, and then he swung Sigivald with a speed that belied his massive form. Barely was I able to dodge the attack, and I did immediately strike back.

"But no matter what strike I used, no matter how fast or agile I was, always did the troll parry my attack. One moment the club was over his head defending my downward strike, then it somehow was there to deflect my foot when I kicked the troll only a moment past. It seemed impossible, and quickly I deduced that sorcery had to be involved. Magic is an art of the mind, and trolls are not known for swiftness in that particular organ, so I doubted that the sorcery came from the creature himself, or from his sleeping companion. It therefore had to be the weapon.

"And so I did focus my attack not on the troll's head or heart—for the wisest course of action when attempting to disable or kill a foe is to strike at one of those portions of the body—but instead on the creature's right arm. Always was the club held in that arm, never once switching. That, too, bespoke enchantment, for several times I attacked in such a manner that switching hands would have been efficacious, but the blinding speed with which the troll parried made that unnecessary.

"After trading a few blows, I made several attempts to attack his right arm, but he proved as skilled at blocking those as he had all the others."

Hilde was now on the edge of the rock on which she'd been sitting. "So how did you win?"

"I retreated briefly to consider my options. As I suspected, once I moved a certain distance from the troll, he paid me no heed. I viewed the ground ahead and saw that he stood on a single large rock—one that I could dislodge while staying outside the sphere of his defense.

"And so I sheathed my sword, found the edge of the rock, gripped it with my fingers, and pulled upward with all my strength. At first, the rock did not budge. But I was determined to repay the favor I owed the stableboy, and so I gathered every ounce of my might and pulled harder. At last, the rock did rip from the earth and upend the troll. Both my opponent and his weapon fell to the rocky ground. Quickly I dashed toward the club and clasped it in my right hand. I could feel the power of the weapon as I gripped it, and I leapt into the air to strike the troll. I rendered the troll insensate with but a single blow, leaving the path free to the Eye of Gerda."

"Did you keep the club?"

Sif chuckled. "I did bring the club back with me to Asgard, along with the jewel. 'Twas Frigga who identified the club as the mighty Sigivald, and I did turn it over to her."

That confused Hilde. "Why didn't you keep it?"

"The sword is my preferred weapon." Sif shrugged. "Clubs are for trolls."

Hilde shook her head. "But if it guarantees victory . . ."

"As Frigga did explain—and as I proved—the enchantment grants whoever *wields* the club victory. The moment one stops wielding it, victory is no longer assured. Besides, with magic, the simpler the spell seems, the more complicated it truly is . . . and it is never reliable, not even in the trustworthy hands of someone noble like Frigga—never mind a foul creature like Loki, or Amora, the Enchantress, or Karnilla, the Norn Queen."

"I guess."

"In any event, even as I gave Sigivald to Frigga, I did provide the stableboy with his gift for his bride-to-be. It was only when he presented it to her and her face fell in shock that the truth did come out."

"So did they get married?" Hilde asked eagerly.

Sif shook her head. "As soon as the boy realized that she had tricked him—and, by extension, me—he refused to marry her."

"That's really awful. She should have just *said*."

"Indeed." Sif got to her feet. "'Tis always better to speak one's mind than keep one's peace, particularly about matters of the heart. When I was your age, I wished to be taught the ways of the sword as Thor, Fandral, and the other boys were. So I went and asked for ingress into the lessons. As a girl, I was not offered such a place, so I spoke my mind."

With a grin, Hilde said, "And when I wanted to come up this mountain with you, I asked!"

"Which," Sif said admonishingly, "is a preferable gambit than simply sneaking along the Gopul River and hoping I would not notice until it was too late."

Hilde looked down. "I know." Then she looked up and smiled. "That's *why* I asked this morning."

"Good girl." Sif hauled her pack up. "Let us continue."

They spent most of the afternoon working their way up the mountain before making camp. Hilde slept peacefully through the night. Sif, for her part, slept very little. She could not ask Hilde to take a watch, and she did not wish them to both be asleep at the same time. Sif did allow herself a quick nap toward sunrise, but that was all.

As they proceeded upward, Hilde climbed up a set of rocks and cried out, "Sif! I found something!"

Sif, who had been behind the girl, climbed faster to catch up.

Hilde had made it up to a plateau, and as soon as Sif joined her, the girl pointed at the rocks on the ground. "Look at this!"

As her teacher, Sif wanted to make sure that the child truly saw what she should have been seeing. "At what am I looking, Hilde?"

"Can't you see it? It's obvious!" Letting out a huff, Hilde pointed at another set of rocks behind her. "See, over there, the rock patterns are just like they are everywhere else." Then she pointed back at the first set of rocks. "But these are all messed up—like someone's been up here disturbing them."

Sif nodded. She too had noticed that, but she was glad that Hilde had also done so.

Hilde then said, "I think I'd better go back to Flodbjerge."

At that, Sif blinked. She had, in fact, been trying to figure out how to break it to Hilde that once they were able to determine the dragon's general location, Volstagg's daughter should return to the village. She had not expected the child to suggest it on her own.

Holding up her hands, Hilde said, "I know what you're going to say, but I can make it back okay on my own. And I already saw the dragon twice—I think that's enough."

Sif chuckled. "You are wise beyond your years, young Hilde. Go forth and return to the village. Upon your arrival, do look in upon Regin, to be sure that he is safe in the storehouse."

Hilde nodded. "I will. Good luck against the dragon!"

With that, Hilde started her long climb down the mountain.

Volstagg's daughter was glad she was able to put Sif's lessons to good use, but the story Sif had told the day before was what really stuck with her.

The truth was that Hilde was frightened of the dragon. And she *hated* that. She wanted to be like Sif, who wasn't afraid of anything.

But she thought about what Sif had said about forcing her

way into a sword-fighting lesson when she had been Hilde's age. Sif had known what she wanted, and she went after it.

Hilde wanted to be like that.

However, the more she thought about it, the more she realized that she'd seen quite enough of Oter. The dragon was big and mean and scary, and Sif had barely managed to survive their last encounter. Yes, Hilde wanted to be like Sif, but she also knew that she wasn't like Sif yet, and wouldn't be for some time. Being able to track a doe and find traces of a dragon's path were a long way from becoming as great a warrior as Sif.

Hilde would get there eventually. Until then, she was content to remain as far away from the big, scary dragon as possible.

Going down the mountain was far faster than going up, and besides, Hilde could move faster when she wasn't slowed down by Sif. For someone so big, she sure moved slowly!

As a result, their day-and-a-half journey up the mountain was less than a day's journey down, and the sun was only starting to set by the time Hilde reached the village.

She went to the council hall to report in to Helena and the others, but she only saw Bjorn.

"Hilde!" he cried upon seeing her enter the hall. "What news? Where is Sif?"

Quickly, Hilde filled in Bjorn on what had transpired.

Nodding sagely, Bjorn said, "You were wise to return. In truth, I had thought it odd that Sif would allow you to go along."

Hilde grinned. "My father says I'm very good at getting my way."

Taking her leave, Hilde set off in the direction of the storehouse. The large building was far away from anything else, and with her newfound awareness of tracking, she saw that there were very few footprints on the ground.

In fact, she saw only two sets—one going toward the storehouse, and one going away from it.

She recalled that the storehouse had gotten very little use of late—which was why Oter hadn't attacked it, and why Sif had thought it a good location for the dragon's brother to hide in.

A wave of cold overcame her as she drew closer to the structure. The spell that kept the fish chilled and preserved until winter was obviously very effective. The handle to the storehouse door was ice cold to the touch, and Hilde had to pull her hand away and blow on it to warm it up before touching the handle again.

Touching the handle more gingerly, she pushed it down. The door clicked open.

"Hello? Regin, it's Hilde—are you here?"

The storehouse was not lit, so sunlight alone illuminated the frost-covered boxes stacked inside.

"Regin?"

Leaving the door open so she could see, Hilde moved between the boxes.

"Regin?"

Eventually, she found a pallet and a blanket—but no sign of Regin.

Frowning, Hilde ran back to the door. She checked the footprints again.

Both sets had been left by the same feet. Based on the amount of wear on the edges of the tracks, the ones coming to the storehouse were almost two days old.

But the ones moving away from it were about half a day old. If they were Regin's prints, he had left in the middle of the night—probably so no one could see him.

Hilde followed the footprints away from the storehouse. Sif had instructed Regin to stay in the storehouse—if he had sneaked out in the middle of the night, Hilde was honor bound to find out where he had gone.

CHAPTER NINE

Sif continued her search for the dragon's lair in the many caves that dotted this section of the Valhalla Mountains.

The signs of the dragon's passing were extensive. The plateaus hereabouts were not wide, and the dragon was of sufficient girth to make navigating on his four legs without causing significant damage to the surrounding terrain difficult. Not that Oter had any great need for stealth or subtlety. As a dragon, such traits were of little use—even less so in such a remote a hiding place.

Sif was able to immediately dismiss several caves as too small for Oter to fit comfortably inside. She inspected each of the larger caves, and knew upon approaching the third such cave that it was the location of Oter's hoard. Afternoon sunlight reflected off the gold that was only a short distance from the cave mouth, glinting in Sif's eye.

Of Oter himself, she found no sign.

The cave was not terribly deep, but was quite wide. The gold and jewels were strewn about the space, taking up the entirety of the cave's floor, but spread out and flattened by the dragon's heavy form taking its rest upon the hoard.

Sif also saw several bones littering the outer edges of the cave.

They were large enough to be those of bears and other creatures that roamed these mountains, and which had no doubt provided food for the dragon. One set of bones was fresh, with bloodstains still upon them. Oter had, it seemed, fed recently.

Those were not the only bloodstains, however—the cave was spotted with the creature's own ichor, no doubt borne from Sif's sword wound.

Moving back to the cave mouth, she closed her eyes and listened. In addition to the sound of the wind and the occasional chirp of nearby birds, Sif also heard the low rumble of water cascading down the mountain.

Since the dragon had just fed, perhaps he now was drinking from the nearby stream.

Unsheathing Gunnvarr, she ran in the direction of the water.

Coming over a ridge, she saw both a stream and the dragon lapping up water from it, her own sword still jutting from his back. The dragon stood near a hollowed-out tree that had been uprooted, and which lay beside the water's edge.

Unfortunately, Sif had been so focused on getting to the dragon that she had neglected her own lessons to Hilde and the other children with regard to sneaking up on one's prey. She had lumbered through the plateau with no more regard for stealth than Oter himself had shown.

The dragon looked up with his horned head as Sif cleared the ridge.

"You again! I had hoped to have another opportunity to rend you limb from limb, little girl! How considerate of you to come to me, rather than forcing me to search the entire town to locate you again."

"Your reign of terror ends today, Oter."

"I have no 'reign of terror,' little girl. I merely wish to ensure that I retain what is rightfully mine!"

"Cursed gold stolen from the dwarves rightfully belongs to no one save the dwarves," Sif said. "And the people of Flodbjerge are indeed terrorized. Call it what you will, but the villagers live in fear of you—and that fear will end today!"

Sif leapt from the ridge to the dragon's head even as Oter's flame singed the bottom of her boots. She took hold of one of the creature's horns as she arced through the air.

Screaming, Oter threw his neck back and forth, but Sif maintained her grip.

To her surprise, the horn itself gave way before her grip did. It broke off with a snap that echoed off the mountain, sending Sif and the creature's now-severed appendage falling to the water below.

Sif landed in the shallow stream with a bone-bruising thud, Gunnvarr in her right hand and the dragon's jagged-edged horn in her left.

Oter's screams echoed through the Valhalla Mountains, to the point that Sif feared the choosers of the slain themselves could hear.

The dragon craned his neck downward and screamed again—his scream this time accompanied by fire.

Quickly, Sif rolled to her right, narrowly avoiding the flames that issued forth from the dragon's maw that boiled away the section of stream in which she'd been lying.

She clambered to her feet, stared at the horn for a moment, then ran back toward the ridge.

She had to remove the dragon from his hoard, and it would do little good to fight him here at the stream. He needed to be defeated in the cave.

Sif jumped onto the hollowed-out tree and leapt over the ridge, narrowly avoiding another gout of flame. Sheathing Gunnvarr and taking the horn in her right hand, she stood upright and hurled it at Oter's head.

The horn ripped into Oter's nostril, causing the creature to once again scream to the heavens.

Sif ran back toward the cave as Oter cried out, "You will pay for this, little girl! My vengeance will be terrible and merciless!"

While Sif's booted feet carried her across the plateau to the cave quickly, the dragon's wings were speedier, and Oter landed at the cave mouth ahead of her. Without breaking stride, Sif dodged to her right as the dragon again tried to burn her.

She rolled and came up to her feet, running toward the dragon's left side. The terrain worked in her favor, as Oter could not maneuver as easily as she could on the narrow plateau, and Sif easily was able to slide Gunnvarr between two scales on his side. She yanked out the blade just as quickly, not wishing to lose another weapon to the creature's hide.

Oter tried to use his tail to strike Sif, but she rolled under that blow as well, coming upright underneath the dragon's belly.

Again she thrust Gunnvarr upward, and again the blade sliced into Oter's scaly hide. The creature screamed in agony, and Sif took advantage of his pain to scramble out from under him.

She leapt onto Oter's back, crawling over to where her own sword still jutted out.

Gripping the hilt with her free hand, she yanked with all her might. The sword came free, loosing quite a bit of Oter's lifeblood with it.

And then Sif leapt up again, to another portion of the dragon's expansive back, and slashed twice, once with each sword.

Imitating the flight of a mosquito, Sif jumped about the dragon's form, slashing each spot with one blade, the other, or both.

With each fresh cut, Sif felt the exhilaration of battle. From the time she was a little girl, she'd dreamt of it, and she still recalled her first true test. She'd sparred plenty of times as part of Tyr's lessons, but that kind of combat had no real stakes.

No, her first real test had come when she had answered Odin's call to arms in Vanaheim, even though she had not been one of the ones Odin had called. But she had gone into battle to face the trolls who attacked the Vanir. In particular, she remembered facing one such troll who had attempted to strike her, but the massive size of his arms made his punches easy to see coming, and Sif's smaller, lithe form had dodged the blows easily. Her own strength had not yet reached its full peak—she was still a girl, not yet the mighty woman she would grow into—but it was still greater than most, and she had been able to triumph against the larger foe.

In that moment, when she had defeated her first enemy in combat, Sif had felt more alive than ever before during her then-brief years. Everything else had fallen to the side—Tyr's disdain, Thor's friendship (more than friendship, actually, though it would be many years before she would realize it), Odin's power, Heimdall's love, and the confusion of the other children of Asgard, who did not understand why a girl wished to join the men on the field of battle.

All of that had burnt away, replaced only by the imperative of stopping those who would menace Vanaheim. She wasn't a girl, she wasn't a woman, she wasn't Heimdall's sister, she wasn't a citizen of Asgard. She was only a warrior, and nothing else mattered but the glory of noble combat. When she, Thor, Fandral, and the other warriors had returned to Asgard triumphant, Heimdall had said to her, "I've always known, sister, that you were as mighty as the men of Asgard, and today you proved it."

Though Heimdall had never said as much in the past, Sif knew that her brother's gift was to see what others did not, and so he had always known that she had the heart of a warrior born.

On that day, she became determined to show it to everyone else, as well.

And so she sought out more battles. And every time she went into combat—whether against trolls, dwarves, elves, giants, demons, orcs, aliens, vampires, her fellow gods, or one of Midgard's many supervillains—she tried to recapture that exhilaration.

"Enough!" The dragon's cries returned Sif to the here and now.

Oter spread his wings and took to the air in the hope of shaking off his foe.

Sif lost her balance, but managed to use the dragon's scales as handholds to keep herself from falling to the ground.

And then she smiled. Why was she trying to stay on the creature's back when it was no longer a sound tactic?

She dove off the dragon, plummeting to the ground. She landed surely on her feet, her might causing the rock to crumble and buckle beneath her boots. Climbing out of the two divots she'd created, she looked up to see Oter circling the cave from above.

"You are a fool, little girl. You would have been safer on my back."

"If I am the fool, Oter," Sif yelled, "why is it that you have left your hoard where I might easily take it?"

Oter's face constricted into a rictus of anguish. "No!"

Grinning, Sif sheathed Gunnvarr and ran toward the dragon's cave, her own sword still gripped in her left hand.

"You will not have my hoard, little girl! No one shall! It's mine, I tell you, *mine*!"

Sif ran into the cave and climbed atop the pile of gold.

Oter landed and shoved his head into the cave mouth. "You will never steal what is mine, little girl—never!"

As the dragon breathed fire into the cave, Sif dove into the pile of gold.

While the many coins and jewels did protect Sif from being burnt, the precious metals also conducted heat. Rapidly, Sif found herself baking in her ruby-colored armor.

But still she waited, braving the agonizing heat, until she no longer heard her foe's exhalation.

As soon as the sound of the flame stopped reverberating in her ears, she cried out in pain and pushed herself out of the pile of gold. Once she gained her footing, she whipped her sword around in the air, hoping to catch Oter off guard, but her vision was blurred from the great heat of the enflamed hoard. Indeed, the cave itself was oppressively hot from the dragon's flames, little better than being amidst the heated gold.

Taking advantage of Sif's failed swing, Oter did something she never expected. Just as her vision cleared, Sif saw the dragon open his giant maw, and she braced herself for the onslaught of flame.

Instead, Oter leaned in and engulfed Sif in his mouth. His jaws snapped shut, the force of his teeth yanking Sif from her feet.

Darkness consumed Sif. As hot and oppressive as the cave had become, it was as nothing compared to the inferno that was the dragon's mouth.

Sif felt the pull of the dragon's throat as the creature attempted to swallow her whole. She thrust her sword downward, piercing the dragon's serpentine tongue.

Light flooded the creature's maw as Oter opened his mouth to scream in agony. Sif yanked out the sword, hoping to take advantage of his cries to escape, but the dragon closed his mouth too quickly.

But her action had resulted in one beneficial consequence—Oter was no longer trying to swallow. Sif reared back with her right hand and punched through the dragon's teeth, her mighty blow shattering his incisors.

Somersaulting through the newly created hole, Sif rolled onto the ground and brought herself upright.

Oter had removed his head from the cavern and was thrashing about the plateau, the many injuries Sif had inflicted adding up significantly. His tail flew back and forth wildly, and Sif was unable to dodge it. The scaly appendage slammed into her side, and Sif went hurtling out of the cave, across the plateau, and down the mountain.

At first, Sif had no control of her actions, and flailed wildly as she tumbled down the mountain. But after several seconds, she was able to grab on to one of the outcropped rocks and halt her descent—though the suddenness of that stop nearly ripped her arm from its socket.

For a moment, Sif simply hung from the rock by her right hand, regaining her composure. She had lost her grip on her sword, and it continued to tumble down the mountain, no doubt lost forever. Luckily, the scabbard Bjorn had provided remained strapped to her back, with Gunnvarr sheathed inside.

Sif reached up and grabbed another stone with her left hand, securing herself on the rock face. She paused for a moment, caught her breath, and then hauled herself upward. Perched atop the rock, she looked up and saw no sign of Oter.

Confused, she continued to climb, remaining vigilant. But

the dragon was nowhere to be seen—not in the sky, nor on the plateau. She did not hear him gloating or breathing fire.

Sif redoubled her efforts, climbing faster. Shortly, she reached the passageway she and Hilde had taken up the mountain, and which led to the outcropping where Hilde had discovered the dragon's tracks. At the top, she unsheathed Gunnvarr and ran to the cave.

She feared that Oter had decided to take advantage of her absence to renew his search in Flodbjerge for Regin.

That fear, at least, was allayed by the sounds she heard closer to the cave—Oter was talking inside it. The stone walls muffled his exact words, but it was definitely the dragon's rumbling voice she heard.

Sif slowed as she drew near, sword at the ready, taking care to move with greater stealth. If the dragon was distracted by something in the cave, she would use it to her advantage.

A few steps from the entrance, she began to be able to make out the dragon's words. His voice was different, the consonants slurred, no doubt due to Sif's violent removal of several of his teeth.

". . . will never depart from you for long. You will always remain under my watchful eye. Nothing shall take you from me, not the foul goddess of Asgard, not my idiot brother, not our pathetic father, not that incompetent bandit, and not the dwarf who turned me into this awful creature when I took possession of you. Soon, we will need to move to a new cave, for this one grows too unstable, but worry not—you will stay mine forever."

Shaking her head, Sif moved quietly into the cave. She inched toward Oter's tail, which moved slowly back and forth near the mouth of the cave.

Sif debated the efficacy of her thinking. Had she retained both swords, her plan would have been a far better one.

Gazing upon the dragon's form, she saw that many of the cuts she had inflicted were already mostly healed. Even her swords, forged as they were from Asgardian metal, did not penetrate far into Oter's hide.

No, the sword was not the best weapon to use against the dragon. And she had proven with her escape from Oter's mouth that her strength was perhaps a greater ally than her steel, particularly given the goal of saving Oter rather than killing him, as Regin had requested.

So Sif raised Gunnvarr over her head and brought it down point-first on the end of Oter's tail, impaling the appendage fully.

The dragon bellowed, his tail pinned to the ground at the cave entrance, but the creature's continued cries only served to make Sif's warrior heart beat faster.

"Why won't you die, little girl?"

"I think, in truth, that I prefer 'foul goddess' to 'little girl.'"

"I will call you 'dead'!" Oter turned his neck and breathed fire. Sif dove to the side of the entrance and easily dodged the flames as they shot through the cave mouth.

Awkwardly, the dragon attempted to remove himself from the cavern, but he was hampered by his pinned tail. He twisted and turned and screamed and contorted—all to no avail.

Then came Sif's fists, for the warrior woman did not stand idle while the creature thrashed about.

"No longer shall you torment the people of Flodbjerge, nor shall you threaten my own life!"

She struck a huge blow to the dragon's jaw, then another to the side of his head.

"For I am Sif, and ever have I been the victor over any foe foolish enough to cross my path!"

Again she struck the dragon, punching downward on his snout and causing his head to bounce off the floor next to his tail.

"And you will not be the winner this day—nor any day after this!"

She kicked the dragon in the jaw, sending his head flying upward, flipping the contorted creature around until he landed on his back atop his hoard.

Jumping atop the dragon's chest, Sif continued to pummel him, punching him again and again, until Oter no longer moved.

Breathing heavily, Sif wiped her brow and climbed down off the dragon's body.

Slowly, Sif stumbled toward Oter's tail. Wearily clasping Gunnvarr's hilt, she yanked it upward. But fatigue sapped her strength, and it took several tries to free the sword.

Eventually, though, she did loose it. After wiping the ichor and dirt off the blade and onto Oter's scales, she sheathed Gunnvarr and wrapped both hands firmly around the end of the dragon's tail.

Regin had said that Oter had to be defeated and removed from his hoard. She had accomplished the first. Now, it was time to do the second.

Gathering every ounce of her waning strength, Sif pulled until her arms felt as if they would fly from her shoulders. She pulled until sweat obscured her vision. She pulled until every sinew of her body cried out with sharp, brutal pain.

She pulled until she felt she could not pull anymore, and then she pulled harder.

Inch by inch, the dragon's heavy serpentine body slid across the piles of gold and jewels, across the rocky ground, and out onto the plateau.

Her strength all but spent, Sif leaned back as far as she could and yanked the dragon's head out of the cave.

As soon as Oter was no longer touching any of his treasured hoard, the dragon did start to glow.

Gasping, Sif stepped backward.

She watched as Oter's snout started to shrink and his wings began to recede. The four short legs disappeared, while the tail split in two. His watery yellow eyes shrank and became blue, while his remaining horn reformed itself into a mop of blond hair.

Within moments, the transformation was complete. Tail had become legs, wings had become arms, and the dragon's face had become a human visage.

Oter was human once again. The curse had been broken.

And not a moment too soon, for her exertions had taken

their toll, and Sif's knees buckled beneath her. She collapsed to the ground, in desperate need of rest.

In a haze, she thought she heard someone coming up behind her.

Had Hilde returned? Who else would be on this mountain?

"Well done, milady," said a familiar voice before something heavy collided with her head and the world went dark.

CHAPTER TEN

Sif was only insensate for a few minutes, but by the time her head cleared, her hands had been bound behind her and she had been seated with her back against the cave wall.

Next to her, Oter was still unconscious, lying naked on the cave's stone floor, also bound.

Standing over her was Regin, with a vicious smile on his face. He now wore Bjorn's scabbard—Gunnvarr sheathed within—leaving Sif unarmed.

"R-Regin? What—"

"I apologize, milady, for the mistreatment—especially given the great favor you have done me. But you might endeavor to impede my actions, and I cannot have that."

Sif's mind remained fogged from exhaustion and the blow she had suffered. She shook her head, trying to clear her mind.

"I must also apologize for the story I spun before you and the council." Regin smiled ruefully. "I did mislead you a bit, but it was necessary."

While he spoke, Sif pushed against her bonds, but Regin had done his knot-work well. She could barely budge her wrists.

Her head still felt as if it were filled with cotton, but she needed to figure out a way to get out of these bonds. She needed to keep Regin talking. "You did not entirely mislead me. The method by which Oter could be reverted to his natural state was exactly as you described."

"Well, of course, because that was the goal. But in furtherance of that goal, I did prevaricate somewhat with regard to my relationship with my father—and my brother."

"What do you mean?"

Regin smiled. "When I told you of how I grew up, I suppose I gave you the impression that my brother and I were happy with Hreidmar, our father." He looked away. "It must be so nice for you Asgardians. Your lives are so pure and simple. Someone attacks Asgard, and you defend it. Odin tells you what to do, and you do it. No one ever defies him, because he's Odin."

"If you believe that, then you are a fool. The All-Father is mighty and wise, but he is not perfect. I myself have defied Odin—alongside Thor, the Warriors Three, and Balder—and we were exiled to Midgard in punishment. Many times have Thor and Loki defied Odin, and he is their father as well as their king." She chuckled. "And if you believe my life is pure and simple, then you know nothing of my life."

"Perhaps. But Odin's punishments for defiance from his offspring are *nothing*—I know this, because the Trickster and the thunder god both still live! My mother, however, was not so fortunate. Tell me, milady, when you were a small girl, did you wake up every morning wondering if this was the day that you would die by the angry hand of your father? Did you and Heimdall cower together in fear every night before going to sleep? If not—and it is obvious that is *not* the case—then I believe I may remain secure in my pronouncement of pure and simple for your life amongst the Aesir."

Sif felt a pang of sympathy, but she tamped it down. This man had attacked her in secret and bound her—he had made himself her enemy, and Sif refused to sympathize with her enemies.

Regin continued. "Our mother defied Hreidmar just as you claim Thor and Loki have defied Odin. But where Thor's worst punishment was—what did you say? Exile to Midgard?—my mother would have longed for something as painless as *exile.* No, she paid for her defiance with her life. And Hreidmar made it abundantly clear that we would suffer the same fate if we were to say anything." He snorted. "Not that it mattered. We lived in Nastrond under King Fafnir, where the only law was not to anger Fafnir. Had we told anyone of Mother's death, there would have been no consequences anyway."

"Nastrond was a foul place indeed. Odin had good reason for destroying it," Sif said quietly.

Regin smiled viciously. "You speak intemperately, milady."

"I speak the truth. You told us that your mother died giving birth to your stillborn brother."

"Mother almost did die that day. The labor was difficult, and the fetus was long dead when she finally birthed it. Hreidmar was furious, as he wanted another child, and so beat

Mother severely. But *that* day she survived. No, it was when she attempted to run away that Hreidmar did finish the task of her murder."

"Were you even attacked by Siegfried the bandit, then?"

"Not attacked, no." Regin shook his head. "After Mother's death, the story continues much as I told it, with one notable exception. The pelt business was lucrative for our father, but not for the pair of us—and not for Hreidmar for very long, either. Whatever profits we made were quickly poured down our father's gullet. At first, he would drink at home, but then he started to go to a local tavern—alone. That was the first time we attempted to run away. But he caught us, and took us with him to the tavern from that day forward."

Sif shook her head. "You are hardly the first children to be all but raised in a tavern."

"Oh, Hreidmar did us a favor by bringing us there. It was how we met Siegfried. You see, we did not encounter the bandit for the first time on the road to Gundersheim, but rather one night at the tavern. Siegfried saw how Hreidmar treated us, and he saw that we feared to confront him ourselves. He suggested that we pay someone to kill him. We agreed, but we were stymied by a lack of coin with which to make the payment. It was Siegfried who told us of a dwarf passing through Nastrond with a hoard of gold that he intended to use to pay for a large patch of land upon which he wished to build a smithy.

"You were correct, milady, when you mentioned that a proper bandit should never attack alone, which was why Siegfried did not wish to attempt to steal the gold alone. In fact, he did not wish to steal it himself at all—for while Siegfried was strong, he was also lame. He did not trust that he would be able to move quickly enough to make an escape following an act of banditry. We were both in need—he of someone to provide whole legs for the act, and we of someone who could rid us of our father.

"So we came to an agreement. The treasure stolen from the dwarf would be split three ways. Siegfried did distract Hreidmar at the tavern while Oter and I stole the gold from the dwarf."

"I take it that you and Oter reneged on the arrangement?"

Regin nodded. "Hreidmar had taught us that loyalty was something to be bought and sold, or received through intimidation. Of what use was it to us? Siegfried offered to kill our father, and what reason did we have for recompense once it was done?"

"But you still killed him?" Sif asked. She had been straining against her bonds, and they were starting to give way. All she needed to do was keep Regin talking while she freed herself.

"Eventually, yes, we did kill Siegfried. The death of our father occurred in much the same way as I described it to you in Flodbjerge, with Siegfried 'ambushing' us on the road to Gundersheim, where we were taking our wares to market. Siegfried acted as a bandit out to steal from us—and as we had predicted, Hreidmar did attack him violently. Siegfried was able to kill Hreidmar with ease—and then he demanded his share of the treasure. Of course, we had it not with us, as we had needed to keep it hidden from our father. We told Siegfried to meet us at a cabin in the Norn

Forest." Regin laughed. "I must confess, milady, that I could not tell you if such a cabin does exist in that forest. It was a creation of my brother and I, merely a place to send Siegfried on a fool's errand."

"You said you killed him, not sent him on a fool's errand."

"That, milady, is because *we* were the fools." Regin started to pace the mouth of the cave. "Siegfried doubled back and followed us to where we had stored the gold. But as soon as Oter entered the chamber where the gold was housed, he started to change. You see, he had been the one to steal the gold. My role had been to guard the dwarf and keep him from interfering. For this reason, the curse was Oter's alone to bear."

Sif shook her head, even as one thumb came free of her bonds. "So there was no charm that left you immune?"

Regin snorted. "I doubt any such charm even exists, but I required it to add verisimilitude to my story."

"Well done," Sif said dryly. Her index finger was now loose, as well. It was only a matter of time. If she could just get her middle finger free, she'd be able to grip the ropes and snap them in two.

"In any event, Oter transformed into a dragon. I was able to escape his wrath, but Siegfried was not so fortunate. The day after I made my escape, I returned to find the place empty of all save a dwarf. That part of my tale was the truth—the dwarf had come in search of his gold, but found only me. He spared me because I had *not* transformed into a dragon, and therefore he believed me to be innocent of the theft."

"So it was not a coincidence," Sif said, "that you came to Flodbjerge to live."

"For *years* I have searched for my brother so I could claim the treasure! My initial belief was that I should have half of it, but I have seen how the people of the village below live in terror of the dragon. *That* is even greater than the wealth that the dwarf's treasure would bring me. I want the *power* that comes with the dragon form. So now, I will claim the entire hoard and become the figure of fear that my brother was!"

Sif continued to struggle to get a second finger free. Whatever else one could say about Hreidmar, he had obviously taught at least one of his sons ropecraft, as Regin's knot was tight indeed.

She needed to stall him further, and so she asked, "And what will being such a figure grant you? The fates of many of the dragons of the Nine Worlds have already been written, and they bode ill for you. Will you become like Nidhogg, condemned to chew on a root of Yggdrasil forevermore, waiting at the gates to Hela's realm? Will you become as the Midgard Serpent, trapped beneath the earth of that world? Will you become like your former monarch, Fafnir, transformed into a dragon and slain in battle with Thor? Stories about dragons invariably have ill endings for those creatures."

"I do not have the ambitions of those creatures, milady. I will be content to have the fools of Flodbjerge look upon me with fear."

"Your ambitions are of no interest to me, Regin. Be assured that if you take this track, you simply will become another dragon that I have bested."

Regin snorted. "Just because you defeated my brother—"

"I speak not of your brother, but of the mighty Lindworm of Denmark on Midgard."

"And you defeated him?"

"I killed the creature before he could wreak any more havoc on Midgard, yes. I had come to Midgard in search of a baby dragon that had escaped from Asgard. I found that it had been given as a wedding gift to Queen Thora when she married King Ragnar Lothbrok. They thought it a harmless pet, but it quickly grew to an immense size and started to consume the livestock of the land.

"King Ragnar had sent many of his soldiers to do battle against the creature, which he had dubbed the Lindworm of Denmark, but those few who returned alive did so without having succeeded. The king's subjects were in danger of starving, for the animals they used to plow the fields and as food were being taken by the dragon.

"You would have liked King Ragnar, Regin, because he, too, dismissed me when I approached him. I told him that I was of the Aesir, and while Queen Thora and most of his subjects knelt before me, King Ragnar only scoffed.

"'You are Thor's bedmate, little girl,' he said to me. 'Of what use are you to me against the Lindworm?'

"I set my jaw as I stared at him and said, 'Thor is sometimes privileged to share my bed, yes, but that is often after we have shared a battle together. I have defeated every foe I have ever faced, as evidenced by the fact that I still live and they do not.'

"King Ragnar stood and cried, 'The men I sent to battle the Lindworm all could make similar boasts before facing the creature. You are just a girl, what could you *possibly* do that they could not?'

"I smiled and said, 'Win.'

"Throwing up his hands, Ragnar said, 'You are a goddess, and I am but a king. Who am I to stop you from going to your doom?'

"What I did not know at the time was that King Ragnar had promised the hand of his daughter, Aslaug, to the warrior who defeated the Lindworm, and he feared my victory, as it would force him to go back on his word, which would damage his reputation amongst his people.

"But nonetheless I struck out into the fields and tracked down the Lindworm. It was not difficult to find him, for he was even larger than your brother was when in his reptilian form, as he had consistently been dining on oxen, cows, bulls, and horses.

"I raised my sword and attacked the creature. The battle lasted many hours, and the Lindworm did wound me grievously, but its underbelly was its weak point, and I was able to strike it there with my sword.

"After killing the Lindworm, I sliced its head from its body and brought it to King Ragnar. Only then did I learn of his promise regarding Aslaug—and so I claimed her as was my right. She was a clever, talented child, skilled in playing the harp. I took her with me across the rainbow bridge back to Asgard and fed her the Golden Apples of Immortality, and to this day she remains one of the musicians who plays for Odin at the palace."

As Sif finished the tale of her battle against the Lindworm, she at last managed to get a second finger free.

Regin gave a small bow. "You are to be commended, milady, for that victory, and for all your others—particularly the one against my brother. But while you may have presented the All-Father with a harpist when you defeated the Lindworm, the only gift Odin will receive this day is your cooling corpse."

Regin walked toward the cave as Sif tugged on her bonds, at last having the maneuverability to add to her strength to the effort.

By the time she snapped the ropes and got to her feet, Regin was inside Oter's cave. Following him in, Sif watched in horror as the very transformation she had observed with Oter a short time ago happened again—only in reverse. Regin's face lengthened, his form grew, his arms flattened and expanded, his legs fused together, and his skin turned a scaly black.

Now fully transformed, Regin looked down upon Sif with eyes as yellow and as watery as his brother's had been, though the surrounding scales were of a darker hue. His voice rang out with the same rumbling tone as his brother's, but the words were sharper and even more brutal.

"I am grateful to you, Lady Sif. You have done what I could

not, which is defeat my brother and remove the curse. In gratitude, I promise you the mercy of a quick death."

With that, Regin reared back his head and prepared to breathe his newfound fire at Sif.

CHAPTER ELEVEN

Propelling herself upward with her legs, Sif did a backflip that kept her from being broiled by Regin's fiery breath.

Regin turned his head upward in the hope of catching Sif in midair, but her flip was far faster than Regin could crane his unfamiliar neck.

Sitting atop the hoard of wealth, Regin continued to try to burn his prey, but Sif was able to stay ahead of his exhalations. He had yet to master them as Oter had.

"Pathetic, Regin." That was Oter's voice.

Sif looked down and saw that Oter was now awake and struggling to sit upright. His speech was no longer the rumbling utterances of a dragon's mouth, but instead the tenor tones of a human one, tinged with a lisp because of his missing front teeth, an injury that had remained through the transformation.

Regin emitted a chuckle that sounded like two rocks grinding together. "So, brother, you are awake. Good. I was hoping you would be able to look me in the eye when I finally rid the world of you."

"I was referring to your idiocy, Regin. You see, the cave in which *my* treasure resides is one I was going to abandon soon because the entrance is unstable. And you just breathed fire on it."

"What are you—"

Regin's words were interrupted by a sharp snapping sound as the rock that made up part of the cave mouth started to crack.

Sif ran over to the bound Oter, threw him over her shoulder, and escaped to the plateau.

Angry, Regin reared his head upward and again breathed fire, but for naught.

Seconds later, the entire cave mouth collapsed, burying Regin within. Outside, Sif tore away Oter's bonds.

"Thank you," he said, "but that won't hold him long. He is not as strong as I was, at least not yet, but he will be able to break free eventually."

"Do not think," Sif said angrily, "that I free you out of any consideration for your plight. I simply do not wish to carry you down the mountain."

"I understand. But *you* must understand that I was compelled to guard the hoard at all costs."

"And for that, you terrorized the people of Flodbjerge?"

Oter shook his head. "I have no enmity for the people of that village, milady."

"Oh, *now* I am 'milady'? It was not long ago, Oter, that I was 'little girl' or 'foul goddess.'"

Oter winced. "Yes, milady, I am sorry. As I said, I was compelled—you threatened my hoard."

"In truth, I threatened no such thing. I care not for gold or jewels or finery. My only interest was in saving the people of Flodbjerge."

Shaking his head, Oter let out a long sigh. "I had no quarrel with those good people, milady, believe me. I have lived in these mountains for some time. I did observe the people of the village covertly, but only to ensure that they posed no threat to my hoard. That state of affairs remained until—"

Sif nodded. "Until your brother came to live there."

"The dwarf's curse is vicious, milady. It amplified my belief that anyone might steal the treasure, but it also knew who I believed to pose the greatest threat to it. Of all those still living, only two people would trigger so intense a response of fear—the dwarf from whom I stole the gold, and my brother, who desired it almost as much as I."

A rumble came from beneath the rocks from the cave-in. Sif knew that it was just a matter of moments before Regin broke loose. "Come," she said, leading Oter toward the ridge.

Oter spoke as they hurried. "The compulsion to find my brother overwhelmed all else. I only was kept from searching the village all at once because I could not bear to be far from my treasure for very long."

"I assumed as much," Sif said with a nod.

The rocks that covered the cave mouth were now shaking faster. Oter glanced back apprehensively, and then regarded Sif with urgency. "He will be free in a moment. You have one advantage against my brother that you did not have against me. After so many years, my hide grew thick and nigh-impenetrable. But Regin's scales are weaker, thinner—you may easily penetrate his flesh with your blade, as you could not mine."

Sif blew out a breath through clenched teeth. "That presents a certain difficulty, I'm afraid. I have no blade at the moment."

"What do you mean? You attacked me with *two* swords!"

She indicated the cave and its about-to-be-reopened entrance with her head. "Your brother took one of my swords when he rendered me unconscious. It is buried along with your erstwhile treasure. And my other sword fell down the mountain."

"That is a bit of an issue," Oter muttered.

"You understate greatly," Sif said dryly. "Nonetheless, Regin both lied to me and used me—neither of these offenses I am like to forgive. And his punishment for the same will be extremely severe."

As if on cue, Regin broke through the cave-in, sending stones flying in all directions. Sif moved to protect Oter from the debris. They were distant enough that the rocks bounced harmlessly off her armor, but Oter was completely unclothed and unprotected.

"You will pay for that indignity, Sif!" Regin cried out.

Sif whirled upon him. "Indignity? You lied to me, misled me, used me as your pawn—and worst of all, you caused the good people of Flodbjerge to suffer and die because of your very presence!"

Regin roared to the heavens, fire issuing forth from his snout. "How dare you take Oter's side after all he did!"

"I take only the side of the innocents who have suffered at the hands of *both* of you! I have no love for your miscreant of a brother—"

Oter whirled on her, taking offense at her words, but Sif ignored him and continued.

"—but at least he was compelled by a curse. You endangered the village while fully in what should laughingly be referred to as your right mind, and you did so for the most base of motives—greed!"

"Not greed, milady, *justice*! Oter did not suffer alone at the hands of our father—we were *both* the victims of his madness! The spoils of Hreidmar's and Siegfried's deaths should have been for *both* of us to share, and Oter took it away from me!"

Oter stepped forward. "You *imbecile*! You thrice-damned *fool*! This treasure would only be considered 'spoils' in the sense that it will spoil your life—as it *ruined* mine!"

Now Regin laughed heartily, more fire spewing forth. "*I'm* the imbecile? You had uncounted wealth—"

Oter interrupted his brother. "Of what use is wealth if it may not be spent? I desired to keep the dwarf's treasure so that we could have all the things that our father denied us. But the curse robbed me of that! Instead, I was trapped in this mountain range, able only to hoard the treasure—never to *use* it!"

"It matters not," Regin said. "The treasure is mine."

"No," Sif said, "the treasure is the dwarf's. And it will be returned to him once I dispose of you, as I did your brother."

"Hardly."

And with that, Regin flew into the air—and then careened past Sif and Oter.

Oter smiled. "It takes some time to accustom oneself to flying."

"So it would seem." Sif grabbed Oter and forcibly sat him next to the ridge. "Remain here. You will be safe."

"What will become of me?"

Sif looked up, trying to spy the dragon, but he had flown beyond her sight—at least temporarily. "If I defeat Regin, then both of you will be brought back to Asgard. Flodbjerge is under the All-Father's protection—it is why I came here in the first place—and Odin will decide both of your fates." She looked down at him. "If Regin defeats me, then I suspect that you will become his next victim in fairly short order. So pray that I win, for Odin will show you far more mercy than your brother will."

With that, Sif climbed atop the ridge, and saw Regin flying back toward her.

"You will die today, milady," Regin cried out as he hurtled through the air. "For millennia, they will sing songs of how Thor's paramour finally fell to Regin the dragon!"

Sif shook her head. "'Thor's paramour?' Is that all you see before you, Regin?"

"That is all you *are*, milady, as King Ragnar told you. Indeed, your story of the Lindworm is the first I have ever heard of such a battle. All the exploits of Sif that I had heard prior to this are solely in concert with a man of greater renown, whether it be Asgardian, mortal, or alien. The songs that they sing of Asgard are all of Thor's might and Balder's prowess and the camaraderie of the Warriors Three. If Sif is sung of at all, it is because of your exploits in the thunder god's bedchamber, not on the battlefield."

Laughing, Sif said, "You know the songs they sing of Asgard well, do you? I care little for them myself, as the measure of a warrior is not in songs that are sung. Warriors will ever be judged by how they fight, and how they win. And I have always fought, *little* dragon, and I have always won."

"Yes, riding through the countryside with a sword in your hand and a cry to arms in your heart. Yet now you have *no* sword. You face me unarmed and unprepared. Do you *truly* believe that there will be any outcome other than your death?"

"I have never believed otherwise. And I have always been right."

With that, Sif leapt into the air and landed atop the dragon's snout.

Regin thrashed about just as Oter had, but his thrashing proved far more dangerous, for his inexperience as a flyer meant chaos from his newfound wings. Both dragon and unwanted rider flew straight up, turned out into the open air, then back toward the mountain, crashing into its side with a jarring impact that rattled Sif in her armor.

Sif and Regin both tumbled down the mountain face, landing on the plateau.

Already fatigued from her battle with Oter the dragon and her struggle to remove his dead weight from the cave, and still smarting from the blow to her head inflicted by Regin, Sif now found her vision swimming before her as she tried to regain both her footing and her composure.

Clambering to her feet, Sif saw two dragons on the plateau. Closing her eyes tightly, she all but willed her vision to coalesce.

Opening her eyes again, she saw only one dragon—but one that was also getting to his taloned feet.

Crying out as she ran toward Regin, Sif jumped and punched the dragon directly in the snout. Another punch to the underside of his jaw sent the creature's head flying upward. He continued moving in that direction, again taking to the air.

Her offensive options limited by the dragon's flight, Sif went on the defensive, dodging Regin's renewed attempts to burn her alive. Regin's aim was far worse than Oter's had been, but Sif was moving much more slowly than usual.

In fact, one of Regin's exhalations did burn Sif's right arm, superheating her armor.

Her face twisting in fury and pain, Sif tore at her armor's right sleeve, ripping off the red-hot metal as she ran toward the mouth of the cave, exposing her sizzling flesh to the cool mountain air. Ignoring the pain that coursed through her arm, she grabbed one of the larger rocks from the cave-in and threw it directly at Regin's head.

The dragon was able to duck his head, but not so the rest of his body, and the rock struck his back. Crying out, Regin flopped to the plateau with an impact that knocked Sif off balance and sent her tumbling to the ground.

As Sif got to her feet, Regin's tail slithered across the rocky ground and collided with her ankles. Crashing back down, the upended Sif landed on her right side.

The entire mountain swam before her eyes. She tried to regain her feet, but the world swam even more every time she moved her head.

Closing her eyes helped, but then she couldn't see her foe.

But opening her eyes made it worse, so she closed them again.

She lay down her head on the cold ground. She needed just a moment, and then she would be fine.

If only her ears would stop ringing and the world would stop moving, she could defeat Regin.

"Sif!"

The voice was familiar and distant.

She risked opening her eyes.

Hilde stood over her.

"H-Hilde?"

"You gotta get up, the black dragon is going to kill that man!"

Gathering up every ounce of willpower, Sif propped herself up on her elbows.

She saw that Regin was looming over Oter, who was standing defiantly against the ridge.

Oter cried out in his lisping voice, "What are you waiting for? Kill me!"

"No need to rush, brother."

"Yes, there is. You must protect the hoard at all costs from any who would take it from you. Yet, you hesitate to kill me."

Regin simply continued looming. "I do not understand. I know I wish to finally kill you after all these years, but I cannot *feel* the emotions any longer."

"No, and you never will. Do you know why, Regin?" Oter laughed. "Because I don't *want* the treasure! I'm no threat to your precious hoard! It's *all* yours! And *that* is all the curse cares about! Your own desires mean *nothing*, Regin. All that you are now is protector of your treasure. And since I am just a pathetic naked man cowering behind a ridge, the curse knows I pose no threat—and so you *won't* kill me. You *can't* kill me!" He shook his head. "Congratulations, Regin. You had the opportunity to live a new life, away from Father and his abuse, away from me and my curse. You had the skills and the freedom to continue the family business, or perhaps start a new one. Anything! Your options were as limitless as the Nine Worlds themselves! Instead, you wasted all this time trying to find me, just to ruin your own life the same way I ruined mine."

While Oter ranted at his confused brother, Sif closed her eyes and tried to focus her mind. Then, she slowly got to her feet. Hilde stood next to her, arms outstretched to help, though she hardly had the strength to hold Sif up.

After she got herself upright, Sif realized that Hilde wasn't trying to provide physical aid. Rather, she had something in her hands.

Squinting to clear her vision, Sif realized that it was her sword!

She snatched it from Hilde's grasp. "How did you find this?"

That led her to a more pressing question. "Why are you here?"

"When I got back to Flodbjerge, I went to check on Regin like you asked—but he was gone. I tracked him to the mountains, and I thought he might be going after his brother. I found the sword on my way up."

"Thank you, Hilde," Sif said. "Now you must go and hide. The curse may realize that Oter is no threat, but it is unlikely to provide the same consideration for you and me."

Hilde nodded, and ran the opposite way on the plateau.

Sif raised her sword with her right arm, ignoring the agony of the burnt flesh. "Regin!"

Craning his neck around to look at Sif, Regin chuckled. "You're still alive, milady? Perhaps you are indeed made of sterner stuff than I thought." Then he once again breathed his flame.

Sif tried to dodge the fire, but her movements were tentative at best, and again she was burnt—this time on both her legs.

"Today is your day, Lady Sif!" Regin cried. "Today is the day that you fall to the sons of Hreidmar!"

Oter spit. "Do not include me in your idiocy, Regin!"

"But I must credit you, brother, for the Lady Sif moves slowly and poorly—all due to your own efforts against her."

Snarling, Sif ran toward the dragon, brandishing her sword. Regin, though, took to the air, and Sif was unable even to strike his tail as the creature flew upward.

Undaunted, Sif again grabbed a rock from the ground—the plateau was now littered with them thanks to Regin's forceful exit from the cave—and threw it with all her waning strength at Regin's head.

This time, the dragon was unable to dodge, and the projectile struck the side of his snout. Dazed, Regin crashed to the plateau.

Again, the impact knocked Sif off balance, but she was able to use her sword to maintain her footing.

Splayed out on the plateau, tail draped over the ridge, Regin muttered, "Damn you . . ."

Sif responded through clenched teeth, as every step had become agony in her fatigue and pain. "No, Regin, you damned yourself."

She strode to the dragon's side and stood before his left wing. Raising her sword, she sliced downward, severing the wing completely.

Regin's screams echoed throughout the mountains and ichor spurted everywhere, while flame spewed from the creature's maw.

One burst of flame headed straight for Oter, who, eyes widening in panic, dove and rolled on the ground by the ridge.

Sif ran back toward the cave. She climbed up the collapsed rocks, gold, and jewels mixed with the broken stone, and onto the top of the cave.

Looking toward the ridge, she saw that Oter was not moving, and a trickle of blood flowed from underneath his head.

Glancing the other way, she saw Hilde hiding behind a rock. Sif was thankful that the girl was safe, at least. While she wished

Hilde had remained in Flodbjerge, she had to admit to being grateful to have her sword back.

The dragon clambered to his feet and stumbled toward the cave.

"You . . . will . . . die . . . this . . . day . . ."

As Sif had hoped, Regin climbed up toward her. Though her legs were badly burnt by his fire, she managed to jump into the air just as the dragon tried to pounce upon her.

She came down and drove her sword into Regin's side. Where her blade had barely managed to penetrate Oter's hide, Regin's hide was as weak as his brother had told her it would be, and the sword went straight through.

Regin collapsed onto the pile of rock and gold.

"Hooray!" came Hilde's voice from below. "You won, Sif, you won!"

"Not quite." Sif's voice was ragged and breathy, and she was barely able to remain upright.

"What do you mean?" Hilde asked, confused.

Sif jumped down from her spot on top of both dragon and cave, the impact making her burnt limbs hurt even more.

"We must take him from his hoard, as I did Oter." She walked over to the dragon's tail, and again started to pull.

As weakened as she'd been after defeating Oter, she was now even weaker—but she had to complete her task. Oter and Regin both had to face Odin's justice, but they would face it as humans—not cursed dragons.

And so she gripped the dragon's tail and pulled.

"The measure of a warrior is not in songs that are sung."

Spots danced before her eyes, but she pulled.

"Warriors will ever be judged by how they fight, and how they win."

The pain in her right arm and in her feet turned the world into a haze, but she pulled.

"And I have always fought."

Next to her, Hilde grabbed a piece of the tail and pulled, as well.

"And I have always won."

Had Sif been buoyed by Hilde's assistance into greater feats of strength? Had Volstagg's daughter provided just enough extra muscle? Sif had no idea—but together, the two of them were able to drag Regin from his treasure.

Moments later, Regin's gaunt form lay once again before them.

With one rather large difference. No longer did Regin have a left arm.

Sif looked down at Hilde. The girl looked up at her from underneath her mop of red hair and smiled.

Satisfied that her work was done, Sif collapsed, blackness enveloping her at last.

CHAPTER TWELVE

When Sif finally awakened, she lay on a pallet indoors—which confused her, as her last memory was of standing on a plateau in the Valhalla Mountains.

Confusing her even more was the bearded face of Volstagg looking down on her and smiling.

"About time you woke up!"

"V-Volstagg? What are you doing here?" She looked around, seeing that she was in a small home. "What am I doing here? Where am I?"

"Which query would you like me to answer first?" Volstagg asked with a chuckle.

"None, actually, as I would much rather know how I came down from the mountain."

Sif pulled herself upright on the pallet, but her head swam as she did, so she quickly laid back down.

Volstagg's avuncular smile turned to a concerned frown as he put a comforting hand on her shoulder. "Rest, fair Sif, as your injuries are quite severe. The local healer says you are not yet ready to move."

Sif looked down and only then registered that her armor had been removed and replaced with a simple gown. Her right arm and both legs were covered in a white salve, which she assumed was to treat her burns.

The door to the house opened, and Hilde walked in, carrying a basket. "Father, I brought lunch for—" Then she noticed that the bed's occupant's eyes were open. "Sif! You're finally awake!"

"So it would seem. Your father was about to inform me as to how I got here."

"Indeed, I was," said Volstagg. "And my dear daughter has been kind enough to provide food, for what is a story without victuals to accompany it?"

Sif rolled her eyes. "Is there anything in your life that does not have victuals to accompany it?"

Grinning, Volstagg said, "Not if I may help it. Come, Hilde, lay out the fine repast you have provided, and I will tell Sif of what transpired while she slumbered."

"It was hardly a slumber," Sif muttered—but she was glad for the food, at least, as she was hungry enough to challenge Volstagg's gluttony.

Hilde sat on the floor, and Volstagg did likewise. (The house shook a bit when the Voluminous One's posterior collided with the floor, reminding Sif of when Oter had impacted with the earth on the mountain.) While Hilde spread out the food on a blanket, Volstagg commenced his tale.

"The story for me begins back in Asgard, when I went to check on Hilde. You see, she and her brother had gotten into a bit of a spat, and had been confined to their rooms by their mother. Alaric, at least, obeyed her wishes." That last was said with a glower at the girl.

Hilde shrank a bit. "I'm sorry, Father, but Alaric took the hunting knife that—"

Volstagg held up a hand. "Yes, Hilde, I'm aware. Your mother told me. We will discuss *that* at another time."

"I take it," Sif said as she swallowed a fruit slice, "that you followed Hilde here?"

"Your brother was kind enough to inform me of Hilde's movements."

"Heimdall knew where I was?" Hilde asked, as if that was a surprise.

"Very little escapes the guardian's notice," Volstagg said with mock sternness. "You would do well to remember that in future."

Testily, Sif said, "Thus far, Volstagg, you have told me little of which I am not already aware."

"Patience, Sif, the Lion of Asgard will arrive at the heart of the tale in due course."

"No doubt, but I wish to still be young when that momentous event occurs."

Volstagg's belly quivered as he laughed heartily before downing a sweetmeat. "I traversed the Gopul River and reached Flodbjerge in due course. Upon my arrival, I was told that my daughter was last seen going to investigate the storehouse to check on a person named Regin, who was apparently the target of a dragon. But at the storehouse itself, I saw only a great deal of fish and felt a great deal of cold. And so I departed, confused, but then saw flame issuing forth from atop one of the Valhalla Mountains."

Hilde's eyes widened. "You *saw* that?"

"My vision may not be as keen as Heimdall's, but even these old orbs may espy flames gouting forth from a place where flames rarely are seen."

Sif regarded Volstagg with a skeptical expression. "Do not attempt to convince me that you hauled your bulk up that mountain."

Drawing himself up to his full height as best he could while sitting on a floor, Volstagg said, "I assure you, Sif, that were I to set my mind to the task, I would be able to scale the mountain with greater ease than you!" His face softened. "However, that proved unnecessary, thanks to my daughter. For even as I approached the foot of the mountain from the bottom, so too was she approaching it from above! And she was not alone."

Sif turned her gaze upon Hilde.

The girl turned away, blushing. "I found a hollowed-out tree near the stream, and I placed you, Oter, and Regin inside it. I used the rope that Regin used to tie up you and Oter to secure the three of you in the tree, and then I pulled you down the mountain using the end of the rope. It took a while, but I managed it eventually."

At that, Sif gaped. "I am impressed, Hilde. That took ingenuity, courage, and strength."

"No, it didn't." Hilde smiled. "I just tried to figure out what *you* would do."

Snorting, Sif said, "In truth, I would have thrown both brothers down the mountain and left them to the Fates."

Volstagg continued the tale. "Hilde and the town council then filled me in on the entire story. I immediately sent a messenger to the dwarves to ascertain the original owner of the gold, since leaving it in anyone else's hands would merely perpetuate the curse."

Sif nodded. "Yes, thank you, Volstagg. Where are Oter and Regin now?"

"Imprisoned and under guard by the citizens of Flodbjerge. There is little love lost there, I can assure you. I have already volunteered Fandral and Hogun to assist in the village's rebuilding efforts."

"When I am well, I will do likewise."

Sternly, Volstagg said, "You will do no such thing. You are injured, and you will heal yourself. Besides, by the time you are well, we will be long done!"

Sif chuckled and shook her head.

Volstagg added, "And when you are well, we shall all return to the Realm Eternal with Oter and Regin as our prisoners. They will face the All-Father's justice."

Sif nodded. "I hope he will be lenient with Oter. He has suffered much, living with the curse so long, and I doubt any punishment Odin could visit upon him would be worse than the memory of what he endured as a dragon."

"If you argue so, fair Sif," Volstagg said, "then it will be like to come true."

Helena opened the door and asked, "How is our hero? Ah, awake, I see! It is good to see you improving, milady."

"Thank you, Helena, it is good to be so seen."

A dwarf walked in behind her. Helena said, "This is Engin. He is the son of Andvari, the dwarf from whom Oter and Regin stole the gold."

"My father," the dwarf said, "is old and infirm, and unable to make the journey, but I gladly come in his place, knowing that my return will mean his redemption."

"Welcome, Engin," Sif said.

"You must be the Lady Sif. Helena has spoken very highly of you. She says that you saved this village from the dragons my father had cursed. Thank you." He looked at Helena. "In exchange, madam, I wish to bequeath half the gold to your village—after removing the curse, of course. Use it to rebuild your town and restore it to its former glory."

Helena was visibly taken aback. "That is—that is very generous, sir."

"Consider it a finder's fee. In truth, Andvari had long since given up on ever seeing his gold again. All his dreams for how he would live out the remainder of his life were tied up in that coin, and the loss of it devastated him. Even receiving half of it back will buoy him more than words can say—but he will not object to you good people receiving a share, as the curse he left on it is what led to the tragedies that have befallen you. A contingent of my people are en route, and they will remove both the gold and the curse within the week."

Sif nodded. "Please, Engin, when you excavate the treasure from the collapsed cave, be you on the lookout for a sword. It belongs to one of the council, a fine man named Bjorn. He loaned me the blade—named Gunnvarr—and I would see it returned to him intact."

"I will see it done, milady."

"You are a good man, Engin."

"I but follow the example of the Lady Sif," Engin said with a bow. "I, at least, have something to gain by my generosity—I will receive half a fortune, and see my father returned to the man he was before the theft of his wealth. You had nothing to gain, yet you gave of yourself—risking your life—so that these people might be safe. I heard Helena refer to you as her hero—and to my mind, this makes you the finest hero of the Nine Worlds."

Sif smiled. "I daresay that many others may also qualify for such a title, but I would never object to being in their company." With looks at both Volstagg and Hilde, she added, "I am in the company of some right now, in fact." She looked at Helena and Engin. "But I am being a poor host. Hilde has gathered a feast for us. Please do join us, lest Volstagg eat it all."

"Of course!" Volstagg said with a hearty laugh. "Food is best shared amongst friends, after all!"

Hilde stared at him. "Since when have you ever *shared* food, Father?"

They all laughed at that. Helena and Engin took their places on the floor and everyone joined in the feast.

THE END

ACKNOWLEDGMENTS

The number of people who deserve thanks for this book are legion, and I hope I manage to get all of them in. I will start with the folks at Joe Books: Robert Simpson (who first approached me with this), Adam Fortier, Stephanie Alouche, Amy Weingartner, and especially my noble editors, Rob Tokar and Paul Taunton.

Huge thanks, as always, to my amazing agent Lucienne Diver, who kept the paperwork mills grinding and more than earned her commission.

Of course, this trilogy owes a ton to the comic books featuring the various Asgardians that Marvel has published since 1962, and while I don't have the space to thank *all* the creators of those comics, I want to single out a few. First off, Stan Lee, Larry Lieber, Jack Kirby, and Joe Sinnott, who created this incarnation of Thor and his chums in *Journey Into Mystery* #83. Secondly, and most especially, the great Walt Simonson, whose run on *Thor* from 1983 to 1987 (as well as the *Balder the Brave* miniseries), aided and abetted by Sal Buscema and John Workman Jr., is pretty much the text, chapter, and verse of "definitive." Thirdly, Kelly Sue DeConnick, Ryan Stegman, Kathryn Immonen, and Valerio Schiti, who chronicled solo adventures for Sif in the *Sif* one-shot and *Journey Into Mystery* #646-655. In addition, I must give thanks and praise to the following excellent creators whose work was particularly influential on this trilogy: Jason Aaron, Pierce Askegren, Joe Barney, John Buscema, Kurt Busiek, Gerry Conway, Russell Dauterman, Tom DeFalco, Ron Frenz, Michael Jan Friedman, Gary Friedrich, Mark Gruenwald, Stuart Immonen, Dan Jurgens, Gil Kane, Pepe Larraz, John Lewandowski, Ralph Macchio, Doug Moench, George Pérez, Don Perlin, Keith Pollard, John Romita Jr., Marie Severin, Roger Stern, Roy Thomas, Charles Vess, Len Wein, Bill Willingham, and Alan Zelenetz.

Also, while these novels are not part of the Marvel Cinematic Universe, I cannot deny the influence of the portrayals of the characters in the movies *Thor* and *Thor: The Dark World*, and on the TV show *Marvel's Agents of S.H.I.E.L.D.* (nor would I wish to deny it, as they were all superb), and so I must thank actors Chris Hemsworth, Sir Anthony Hopkins, Idris Elba, Ray Stevenson, and most especially Jaimie Alexander (who is the perfect Sif), as well as screenwriters Shalisha Francis, Drew Z. Greenberg, Christopher Markus, Stephen McFeely, Ashley Edward Miller, Don Payne, Mark Protosevich, Robert Rodat, Zack Stentz, J. Michael Straczynski, and Christopher Yost.

Also, one can't write anything about the Norse gods without acknowledging the work of the great Snorri Sturluson, without whom we wouldn't know jack about the Aesir. In particular, I made use of the *Völsunga Saga*, which recounts the original story of the dragons on which this novel is based. Additional thanks must go to Saxo Grammaticus, from whose *Gesta Danorum* I (very, very liberally) adapted Sif's tale of her battle against the Lindworm of Denmark.

Thanks to my noble first reader, the mighty GraceAnne Andreassi DeCandido (a.k.a. The Mom). And thanks to Wrenn Simms, Dale Mazur, Meredith Peruzzi, Tina Randleman, and especially Robert Greenberger for general wonderfulness, as well as the various furred folks in my life, Kaylee, Louie, and the dearly departed Scooter and Elsa.

MARVEL

WARRIORS THREE

GODHOOD'S END

BOOK 3 OF THE
TALES OF ASGARD TRILOGY

KEITH R.A. DECANDIDO

GODHOOD'S END

BOOK 3 OF THE TALES OF ASGARD TRILOGY

KEITH R.A. DeCANDIDO

JOE BOOKS LTD

For Wrenn, who combines Fandral's beauty,
Hogun's determination, and Volstagg's joy.

PRELUDE

At the center of the Nine Worlds is Yggdrasil, the world tree, linking them all via its mighty roots and powerful branches.

Thousands of years ago, the Aesir of Asgard did cross the Bifrost—the rainbow bridge—to Midgard, which its inhabitants call Earth. Many of the people of Midgard did view the powerful warriors of Asgard as gods, and so worshipped them as such.

The thunder god, Thor—son and heir to Odin, ruler of the gods of Asgard—had been a callow youth, but in adulthood had become a fine warrior. Upon proving himself worthy to Odin, Thor was awarded Mjolnir, the mighty Uru hammer that became his trademark weapon thenceforth—and which would serve him well in the battle to come.

A night not long after Thor was granted Mjolnir also marked the eve of a journey to the Ydalir, a section of Asgard on which trolls were encroaching. Honoring the Aesir's tradition, Thor held a feast for his comrades in arms in Bilskírnir, the great hall Odin had gifted to Thor.

One of those comrades was Fandral. Thor and Fandral had trained together in the art of swordplay with the thunder god's older half brother, Tyr.

Another was Volstagg, who was much older than Thor, and who had been a decorated war chieftain in Thrudheim.

Fandral was regaling some of their other comrades with tales of his death-defying battle against Thrivaldi, the thrice-mighty. "With my longsword, I did pop out one of the beast's eyes—and then with a second thrust, out came the other. The beast's head could see no more!"

Then Fandral paused for effect. "A pity, then, that the beast had nine heads. For Thrivaldi was called 'the thrice-mighty' with good cause! Had he only the three heads, he would simply be 'the mighty.'"

When Fandral was done with his tale, Volstagg stepped forward. Thor had been a boy when he had first met Volstagg, who had then carried a trim, muscular figure. Now, though, his form had become a bit rounded, and Thor did note that Volstagg's plate was far fuller than that of anyone else in the hall. Nonetheless, Volstagg still stood taller than all in the room. "If there's anything I cannot bear," he said of Fandral, "it is a warrior who exaggerates his accomplishments!"

A young man named Hogun, who had only recently come to Asgard, spoke softly. "I have heard many of your tales, Volstagg. They are far less believable than Fandral's."

"Nonsense! Truly did I slay the Utgard Boar with my bare hands!"

Hogun frowned. "I seem to recall that when you told me the story on the night we met, you had used your sword."

Fandral laughed. "In truth, kind Hogun, I suspect the braggart did slay the boar solely that he might add him to his feast."

Volstagg glanced down at his plate, laden with a varied sampling of the victuals available in Thor's hall. "Do not mistake appetite for indolence, young braggart."

"Nor do I mistake you for a warrior! Were it not for your friendship with Thor, I doubt you would even be permitted to sit at the high table in Odin's banquet hall."

Thor had stayed out of the conversation. While he did not know Hogun well, he numbered both Volstagg and Fandral amongst his friends. But at this slight against Volstagg, he did join in. "Hold, Fandral; your words cut me to the quick, and do likewise to the All-Father. None may sit at Odin's table who are not worthy."

To his credit, Fandral looked abashed, and he bowed low. "My apologies, Thor, I meant no offense. I meant only to say that when I sit at the high table, I shall have truly earned it!"

"Pfah." Volstagg idly grabbed a piece of meat off his plate and stuffed it into his mouth. "I find that very unlikely. Were you able to beard Svafnir in its lair?"

"With my eyes closed," Fandral said with a chortle. "Were you able to defeat the monstrous sea serpents in the river that flows on either side of the Isle of Love?"

"No," Volstagg replied, "but only because I have no need to travel to such an island, as love is my constant companion."

"Given your love of food, that surprises me not," Fandral said nastily.

Volstagg slammed a fist on the table. "I speak of my noble wife, Gudrun! The finest flower in all of Asgard!"

Thor quickly stepped in before his two friends came to blows. "Hogun, why not regale us with a tale of your own?"

The dark-haired youth quickly shook his head. "Nay, my prince, I have no such tale to tell."

"Not even the story of how you came to fair Asgard?"

Hogun allowed himself a small smile. "I walked, sire. And eventually did arrive here, where now I apprentice to a stonemason in hopes of becoming an artisan."

Volstagg ate another morsel, this off Thor's plate, and Fandral sneered. "Does this Gudrun not feed you, that you must eat everything in sight?"

Whirling on Fandral, Volstagg cried, "Do not again speak ill of my beloved wife! I was slaying trolls when you were still in swaddling clothes!"

"Boring them to death with your boasts, no doubt."

"Do not mistake my exploits for boasts, boy. Such is my might and cunning that I could travel to Niffleheim, pat Fenris on the head, and not lose a fingernail in the doing of it!"

Fandral snorted derisively. "Not before I did it first, ponderous one!"

Seeing an opportunity to end the argument, Thor said, "A wager! What better end to my feast than a quest that will resolve a bet between warriors?"

"Then it shall be done!" Fandral cried. "I will show this fool for the popinjay that he is!"

Volstagg nodded. "We will leave at first light."

Thor winced. "Alas, I may not accompany you, as we ride to the Ydalir tomorrow."

"But you must come!" Fandral said. "Needs must we have someone impartial to judge the competition."

Looking at the young, dark-haired man, Thor asked, "What of Hogun?"

"Yes!" Volstagg said. "I would trust Hogun to be fair about it when I am victorious."

Fandral glared at Volstagg, then smiled at Hogun. "He is friend to us both and therefore loyal to neither exclusively. While there is little on which I would agree with Volstagg, I do agree that Hogun is a good lad."

Hogun bowed his head. "I would be honored."

"Then it's settled," Thor said.

Fandral grinned. "Be you at the docks of Ormt at first light, Voluminous One—if you've still a belly for this once you've sobered up."

Volstagg laughed derisively. "I'll be there, child. Just don't make me drag you out from behind your mother's skirts come daybreak."

And so it came to pass the following morning that three comrades met at the docks of Ormt.

Fandral thought of the glory that would be his when he made a fool of old Volstagg.

Volstagg thought of the meal that Gudrun had packed for him while muttering about her idiot husband going on fool quests when there were chores to be performed.

Hogun kept his thoughts to himself.

They set sail for Niffleheim as the sun rose, and ere long they came to the shores of that land of the dishonored dead.

Though only the bravest or the most foolhardy traverse from one world to the other, it was an open question which description applied to the old warrior, the young swordsman, and the quiet boy.

Along the way, Volstagg told Hogun the story of Fenris.

"Fenris is a giant wolf—the child of Thor's adopted brother, Loki, and the giant Angerboda. Loki, I must say, has the most bizarre offspring. In any event, Fenris was too dangerous to be allowed to roam unfettered, so Odin decreed that he be bound."

Fandral interrupted the story. "It was more complicated than *that*, of course, because no bond could hold the giant wolf. And the wolf is wily and not easily trapped. It was my former teacher, Tyr, who finally was able to bind Fenris—though at the cost of a hand."

Now Volstagg interrupted. "It was more complicated than that, of course."

Fandral sneered.

Volstagg went on. "The wolf could not be held by any bond created by Asgard, and so the All-Father did as he often would when he needed craftwork: he travelled to Nidavellir and commissioned the dwarves. They, who had forged so many weapons—from Thor's hammer to Balder's shield—could easily construct a leash for Fenris."

"And they created Gleipnir," Fandral continued. "So thin as

to be invisible, so sharp as to slice in two any object, it remains wrapped around the neck of Fenris. Should he strain Gleipnir too far, his head will be cut from his body."

Hogun frowned. "Then why is he so dangerous?"

"To be close enough to pat him on the head is to be close enough to be mauled by him," Fandral said.

Volstagg added, "Plus, as I said, he is wily."

"Actually, *I* said that," Fandral replied angrily.

Ignoring him, Volstagg said, "Fenris will try to trick us into removing Gleipnir."

When the comrades arrived at the misty plains of Niffleheim, they were beset almost immediately by half a dozen Ice Giants, who served Ymir.

Before Fandral could react, Volstagg moved upon them, wielding his blade with tremendous strength, for while Volstagg's size was only partly muscle—his middle was growing larger as he aged—he remained the Lion of Asgard.

He broke three of the Ice Giants in two with his mighty attack, and beheaded the other three.

"I must confess, Volstagg," Fandral said slowly, "I did not believe you had such fire in you for aught save feasting."

Volstagg's response came between ragged breaths, for in truth the effort had fatigued him more than expected. "The Lion of Asgard is a man of passion, child, in all things. Now let us continue—Fenris awaits!"

They moved onward, but were again stopped on the misty roads of Niffleheim—this time by a Rock Troll.

"Smell Aesir, I believed I did," the Rock Troll rumbled. "Die, you will, by the hand of Glarin of the Sword!"

Hogun's eyes went wide. "I have heard tales of Glarin of the Sword. It is said that none may defeat him as long as he grips his blade."

Fandral simply grinned, holding his own sword aloft. "You obviously misheard, good Hogun, for that is what is said of me!"

"First, you shall be, blond one," the Rock Troll said. "Your comrades, next."

"Hardly." Fandral ran toward Glarin. "Have at thee!"

The sword fight was the greatest in which Fandral had ever engaged. Never before had he been so challenged—not even in his earliest days, training under Tyr.

Every thrust of Fandral's, Glarin did counter. Every strike of Glarin's, Fandral was barely able to parry.

Only after a seeming eternity of fighting did Fandral note that Glarin occasionally left open his right side. It was but for a moment when he did an upward thrust, and it took Fandral several tries before he even could attempt to take advantage of it.

But eventually, he did so, slicing his blade through the Rock Troll's leg.

Glarin of the Sword cried out in agony as a filthy ichor spewed from his earthen skin.

"Wound me, you have! Never before this has happened!"

"And never again shall it happen," Fandral said as he cleaved Glarin's head from the rest of his rocky body.

"Impressive, young Fandral," Volstagg said. "Never before have I seen such swordplay—not even my own."

Fandral bowed before cleaning his sword. "The Lion of Asgard does me privilege."

"You are both great warriors," Hogun said. "It is my honor to judge your competition."

"Yes." Volstagg said the word quietly, and briefly became lost in thought before brightening once more. "Come! The wolf awaits!"

Farther they did travel, and soon reached the third root of Yggdrasil that linked Niffleheim to the rest of the Nine Worlds. Gnawing at the root was a giant, green dragon.

"'Tis Nidhogg," Fandral whispered almost reverently.

"I have heard tell," Hogun also whispered, "that he gnaws on both the root of the world tree and the souls of the dishonored dead."

Volstagg, uncharacteristically, said nothing. He hoped they would be able to avoid the wyrm—that it would be too occupied with its gluttonous task to be concerned with two warriors and a lad.

But it was not to be. As soon as they approached, the dragon reared back its scaly head.

"Run! Quickly!"

At Volstagg's urging, all three moved as fast as their legs would carry them.

Nidhogg, though, needed no legs to move, for he had wings, and he did use them to overtake Fandral and Volstagg in an instant.

Helplessly, Hogun watched as his friends were slammed to the ground and held there by Nidhogg's mighty claws.

"R-run, Hogun! Save—save yourself!" Volstagg uttered as the dragon's claw crushed his massive frame.

Fandral, equally strained, added, "No sense in all three of us dying! Return to Asgard! Tell them we fought valiantly!"

For several seconds, Hogun simply stared as he watched both of his friends brought low by the dragon. And for a moment, he saw in his mind's eye two other people dear to him, who had been crushed by the might of a massive creature.

He had been frightened then, unable to act. And he had sworn to never again put himself in such a position. Yet here he was, and he would *not* let Volstagg and Fandral suffer the same fate as his cousins.

Unsheathing the dagger that was all he had left from his father, Hogun cried out in anguish and attacked.

Nidhogg had not even acknowledged Hogun, perceiving him as unarmed and not a threat. That proved a dangerous mistake, as Hogun plunged his father's dagger into the creature's wing.

Screaming with an unearthly howl, Nidhogg did then fly away brokenly, unwilling to work so hard for food when Niffleheim provided all he desired without effort. More souls would try to escape Hel soon enough, and Nidhogg needed only to be ready to consume them. These two—or, rather, three—warriors had seemed a decent distraction, but not enough to keep the dragon from his task.

Hogun helped Fandral to his feet. Volstagg clambered upward of his own accord.

"You have the thanks of the Lion of Asgard," Volstagg said.

"And the confusion of both of us, I would think," Fandral added. "I thought you an aspiring artisan?"

"I am," Hogun said quietly. "I prevaricated last night when I told Thor that I had no story to tell of coming to Asgard beyond that I walked. In truth, my tribe was massacred, and our standard stolen, by a creature known as Mogul of the Mystic Mountain."

Volstagg nodded. "I've heard tales of that tyrant, but always believed them to be false—and Mogul himself but a legend."

"He is no legend, Volstagg," Hogun said bitterly. "He killed my family and scattered my tribe. I know not how many still live, if any. My twin cousins and I survived. They were older than I, and noble warriors. They attempted to do battle against Mogul, but his slave, the Jinni giant, did take their lives. I froze, unable to help them."

Volstagg put a hand on Hogun's shoulder, but the young man shrugged it off.

"You were but a youth," Volstagg said, "who saw his family destroyed. There is no shame in fear, young Hogun, especially to one untrained—"

"I *was* trained! You do not understand, Volstagg—I was raised to be a warrior and weapon smith, like my father." Hogun held up the dagger, still dripping with Nidhogg's blood. "He crafted this dagger as a gift for me after I made my first kill. But when I saw my dear cousins laid low by the Jinni, I forgot all my training and saw only death. And so I ran." He looked up at Fandral and Volstagg. "I swore never to put myself in such a position again. I came to Asgard, where I knew I could lose myself amongst the Aesir and use my smithing skills to become an artisan."

"Then why did you come with us?" Fandral asked.

"For the same reason I befriended you both, and wished to do so with Thor."

Volstagg spoke with grave understanding. "You may take the boy out of the warrior, but you may not take the warrior out of the boy. You heard the siren call of battle."

Hogun nodded. "Still, I thought I could keep to my vow. I was merely to judge which of you would pet the Fenris Wolf's pelt first. But when I saw you both in danger, just as my cousins were—"

"Then you acted," Fandral said with a grin. "The measure of a warrior lies not merely in his victories, but also in how he recovers from defeat. After all, even the finest warrior may lose a battle—it is only the poor ones who lose the same way twice."

Volstagg regarded Fandral with amusement. "That almost approached profundity, boy." But he spoke the words with none of the previous night's acrimony.

"Your words are kind," Hogun said grimly, "yet still I have broken my vow. But had I not, I would have let two good men die. I see no good in any of this."

"I see one good," Volstagg said. "I see us. Last night we were three fools in a feasting hall. Today, we are three warriors out to make a fool of the Fenris Wolf. But hang our wager! Instead, we shall work together—the three of us—to pat Fenris on the head and live to tell the tale!"

"Agreed," Fandral said with a smile.

Hogun did not smile, but he did nod his head. "Agreed, as well. Let us beard the wolf together."

And so the Warriors Three did march into danger for the first, but far from the last, time . . .

CHAPTER ONE

Thjasse plotted.

For some time, he had served as lieutenant to Hrungnir, who ruled a contingent of Frost Giants in Jotunheim. Hrungnir had two advantages over the average Frost Giant: he was cleverer than most, and he possessed Goldfaxi, the second-fastest steed in the Nine Worlds.

Though Hrungnir was indeed cleverer than *most*, there was at least one who fancied himself cleverer still, and that was Thjasse. However, Thjasse did not have Hrungnir's strength or skill in fighting—Hrungnir was, after all, nicknamed "the Brawler" for cause. Nor did Thjasse possess Goldfaxi.

However, Thjasse had another gift that was rare amongst the Frost Giants: patience. He knew that rule based on the speed of a horse was, by nature, a fleeting one. Plus, Hrungnir's ego would, Thjasse was sure, eventually get in the way.

And indeed, it did. Hrungnir challenged a stranger riding a great horse to a race of steeds, and Goldfaxi lost. Later, Hrungnir was told by Loki, the God of Mischief, that the stranger had been Odin in disguise, and the mount Sleipnir, acknowledged by all to be the fastest horse in the Nine Worlds.

Rather than accept defeat gracefully, than admit that he had been fooled, Hrungnir let his vanity get in the way, and led an invasion of Asgard—which was repelled by half a dozen of the Aesir's finest warriors—and then kidnapped Odin's wife, Frigga, bargaining with her life for a one-on-one battle with Thor.

Hrungnir had been aided in his battle by enchanted armor provided by Loki, but the God of Mischief earned his title, for after a certain point in the battle the armor lost its enchantment, and while Thor was badly battered, he was still victorious over Hrungnir.

Though his side was defeated, the loss worked in Thjasse's favor, as Hrungnir's fall meant Thjasse's own rise.

Still, Thjasse had no love of the Aesir or of Asgard. Like most Frost Giants, he still felt the sting of Odin's slaughter of Laufey, and of the gods' constant harassment of the Frost Giants. He wished the Aesir gone.

However, Thjasse knew better than to try a frontal assault. Many Frost Giants, from Laufey to Utgard-Loki to Hrungnir, had attempted such—and they had all failed. Even though his people were bigger and stronger, the Aesir were equally mighty, and even cleverer besides.

Thjasse knew that brute strength would not be the way to defeat the Aesir—their defeat would instead require guile.

Over the weeks that he spent consolidating his rule, Thjasse learnt all he could about the Aesir—and, from his observances over the years, he already was aware of quite a bit. He soon identified the Aesir's greatest weakness: their reliance on the Golden Apples of Immortality. Without them, the gods of Asgard would slowly grow weak and infirm. And if he could eliminate the restorative effects of the apples, once the Aesir had been sufficiently weakened, he would strike.

The difficulty would be in getting the apples away from their keeper. It was Idunn who was tasked with guardianship of the Golden Apples, and she took the duty quite seriously.

Thjasse had come up with a plan to distract Idunn and allow the apples to be removed from her purview, but it would require a disguise. While the Frost Giants commanded many magicks, the ability to change their shape was not amongst them. Luckily, there were those amongst the gods who had no love for their fellow Aesir and who could be tricked into aiding Thjasse.

There were five spellcasters who had the ability to help Thjasse, at least in theory. One—Frigga—was out of the question. Even leaving aside the fact that she was the All-Father's wife, after being held hostage by the Frost Giants, she would never do anything to aid them.

However, that still left Loki, Amora, Karnilla, and Lorelei—all of who had some animus for the Asgardians and who could possibly be suborned to Thjasse's cause.

All things being equal, Loki would be the perfect cat's-paw, as he was born of the Frost Giants—the son of Laufey himself. But for all that he had claimed to be helping, Loki had been as responsible for Hrungnir's fall as Thor and Odin had been, and Thjasse could not trust that the Trickster would not have a hidden agenda that would be harmful to the Frost Giants.

Then there was Karnilla. But one of Hrungnir's last campaigns before becoming embroiled with the Aesir had been to terrorize a farm on the outskirts of Nornheim, the realm that she ruled—and for that matter, Karnilla had once been kidnapped and humiliated by Utgard-Loki. Thjasse doubted he would be able to rely on the Queen of the Norns to be anything but an enemy to the Frost Giants.

Amora, who sometimes went by the name of "the Enchantress," was a possibility, as Thjasse had no particular issue with her. But she was as much a schemer as Loki was, and just as likely to twist Thjasse's ambitions to her own ends.

That left Amora's sister, Lorelei. She had all of her older sister's power, but none of her ambition.

Lorelei, Thjasse thought, would be ideal.

His first stop was the kitchen in Hrungnir's castle.

True, Thjasse ruled it now, but he still thought of this ramshackle structure that barely could be considered a castle as Hrungnir's. Badly maintained and aesthetically unpleasing, it symbolized Hrungnir's rule perfectly.

Long term, Thjasse planned to have a new castle constructed, but that was a lengthy project that would be difficult to implement until after he'd proven himself a strong ruler.

Which he would do after bringing down the Aesir.

Toiling in the kitchen, as ever he did, was Kare. No one was quite sure from where Kare had come. Some said he was the offspring of a Frost Giant and a woman from Vanaheim, which, if nothing else, explained his tiny stature. Kare was routinely harassed and ridiculed by the other Frost Giants, and Hrungnir had assigned him to the kitchen mostly to keep him out of sight.

Thjasse had no idea why Kare remained with the Frost Giants. Diminutive enough to pass for a very tall Vanir, he would likely not have been subject to the same harassment in Asgard, Vanaheim, or Nornheim that he was in Jotunheim.

Kare was cleaning the ale mugs when Thjasse entered the kitchen.

"Whatever it is," Kare said without turning to see who entered, "just take it and go."

"I'm here for you, Kare."

At the sound of Thjasse's voice, Kare turned around. "Finally getting rid of me? Never understood why Hrungnir kept me around, to be honest."

"Actually, I have a task that I need you to perform—one that only you can do."

"Need someone to get into a crawl space?"

Thjasse shook his head. "Not exactly. You are a critical portion of my plan to destroy the Aesir once and for all."

Kare had sounded almost bored, and definitely cynical. But at the words *destroy the Aesir*, he brightened. "What do you need me to do, Thjasse? You have but to name it."

"No love for the Asgardians, eh?" Thjasse asked with a grin.

"Suffice it to say that any plan that ends with their destruction is one that I would be honored to be a portion of, critical or otherwise."

And that, to Thjasse, explained why Kare tolerated being in Jotunheim.

The next night, on the outskirts of Asgard, Lorelei was having fun.

For Lorelei, fun consisted of going to a tavern and watching the men therein fall all over themselves trying to get her into their beds. Sometimes, she would pick one to win that particular contest.

Tonight, however, she was interested only in the attention. Once she had grown bored with the flirting and the inevitable brawl had ended, she departed.

She had chosen this particular tavern because it was a pleasant walk through a small, wooded area to her own home, and she always enjoyed being amidst nature—especially after being in a tavern with so many drunken louts.

Not that the louts weren't entertaining in their own right—but communing with nature was so much more enjoyable.

However, on this night, the peace and quiet of her walk home was interrupted by a tall man who stepped out from behind one of the trees. A snarl on his face, he cried out, "You!"

"Do I know you?" the red-haired woman asked. She met so many men, and they were all so completely interchangeable, that she had no real need to remember them.

"You don't even *remember*? You *destroyed* my life!"

"Obviously not," Lorelei said with disdain, "as you are clearly alive and standing before me."

She tried to continue on her way, but the tall man blocked the path. "You seduced me with one of your spells, and then my wife learnt of it! You ruined *everything*!"

While Lorelei could not recall being involved with this particular individual, she recognized the accusation, at least. But she had lost track of the number of married men she had seduced over the centuries, and of the number of marriages she'd shattered. Either way, though she could not specifically recall seducing this man, his story had at the very least a certain verisimilitude about it.

However, it was not Lorelei's problem that he had been too weak to resist her. She muttered a spell that would loosen the paving stones under the man's feet.

But before she could complete the spell, the man grabbed her in a crushing grip.

"I will have my revenge!" he cried, and he was now close enough that she could smell the ale on his breath.

"Unhand me, lout, before—"

Then the tall man clamped a meaty hand over her mouth. "Oh no, witch, you'll not use your honeyed voice on me again! In fact, I think I'll rip your head from your body, so no man may suffer from your sorcery ever again!"

Lorelei's eyes widened and she struggled, trying to break free. His grasp on her body was sufficient to keep her from tracing sigils and from mouthing a spell. But just as the man pushed Lorelei's head backward with the intent of ripping her neck in two, a giant leapt from the nearby trees.

Thjasse had waited until Kare had actually put Lorelei's life in direct danger before acting. Once that happened, he came out from the other side of the oak behind which he and Kare had been lurking in wait for Lorelei.

"Unhand her!" Thjasse cried and grabbed Kare's diminutive arms, tearing his hands away from the woman.

As Thjasse had instructed, and as they had rehearsed, Kare then said what he was supposed to: "You will not keep me from my vengeance, Frost Giant!"

Thjasse then pulled his axe from its holster on his back and raised it overhead.

Kare looked shocked and frightened. Thjasse couldn't blame him: this was *not* what they had rehearsed. The small giant's last thought before Thjasse cleaved his head from his body was to wonder why Thjasse had betrayed him thus.

For his part, Thjasse had no use for so tiny a giant. Besides, Lorelei's gratitude would be far greater if Thjasse killed her tormentor rather than, as he and Kare had discussed, just driving him off.

Lorelei stood in a defensive posture, staring at Thjasse.

Thjasse dropped his axe to the ground and held up his hands. "I mean you no harm, Lorelei."

"You know who I am, Frost Giant—that puts you at an advantage."

"My name is Thjasse."

"I do not care for your name," Lorelei said testily, "but I do care to know why you act thusly."

"And how is that?" asked Thjasse, having expected gratitude from this vapid sorceress.

"Why you killed that man. The Frost Giants are not known for *saving* the lives of the Aesir."

"In truth, lady, I came to this road with the intent of asking for your aid. I have need of magicks that only Lorelei might supply."

Lorelei sneered at him. "And you think that I will provide these magicks?"

"I think that I have saved your life. I know not who this gentleman was, but though he be puny by my standards, he seemed to be much larger than you, and had I not been here craving a boon from you, your life would likely now be forfeit." Thjasse stepped toward Lorelei, who flinched. "We Frost Giants keep our word, lady—and we react poorly to those who do not."

Despite her apprehension, Lorelei stuck out her chin defiantly. "I have given you no word to keep, giant. I did not ask you to interfere in my business." Then her face softened. "However, I cannot deny that you have done me a service, however unintentional. And in any case, you might *have* harmed me after killing this idiot. That you haven't speaks well of you—far better, in fact, than of most Frost Giants. Therefore, I will at least hear your request."

Thjasse gave a small bow. "The lady is generous." He also knew that Lorelei would keep silent about this, for she would not want it known that she had needed the help of a Frost Giant to stop a revenge-obsessed male. "While we Frost Giants have many magicks at our command, we lack the ability to disguise ourselves."

"I see. And whom do you wish to be disguised as?"

"Loki."

For a moment, Lorelei said nothing.

Then she burst into mellifluous laughter. Thjasse could see how the tiny ones saw her as aesthetically pleasing.

"Oh, Thjasse, I might well have granted that request even were I not in your debt. I have no love for Odin's adopted son, for a multitude of reasons. I assume your plan involves doing some harm to the Trickster?"

Thjasse nodded. "After a fashion."

"Then hold you still, giant, for in a few moments even Frigga would not be able to tell that you are anyone but the son of Laufey."

Idunn sat in her home, near the tree on which the Golden Apples grew.

She was reading a book of poetry that Thor had brought her back from Midgard, a collection of poems by a mortal named William Blake. He created stylized illustrations and worked the words around them, and she found his work to be quite compelling and relaxing.

Idunn had once thought her job as caretaker of the Golden Apples of Immortality to be a simple task, but the centuries had proven it to be anything but. Often was she the target of those who would try to gain the apples' power for themselves. At other times, she was inveigled by those who would try to get her to favor one god over another.

But Idunn's neutrality was sacrosanct. All of the gods received the apples equally. None were favored, none were shunned. That was how balance was maintained.

She had just finished a volume called *Songs of Innocence*, and debated whether or not to continue with the companion volume, *Songs of Experience*. It seemed that this mortal poet had similar views on balance as her own.

However, Idunn did grow tired, and also considered the possibility of sleep.

Then, she sensed someone approaching her home.

Rising from her couch, she went to the door and opened it to find Loki standing on the other side.

"What brings the God of Mischief to my doorstep?"

"'Tis Frigga, my lady," Loki said without preamble. "You will recall that she recently did battle with the Frost Giant Hrungnir?"

"I have heard of such a battle, yes." Idunn generally did not concern herself with the doings of her fellow Aesir, preferring instead to stay above it all, to maintain her neutrality. But gossip still did move at great speeds throughout the Nine Worlds, and Thor's duel with Hrungnir following Odin's wife's battle with that selfsame giant in the mountains had been the talk of all Asgard.

"Unfortunately, Mother downplayed the actual injuries she

suffered—not only at Hrungnir's hands, but also while a prisoner of the Frost Giants. Hrungnir's lieutenant, Thjasse, was quite cruel to her."

Idunn was dubious. "What, then, do you expect of me, Loki?"

"I require an apple to feed her. Without it, she will surely die."

For a moment, Idunn hesitated. "You understand, Loki, why I might have difficulty understanding why you would be the one to run this errand."

Loki looked away in annoyance. "Because my mother is a stubborn fool!" Then the Trickster got himself under control. "She has not informed the All-Father of how poorly she is doing for fear of worrying him, and the one-eyed imbecile is falling for it. Meanwhile, Thor is also recovering from his injuries, and even were he bright enough to see how she is truly suffering, he is not currently in any position to notice."

At that, Idunn chuckled. "That sounds very much like the Loki I know." Then her face hardened. "The same Loki who once burnt my home to the ground in order to steal the apples."

"Will you not forgive a youthful indiscretion?"

"Hardly that, given that it was not so very long ago, Loki." She shook her head. "In any case, I will not give you an apple to bring to Frigga. I shall take one to her myself—but not before I weave a spell that will keep Loki from coming anywhere near the apples that remain behind."

Loki made a low bow. "I would expect no less. I ask only that you hurry, as Mother needs your aid sooner rather than later."

Within a few minutes Idunn had gone, several apples in hand, but only after casting a spell that would keep the adopted son of Odin from touching the apples. This suited Thjasse fine, as he did not intended to remain as Loki. Thjasse spoke the incantation that Lorelei had provided, and transformed back into his own, larger form. He quickly gathered all of the Golden Apples in a magickal sack that he had procured decades ago and that could hold an infinite number of items.

It would take a month or two, but Thjasse was patient. He knew that the Aesir would grow old and infirm, and become the easiest of targets for his forces.

CHAPTER TWO

Thjasse had timed his theft so that it occurred on the eve of Idunn's delivery of the apples to the gods, so the Aesir were denied the magickal fruit immediately. But the effects of the theft of the apples became apparent far faster than anyone, even Thjasse, could have suspected.

When Idunn reported the apples missing—after going to visit Frigga only to find that she was in perfect health—Odin's first task was to send Balder to determine where the apples had been taken. And by whom.

The first person to notice that more was amiss beyond the theft itself was the Healer Royal. Three days after Idunn was fooled by the false Loki, the healer made her rounds to check on both Thor and Sif.

Thor was still recovering from multiple broken bones and a great deal of bruising from his battle with Hrungnir, who had been wearing enchanted stone armor during their duel.

But when the Healer Royal examined Thor this day, she noticed that he had made no more progress in healing whatsoever. The bones that had been mending normally had not changed in the past three days.

"What is the prognosis?" Thor asked. The Healer Royal knew

that Thor had spent some time sharing his existence with a mortal physician, and had some knowledge of the medical arts, so she was unable to prevaricate as well with him as she might have with other patients.

"You are continuing to heal, albeit a bit more slowly." She smiled. "I suggest that you try not to rush the process. I know that the God of Thunder takes his role as protector of both Asgard and Midgard seriously, but attempting to be more active than is wise will only keep you in that bed for even longer."

Thor actually smiled at that, which meant that the healer's guess was accurate—he was attempting to be more active than was wise given how far along in his recovery he was.

"It was a saying on Midgard," Thor said, "that doctors make the worst patients. While I can no longer be considered to be a true healer, it seems I still have that instinct to rush things."

"You were a warrior before you were ever a healer, Thor," she said, putting a hand on his shoulder. "Your instinct is to return to battle."

He nodded. "Particularly now, when Asgard has been robbed of one of its finest treasures."

The Healer Royal moved on to Sif, who had fewer broken bones than Thor, but who did have burns on her arms and legs following her battle against two different dragons in the Valhalla Mountains. Sitting by her side was Hilde, one of the many children of Volstagg the Voluminous and his wife, Gudrun. Hilde had aided Sif in her battle against the dragon brothers.

To Sif, the Healer Royal simply said, "Things are progressing as normal." Sif would not be satisfied with any answer other than one of full healing, and she was an even worse patient than Thor.

"I need to return to the battlefield!" Sif said through clenched teeth. "And yet, I now feel even *weaker* than I did when you began your ministrations!"

"It takes time, Sif," Hilde said. "I remember once when I broke my arm after Alaric and I got into a fight with a couple of other kids who were making fun of Father. It took *forever*, mostly 'cause I didn't rest like the healer told me to."

Sif glowered at the girl.

The healer gave Hilde a grateful look, then turned back to Sif. "I will attempt a different salve for your burns." She then applied the very same salve that she'd been using for centuries.

"Thank you," Sif said testily.

"I'll make sure she's okay," Hilde added with a smile.

"That is not necessary," Sif said. "I appreciate your help, Hilde—both here and in Flodbjerge—but—"

"But nothing. If I go home, Mother will just yell at me for not staying in my room when she said to. I'd rather stay with you."

Recalling her own youthful indiscretions that had led to long imprisonments in her room, Sif sympathized with the girl's plight. And she had proven herself to be a valuable companion. "Very well. For now."

Hilde brightened. "Thanks!"

Confident that Hilde would, at the very least keep Sif from

making herself worse, the healer departed Sif's home, and was met on the doorstep by a messenger from the palace.

"The All-Father wishes to see you immediately, lady," the messenger said.

"I wish to see him as well, so this is fortuitous." She had just been wondering how soon she would be able to gain an audience with the ruler of Asgard.

The messenger escorted the healer to the central part of Asgard, past the Museum of Weaponry and the Hall of Heroes to the Warriors' Walk, eventually reaching the steps of the throne room.

The healer entered to find Odin alone, save for Heimdall. She wondered what might take the guardian of the rainbow bridge away from his post at the mouth of the Bifrost.

The answer to her query was soon in coming, for as she walked closer to the throne, she heard Heimdall speak with a stricken voice.

"I fear, All-Father, that I may no longer be capable of performing my duties as guardian of Asgard."

"Do not be foolish, Heimdall," Odin said, and the healer detected an odd tone in his voice—almost as if the All-Father was in pain. "Never have I had reason to doubt your loyalty and steadfastness."

"It is not those qualities that I am lacking in, my liege, but rather my physical ability. I can no longer see as far as Varinheim or Skornheim, and the outskirts of Niffleheim are similarly invisible to me now. No longer can I hear the running of the Gopul River or the calls of gulls that fly over the Sea of Marmora."

"Perhaps your abilities are declining, noble guardian," Odin said, "but even a diminished Heimdall is superior to any other who might replace you. Return to your post, and be vigilant. Keep your enchanted sword, Hofund, at your side and the Gjallarhorn on your back. Be ready for all that might menace the Realm Eternal."

Heimdall fell to one knee. "As my liege commands."

Odin looked past Heimdall and saw the newest arrival. "Ah, healer, welcome. I would have words."

"As would I with you, All-Father. I would ask your indulgence and have Heimdall stay a moment as well, for his current issue may be related."

That surprised Odin, and he nodded. Heimdall stood at parade rest while the healer approached the throne. Quickly, she filled in Odin and Heimdall on Thor's and Sif's sudden lack of progress in healing.

"In addition," she said, "in the past three days, I have received far more complaints of everyday ailments than is normal for a three-*month* period."

"And you have another," Odin said, "for I summoned you here to discuss an issue with my back. There is a pain in the small of it that vexes me whenever I rise or sit."

The healer nodded. "My Lord Odin, I cannot believe that it is a coincidence that these issues began immediately upon the theft of the Golden Apples."

"Nor I."

Another messenger came into the throne room. "Forgive me, All-Father, but I bear urgent news of Balder the Brave!"

"Step forward," Odin said, a protest at being interrupted dying on his lips. Since Balder had been sent to investigate the theft of the apples, his fate was of great import.

The messenger knelt before the throne, and then stood hesitantly.

"Speak, lad!" Odin bellowed. "Give us news of the Brave One!"

"Please, my lord, be aware that I merely convey what I was told."

"Of course. Be on with it!" Odin began to lose patience.

"While returning from Nornheim where he did question Queen Karnilla, Balder did injure himself while mounting his horse."

Under any other circumstances, Odin would assume that this was a trick on the part of the Norn Queen, the latest in her many attempts to win Balder for herself.

But in light of what the Healer Royal had told him—not to mention his own back pain—he found the messenger's words convincing.

"I was told that the Norn Queen did swear by the Gjoll that she had no part in either Balder's injury or the theft of the apples, and that she would care for Balder."

"Very well. You may go."

The messenger departed quickly, relieved that Odin's anger at this news had not been greater.

Odin's anger was still quite sufficient, however. "Summon the Warriors Three immediately!" With Thor, Sif, and Balder injured, Odin needed the counsel of the finest of his remaining warriors—that meant Heimdall as well as Fandral, Hogun, and Volstagg.

"They are returning to Asgard from the city of Flodbjerge, my liege," Heimdall said. "After my sister Sif's battle with the dragons there, Volstagg did volunteer himself and his two companions to aid the town in repairing the damage brought about by the creatures."

"Of course." Odin had completely forgotten about that, but now that Heimdall had reminded him, he recalled Fandral informing him of this a week earlier.

"But they have completed their work and are traversing the Gopul River even as we speak. They should return within the hour."

Sure enough, the trio arrived in the time frame indicated by the guardian.

"What has happened?" Fandral asked urgently. "As soon as we entered the gates, we did sense that something was rotten in the city of Asgard."

Normally, Odin would have risen from his throne, that he might speak with even more authority, but doing so was painful at the moment, and so he remained seated.

"Indeed, noble warriors," the All-Father said. "The Golden Apples have been stolen!"

Odin related what had happened, concluding by saying, "It would seem that the theft of the Golden Apples has consequences that reach further than simply denying us our immortality. It should have taken many months before any ill effects were detected, but after three days, we are *all* feeling poorly. Even I have succumbed to minor ailments that would normally be beneath me."

"Truly," Fandral said, "it is a dark day for Asgard."

Volstagg shook his head. "It would seem that sorcery is afoot."

Heimdall then spoke. "*You* three seem to have felt no ill effects."

Fandral nodded. "After Volstagg did volunteer us to aid the people of Flodbjerge, Hogun and I arranged for our delivery of apples to come early, that we might partake while we worked to reconstruct the village for those good people."

Volstagg added, "We dined on the apples three days ago, on our usual schedule." He grinned. "They went quite well with the fish stew prepared for us at Flodbjerge. Truly, it was a fine feast!"

Odin rubbed his bearded chin. "Then let it be known that the three of you are the only Asgardians who have yet to suffer from whatever has affected us all."

Hogun said, "It may be only temporary, my liege. We should assume nothing until the cause is determined. Idunn said that the person who stole the apples was disguised as Loki. Are we sure the Trickster himself is not responsible?"

"I did not believe so," Odin said, "for Idunn was sure that she had proofed the apples against being approached by my son. But Volstagg is correct that this has the stench of sorcery—of a type that Loki practices all too often."

Heimdall shook his head. "Forgive me, my lord, but Loki has not left his keep since you confined him there following the trolls' invasion of Asgard. It is possible that he has escaped since then, as my eyesight has suffered, but before the apples were stolen, my abilities were as strong as ever, and I spied no departure by the Trickster."

Odin nodded. Loki had conspired with a group of trolls to penetrate the city walls of the Realm Eternal, and further, had kept Thor from using his Uru hammer, Mjolnir, during the ensuing battle. As punishment for this affront, Odin had confined Loki to his keep for a full month. That month was almost expired.

"I do not doubt your word, nor your eyes—at least not before the current crisis—but I also do not doubt the guile of my adopted son. I am not convinced that he was not a participant in Hrungnir's plot against the Realm Eternal. The armor in which the giant was encased when he dueled with Thor *also* had the stench of Loki's trickery."

Heimdall nodded. "You believe he was able to escape from his keep without my detecting it?"

"I believe that Loki should be interrogated to determine the truth." Odin turned to the Warriors Three. "Hogun, Fandral, Volstagg—I hereby charge you with bringing Loki before my presence, that he may explain what role, if any, he has played in this."

Fandral and Hogun both knelt. "It will be done, my liege," Fandral said.

After a moment, Volstagg also knelt, but then he didn't move. "It would seem that the Lion of Asgard is . . . unable to rise to the occasion."

Laughing, Fandral said, "Perhaps we should place some food on the far side of the room. No doubt that would give the Lion a leg up."

The Healer Royal stepped forward. "Please, my lords, do not jest. I do believe that Volstagg's need is true."

Only then did Fandral look at his old friend's face. Normally, Volstagg's visage was jovial—no matter whether he was in battle, in the dining hall, or simply traversing the streets of the Realm Eternal, the Voluminous One took joy in life.

But now, Volstagg's face was twisted in pain. He truly could not move his legs to bring himself upright.

"It would seem," Heimdall said slowly, "that whatever spell was cast upon the apples, it eventually affects even those who did partake of them recently."

Quickly, Fandral grabbed one of Volstagg's arms, while Hogun took the other.

With a mighty heave, they brought Volstagg to his feet.

"Come, my friends," Volstagg said between deep breaths, "let us away to Loki's keep. If he is responsible for the sorcery that has left the Lion of Asgard so helpless that he cannot even take to his feet, I would know about it, and see him thrashed!"

Fandral chuckled. "I had thought a feast would be all that would be required, but you speak true, old friend."

"Let us go," Hogun said urgently.

CHAPTER THREE

"I am telling you fools that I have done *nothing*!"

Loki might normally have gesticulated wildly upon saying those words, but at present, his arms were pinned to the floor of his keep, along with most of the rest of him.

Upon arriving, Fandral had immediately pushed Loki to the floor, Hogun had kicked him, and then Volstagg had sat on him.

The Trickster now remained in that ignominious position under Volstagg's outsized rump while Fandral and Hogun searched the keep.

"And of course," Volstagg said while munching on a date that he had found in a bowl in the sitting room, "Loki always speaks the truth."

"Hardly," Loki muttered, "but I've no reason to prevaricate now."

"Loki *needs* no reason to lie," Volstagg said. "It comes as naturally to him as breathing."

"And as naturally as gluttony comes to you, Volstagg," Loki said. "I ask again that you remove yourself."

"Once my compatriots have satisfied themselves that the Golden Apples are not here, I will consider your request." Volstagg popped another date into his mouth.

Loki grew frustrated. "I'm sure Heimdall has already informed you that I have not left my keep since Odin confined me here! Your energies would be far better spent seeking out the *true* culprit—before the ill effects start to show themselves."

"They already have," Fandral said as he checked under Loki's couch. "Heimdall's eyesight is dimmed, Odin's back is weakened, and Balder has lost his coordination. Plus, Thor's and Sif's healing progress is slowed considerably."

"I see," Loki said. Then he saw Hogun pick up a figurine. "Do not *touch* that!"

"Why?" Hogun asked grimly.

"It is crystal. You might break it."

Placing the figurine gently back on the end table, Hogun said, "The house does look very . . . lived in?"

Loki sighed. "The sprites who are charged with keeping the place neat and clean are instructed to do so only when I am absent. Convincing them to do otherwise during my house arrest has proven rather difficult."

Fandral dug through the couch's cushions. "It is indeed a dark day in Asgard, for Loki has admitted that something is difficult for him."

"Very droll, Fandral. I convinced them to clean the kitchen once, but since I have returned from Jotunheim—"

Loki cut himself off, cursing himself for a fool. He blamed the stress of Volstagg's weight crushing him for such an obvious blunder. That, and he'd been having trouble focusing the past few days . . .

"So Odin was correct," Hogun said as he investigated the wardrobe, "and the Trickster did indeed break his sentence to venture to Jotunheim."

"No doubt," Fandral added, "to provide the enchanted armor to Hrungnir, in which he did battle with Thor."

"Yes, yes, yes, you're all very clever for figuring out what I practically told you in so many words. Nonetheless, I have not ventured outside the keep since then, precisely *because* of what happened in Jotunheim. I aided Hrungnir, and he repaid my generosity by kidnapping my mother." Loki actually smiled, though doing so while weighed down by Volstagg's girth was difficult. "Why do you think the enchantment on Hrungnir's armor ceased after a time?"

Gazing at his comrades, Fandral said, "Loath though I am to agree with the Trickster, his words do have the ring of truth. If there is any in the Nine Worlds for whom Loki might have affection, it is Frigga."

Hogun stepped forward. "There is another reason why I believe Loki speaks the truth."

Loki rolled his eyes. "Besides the fact that I *am* speaking the truth, you mean?"

Ignoring him, Hogun pointed at Loki's head. "Behold his hair. There is silver amidst the black. I do not believe that vain Loki would ever permit such a blemish if he could possibly help it."

"Perspicacity incarnate," Loki muttered. "May I have this great blundering oaf removed from my person now?"

"Of course." Volstagg slowly got to his feet, making sure to shift his weight repeatedly to make the experience as uncomfortable for Loki as he could. After all, even if the Trickster wasn't responsible for the theft of the apples, the Lion of Asgard could hardly call him *innocent.*

Clambering unsteadily to his feet, Loki made a show of brushing his clothing off. "Now then, if you'll kindly excuse me, I have—"

"Oh no," Fandral said. "I am afraid, Loki, that your presence is requested in the throne room."

Loki let out a very long sigh. "Have we not already discussed this? I am a victim of this incident, not the perpetrator."

"Nonetheless," Hogun said, "Balder is recovering from his injuries in Nornheim, and Thor and Sif are likewise incapacitated. Odin requires *all* who might be able to assist in this crisis. Even you."

Volstagg added, "Besides, there is obvious sorcery afoot. You are an expert in such matters, are you not?"

"Have you forgotten that Odin himself confined me to my keep?" Loki asked in a final attempt to avoid being in the presence of his adoptive father.

"We forget nothing." Fandral grinned. "Including Odin's instructions, which were to bring you to him. Come, let us away to the throne room."

* * *

After sending the Warriors Three on their errand and Heimdall back to his post at the Bifrost, Odin allowed the Healer Royal to examine him. She said that the muscles in his back had tightened and pulled, and she applied an ointment that burnt a bit, but then provided near-instant relief. She said that it would relax the muscles in question, and she advised him to not strain his back overmuch.

"Easier said than done, I'm afraid," Odin said wryly.

"At the very least, do the best you can." The healer smiled then. "At least you are attending to my advice with more openness than Thor or Sif."

"That is not surprising," Odin said. "They are warriors. Being able of body is paramount for them to be what they are."

"Perhaps," the healer said cautiously, "but there is no greater warrior in the Nine Worlds than Odin."

Odin chuckled indulgently. The healer was privileged to see this quieter, more thoughtful side of the All-Father, as it was one rarely seen by those he ruled.

"Once," he said, "that may have been true, but the time when I would lead the forces of Asgard to war are long past. I am a king, now, and a king's responsibility lies here in the throne room, not on the battlefield. It also means that I appreciate the value of sitting."

"No doubt." The healer gathered her belongings and prepared to leave.

A page boy entered the throne room. "My liege, Lorelei, the sister of Amora, wishes an audience."

That surprised Odin. He could not recall a single occasion prior to this when Lorelei had requested an audience with the All-Father.

"Send her in," Odin said, his curiosity piqued.

After wishing the Healer Royal well, he awaited Lorelei's entrance. The woman entered, dressed in a cloak with a hood that obscured her face.

"Speak, Lorelei, and tell me what brings you to the throne room of Odin."

Dropping to her knees and prostrating herself before the throne, Lorelei said, "I beg the All-Father's forgiveness! I have committed a grievous wrong!"

Knowing that Lorelei possessed some skill with sorcery—nowhere as powerful as her older sister, but formidable nonetheless—Odin spoke his words softly. "Rise, Lorelei, and speak. Tell me what wrong you believe you have committed."

"I was returning home after spending some time at a local tavern, when I was accosted by a strange man. I know not his name nor why he assaulted me, but he grabbed me and clamped a hand over my mouth, and pinned my arm with his other so that I could not cast a spell to save myself."

"And this man did not say why he attacked you?" Odin asked.

Lorelei shook her head. "I know not, my liege. But before he could commit further harm to me, a Frost Giant did save me!"

Odin frowned. "That is . . . peculiar behavior for a Frost Giant."

"I thought the same, and moved to defend myself against

further attack from him, but he did not pick up where his victim left off. It turns out that the Frost Giant had been following me with the intent of asking me for a favor when the strange man ambushed me. The giant said that he saved me in the hopes that I would do said favor."

"And did you?"

Lorelei had been looking down at the floor, the hood of her cloak and her scarlet tresses serving to obscure her face. Now she looked away, ashamed. "I did, my liege. I am sorry, but the man would have killed me, and Thjasse—"

Odin straightened. "You were saved by Thjasse?"

Now Lorelei turned and looked directly at Odin. The All-Father noted that the woman's visage had more lines than he'd ever seen before.

"You know this Thjasse, All-Father?"

"I do. He was the lieutenant of Hrungnir, the base villain who challenged my steed to a race, and when he lost, kidnapped Frigga and forced Thor to fight him. I had been informed that Thjasse had replaced Hrungnir." Odin rubbed his chin for a moment, then turned his one good eye on Lorelei. "Continue, Lorelei. What favor did Thjasse ask of you?"

"To disguise him as Loki, my liege."

Unable to help himself, Odin chuckled. "I admire the audacity, at least. And you agreed?"

"He did save my life, All-Father, and what's more, I have no love for your adopted son. Loki did treat me poorly once upon a time, and I believed that Thjasse's plot would bring ill to the

Trickster. Those two reasons were more than sufficient." Lorelei looked away again. "Or so I thought. I did not imagine that he would then use that disguise to contrive to steal the Golden Apples!"

"So you know of that. Thjasse did not inform you that such was his purpose?"

"No, my liege! Had I been so informed, I would never have agreed—no matter that he saved my life." She threw the cloak back, revealing not only a more wrinkled face than she had ever had, but also streaks of silver amidst the red in her hair. "I cannot bear to live looking like *this*. The mirrors of my home are all taken down so I will not be forced to look upon my newfound hideousness."

"Your vanity serves you ill, Lorelei. Would that you had thought to query Thjasse more aggressively. Tell me now—is changing his shape to that of Loki the *only* favor you did for Thjasse?"

"I swear, my liege, by the Gjoll, that is all I provided for him."

Odin noticed that that was the only part of her story that she would swear that oath by.

The All-Father was tempted to punish Lorelei, but he stayed his hand. Truly, she was a victim in this. No doubt her initial attacker had been a pawn of Thjasse, as well.

No, Hrungnir's former lieutenant was the true enemy of Asgard.

"Go, Lorelei!" Odin pointed to the egress. "Return to your domicile and think upon what you have done this day. And hope that Odin and the remaining warriors of Asgard may correct this calamity, or you will find that the visage that stares back at you in your looking glass will cause you even greater revulsion ere long!"

Even as Lorelei fled the throne room, Odin pondered. Thjasse had needed to look like Loki in order to make Idunn think Loki was the perpetrator of this crime. But the Frost Giant had not simply stolen the Golden Apples. Something else had been done to them to cause this sudden downturn in the health and welfare of the Aesir.

Odin found his musings interrupted by the return of the Warriors Three, with the son of Laufey in tow.

"Greetings, Father," Loki said bitterly. "I am informed by these three louts that you wish my counsel in these trying times. Or do you still believe that I am responsible?"

"That would depend." Odin looked at Fandral. "What say you three?"

In response, Fandral said, "Hogun did observe that Loki's hair is showing signs of silvering. Were he responsible for this calamity, he would, at the very least, have attempted to shield himself from its effects."

"Or," Hogun added, "failing that, he would at least disguise those effects from others."

"I am still not convinced that Loki is innocent," Odin said. "Approach the throne!"

The four of them did so. Fandral and Hogun knelt down. Volstagg and Loki did not, the former out of necessity—he did not wish to be helped up a second time—the latter out of contempt.

"What must I do to convince you that I did not steal the Golden Apples?" Loki asked plaintively.

"Nothing you say can convince me, my son." Odin paused, and let Loki squirm for a moment before continuing. "Because I already know that you did not steal them. Idunn bespelled the apples so that you could not approach them, and I have just learnt that the Frost Giant Thjasse in recent times contrived to disguise himself as Loki."

"Thjasse?" Loki spat upon the throne room floor. "That crafty Frost Giant is making a play for Hrungnir's position, is he?"

"He has, in fact, already made it," Hogun said. "Since Thor defeated the Brawler, the Frost Giants who swore fealty to Hrungnir have turned their loyalty to Thjasse."

"Not surprising. Thjasse was truly the brains of the outfit in any case." Loki turned back to the throne. "If you know I did not steal the apples, Father, then why do you say you are not convinced of my innocence in this matter?"

"Because the Golden Apples were not merely stolen. Their theft has enacted a spell that is causing all of us to suffer ill effects that should take months, not days, to transpire. I know the magicks of the Frost Giants, and they are not capable of so complex a spell as would be required for such a consequence."

"And you believe I would cast such a spell?"

"Perhaps." Odin leant forward in his throne, wincing briefly from the pain. "I am, at the very least, certain that you *could* cast such a spell."

For a moment, Loki considered attempting to continue to protest his innocence, but he decided to provide the truth. At this point, to conceal his trickery would only make it worse when it was inevitably discovered who had cast the spell on the apples weeks before.

"You are correct, of course."

Fandral immediately unsheathed Fimbuldraugr, his longsword, and placed the tip of the blade very close to Loki's throat. "You will pay for this treachery, Trickster!"

At the same time, Hogun unsheathed his own knife, though he said nothing—his facial expression, however, spoke his contempt quite eloquently.

"What," Volstagg said, "would possess you to do such a thing? After all, you are as affected by the spell as any of us."

"Well, *obviously* my intention was to have the apples stolen at a time of *my* choosing, when I would of course protect myself from the spell, as Fandral did suggest."

Odin spoke before any of the Warriors Three could express their outrage. "And what is the nature of the spell, Loki?"

"I should think that would be obvious," Loki said with a smile, deliberately ignoring Fandral's sword point at his neck. "Should the apples be removed from Idunn's care, all those who have consumed them would see the apples' restorative qualities reversed."

Volstagg frowned. "You said you could protect yourself from the ill effects."

Shrugging, Loki said, "Yes, of course."

Fandral grinned, sword still raised. "That begs the question of why you haven't yet."

"Because for the counterspell to be effective, one must have possession of the apples. I do not." Loki sighed. "I even attempted to cast the spell in any event, but I last consumed the apples too long ago. Not enough residue of them remains for the spell to be effective."

Odin stroked his beard thoughtfully. "Might the spell be cast on one who has consumed the apples recently?"

"And who might have done that?" Loki asked.

"Us," Hogun said simply.

"We have been in Flodbjerge for the last fortnight," Fandral said, "aiding the people in rebuilding their city, and had arranged with Idunn for early delivery of our apples. But we did not eat them until the appointed time, which was the condition under which Idunn would so deliver them."

"Then you are fortunate," Loki said. "Perhaps I may be able to shield you from further deterioration."

Odin smiled. "It seems, my son, that your counsel *is* proving useful." Then the smile fell. "But it would not have been needed had you not committed a crime against Asgard in the first place."

Loki was about to step forward, but Fandral still had his blade poking at the Trickster's throat. Sparing a contemptuous glance at the blond warrior, Loki then glared at Odin. "It was no *crime*. A bit of mischief is all it was—the All-Father might recall that Loki is the god of such."

"God of Mischief, yes, and also the God of Lies, and I believe you take the latter far more seriously than the former."

Putting a hand to his heart, Loki smiled. "You wound me, Father."

"I describe you, my son." Odin leant back in his throne. "If Loki's spell functions as it should, then the Warriors Three will be the only gods of Asgard at full fighting strength. It will fall upon yon trio to beard Thjasse in his lair and retrieve the Golden Apples, lest this thievery spell disaster for the Realm Eternal! So be it!"

Loki stared at Fandral. "I will require you to lower your sword."

Fandral grinned and did so. "For now."

"Stand you together," Loki said. "Volstagg, you may waddle as you see fit, but stand beside your fellows."

"Have a care, Loki," Volstagg said, "for the Lion of Asgard has need of a new chair, and you have already proven yourself to be an excellent seat."

Loki scowled, and unconsciously rubbed his own backside, still sore from when Volstagg had sat upon it.

The Warriors Three stood side by side before Loki, who gathered the energy needed to cast his spell.

As he did so, Loki thought it wise to provide a warning. "Be you advised that the duration of this spell is impossible to determine. Had you consumed the apples within the past hour, I could guarantee complete immunity. As it stands, I have no method by which I may determine the spell's effect.

In midbattle, you may find yourself suddenly quite infirm." He glanced at Volstagg. "Or rather, *more* infirm."

Fandral looked sideways at Volstagg. "Don't."

Smiling, Volstagg said, "Merely wondering how well the green raiments of Loki would match the drapes of our sitting room."

"Yes," Fandral replied, "but the purple in his face from prolonged exposure to your underside would surely clash."

"True," Volstagg said with a sigh.

Loki rolled his eyes. "If you're *quite* finished."

"Merely waiting for you to start," Fandral said.

"Then start I shall." With that, Loki mouthed the words of the counterspell.

After a moment, the trio were covered in a warm, golden glow. When the incandescence faded, they looked at each other.

"I feel no different," Volstagg said.

Hogun, though, nodded. "I do. It is the same suffusion of strength that comes when I eat the apples themselves."

"I feel it as well," Fandral said.

"That is a sign that it was successful," Loki said. "Now then, if you'll excuse me—"

"Do not imagine," Odin said, "that you are departing, Loki."

"Only to return to my keep, Father." Loki grinned. "I believe I am under house arrest."

"Indeed." Odin gestured contemptuously at his adopted son. "Be you gone, then, Loki, and await further instructions."

"Instructions?"

"I might have need of you further as the situation progresses."

"Might you now?"

Fandral put his hand to Fimbuldraugr's hilt. "Need I unsheathe my sword once again, Loki?"

"Hardly." Loki gestured, and cast a teleportation spell.

Nothing happened.

Loki found it suddenly extremely difficult to catch his breath. "I do—do not—"

"It would seem," Volstagg said with a mirthful chuckle, "that you have forgotten the effects of your own spell."

Loki cursed himself, realizing that the Voluminous One was right—the effort of casting the counterspell had left him too fatigued to teleport.

"Since you are unable to hie yourself directly to your keep," said Odin, unable to keep the amusement out of his voice as he spoke, "perhaps you might tarry here a while?"

"I seem to have little choice." Loki spoke through clenched teeth. The keep was too far to walk—he had been brought to the throne room on the back of Hogun's horse, and he doubted the Grim One would lend him the steed to return.

Fandral saluted Odin with Fimbuldraugr. "We will hie ourselves to Jotunheim immediately."

"In point of fact," Hogun said, "we will hie ourselves to Jotunheim at first light. Night is falling, and the road to Jotunheim is fraught enough when the sun shines."

"Hogun is wise." Volstagg pointed a finger upward. "But come the morrow, Thjasse will rue the day he violated the Aesir. The Lion of Asgard swears it!"

"Go you with my blessing," Odin said. "I will see you off at the royal stables at dawn. After that, I shall address the Aesir and assure them that all will be well."

"Will they know the truth?" Fandral asked.

Odin shook his head. "The whole truth would cause undue panic. I shall say simply that the apples have been bespelled and that the Warriors Three are seeking a counterspell to deactivate it. The apples are being hidden from Asgard until then."

"Very wise, All-Father," Hogun said.

As the trio headed to the egress, Volstagg said, "It is good that we do not leave right away. I have not been home since leaving for Flodbjerge, and I would see Gudrun and the children. Besides, we will need to provision for our journey."

Fandral smiled. "And only the wife of Volstagg can prepare sufficient foodstuffs to feed the Lion's great belly?"

"Indeed!" Volstagg said with a grin.

"Just be sure," Hogun said, "that you do not sample all of the provisions before meeting us at the city gates, lest there be none such remaining for Fandral and I."

"Now then, what manner of friend would I be if I allowed you to taste food I had not first tested so to be sure that it was worthy of your gullet?" Volstagg chuckled, his belly quivering. "Now, let us go and rest, for tomorrow, we save the Realm Eternal!"

CHAPTER FOUR

At dawn, the Warriors Three set forth.

Volstagg spent the night before their journey telling stories to his children. He had only intended to tell them one story, but they asked for two more before they finally fell asleep. Then he enjoyed a peaceful night's rest beside his wife, Gudrun.

Fandral spent the night before their journey in the company of a brunette woman named Ella. He had intended to spend the evening with a blonde named Helga, but she felt poorly—no doubt suffering the effects of the spell on the apples. Then he had approached a redhead named Morenn, but she needed to care for her sick brother. Luckily, he only called Ella "Helga" once, and Fandral had breathed the name heavily enough that it probably sounded like "Ella" in any case.

Hogun spent the night before their journey alone, sharpening his weapons.

Volstagg had his family and his food. Fandral had his charisma and his charm. But Hogun had only the memory of a slaughtered family and his own inaction in the face of that. Although he would go to Hel and back for Asgard, though he would brave any foe alongside Volstagg and Fandral—as well as Thor and Sif and Balder—and though he would die for Odin, he still feared to grow close enough to anyone lest he lose them the way he had lost his people to Mogul of the Mystic Mountain.

His boon companions were the only ones he came close to caring about, but he would let those emotions go no further than his comrades in arms. He had loved once, and lost everything. He could not bear to let that happen again.

At dawn, Fandral and Hogun arrived at the royal stables. Odin was already there, as was the stablemaster and Odin's vizier. The vizier, however, looked out of sorts.

Fandral's elegant, golden-maned horse, Gulltoppr, whinnied at the sight of his rider, while Hogun's steadfast, dark-maned steed, Kolr, stood more calmly. Iron Shanks, the long-suffering mount of Volstagg, chewed casually on hay he had pulled from the bales.

"Where is Volstagg?" Odin asked.

Fandral grinned. "You told him to be here at dawn, so he is like to arrive approximately a quarter hour past then, at the earliest."

"No doubt testing the provisions to make sure they are of adequate quality for our journey," Hogun said dryly.

Turning to Odin, Fandral said, "My liege, is Loki still in the palace, or was he able to hie himself back to his keep?"

"Hm?" Odin stared blankly at Fandral for several moments. "Oh, Loki, of course. Yes, he returned home in the night. However, I have tasked Hugin and Munin with keeping watch over his keep, to ensure that he does not escape. Heimdall's eyes are not up to the task at present."

Fandral nodded in agreement, and exchanged a look of concern with Hogun. Odin's blank stare spoke ill of his ability to rule Asgard properly.

"We shall proceed with dispatch, my liege," Fandral said. "This attack on Asgard will be avenged and righted."

"I have no doubt of that at all, Hogun—and Fandral." Odin quickly corrected himself, which did nothing to ameliorate Fandral and Hogun's concerns.

"Ho, my friends!" came a booming voice from down the road.

Hogun and Fandral turned to see Volstagg lumbering toward them, his daughter Hilde by his side. The girl carried a large sack, filled with victuals for the journey.

"I have spent the evening with my family, and Hilde has kindly agreed to see us off."

"And aid with the fetching and carrying," Hogun added.

"Of course. Why else does one have children?"

Fandral shuddered. "The Fates willing, I shall never know."

Noting the ease with which the girl handled the large sack, Hogun stroked his mustache thoughtfully. "Hilde seems unaffected by the loss of the apples."

"None of the children are," Volstagg said. "The resiliency of youth. Besides, the true benefits of the apples hardly apply to the young."

The stable master said, "All of your mounts are fed, washed, and watered, my lords."

"Excellent!" cried Volstagg. "I'm sure that Iron Shanks will race to Jotunheim so we may beard the foul Thjasse in his lair."

"Assuming," Fandral stage-whispered, "that the steed survives the journey."

Volstagg drew himself up to his full and considerable height. "Iron Shanks has served me quite well lo these many years!"

"It is a wonder he has not collapsed from exhaustion, then." Fandral laughed as he mounted Gulltoppr.

Before likewise climbing atop Kolr, Hogun walked over to Hilde, who was tying the provisions sack to Iron Shanks's saddle.

As soon as she saw Hogun, Hilde jumped and made a slight squeak, dropping the provisions onto the ground. Sheepishly, she picked the sack up and tried to sound casual. "Yes, Hogun?"

"I was wondering if you might do us a favor, Hilde."

"*Anything*, Hogun, just name it!" Hilde winced at her words, as she sounded a little *too* enthusiastic to help Hogun.

Hogun glanced briefly at Odin. "The All-Father is affected by what has happened."

"The theft of the apples. Father told me on the way here."

"He did not tell the other children?" Hogun asked apprehensively.

Hilde shook her head. "He only told me because he said that after helping Sif against the two dragons, I was trustworthy."

Hogun actually almost smiled at that. "Yes—while we aided with the repairs, the tales of your bravery were the talk of the people of Flodbjerge."

"Really?" Hilde's eyes went wide. "Nobody's ever told stories about me before!"

What little smile Hogun had given disappeared. "Do not

embrace such tales, Hilde. A true warrior seeks not approbation, but only the satisfaction of a task well performed. Glory is for the bards and the attendees of feasts."

Abashed, Hilde said, "Of course."

"Excellent."

Hilde finished securing the provisions sack, and then Hogun brought her over to Odin.

"My liege, Hilde will accompany you and the vizier back to the throne room."

"For what purpose, Fandral? No, Hogun! My apologies, Hogun, my memory seems to be slipping."

"I believe you have answered your own question, All-Father," Hogun said dryly.

"Indeed. You are wise indeed, Grim One. As Volstagg said, the children are less affected by this calamity." Odin looked down at Hilde. "Your service will be quite welcome, child."

Hilde got down on one knee and bowed her head. "It is my honor to serve, All-Father."

Odin smiled. "Rise, child. Volstagg has raised you well."

Volstagg chuckled. "All credit should go to Gudrun, truly. Now then, let us away!" The Voluminous One attempted to clamber atop his steed, but it took several attempts at climbing, sliding, heaving, and crawling before Volstagg at last managed to get himself atop Iron Shanks.

The horse, for his part, continued to chew hay, barely even registering the considerable weight that had been added to his back.

Shaking his head, Hogun mounted Kolr and said, "We will return with the apples as fast as we are able!"

"Fare you well, dashing Fandral, grim Hogun, and rotund Volstagg!" Odin raised his scepter. "May the Fates guide your path to victory and the saving of the Aesir!"

Fandral cried, "Hyah!" and gave Gulltoppr a gentle nudge with his thighs. The horse galloped forward.

Hogun simply whipped the reins gently, and Kolr did follow, also at a gallop.

"Ho, Iron Shanks, let us away!" But Volstagg's words had no effect, and Iron Shanks continued to eat his hay.

Eventually, Volstagg was able to inveigle his mount to move, albeit not at a gallop. By the time the horse caught up to the other two, Kolr and Gulltoppr were at the Sea of Marmora, drinking from it.

"Ah, excellent—a respite," Volstagg said. "It seems that Iron Shanks requires an iron fist to propel him forward."

"Or perhaps a less weighty rider?" Fandral grinned.

Urgently, Hogun said, "We must make better time. Fandral and I have been waiting here for half an hour. If your mount does not increase his speed, it will take most of the day to go through dwarves' country and past the Forest of Sigurd to Jotunheim. It would behoove us to move *quickly.*"

"Of course, of course," Volstagg said. "Worry not, my friends, Iron Shanks has now fully digested his hay from the stable. At this point, I can guarantee he will be as fast as ever."

"In that case, we may never reach Jotun—"

Fandral cut himself off when he noticed something strange in the air.

He glanced at Hogun, who simply said, "I sense it, as well."

And then, a moment later, a Storm Giant appeared before them. He was red of hair, with a beard thicker even than Volstagg's.

"Ha! I see Asgardians invading my domain! You shall become prisoners of King Rugga!"

Not only had the three warriors been caught unawares, but the horses had been, as well. Iron Shanks and Gulltoppr both lifted their forelegs and whinnied in surprise, while even the usually calm Kolr bucked a bit.

Instinctively, Fandral and Volstagg moved to calm their mounts, and the Storm Giant grabbed them both with one massive hand.

Hogun took advantage of the confusion and dived into the Sea of Marmora.

Fandral found himself completely lost within the massive hand of the giant, unable to even reach for his sword, much less wield it.

Volstagg's greater girth had at least kept his mouth free, though he, too, was unable to break the giant's grip, nor use his arms or legs. "Fie upon you, Storm Giant! Release the Lion of Asgard at once, or face terrible consequences!"

"Do not squirm, little godlings, for it will be for naught! None may break the iron grip of King Rugga!"

With a bitter chuckle, Volstagg said, "In truth, ne'er has Volstagg been called 'little' before."

"Silence, *little* godling!" Rugga cried, and looked around the shore of the sea. "I spy three horses, yet see only two little godlings. Where is your comrade?"

"Of what comrade do you speak, Rugga?" Volstagg asked, feigning confusion. "Noble Iron Shanks serves as our pack horse, for our journey ahead is long, and must be properly provisioned. The remaining two horses serve my old friend Fandral and myself."

Rugga let out a slow breath, the stench of which nearly rendered Volstagg faint. "Very well. We shall return to my throne room, where you will answer all of my questions or die!"

"What of our horses?" Volstagg asked.

"What of them? They are too small to eat, and I have no hands to carry them."

Only after Rugga had stomped off did Hogun break free of the sea. Drying himself off with one of the blankets they had brought along, Hogun briefly pondered how the Storm Giant could have snuck up on them. King Rugga, like all Storm Giants, was considerably larger than any Asgardian.

But then Hogun recalled a story Thor had told him once about his youth. He and Loki had found their way to the realm of the Storm Giants, and there they had been tricked by the giant's ruler, Utgard, who fooled the brothers with illusions and trickery.

Obviously, Rugga had used similar trickery to approach the trio unawares.

Still, Storm Giants were far from Asgard's finest thinkers. Rugga had made off with his prisoners without even searching for Hogun, leading Hogun to think the giant king had not properly observed the number of his foes. Hogun intended to make Rugga regret that decision.

Hogun also knew the warriors could ill afford this delay. With every hour that passed, the situation in Asgard grew more dire.

Quickly, Hogun led the three horses to a giant oak and secured all of them to it. They had been fed and watered, at least, and now they would have the opportunity to rest. Which was fortunate, as Hogun knew that once he effected his rescue, they would need to ride the mounts hard and fast to get to Jotunheim and Thjasse's castle.

Though he was a master tracker, Hogun in truth needed no great skill to follow the path of Rugga. While the Storm Giant may have used spells of misdirection to mask his attack, he had taken no such precaution with regard to his retreat.

The verdant hills around the Sea of Marmora provided plenty of cover, allowing Hogun to move silently. Not that Rugga was like to hear him, but stealth was nonetheless warranted. Hogun knew not the situation, and he needed information on where Fandral and Volstagg were being held before he could rescue them.

Eventually, he came to Utgardkeep, the very same castle that Thor and Loki had visited as youths. The structure was massive and imposing, but built specifically for giants, and though the gates were locked, Hogun was easily able to slide between the space between the door and the floor.

Hogun moved through the enormous halls. He heard the sounds of eating and drinking, and snuck in that direction to see several giants enjoying a meal. Of Rugga, there was no sign.

He proceeded through some other corridors, struggling to keep track of his movements. Normally, Hogun could retrace his steps through a labyrinth while blindfolded, but the sheer size of this keep made it difficult to recall landmarks. It was an endless stream of corridors that felt like huge caverns, leading to rooms that were even larger.

It was the voice of Volstagg that drew Hogun to what he soon learnt was the throne room. Climbing over a hinge and entering in the space between the door and the wall, Hogun saw a large table in front of a massive throne. Atop the table were two giant bell jars.

Volstagg was inside one jar; Fandral in the other.

As a youth, Hogun's inaction had led to the deaths of his cousins. In the millennia since, Fandral and Volstagg had become closer to him than any of the blood relatives of his youth—including even those two cousins. He would not see his fellow warriors die this day.

Rugga's voice echoed off the walls, loudly enough that Hogun felt the vibration of his words in his very bones.

"I have heard that Asgard has lost the Golden Apples of Idunn, and that the Aesir already begin to grow decrepit and infirm. Is this so?"

Fandral regarded the giant with amusement. "Does dashing

Fandral look infirm, King Rugga? I assure you that I am at the peak of health."

Rugga turned to Volstagg. "The same cannot be said of your companion."

"I assure you," Volstagg said archly, "that the Lion of Asgard is second to no god in either strength or vitality!"

"Perhaps my plan is a wise one, then," Rugga said with a grin.

"Hardly that," Fandral said, "for those rumors you heard are false. The apples have been hidden for safekeeping, but there is no danger to Asgard."

"However," Volstagg added, "there is grave danger for any who may be foolish enough to attack Asgard, for the Realm Eternal's guardians are at the ready to repel any invaders. Why, only recently I had the privilege of fending off an invasion of trolls into Asgard's very city walls! Bravely did I wade through the trolls, vanquishing them right and left!"

Rugga laughed, and the bell jars that held Fandral and Volstagg rattled. "You? Single-handedly held off a troll invasion?"

"Well, not single-handedly, as I did receive some *small* assistance from my friend Fandral here, as well as a few others, including Balder the Brave, Hogun the Grim, Thor the Thunderer, and of course, the Lady Sif. Doughty warriors all, and I assure you that they were all honored to follow my lead."

While Volstagg blathered on, Hogun made a survey of the throne room. The path he had taken through the keep could be backtracked, enabling the three of them to escape, but this would only work if Rugga himself was incapacitated and unable to alert his fellow Storm Giants that the prisoners were free.

"Then of course, there was Hrungnir. No doubt you are aware that the Brawler did challenge Odin and was firmly routed. In jealous anger, Hrungnir did lead an invasion across the Ida Plain, and the Lion of Asgard led the charge to repel his forces! One by one, each Frost Giant did fall before the mighty fists of Volstagg!"

Hogun was grateful that Fandral refrained from his usual amused rejoinders in response to Volstagg's braggadocio. Rugga had focused all his of attention on Volstagg's story, and was beginning to be convinced that Asgard was not as vulnerable as he had heard—or as it truly was.

Rugga stroked his thick red beard. "You say that . . . that Thor did aid you in your battles?"

"Oh yes," Volstagg said with a firm nod. "In fact, one might say that Thor is Volstagg's protégé. I taught the lad everything he knows."

Fandral finally spoke up, for he saw the fear in Rugga's eyes. "In fact, Thor will not be pleased when he learns that you have captured Volstagg and me, as we are two of his closest friends."

Rugga looked away. "I recall his fury when I kidnapped Sif many years ago."

Volstagg chuckled. "I would never presume to say that his love for Fandral and me is as great as his love for the Lady Sif, but still . . ."

Finally, Hogun saw something that might be useful in tripping up the giant—literally—and, moving with all the stealth at his command, he worked his way to the base of Rugga's throne.

"Perhaps you are telling the truth," Rugga said.

Volstagg drew himself up to his full height inside the bell jar. "'Perhaps'? Are you calling the Lion of Asgard a liar? I have never been so insulted in all my life."

Fandral muttered, "I've certainly tried . . ."

Rugga pointed a large finger at Volstagg. "But you might also be lying to protect yourselves. The gods of Asgard may indeed be weak, and are boasting now to keep themselves from being attacked while they're vulnerable."

Volstagg made a *tch* noise. "Ridiculous! What need have gods to exaggerate their accomplishments?"

"If the apples are stolen?" Rugga grinned. "A great need indeed!" The Storm Giant king rose to his feet—

—and thrust his arms outward as he tried to maintain his balance. Screaming in confusion, he fell forward, his massive head colliding with the table with a bone-jarring thud.

The two bell jars became upended, and Fandral and Volstagg struggled to maintain their own equilibrium as their prisons shook, fell, and rolled.

From the floor near the base of the throne, Hogun cried, "Move quickly, my friends! I cannot guarantee that King Rugga will remain insensate for very long!"

Fandral's bell jar had tipped over onto its side, so he was able to easily crawl out and go to the edge of the table, where he could see Hogun standing proximate to Rugga's feet.

And where he could also see that the laces of Rugga's massive boots had been tied together.

Laughing heartily, Fandral said, "I may now say that I have lived to see the day that Hogun the Grim achieved victory on the battlefield by engaging in a child's prank."

"A weapon is a weapon," Hogun said flatly. "If it allows one to win the day, what matters its origin?"

"Indeed."

"Fandral!"

Turning, Fandral saw that Volstagg had tried to crawl out of his jar, but had only made it as far as his chest before becoming stuck.

"Quickly," Hogun said, "free his obeseness before the other giants become aware of what has transpired!"

Unsheathing Fimbuldraugr, Fandral went over to Volstagg's prison and held the sword high, the hilt pointing downward. "Hold very, very still, my corpulent friend."

With a single blow, Fandral's might and Fimbuldraugr's hilt combined to smash the glass, which scattered across the table.

"Let us make haste," Fandral said, using even more of his considerable strength to help Volstagg to his feet.

"Indeed," Hogun said. "I shall lead the way!"

CHAPTER FIVE

Throughout the day, Odin kept receiving messages from people wondering where the Golden Apples were. Hilde was even more surprised to learn that while the messages were coming at a greater rate now than they had been, there had been a steady stream of them since the apples had been taken.

As Odin spoke to one messenger, Hilde went to the vizier, who had come to the throne room to meet with Odin about something involving the kitchen-staff supervisor.

"Vizier?"

The elderly advisor said nothing at first, but continued to stare blankly.

"Vizier?!" she said more loudly.

"What? What? Oh, yes, child, my apologies. What is it?"

"Maybe Odin should, I don't know, talk to *everyone*? Make a big announcement?"

"Hmmm." The vizier stared again, but this time he seemed to actually be pensive, rather than simply absent mentally. "It might not be a bad idea. When next I go to the throne room, I will suggest it."

Hilde winced. "You *are* in the throne room."

"I am?" The vizier looked around, as if realizing for the first time where he was. "Od's blood, I need to be at the hall of records!"

The vizier turned and left the throne room, followed immediately by the messenger.

Odin turned to face Hilde after the messenger departed. "Hilde, what brings you here?"

"Um, you asked me to stay with you, Lord Odin."

Nodding in remembrance, Odin said, "Yes, yes, of course. Thank you, Hilde."

"I—I was going to suggest something to the vizier, but he left."

Again, Odin nodded. "What do you suggest?"

"Give a speech to the people of Asgard. Let them know what's happening. Or, I guess, the cover story of what's happening. I mean, everyone's asking anyhow."

"Yes, of course! I'd intended to do that very thing." Odin put a large hand on her small shoulder. "You are wise beyond your years, Hilde." Odin got to his feet, and then nearly fell over. "Ahh, my back."

Hilde ran to help him, but he held up a hand and spoke sharply.

"I am the All-Father of Asgard! I will rise to my feet on my own!"

At Hilde's reaction, Odin softened.

"My apologies, child, I did not mean to frighten you."

"I'm not frightened!" Hilde lied. "I was just surprised."

"Summon the messengers! Let the word go out to all of Asgard that the All-Father will speak before the Aesir!"

Within two hours, Odin stood on the stage of the great amphitheater. For many millennia, the amphitheater had been the site of hundreds of important events in Asgard, from games and challenges, to mustering for wars.

Odin recalled the first time he had stepped onto this stage after ascending to the throne. The forces of Vanaheim were marshaling against Asgard, thinking the upstart king to be weak. Odin gathered the warriors of Asgard in the amphitheater and told them that they would not lose this battle, and that the Vanir would rue the day they challenged the Realm Eternal.

His words had been prophetic, for Asgard won the day, and centuries later, Odin would seal an alliance with Vanaheim with his marriage to Frigga.

He seemed to recall an ultimatum delivered to Frigga's father, Freyr, but now Odin found he could no longer summon the details to mind.

Backstage, Hilde stood, nervous. Her first time in the amphitheater had been when Odin was lost and believed dead in the fight against Surtur. It was here that the Althing had been held to determine who would rule Asgard in Odin's absence. It was Balder who was selected, and Hilde remembered that he had done a good job until Odin's return.

Since that time, Hilde had seen a bunch of such gatherings,

and though a huge crowd had gathered to hear Odin's words, this was the quietest she'd ever heard such a large number of people be. Oh, people were talking amongst themselves, but it was a nothing but a low rumble.

That scared Hilde even more than Odin being forgetful.

Odin stepped forward and raised both of his arms. "People of Asgard, attend!"

The crowd quieted down after a second.

"As most of you know, the most recent delivery of the Golden Apples of Immortality has been delayed. Unfortunately, there is a threat to Asgard itself—and also to the apples. Many of you will recall that the Realm Eternal was subject to an attempted invasion by the Frost Giant known as Hrungnir. While my son Thor was able to defeat Hrungnir, the Frost Giants were unlike to remain leaderless for long. Hrungnir's lieutenant, a canny giant by the name of Thjasse, has taken over, and he has set his sights upon the Golden Apples."

Now Hilde heard murmurs throughout the amphitheater.

"Rest assured," Odin continued, "that the warriors of Asgard are even now working to remove the threat. But until that time, the apples *must* remain hidden in a secure location."

One person yelled from the audience, "But Thor's hurt!"

"So's Sif!"

"And nobody's seen Balder!"

"Where are the Warriors Three?"

Again holding up both arms, Odin caused the people to grow quiet once again. "While it is true that both my son and the

Lady Sif are abed with injuries, rest assured that Balder, Hogun, Fandral, Volstagg, and noble Heimdall are all performing missions to ensure the continued safety of Asgard. Why, even Loki and Lorelei have been aiding us in our hour of need."

A quiet murmur went through the crowd, and Hilde wondered if it was such a good idea to mention Loki.

"So go forth to your homes and rest assured that the situation is in hand! The apples will be restored ere long, and the lives of the gods will return to the way they were, and ever shall be."

Odin stood for a few more seconds, and then awkwardly walked away from the stage.

Hilde put on a smile for Odin's sake. "That was really good, All-Father." She was even telling a partial truth. "At least now people know what's going on, kind of."

"Thank you, Sif," Odin said.

Wincing, Hilde said, "I'm not Sif, All-Father."

"What? Of course you aren't. Who said you were?"

"I—" Hilde let out a long sigh. "We should go back to the throne room."

"Indeed," Odin said. "The vizier said he wishes to speak to me about the kitchen-staff supervisor."

Hilde considered and rejected the notion of correcting Odin. She wasn't sure that by the time they got there the All-Father would even remember the sentence he had just uttered, much less recall one way or the other the nature of his conversation with the vizier regarding the kitchen-staff supervisor.

Hilde just hoped that her father, Hogun, and Fandral could retrieve the apples soon, as it was becoming increasingly obvious that Odin would not be in any condition to rule Asgard until he was restored by the apples.

CHAPTER SIX

Hogun was pleased that retracing the route he had taken into Utgardkeep got the three of them out. Stealth was still the order of the day, so they were not slowed down by Volstagg, especially since the Voluminous One was kind enough to remain quiet during the escape.

Fandral was relieved that the horses were still tethered to the oak where Hogun had left them. Gulltoppr had been the finest steed Fandral had ridden in all his days, and he would be loath to lose the horse.

Volstagg was grateful to see that the sack of provisions was still attached to Iron Shanks's saddle, as he was starving.

As Hogun mounted Kolr, he glowered at Volstagg. "We do not have time for you to stuff your face!"

"Fie upon you, Hogun!" Volstagg said through a mouthful of jerky. "Manipulating a foolish giant is hungry work!"

"'Twas I who did all the actual work of finding you—sneaking past the giants, formulating an escape, and actually defeating the giant."

Swallowing the jerky and stuffing a large fruit into his bearded mouth, Volstagg said, "And were it not for my verbal distraction, King Rugga would easily have seen you stumbling about on the floor."

"Unlikely."

Fandral shook his head. "It matters little, my friends. What *does* matter is that we are free of King Rugga, and we must now tarry no longer. All of Asgard is depending upon our skills this day, and we must not let them down!"

Volstagg swallowed another fruit virtually whole. "You speak true, my friend. I believe this will suffice for the nonce." He clumsily hauled himself onto Iron Shanks's back. "Let us away!"

They continued on the outskirts of Nidavellir, and even at this distance, they could smell the smoke from the dwarves' forge. Thor's Uru hammer, Mjolnir, had been forged in that great furnace, as had many other magickal weapons.

To Fandral and Hogun's relief, Iron Shanks was able to keep up with Kolr and Gulltoppr, and when Fandral said as much, Volstagg snorted. "Of course. I *did* say he would."

"You also said that you single-handedly defeated the trolls and Hrungnir's giants."

Volstagg made a dismissive gesture. "Merely a minor bit of exaggeration to convince King Rugga of the truth of my words. Modesty did not become me under those circumstances."

Fandral laughed. "And how, old friend, would you even be aware of what modesty is like, given how rarely you have experienced it?"

It took most of an hour to get around Nidavellir and enter the Forest of Sigurd.

Sensing the fatigue in his mount, Fandral said, "It is well that we have reached the forest, for Gulltoppr could use a respite."

Hogun nodded. "We will proceed at a canter through the woods."

"Not for too long, I hope." Volstagg gave his steed a pat on the side. "Iron Shanks wishes to fly free and unfettered to bring the Lion of Asgard to battle more quickly!"

Dryly, Hogun said, "'Quickly' is rarely the word that may be used to describe how Volstagg springs into action."

"Though," Fandral added, "it very adequately describes how Volstagg approaches the dinner table."

"Ah, my friends, have you not learnt?" Volstagg chuckled from atop his mount. "The secret to life is to approach all things with enthusiasm, joy, and speed, whether 'tis dining, fighting, loving, or . . ."

Fandral grinned. "I certainly can appreciate the value of rushing into fighting, but loving? I would say that should be approached slowly, and with care."

With mock-gravity, Volstagg said, "It is obvious, Fandral, that you are not married."

"Nor do I have any intention of being so."

Volstagg chuckled. "You may enjoy your bachelor ways, Fandral, but all the pleasure I encounter from the consumption of food or the clash of swords is nothing compared to the sheer unbridled joy that fills my very heart when I return to hearth and home. Knowing that Gudrun and the children are waiting for me is what drives me to live every day."

Fandral and Hogun exchanged a glance.

"Did you notice, Hogun, that Volstagg's voice deepened in tone?"

"I did, Fandral. It would seem the Voluminous One's voice raises when he exaggerates his exploits, yet lowers when he speaks from the heart."

"We do not hear that lower voice often, do we?" Fandral asked with a grin.

"No," Hogun said, "but his heart must go through quite a bit of girth to be heard."

Volstagg harrumphed in annoyance at the teasing, and squeezed Iron Shanks with his thighs so he'd canter a bit faster, moving ahead of his fellows.

Volstagg was contemplating whether or not to suggest taking a pause to eat—on the one hand, they *were* in a hurry, and King Rugga's assault had delayed them; on the other, he was getting peckish, as it had been an hour or so since last he'd eaten—when Hogun cried, "Ambush!"

Three dwarves leapt from the trees, and within moments had surrounded them. Iron Shanks and Gulltoppr both stopped their forward motion; Kolr skittered a bit, agitated by the new arrivals, but Hogun got him under control quickly by tugging on the reins.

At first, the Warriors Three allowed themselves to relax. The dwarves were allies of the Aesir, after all. But the trio of dwarves who surrounded the warriors did not lower their weapons upon recognizing the Asgardians.

Slowly, Fandral said, "Step aside, please. We are on official Asgardian business—charged by Lord Odin himself!"

One of the dwarves grinned maliciously. "What care we for that?"

Another dwarf spoke. "We have heard that old One-Eye is weak—that Asgard's strength is no more."

The third said, "So now we strike. No more caves and caverns for us—no, the dwarves will rule the shining city!"

Hogun said, "King Eitri is Odin's ally and friend."

"King Eitri," the first one said, "may do as he wishes."

"Indeed," said the second one, "he wishes we were not here with weapons we stole from his forge."

"But we are," the third one said. "And with our weapons, we will take the shining city!"

Unsheathing Fimbuldraugr, Fandral said, "To achieve that goal, rebellious dwarves, you will have to get through us."

"Our intent from the start, that was." The first one raised his weapon, a great axe. "I am Helger, future ruler of Asgard!"

"Not if we have anything to say about it," Volstagg said, even as Fandral rode Gulltoppr straight at Helger.

Normally, having the high ground and also being in motion would give Fandral the advantage, but as he rode toward Helger, the dwarf swung his axe with unworldly speed, deflecting Fandral's blow hard enough that Fandral almost lost his grip on his longsword.

The second dwarf wielded a short sword and swung it at Volstagg, who, although prepared for it, was yet unable to dodge the blow and fell from Iron Shanks's back even as blood spurted from a wound opened on his right arm.

The dwarf stood over Volstagg and said, "Do not move, fat one."

"You caught the Lion of Asgard unawares. Your speed is quite impressive."

"Eitri's forge is filled with many treasures, including these weapons that do permit us the speed and abilities to make defeat impossible."

"Did you perhaps question why those weapons remained in Eitri's forge and were not brought out for use by all dwarves?" Volstagg reached across his expansive chest with his left arm to clutch his right where it was wounded, hoping his strong grip would stanch the bleeding.

"What does it matter?" the dwarf asked angrily. "Ours the weapons are now, and ours Asgard also will be!"

The third dwarf attacked Hogun with a mace, and while Hogun was fast enough to deflect the dwarf's blow, he was unable to strike back, as the dwarf parried with infernal speed. Hogun attempted again to strike, but though he too had the high ground, he could barely hold his own.

And then the dwarf hit Kolr in the right foreleg with the mace, and the mount bucked and whinnied, raising his forelegs in anguish. The sudden motion sent Hogun flying into a nearby tree. Impossibly, the dwarf stood over Hogun almost at the same moment that Hogun landed upon the ground.

Helger swung his axe at Fandral, who quickly leant backward

from atop Gulltoppr to prevent decapitation. Fandral rode the horse forward a bit, then turned the mount around to face Helger once again.

"Already lost, you have, goldenhair. Blackhair and the fat one lie defeated at our feet. Next, you shall be."

"As long as we draw breath, Helger, we warriors of Asgard are *never* defeated. And even after, sometimes! So have at you, dwarf! And damned be him that first cries 'Hold, enough!'"

Fandral rode his steed toward Helger, but while they exchanged strikes, neither scored a direct blow.

Both Hogun and Volstagg tried to move, but the two dwarves who stood over them made it clear that would be unwise.

The two Asgardians then exchanged knowing glances. Helger's friends dared not remove themselves to help Helger for fear of Hogun and Volstagg rejoining the battle. But that left Fandral alone to face the dwarf.

Helger tossed the haft of the axe from hand to hand. "The inevitable you are delaying, Asgardian."

"I was about to say the same thing to you," Fandral said as he again turned Gulltoppr around.

They faced each other for a moment, reminding Fandral of bullfights he'd seen on Midgard, except that Helger waved an axe rather than a large, red cloth. He also recalled that the bull usually lost those fights.

Forward Fandral charged, Fimbuldraugr raised high.

But instead of striking downward, he leapt up and over, easily clearing the quick swing Helger made with his axe toward

Fandral's head—or, rather, toward the empty air where Fandral's head had been.

Flipping up and over, Fandral landed on his feet behind the dwarf and swung his sword at Helger's back.

Amazingly, the dwarf managed to thrust his axe behind his back with blinding speed, deflecting the blow. The weapons were enchanted, indeed.

At least, up to a point. While the axe did prevent Fandral from slicing into the dwarf's back, it did not prevent the Asgardian from slicing into the axe's haft, which shattered in two, the blade falling to the grassy ground with a thud.

Helger whirled around, staring at the broken haft in his hand, now little more than a splintered club. "This is not *possible*!"

"As Volstagg said, there was perhaps a reason why your weapons were kept in Eitri's forge."

The dwarf pulled a sword from a scabbard that Fandral hadn't even noticed up to that point, so focused was he on the axe.

"It matters little. You will die this day, goldenhair."

Grinning, Fandral said, "Many have faced me with a sword and said those words. All of them were quite mistaken."

Helger said nothing in reply, and simply ran forward, swinging the sword with an easily parried overhead strike.

Fandral was relieved to see that Helger wielded this sword with simply average speed. This was obviously the dwarf's own blade.

So Fandral made a quick side strike, but the dwarf parried that, as well. Though he no longer wielded an enchanted weapon, he still had plenty of skill with the sword, and Fandral quickly realized that Helger was not to be underestimated as an opponent.

But neither was Fandral.

Over several strokes, they took each other's measure. Helger's techniques were broad but quick, and Fandral found no openings.

But Helger was unable to score any strikes upon Fandral's person, either.

However, the dwarf did push Fandral back toward one of the larger oaks of the forest. Surrounded by inclines on either side, it formed a bit of a cul-de-sac, and Fandral found himself backed into it.

When he was a youth and training in swordplay with Tyr, one of the things the warlord had always drilled into his charges was that whenever a foe advances upon you, do not let that opponent drive you straight backward. "Always," Tyr had said, "shift yourself to your left or to your right. Do not let your opponent control the battle, but force him to change direction with you."

While Fandral had forgotten that particular lesson as he found himself backed against the thick oak, he did recall another: "Use the entire ground available to you."

So Fandral leapt up onto a low-hanging tree branch.

Helger stared in surprise, not expecting such a maneuver.

Fandral took advantage and, balancing himself on the thick branch, swung downward toward the dwarf's head.

Somehow, Helger managed to get his sword up in time, but then Fandral swung for the dwarf's neck. Helger awkwardly blocked that as well, but the parry set the dwarf off balance, and he stumbled.

Thinking to press his advantage, Fandral shuffled farther down the branch to get into a better position to strike once again.

But the dwarf recovered his footing and slashed wildly, missing Fandral entirely and instead slicing into the branch itself.

Fandral's laughter at the dwarf's poor aim was short lived as the branch shifted beneath his feet. While Helger hadn't been able to slice through the thick wood, his blow had weakened it to the point where it could no longer support the weight of the Asgardian.

As the bough bent, Fandral leapt off of it, using the branch the way divers on Midgard used boards in their swimming pools. Doing an impressive front flip (if he thought so himself), he landed on the other side of the dwarf.

"Well played!"

Helger declined to reply, instead pressing his attack. This time, though, Fandral remembered his training and shuffled to the left, forcing Helger to also change direction.

Onward they dueled, moving swiftly about the clearing. The clanging of sword on sword echoed off the trees.

At once, Fandral was both thrilled and concerned. The latter because he had come very close to defeat on more than one occasion in this clash. Helger was as fine a swordsman as Fandral had ever faced, and the dwarf's sword came far closer to tasting Fandral's blood than the blond-haired Aesir was at all comfortable with. The former, in truth, for the same reason. This was the finest duel Fandral had fought since he, Hogun, and Volstagg's first journey together in pursuit of the Fenris Wolf, when Fandral had faced Glarin of the Sword.

But Helger did not have any sorcerous advantage on his side, as Glarin had. Not since Helger had lost his magickal weapon.

They continued to clash until Fimbuldraugr's pommel met with the hilt of Helger's sword, and both combatants found their weapons temporarily interlocked. Helger pulled, and Fandral pulled, yet the weapons did not disentangle, and neither combatant would let go of his hilt.

So Fandral kicked Helger in the stomach.

But Helger did not let go, and as he stumbled backward, he pulled Fandral with him, and the two fell to the ground.

For a moment, both Aesir and dwarf were caught in a tangle of arms, legs, and steel, but Fandral managed to extricate himself and get to his feet.

Helger did likewise, but their swords were still entwined on the ground.

They exchanged a quick glance, then both dived for the swords.

Instead, they crashed into each other, Fandral's head striking Helger's chest. Thinking quickly, Fandral grabbed Helger's shoulders and tried to throw him aside, but Helger grabbed Fandral's arms and counteracted Fandral's move.

For several seconds the two grappled, neither able to gain the upper hand.

Fandral then leant back, surprising Helger, who had expected Fandral to push or twist, not to retreat. But that moment of surprise was enough for Helger to loosen his grip for but a second, and Fandral pressed that advantage, throwing Helger onto his back and pinning his shoulders.

Now crouched atop Helger's chest, Fandral punched the dwarf twice in the face. Blood flew from his foe's nose, and Fandral could see in the dwarf's eyes that the blows had made him insensate, at least, for a moment. Leaping to his feet, Fandral dashed to where their swords had fallen and extricated Fimbuldraugr before tossing Helger's sword into the forest.

Holding up the blade, Fandral said, "Yield, Helger! There is no dishonor in surrendering to a superior foe! Surrender, and we shall grant you leave to return to Nidavellir—or elsewhere, if you prefer not to return to Eitri's domain."

Helger laughed mirthlessly. "Superior foe, goldenhair? Hardly. Never will I yield to the likes of you!"

"So be it." Fandral said the words sadly.

Inevitably, Helger charged at Fandral. Just as inevitably, Fandral ran him through with Fimbuldraugr.

Helger's face twisted as the life fled from his body and his soul fled to Hela. Fandral lowered his arm, and Helger's body slumped to the ground, blood pooling underneath and soaking into the dirt and grass.

Fandral turned to face the other two dwarves, who still held their weapons on Volstagg and Hogun.

"Your leader is dead. The weakness of your weapons has been exposed. A choice have you: take his body and abandon all thoughts of invading Asgard, or suffer the same fate as he."

The two dwarves looked at each other.

Then they looked at Fandral.

Then they looked at Helger's dead body.

Then they looked at Volstagg and Hogun. The Voluminous One was smiling beatifically. The Grim One simply scowled. It was an open question which expression frightened the dwarves more: the two warriors', or the look of sad determination on Fandral's visage.

And then, finally, they threw down their weapons.

"Wise choice." Only then did Fandral walk over to Gulltoppr and remove a cloth from the saddlebag with which to clean Fimbuldraugr.

One dwarf grabbed Helger's legs, while the other grabbed him under the shoulders. The latter said, "'Twas all Helger's notion, truly. 'Don't do it,' we said. 'Bad idea,' we said. 'The Aesir are nasty,' we said. But he *would* insist!"

The other dwarf whispered, "Will you be *silent*?"

Hogun leapt to his feet. Volstagg clambered upright somewhat more laboriously.

"Are you well?" Fandral asked his comrades as he wiped the dwarf's blood off his steel.

Concerned at the look on Fandral's face, Volstagg said gently, "That was to be my question for you, my friend."

Fandral smiled grimly. "I am victorious, Volstagg. Is that not all that matters?" But then the smile fell. "I merely lament the loss of an excellent swordsman. He was as fine a foe as ever I have faced. I was loath to end him, for were our task not so critical, I would gladly have dueled him until Ragnarok. I dislike the waste."

Hogun put a hand on Fandral's shoulder. "Our task is indeed critical, and we must move on."

Nodding, Fandral mounted Gulltoppr.

Checking Kolr to make sure the mace blow had not injured the steed too badly, Hogun said, "We must ride as quickly as the forest will allow."

As he hauled his bulk onto Iron Shanks, Volstagg said, "While the dwarf was indeed decent with his blade, I'd hardly rank him in the category of 'excellent.' In truth, I saw much finer swordsmen in Thrudheim in my youth. I can assure you, good Fandral, that you would have thrashed any of those swordsmen with even greater ease than you thrashed this dwarf. Although not, of course, as easily as I did thrash them back in the day."

Unable to help himself, Fandral laughed. "Without even benefit of a weapon, I'd wager?"

"Of course not, for the Lion of Asgard was able to rend his foes limb from limb with his bare hands!"

And so the Warriors Three continued onward toward Jotunheim.

CHAPTER SEVEN

Hilde had had no idea how much *work* being ruler of Asgard was.

What impressed her the most, though, was how well Odin handled it when in front of people.

When the various chamberlains and ministers and bureaucrats came into the throne room with issues that required a decision from the All-Father, Odin actually managed to thoughtfully consider each request and make a decision.

However, Hilde soon realized that it wasn't as impressive as she'd hoped. For starters, it was obvious that each of the petitioners were confused as to why it was taking Odin so *long* to come to his decisions.

It was the minister in charge of Asgard's thoroughfares who finally voiced those concerns. "It is a simple question, Lord Odin," he said testily. "May I replace the paving stones near the Temple of Titans? They were badly broken during that rather unfortunate battle with the trolls last month. Your son's lightning and the Lady Sif's sword strikes were particularly damaging—not to mention Volstagg's very weight. Honestly, I wish I could ban him from the city altogether. In any event, All-Father, it is a simple question that only requires a simple answer, not the dillydallying of—"

"*Silence*!"

The minister recoiled as if he'd been slapped.

"You will cease your prattle, minister, lest Odin forget that you are a valued member of his court, and instead treats you like the babbling buffoon you make yourself out to be this day! Know you that I consider *all* entreaties to the throne, and do not wish to rush into *any* such that affect the well-being of the Realm Eternal—even so *inconsequential* a matter as yours!"

Immediately falling to his knees, the minister said, "My deepest apologies, Lord Odin. I misspoke only out of surprise and concern, as you usually reply to my entreaties with more . . . dispatch."

"These are trying times, minister," Odin said gravely. "The Golden Apples are . . . endangered, and we must be vigilant. No decision may be made lightly. However, in this case, I believe that it would be well for the paving stones near the Temple of Titans to be replaced. So be it!"

Getting to his feet, but continuing to bow, the minister said, "My thanks, Lord Odin." He swiftly left the throne room.

As soon as he was gone, Odin slumped in his throne and let out a low moan.

Hilde grew even more frightened. She had seen many things in her years, from a freed Fenris Wolf, to Malekith's attempt to take over Asgard, to Sif fighting two dragons, but even with all that, the thing that scared her more than anything else was seeing Odin look and sound exactly like her father did after a big meal.

"That was really impressive," she said, trying to buck the All-Father up.

"It was also extremely difficult, Hilde."

Odin spoke in a raspy whisper, though Hilde was grateful that he at least got her name right. Over the course of the past several hours, he'd called her Sif, Frigga, Idunn, Brunnhilde, and Jane.

"Is anyone else supposed to come by?" she asked.

"Even if there is, I shall have my vizier reschedule them. I must have the bedchamber royal prepared, as needs must I sleep for a time to recover my faculties."

Before Odin could give that order, however, the door to the throne room opened and the vizier entered, followed by two women. Hilde recognized them—one was Yngvild, the wife of the blacksmith, the other, her sister. Alaric sometimes played with their children. Hilde never joined them because their oldest child, Menglad, was kind of a creep, and Alaric always got creepier when Menglad was around.

"Forgive me, All-Father," the vizier said without prompting upon walking in, "but Yngvild and Erika have been waiting all day, and they say their need is urgent."

Odin let out a long sigh, and his head slumped forward a bit more.

The vizier took that for a nod of assent, and led the two women before the throne. Hilde winced, as she was pretty sure that Odin wanted to say no, but was too tired to even do that.

Yelling at the minister had taken a lot more out of him than she would have believed possible.

The two women got down on their knees, and Erika said, "We apologize for the intrusion, Lord Odin, and we would not disturb you during this crisis if our need were not so great."

Wearily, Odin managed to utter the word, "Speak."

Yngvild nodded and did as she was bid. "My sister and I have four children between us, and three of our children, as well as my husband the blacksmith, are very ill. The Healer Royal has been by to see them, but none of her remedies have had any effect. They *need* the apples."

Quickly, Erika added, "We understand why you must keep the apples hidden from the giant, but our need is great."

For several moments, Odin simply stared blankly with his one good eye at the two women. "I—"

But then he trailed off.

Hilde finally stepped forward. "You must forgive the All-Father, but he has spent most of the day reinforcing a very powerful spell!"

Erika and Yngvild exchanged confused glances. "I'm sorry?"

"It—it isn't just the giant Thjasse who is after the Golden Apples of Immortality. He's convinced a dragon to help him out! It's an evil dragon named Regin, and he has the power to . . . to sense the apples, no matter where they are! You see, that's why Lord Odin had to hide the apples—not just physically, but to make it impossible for the dragon to *sense* them, as well. It takes a *huge* spell, and it's so complicated that Odin can't take any of the apples away from the hiding place. If he does, it'll ruin the spell!"

"Oh dear."

Biting her lip, Hilde said, "I'm so sorry about your husband and kids. I know my brother likes them a lot."

Yngvild frowned. "You are Alaric's sister?"

Hilde nodded.

"Honestly, I think your brother is a terrible influence on poor Menglad. He's a much better behaved boy when Alaric isn't around."

Erika put a hand on her sister's arm and gave her a scolding look. "Now isn't the time for that, Yngvild."

Under any other circumstance, Hilde might have giggled.

Odin finally spoke, albeit in a very heavy voice. "Even as we speak, noble ladies, the Warriors Three are journeying to defeat both Thjasse and . . . and the dragon. Once we have received word that they have been victorious, you may rest assured that the blacksmith will be the first whom I ask Idunn to supply when the apples are retrieved."

Still kneeling, the two women bowed their heads to the floor. "We thank you, Lord Odin," Yngvild said.

"And our thoughts are with Hilde's father and his two companions," Erika added. "May their sword arms be strong and their horses swift."

Getting to their feet, the blacksmith's wife and her sister departed from the throne room.

Once they were gone, Odin turned his weary gaze upon

Hilde. "Well spoken, young Hildegard. The Realm Eternal owes you a debt it may never be able to repay."

Hilde blushed. "Thank you, All-Father. I'm just trying to help."

Slowly, and with a very loud groan, Odin got to his feet. "Now then, prepare the bedchamber royal!"

As Odin worked his way to an obviously very badly needed nap, Hilde wondered how her father, Fandral, and Hogun were doing. If they didn't get back soon, people were going to start *dying*. And as much as she didn't like Menglad, she didn't want him to even be sick, much less dead.

Nervously, she went to the kitchen in hopes of getting something to eat. She had nothing like her father's appetite—no one had anything like Volstagg's appetite—but she was getting hungry. And she had the feeling that her crazy dragon story wasn't the last time Odin was going to need her help before this was over.

CHAPTER EIGHT

"And then, of course, I had to teach the brigand a lesson. No one insults my Gudrun and gets away with it for long, and so I thrashed him within an inch of his life."

Fandral chuckled at Volstagg's words as they travelled the road that would take them around the final mountain before entering Jotunheim. "Was that before or after one of your hands was bound behind your back?"

Volstagg harrumphed. "Have you not been paying attention? *Both* my hands were behind my back!"

The trio rode single file along a path that went around the mountain. It was barely wide enough for the horses, with the mountain on one side of the path and only a cliff and air on the other side. Hogun took the lead, keeping a keen eye out for any more ambushes. Fandral took the middle, being amused by Volstagg's latest story of derring-do.

Astride Iron Shanks, Volstagg took up the rear, as was his wont. The uncharitable would say that he always chose to take up the rear out of cowardice—or because his bulk made it necessary for him to lag behind. Volstagg himself always insisted that it was safer for his opponents if he was kept from thrashing them all alone.

"So," Fandral said, "if both your hands were bound behind your back—and assuming that your hands could actually be brought to meet behind your girth—how, precisely, did this thrashing occur?"

"With kicks of great strength and power, of course! As a youth long ago, I was trained in the art of kicking by the legendary Sparka, master of the pedal arts. Employing the training given me by that great practitioner, I was able to smash the fool's leg with a kick to the knee, then quite literally take his breath away by directing my foot into his belly. He doubled over, trying desperately to catch his breath. In fact, during that very encounter, I finally understood one of the lessons the great Sparka had taught me in those days of my youth. You see, he referred to the kick to the upper part of the belly as the troll and the moon."

Fandral frowned. "Why would he call it that?"

"That, in fact, was my question to him, and so I did query him on the very subject. But he did not answer, and I—a brash, impetuous youth at the time—did not see it. However, when I kicked the brigand in the belly, he doubled over, unable to catch his breath. Then, at last, I understood the story. For you see, a troll is not a particularly bright specimen. And a troll might see the reflection of the moon in the water and grab for it. But the very act of grabbing it disrupts the water and the reflection disappears—at least until the water settles, at which point the moon returns. The troll continues to grab for the moon but is never able to grasp it."

His head now swimming, Fandral asked, "And what has this to do with a kick to the stomach?"

Volstagg grinned. "A properly placed kick will cause its victim to double over with an inability to catch his breath—he can no more gain a foothold on his breathing than that troll may gain a grip on the moon's reflection."

Nodding, Fandral said, "Ah, I see."

"And that is how I put the lessons of Sparka to use in that tavern."

"I find parts of this story difficult to credit, old friend," Fandral said with a chuckle.

"Only parts of it?" Hogun muttered as he gazed around the corner of the latest bend in the path.

"Ha!" Fandral acknowledged Hogun's skepticism, and then continued, "First of all, I doubt that this Sparka truly exists."

"Oh, he does," Hogun said.

Fandral did a double take. "How's that?"

"Volstagg speaks true when he says that Sparka was a master of the art of the kick. He was a legend amongst my people. According to that legend, his hands had been badly broken and did not heal properly, so he was unable to fight with them, nor could he properly hold a weapon. So he learnt how to balance himself, and then trained himself to kick in a manner that would cause the most harm to his opponents."

"I am not surprised," Volstagg said, "that Sparka's fame reached the land of your birth, Hogun."

"Oh yes," Hogun said. "And those stories all ended with

Sparka's death at the hands of Rimthursar, right before Odin defeated him."

Fandral whirled his head around to face Volstagg from over Gulltoppr's rump. "As I recall, you were an infant when Odin did battle with Rimthursar."

"Bah," Volstagg muttered. "What does it matter? It was all some time ago. In any case, that was the least of my problems. You see, I had thought the brigand to be alone—but he had friends."

"It is the way of brigands to have friends," Fandral said thoughtfully, "though I cannot for the life of me comprehend how that is so. After all, brigands are often disagreeable."

"So are their friends," Hogun muttered.

"Indeed!" Volstagg chuckled. "And these friends were *quite* distressing. They surrounded me and informed me that they would be hastening my journey to Hela's realm."

"Obviously," Fandral said dryly, "they were unsuccessful."

"Well, obviously, yes. I did warn them. I said, 'Be wary, my friends, for the Lion of Asgard's disagreement with your friend is over and done with. I have no quarrel with you, and it would pain me greatly to cause any of you harm.' Naturally, the brigands did not heed my sage advice—brigands almost never do—and they challenged me. So I did, very reluctantly, thrash them, as well."

"All three of them?" Fandral asked.

"I believe I said there were six," Volstagg replied with a nod.

Fandral grinned. "In fact, you gave no number, but I'm not surprised at you raising the figure from my guess."

"Regardless, I grabbed two of them and slammed their fool heads together."

"An impressive accomplishment," Fandral said, "with both hands bound behind your back."

Without missing a beat, Volstagg said, "Oh, by the time the ten friends had surrounded me, I had had the opportunity to rend my bonds with the assistance of a kitchen wench in the tavern, who was carrying a knife. In any event, what matters is that all dozen of them fell by my hand, at which point I gladly bought a round for everyone in the tavern who was still conscious."

"A fine tale," Fandral said, "worthy of being made into a song."

"Yes, well, I did approach that bard who plays at the tavern about putting the story to song, but he seemed strangely uninterested."

"Imagine tha—"

"Hold!" Hogun interrupted Fandral, holding up his hand and bringing Kolr to a halt.

Behind him, the other two also stopped.

"There's an ambu—"

The rest of Hogun's words were cut off by a giant log that swung down from a nearby tree, knocking both Hogun and Fandral off their mounts.

A troll leapt down from the same tree, cackling.

"A prize, a prize, a prize! Nay, two prizes! Two Aesir are mine, with the rest to follow!"

"Hardly, knave!" Volstagg said. "You may have defeated Hogun the Grim and Fandral the Dashing, but still have you Volstagg the Voluminous to contend with. You will find that defeating me is a far greater challenge."

"No challenge at all!" the troll cried. "Asgard is ripe for the taking!"

"Your fellow troll, Baugi, made such an attempt not long ago, and—with some small aid from my comrades—I did thrash him and banish him back to the Realm Below."

"Ah, yes, but Baugi was a fool, and I am not! Besides, Asgard is weak! Thor is abed following a battle with Hrungnir, and Sif is the same after warring against dragons. As for Balder, he is trapped in Nornheim, no doubt a prisoner of Karnilla. And now the Warriors Three have been brought low. Tell me, fat one, would now not be the best time to take Asgard?"

"You have *not* brought low the Warriors Three, my dear troll, for as you can see, only two lie wounded on the path thanks to your treacherous attack. We are not referred to as the Warriors Two, after all."

"And what will you do that these two could not?"

"Oh, I could easily wring your neck—but that would not be sporting, now, would it? After all, the Lion of Asgard's fury is a terror to behold, and I would not unleash it if it were not necessary."

The troll moved toward Volstagg, who was still mounted on Iron Shanks. "Sporting, you say? Do you propose a wager?"

Volstagg had, in fact, been stalling in the hope that Hogun or Fandral would come to their senses and leap into battle from behind, thus catching the troll unawares, but they lay still upon the dirt. He was grateful that the log had not, at least, struck them with enough intensity to knock them over the cliff. Even as strong as they both were, Volstagg's boon companions would like to have been killed by such a fall.

However, he was hardly about to pass up the opportunity the troll was providing. "A wager indeed! Shall we compete in feats of strength? Feats of bravery? Feats of appetite?"

"I would hardly engage in a contest of appetites with one of your girth, fat one."

Unable to help himself, Volstagg smirked. "You are wiser than you appear, troll—though that would not be difficult."

"I doubt the same can be said for you, as it is said that one who boasts is a great fool indeed. So I challenge you to a battle of wits! We shall each ask the other a riddle."

Volstagg nodded. "A fair and good competition!"

"If you are ill to the task of answering my riddle, the three of you shall go over the cliff, and I will continue to Asgard and conquer it."

"If you're able, yes. And should your reply to my conundrum prove to be incorrect, you will return to the Realm Below and allow the three of us to go on our merry way."

"And what way might that be, Voluminous One?"

"Is that your first riddle, troll, or an attempt to gain intelligence?"

The troll grinned. "I would never seek intelligence from you, vainglorious Aesir."

"Because you know the Lion of Asgard would never reveal such secrets to one such as you."

"No, because the Lion of Asgard is, as I said, a fool. Which I will prove ere long."

Volstagg chuckled. "If we each answer each other's riddle, what then?"

"We continue until one does not."

"Agreed."

The troll moved closer to the prone forms of Hogun and Fandral. "Do not attempt to cheat, Asgardian, for if I detect any indication of such, over the cliff your friends shall go."

"My good troll, the Lion of Asgard would *never* cheat! Speak your riddle, and I shall dazzle you with my quick delivery of the answer."

"Very well. What begins its journey on four legs, continues it on two, and ends it on three?"

Volstagg shook his head. If the troll thought him *this* dense, this contest would end quickly. "A mortal journeying through life—four legs while crawling as an infant, two legs through childhood and adulthood, and with a cane as a third leg in the infirmity of old age. Perhaps you thought I would struggle with the final aspect of that, but I have known many mortals of Midgard in my time, and seen them age and die."

"Very well," the troll said bitterly, for he had indeed believed that Volstagg's immortality would prevent him from eliciting the meaning of the final third of the riddle. "Take your turn!"

"A man came upon a family inside a fishing boat. He asked

the family, 'How fare you?' In response, they said, 'What we catch, we throw back, but what we do not catch, we keep.' To what were they referring?"

The troll rubbed his chin, and then grinned. "Lice."

"Well played," Volstagg said. He had not expected a denizen of the Realm Below to know of the difficulties that those who sailed had with head lice. Volstagg himself had had plenty of experiences with lice during the seafaring of his long-ago youth.

Leaning in closer to Volstagg, the troll asked, "What has a single eye but can see nothing?"

"Assuming you are not making a jest at the expense of the All-Father, I would say a storm."

Snorting, the troll said, "I would have expected you to say 'a potato,' but your answer will do."

Volstagg stroked his beard thoughtfully. "What runs, but never walks; has a mouth, but does not speak; has a bed, but cannot sleep; and has a head, but is incapable of weeping?"

This one stumped the troll for many seconds, and for a moment, Volstagg allowed himself to think he had won. But then the troll snapped his fingers and cried out, "A river!"

"Indeed," Volstagg said dolefully.

"How far may a stag walk into the Forest of Sigurd?"

"My children could answer that one," Volstagg said disdainfully. "Halfway. After that, the stag is walking *out* of the forest. Feed me and I grow, but give me water and I die. What am I?"

"A fire. Where may you find roads with no carts, forests with no trees, villages with no houses, and rivers with no water?"

"A map. What has arms but no hands, and a face but no head?"

"A clock. What has a head and a tail, but no body?"

"A coin." Volstagg was starting to actually enjoy this, though he was always mindful that the lives of Hogun and Fandral hung in the balance. "What question can never be answered in the affirmative?"

The troll was at a loss at first, but when he turned away to ponder, he saw Fandral and Hogun still insensate and the answer came to him. "'Are you asleep?' What turns everything around, but does not move?"

Volstagg actually struggled with that one a moment before it came to him. "A mirror. I am a container with no corner or side, but I hold a golden treasure inside me. What am I?"

"An egg—like which I will break you when I win this contest, fat one."

Volstagg chuckled. "Sticks and stones, droll troll." He did not add that this was one contest where words *would* hurt. "Speak your next conundrum!"

The troll sighed. "It is boneless, straining against that which covers it. It may be gripped with one's hands in an endeavor to bring satisfaction. A woman may cover it with her apron. What is it?"

"Dough," Volstagg said simply.

"You didn't disappoint on that occasion," the troll said with a chuckle.

Out of the corner of his eye, Volstagg noticed Hogun stirring.

And so he decided to use the most difficult riddle he knew. In truth, he had not expected to need it, for he had never dreamed that this, or indeed *any*, troll would have the intellectual wherewithal to last this long in such a contest.

Volstagg had first heard this riddle centuries ago on Midgard, and he'd challenged each of his children with it once they were old enough to figure it out. Hilde was the only one of his children to get it right away.

"An Aesir arrives at two doors. One door will lead to Asgard and freedom, the other to Niffleheim and death, but the warrior knows not which is which. Each door has a guardian—one who always lies, the other who always tells the truth. But again, the Aesir does not know which is which. What is the one question the warrior may ask that will lead him to the door to Asgard?"

The troll frowned. "What?"

"Shall I repeat the—"

"No!" The troll paced angrily and muttered to himself. "One lies, and one tells the truth. But you don't know which is which. So you can ask them anything, but you don't know if it's the liar or the truth-sayer."

Volstagg watched with amusement as the troll turned the problem over in his head, pacing back and forth in an ever-longer parabola, to the point where he wondered whether the troll might pace all the way over the cliff.

His own older children had struggled with this riddle also, and in fact, the troll's mutterings and perambulations were almost a perfect match for those of Alaric when Volstagg had posed the riddle to him years before.

The troll proposed and rejected to himself many possible questions for the hypothetical warrior to ask. At last, his shoulders slumped, he ceased his pacing and stood before Volstagg, abashed. "I do not know the answer. Tell me."

Smiling, Volstagg said, "The question the warrior must pose is to ask one of the guardians the following: 'If I ask your fellow guardian what door he guards, what will he say?' If he says, 'Asgard,' then the guardian you asked guards Asgard, for either he is the one who tells the truth—in which case his companion will lie and say 'Asgard'—or he is the one who lies—in which case the other guardian is the truth-speaker, and the guardian to whom you spoke has lied about what his companion will say. If the answer is 'Niffleheim,' then the other door leads to Asgard, for the same reason."

"You tricked me!"

Volstagg drew himself up to his full height. "I did no such thing! I posed a riddle, and you failed to answer it! Now then, return yourself to the Realm Below. Fandral, Hogun, and I have important business of Asgard to attend to, and your foolishness is keeping us from it!"

The troll, however, was unimpressed by Volstagg's bellowing. "I repeat, Aesir, you tricked me, weaving fell magick with your words, and I shall not stand for it! You will die, as will your fellows!"

"I think not."

Whirling around at the new voice, the troll saw that Fandral was standing upright, pointing Fimbuldraugr at the troll's chest.

"So, you're awake, goldenhair. Not for long will you—"

"Volstagg did wager with you, and you did agree to abide by it. It is difficult enough to trust the word of trolls, but if you go back on your promise now, the word of trolls will evermore mean *nothing* throughout the Nine Worlds."

The troll hesitated.

Volstagg added, "Will you truly damn all trolls with your actions? Your kind have always fulfilled their bargains. To destroy that tradition now would—"

"Enough!" The troll shook his head. "I will return to the Realm Below as promised. But know that some day I will have my vengeance upon Volstagg the Voluminous for his verbal trickery this day!"

"Will you, now?" Fandral asked in a dangerous voice.

"As you so generously reminded me, Asgardian, we trolls are known for our bargains. I will allow you passage through the mountain unmolested, but I also promise you this: the insult I have borne this day will ne'er be forgotten by me or mine." He stared at Volstagg. "There will come a day when you least expect it, fat one, that you will find the blade of a troll penetrating your corpulence. That day will be your last."

With that, the troll leapt back up into the tree from which he'd engaged his ambush.

"Disagreeable fellow, is he not?" Volstagg asked.

From the ground near the cliff, a moan escaped Hogun's lips.

Fandral dashed to his side and helped the Grim One to his feet.

"Are you well, old friend?"

Slowly, Hogun nodded. "The ringing in my head should abate with time. And even should it not, it would matter little, for we must be away and quickly. With each hour that passes without the apples, Loki's spell brings the Realm Eternal closer to ruin."

As he mounted Iron Shanks, Volstagg harrumphed. "Well, we would have arrived by now if you two weren't lounging about, leaving me to do all the hard work."

Rolling his eyes as he mounted Gulltoppr, Fandral said, "Naturally."

Leaping atop Kolr, Hogun urgently said, "Let us *go*. We must tarry no longer!"

And so the trio rode up the mountain path. The road was too narrow for a full gallop, but they did canter much faster than they had earlier, out of fear for how Asgard was faring without the apples.

CHAPTER NINE

Hilde wasn't sure what she should be doing now that Odin was asleep. The vizier had also taken to his bed, and the guards outside the throne room had been instructed to turn away all who approached and give them instructions to return when Odin awakened. The only exception to that order would be the return of the Warriors Three.

She felt weird just sitting inside the big throne room all by herself, but she couldn't really go home. Mother was still annoyed at her for leaving without permission to follow Sif, and Alaric was sulking around the house. He was mad because everyone was talking about Hilde and Sif's adventure in Flodbjerge, and about how great Hilde had been to help the mighty Sif like that, but nobody ever talked about how Hilde had gone on that adventure by sneaking out of her room, and that she had been confined to her room because she had beat up Alaric.

Of course, when Alaric was bemoaning Hilde's newfound fame, he neglected to mention that the only reason why Hilde had beat him up was because he had ruined the hunting knife that Father had promised to her . . .

Either way, going home was a poor option for Hilde, what with Mother's anger and Alaric's whining. So she decided instead to check on Sif.

When she arrived at Sif's home, Hilde was disappointed to see that the warrior was asleep. Hilde was about to turn and leave, but in a groggy voice, Sif muttered, "Who's 'ere?"

"It's Hilde."

"Good. 'F 'twas an 'truder, I haven't strength to kill 'em."

Rubbing her eyes, Sif sat up in her bed, wincing in pain.

"Your arms and legs still hurt?" Hilde asked.

"Indeed. They *were* improving, but over the past four days, everything has grown worse."

Hilde shook her head and sighed. "I hope the Warriors Three get the apples back soon."

"What?"

Now it was Hilde's turn to wince. Sif had probably noticed that she hadn't gotten her monthly allotment of the Golden Apples, but she hadn't heard the details. "Um, it's nothing."

Sif's hair was tousled, her eyes bloodshot, her face wrinkled, and her skin pale. She looked as pathetic as it was possible for her to look. And *still* she glared at Hilde in a manner that made the girl extremely apprehensive.

Very slowly, Sif said, "Tell me."

With a sigh, Hilde sat at the foot of Sif's bed and filled her in on what was going on.

Sif moved to throw the bedclothes off herself.

Leaping to her feet, Hilde asked, "What are you doing?"

"I cannot simply tarry in my bed while your father, Fandral, and Hogun work to save Asgard. I must—" But as soon as Sif's feet touched the floor and she shifted her weight onto them, she collapsed.

Hilde moved to aid Sif, but the warrior held up a hand. "I will be fine."

"Sif, you're *injured*. You can't help anyone if you can't even stand up."

Bracing herself on the bed, Sif clambered to her feet. "I am perfectly capable of standing—"

Again she shifted her weight from her arms against the bed to her feet on the floor.

Again she collapsed.

"—on my own," she finished dolefully.

"Sif . . ."

"Yes, yes." Once more, she braced herself on the bed and hauled herself upward, but this time it was to lie back down upon it. "As I said, I have grown worse. I was able to stand for several minutes only a day ago."

"So has everyone else—gotten worse, I mean." Hilde stood now by the side of Sif's bed. "It's the spell."

"It is well that Loki has used his magicks to aid the Warriors Three. Even with that, I may well sever his head from his body when next we meet for reducing me to *this*."

"It's not Loki's fault." Hilde sighed. "Look, you were badly hurt by those two dragons. You'd probably still be stuck in bed right now even if Loki hadn't been involved."

"Do not underestimate the appeal of severing Loki's head, Hilde," Sif said with a smile.

They sat a bit longer until Sif, exhausted from the ordeal of trying to stand, fell asleep again.

Tiptoeing out of the house, Hilde decided to also check in on Thor.

The thunder god was actually awake when Hilde came in. He was reading a codex book that looked like the type they made on Midgard. Father had brought back several such books when he'd visited that world. It didn't surprise Hilde that Thor had such tomes—he spent a considerable amount of time on Midgard, after all.

Thor put aside the volume when Hilde entered and gave her a big smile. She glanced at the book and saw that it was called *Riders of the Purple Sage.*

"Ah, Hilde! I had hoped to see your father and his boon companions, but I will gladly accept your company! How fare you?"

"I'm okay. What's that you were reading?"

Glancing down at the book, Thor's smile became even warmer. "'Twas a gift from one of my fellow Avengers, Captain America. It is an adventure story that is worthy of the great battles of Asgard. As I am trapped in this bed until my bones do mend, it is a pleasant palliative. But speak! Tell me why neither Balder nor the Warriors Three have graced the thunder god's presence this day!"

"Well, they all are busy on a mission for the All-Father."

The smile fell. "A mission? What events have bestirred about Asgard that require their strong right arms?"

So for the second time that afternoon, Hilde regaled a hero of Asgard with the tale of Thjasse's theft of the Golden Apples.

Thor shook his head. "I should have known that there was a sorcerous explanation for my sudden slow healing—and that there was more to the missing apples than I had been told. And I also should have known that the Frost Giants would not be content to lick their wounds after I defeated Hrungnir." He threw off his bedclothes.

Thrusting out a hand, Hilde said, "No, Thor, don't!"

However, the thunder god didn't even make it as far as Sif had. Sweat beaded on Thor's brow as he tried to rise from the bed, every movement causing him great anguish.

"Hel's teeth," Thor muttered. "Calamity has fallen the Realm Eternal, and her champion is lying abed like the meanest slug."

"You're not a slug, Thor, you're hurt. You need to heal."

Thor shook his head. "So the Healer Royal has informed me repeatedly." He put a large hand on Hilde's small one. "My thanks, young Hildegard, for informing me of the goings-on. And I am grateful that you are assisting Odin."

"That was Hogun's idea," she said proudly.

"Wise is the Grim One. I owe much to him." Thor sighed. "Why, I recall one occasion when several warriors of Asgard set sail to determine who had cracked the great Odinsword. The danger was great, for any who could crack the Over Sword of

Odin could do incomparable damage to the Nine Worlds. For that reason, we were accepting of any who might wish to join us, even a few brigands. Indeed, my treacherous brother Loki was cocaptain of the mission with me, for we neither of us wished to see the destruction of everything."

"Hogun was on the mission?"

"Aye, and your father, and Fandral. As were two of those brigands I mentioned—Magrat and Kroda. They attempted to kill me just as our journey commenced, but Hogun did wordlessly stop them. He simply threw his dagger between them without a word, stopping their attempted assassination. While he let them live, that they may continue to battle for the safety of the Realm Eternal, he also made it clear to them that he was watching, and would brook no more perfidy from them."

"Then what happened?"

"We sailed through the Nine Worlds, facing the stone dragon of Utgard and Queen Ula of the flying trolls. Loki did also mutiny 'gainst my command rather than risk facing the stone dragon, and only Balder and the Warriors Three stood by my side. But it was enough, as Fandral's swordplay, Hogun's fierceness, and your father's girth joined forces with Mjolnir and me to cease the mutiny, even as Balder was able to destroy the dragon, thus negating the need for mutiny." Thor smiled happily. "That was the start of a long string of adventures I went upon with that noble trio. We faced Harokin, the bold, and Fafnir, the dragon, and Mogul of the Mystic Mountain. Never could I ask for better companions, whether in battle or in the mead hall."

Hilde grinned. "I bet my father is much more skilled in the mead hall."

"Indeed." Thor chuckled. "Would that I could fight by their side this day."

"Father said the same thing when you went off to fight Hrungnir."

Thor shot Hilde a look. "Did he?"

Nodding, Hilde said, "I mean, there's always more adventures to be had, more battles. It'd be great if you could all fight together all the time, but it doesn't work that way. Sometimes you're on Midgard with the Avengers, sometimes they're off fighting one bad guy while you're off fighting another one. It's just the way it works."

"You are indeed wise beyond your years, Hilde. I see why Volstagg speaks of you with such pride—as Sif does, as well."

"Father talks about me with pride?" Hilde's eyes widened. "*Sif*, too?"

"Indeed."

"Wow."

Suddenly, Thor let out a massive yawn—one so huge that Hilde thought for a moment that all of the air was being sucked out of the thunder god's bedchamber.

"My apologies, young Hilde, but it seems that the medicines prescribed by the Healer Royal are once again taking their toll. Needs must I rest."

Getting up from the foot of the bed, Hilde said, "I'm glad you're doing okay."

"In fact, I am rather far from that state, and fear that my condition will grow far worse if the Golden Apples are not recovered. But I have faith in the Warriors Three, just as I did centuries ago when we did battle against Fafnir, years ago against Surtur, and more recently against Hrungnir."

Hilde silently hoped that Thor was right. But if the apples weren't returned soon, she feared that neither Thor nor Sif—nor Balder, recovering in Nornheim—would heal their wounds. Odin was becoming more mentally fragmented, and Heimdall's ability to guard the rainbow bridge was deteriorating.

She headed back to the throne room, hoping that there wasn't another crisis, hoping that Odin would be able to continue to take his nap—

—and mostly hoping that her father, Hogun, and Fandral would save them all.

CHAPTER TEN

The castle of Hrungnir was singularly unimpressive.

"Thor had said that the giants' redoubt was lacking," Volstagg said as the trio approached over the snowy ground of Jotunheim, "but he truly undersold it."

"The place seems quiet, as well," Fandral said. "Perhaps when he took over leadership, Thjasse found a new place to house his rule."

"That would be unfortunate," Hogun said tightly. "Then we would be forced to search all of Jotunheim for the apples."

Volstagg indicated the land around the castle with one hand. "Behold all the debris. Broken stone, shattered trees—Thor did not exaggerate when he said it was a mighty battle 'tween him and Hrungnir."

With a grin, Fandral said, "Yes, well, we all find it better to leave exaggerations in tales of battle to *you*, who are so much more practiced in the art." Before Volstagg could respond to that slander, Fandral continued, "Regardless, we must search the keep. Even if Thjasse has abandoned it, there may be clues to his whereabouts."

"Agreed." Hogun had just nudged Kolr to gallop toward the castle when he noticed movement inside it. "Hold!"

The other two warriors followed Hogun's gaze, seeing movement in the outsized windows of the redoubt.

Moments later, ten giants stomped out from underneath the castle's portcullis.

"I smell Aesir!" one of them bellowed.

"You Asgardians are trespassing on Frost Giant land!" another cried. "You'd be well to turn tail and depart, lest you meet the same fate as the last person from your foul city who dared intrude upon us."

Fandral said, "As I recall, the person in question soundly defeated your leader, which led directly to his ouster."

A third giant chortled. "Yes, and then he needed to be aided in his departure by a feeble woman."

"Have a care, Frost Giant," Volstagg said in a low voice. "Speak ill of any man of Asgard if you wish, but do not presume to insult any lady from the same, least of all the Mother of Asgard!"

"If she is your mother," said a fourth, "'tis no wonder you're all fools and braggarts."

Before the banter could continue, Hogun spoke plainly. "Where is Thjasse? We would have words with him."

"I am Anborn," the first giant said. "I lead the Frost Giants who currently occupy this castle."

Hogun nodded. "Meaning Thjasse is not here."

"Where Thjasse is," Anborn said, "you will never find him."

Fandral grinned. "Do not underestimate our ability to track our foes, Anborn."

"Oh, I have no doubts regarding that, Asgardian. I have heard tales of Hogun the Grim and how he once tracked a leaf across the entirety of Skartheim. But no, I say that you will never find Thjasse because the three of you will be going straight from our domain to Hela's."

Unsheathing Fimbuldraugr, Fandral said, "Be warned, Anborn, that we are on a mission from Lord Odin himself, and it is one of grave import. Thjasse has done grievous harm to Asgard, and neither I, nor Hogun, nor Volstagg will rest until that harm is reversed."

Hogun added, "And we are not like to let a mere ten giants stand in our way."

"Mighty Volstagg has already triumphed over dwarves, trolls, and Storm Giants—with the aid of his boon companions, of course," the Voluminous One generously added, indicating Hogun and Fandral. "Do you imagine that any of us would have difficulty defeating you, as well?"

"Oh, if boasts and arrogance were weapons, we would be defeated already," Anborn said. "Alas, you will have to make do with those tiny blades you carry."

Foregoing his sword, Hogun unsheathed his mace. Both he and Fandral rode toward the giants.

Volstagg, however, stood his ground atop Iron Shanks. "This is your last chance to surrender, Frost Giant! Do so, and we will spare you from being thrashed soundly! Fail to do so, and you will not live to regret the action!"

Anborn's response was to shout, "Destroy them!" at the top of his lungs.

Shaking his head, Volstagg said, "Why do they never choose surrender? It's so much neater and simpler."

Squeezing his ample thighs, Volstagg urged Iron Shanks forward.

The steed did not move.

"Curse you, horse, *move*!" Volstagg bellowed.

Again he squeezed his thighs, but Iron Shanks lowered his head and licked the snow on the ground.

"Confound you!" Now Volstagg kicked the horse, something he did only when absolutely necessary.

But Iron Shanks remained recalcitrant.

"There is glory to be won! Giants to be defeated! Asgard to be saved!"

Iron Shanks continued to lick the snow.

"Curse you for being the only horse in the Nine Worlds who can properly carry my magnificence." Volstagg grumbled, and decided to dismount so he could join the battle properly. However, his left foot got caught in the stirrup. Pinwheeling his arms, he attempted to keep his balance, but it was a lost cause, and he fell facedown in the snow.

Meanwhile, Kolr and Gulltoppr showed more interest in joining the battle than Volstagg's mount did. They both galloped directly at the ten Frost Giants, Fandral and Hogun raising their weapons high from their seats on the horses' backs.

The tallest pair of the giants broke out in front of the other eight as they ran abreast toward the stampeding warriors.

With only a quick glance and a nod at each other, Hogun

and Fandral veered away from one another, the former toward one giant, the latter toward the other. The pair of warriors had been fighting together for so long that they no longer needed to communicate strategies with words—a mere look, and each knew what the other was thinking. Indeed, most of those strategies were but for the two of them, as Volstagg's own participation in their battles was always fraught with complication. Both men were second to none save perhaps Gudrun in their love for the Voluminous One, as well as in their respect for his prowess once he got onto the battlefield—it was getting him there that was sometimes problematic. And often, Volstagg employed his own unique tactics. Either way, Fandral and Hogun often had to fight as a pair for one reason or another, and they did so now with the ease of many centuries' practice.

Both horses were now at a full gallop, and the two giants were caught unawares by so brazen, and so speedy, an attack. Each tried to swing at the Asgardian nearest them, but each flailed only at air as the two riders moved swiftly past.

As they went by, Fandral struck his giant's left leg with his sword while Hogun did the same to his giant's right leg with his mace.

The two giants each cried out in pain and reached down to clutch their wounded legs, only to each lose their balance in much the same manner as Volstagg had while trying to get off his horse. They tumbled, falling toward each other, their heads colliding with a *thud* that echoed off the walls of the castle.

Even as both giants fell to the ground, sending snow flying

into the air, Hogun and Fandral rode on to face the other eight.

The riders narrowed their path, heading straight for the middle two giants, both Kolr and Gulltoppr running at a full gallop.

And then they rode straight between two giants' legs and toward the keep.

"Damn them!" Anborn cried. "Olav, Niels, take care of the fat one! The rest of you, after them!"

Olav and Niels nodded and moved toward Volstagg, who was still struggling to untangle himself from Iron Shanks's stirrup.

Anborn led the other five giants toward the castle. He was not pleased that the Warriors Three had only been there a few moments and yet had taken down two of the giants' number. Thjasse had left Anborn with strict instructions to kill *any* Asgardians who came to investigate the theft of the Golden Apples.

In truth, Anborn had been hoping that Balder or Sif would travel to Jotunheim to avenge the Asgardians. Balder had humiliated Utgard-Loki in his time, and Sif was rather comely by Aesir standards—Anborn would have enjoyed toying with her.

But alas, he was stuck with these three fools. Hardly the cream of Asgard's crop, and he expected that he would be able to deal with the vainglorious idiot, the dour warrior, and the fat fool with relative ease.

Inside the keep, Hogun and Fandral rode through the massive corridors, eventually finding themselves in the dining room. In the center was a massive oak table.

Grinning, Fandral unsheathed Fimbuldraugr, rode to one end of the table, and leapt from his horse to a position about halfway up the table leg. He hacked away at the leg with his sword until the leg snapped in two with a mighty crack.

Hogun, seeing Fandral's plan, rode his horse to the other end of the table.

The now-unsteady table rocked a bit, having lost a quarter of its support, but remaining upright for the moment. Fandral leapt down next to Gulltoppr, bending his knees and rolling over to an upright position before hopping back onto his horse. He had once made the mistake of leaping from a second-story window—a much shorter distance than what he traversed this day—right onto Gulltoppr's saddle, and the suddenness of his impact, as well as the location of same, left him barely able to walk for the next week. Since then, he'd made it a point to only leap from such heights to the spot *next* to his noble steed, especially given the sheer number of bedroom windows through which he'd needed to escape upon the unexpected return of angry husbands . . .

Fandral rode to the other leg on his end of the great table. He performed the same task with more dispatch this time, and that half of the table came crashing to the floor, sending cutlery, dishes, and mugs flying about the room.

Landing next to his horse once again, Fandral leapt atop Gulltoppr and sped to the other end of the table to join Hogun. His partner was already standing at the base of one of the still-intact legs, and Fandral moved to the other. Now they just had to wait.

In the distance, Hogun could hear the giants stomping through the keep, trying to figure out where the two warriors had gone.

Eventually, one giant stuck his head in the dining room. "What in Ymir's name happened *here*?" the giant bellowed upon seeing the broken table and scattered utensils.

Another giant joined him. "What's goin' on, Harald?"

"It's another mess. Can you believe this, Hrolf? And with Kare gone, who's gonna clean it up now?"

"Betcha Thjasse makes *us* do it 'cause we found it."

"Well, Thjasse ain't here, and Anborn better not try that with me. Otherwise, I'll tell Thjasse who it was who *really* broke his favorite axe last month."

Hogun and Fandral glanced at each other. Hogun mouthed the word *wait*.

Hrolf and Harald came into the room as they talked. Once both giants were standing at the broken end of the table, Hogun yelled, "Now!"

The two intact legs were at an angle, thanks to the table's current downward slope. Fandral and Hogun pulled the intact legs with their considerable strength in order to straighten them, which in turn pulled the broken end of the table upward right at Hrolf and Harald's jaws.

"Urk!"

"Ow!"

After straining to lift the table as high as they could, Hogun and Fandral let go of it, sending the far end of the table back down toward the floor, colliding with the tops of Harald and Hrolf's heads on the way down.

The two giants fell to the floor with a bone-jarring impact, their heads now underneath the table, and neither moved.

"That's four giants taken care of," Hogun said, "with two more outside for Volstagg. That leaves four for us."

Grinning, Fandral said, "Come, let us see what other traps we may lay for them!"

"There is one more we may lay here." Hogun pointed to the ceiling, where a candelabra hung by a chain.

Looking up, Fandral saw the possibility and laughed. He leapt atop Gulltoppr, using the steed as a jumping-off point to hop onto the intact end of the table; from there, another mighty jump brought him to the candelabra.

Climbing up the sconces, he saw that the links in the chain were old and worn, and badly maintained—much like the rest of the castle.

Using his dagger, Fandral sliced through the weakest of the links, severing it. The metal was strong enough to hold for now, but Fandral could see the slow buckle that breaking the link had caused.

He retraced his leaps back down the sconces, thence to the high part of the broken table, and down to the floor. "I estimate it will be a quarter of an hour at most before that comes crashing down on its own." He smiled. "Sooner if, say, a giant comes into the room with his heavy tread."

Hogun nodded. "Well done. Let us away."

Leaping back onto their horses, the pair rode through the dining room and several more massive corridors before reaching the kitchen.

In truth, Hogun smelled the kitchen before arriving at it. "This Kare, who Harald had said was now gone, apparently has been absent for several days."

Putting his hand over his nose, Fandral nodded. "Agreed. Perhaps try somewhere else?"

Hogun shook his head. "Nay, this is the perfect place to lay siege to the Frost Giants."

Outside, Volstagg continued his struggle to extricate himself from Iron Shanks's stirrup, his primary impediment being his inability to actually reach his feet with his hands. Yanking on the stirrup with his imprisoned left foot did no good, and no matter how much he tried to bend himself in two, his arms were simply not long enough to reach around his girth.

This was why the Lion of Asgard only wore boots that he could simply step into. That tendency had gotten him into trouble, of course. There was the one occasion when he had accidentally stepped into Gudrun's house shoes and had gone to see Lord Odin while wearing them. In all the years Volstagg had known the All-Father, it was the only time he'd heard Odin laugh so hard as to have trouble breathing. Thor and Balder, of course, guffawed; Fandral and Sif were also amused, and even Hogun had cracked a smirk.

Then, of course, there was the time that Svein and Alaric had put applesauce in his boots.

Finally, it occurred to Volstagg how to free himself: slide out of his boots. Only his left foot was entangled, after all, and he had become quite skilled at removing one boot with the other foot. Before he could indulge in this course of action, however, he heard the pounding of large feet upon snow-covered ground.

"Well, Olav, look here," one of the two Frost Giants who approached him said. "It's an Aesir already tied up for us."

"Too bad he isn't gagged, eh, Niels?"

"Be grateful, varlets, that I am bound, for you would surely be receiving a beating of the highest order from the Lion of Asgard!"

Olav look at Niels. "See what I mean? The hot air from his boasts'll prob'ly melt the snow."

"Let's put him out of our misery once'n for all."

Niels was about to put his words into action and grab Volstagg. However, Iron Shanks chose that moment to streak off at a full gallop, dragging Volstagg along with him, through the snow.

"Get them!" Olav cried.

"Oooooof! Ack! Apf!" Volstagg spit snow from his mouth as he bounced along behind the speeding mount.

The two giants had strides far greater than that of the horse, but the horse was quite swift, and also more agile. Iron Shanks regularly changed direction—which did nothing to make Volstagg's situation any happier—and the two giants darted about trying, and failing, to snag the steed.

At one point, Iron Shanks dashed between Olav's legs, and

Volstagg saw his opportunity. Reaching out, he gripped the giant's leather boot.

Volstagg's plan had been for the giant's bulk to provide a counterweight, thus forcing Iron Shanks to stop his forward motion. At worst, the jolt of Volstagg being tethered to something solid—and few things were more solid than a Frost Giant's leg—might serve to at least yank Volstagg's foot free of the entangled boot.

Neither of those circumstances came to pass. Instead, Iron Shanks kept going, taking the Frost Giant with him.

Volstagg's grip was strong enough that Olav's leg was upended. After a moment, Iron Shanks's speed forced Volstagg to let go, but by then Olav was completely off balance, and he fell to the ground.

As the Frost Giant fell, Volstagg heard a nasty crack. If he was very lucky, Olav had simply broken a bone on a rock.

That left only Niels to contend with.

Iron Shanks galloped toward the stump of what looked to have once been the base of a giant oak. Volstagg tried the same stratagem he'd used with Olav's foot, figuring the stump to be better rooted to the ground than the giant had been.

In that, he was correct. He was able to grab hold of the stump and stay there.

His left boot and his horse both continued on, unabated.

Volstagg had hoped to catch his breath and wipe the snow and dirt from his face, but Niels did not leave him with ample time for such an indulgence. The giant was almost upon him, so Volstagg reached for the first thing he could grab: a massive splinter that sat on the ground near the stump.

Even as Niels reached down to pick Volstagg up, the Lion of Asgard used all his might to shove the splinter into the giant's foot.

To Volstagg's shock, the splinter went all the way through Niels's foot and into the ground, effectively pinning the giant there.

Screaming in pain, Niels reached down to move his foot, which only made him cry out more pitifully.

Looking around, Volstagg saw that there were several such splinters. He picked one up. "Zounds! 'Tis petrified! What power could have so pulverized a petrified tree?"

Through gritted teeth, Niels said, "Hrungnir's stone armor." The giant was trying and failing to pull the splinter from his foot, but the splinter went too far into the frozen ground, and besides, while the splinter was large by Volstagg's lights, to the giant it was too small to even get a grip on.

"Ah, of course." Volstagg nodded. "The magickal armor that did such harm to Thor. I am not surprised that it could ravage this oak. Very well, then."

Getting to his feet, Volstagg immediately regretted the action, as he wore only one boot. The unshod foot stepped into the snow, which reminded Volstagg unfavorably of that time two of his sons had put applesauce in his boots.

Still, he *was* the Lion of Asgard, and it was unseemly for him to be put out by so minor an inconvenience as a wet foot.

Brushing the dirt and snow off of himself, Volstagg found another splinter of petrified wood, larger and sharper than the one currently embedded in Niels's foot.

"Now then, my good giant, the time has come to speak of important matters."

Snarling, Niels said, "I've nothing to say to you, Asgardian."

"Not even to tell me where Thjasse is?"

"*Especially* not that!"

"Pity." Volstagg took the splinter and shoved it into the giant's other foot.

"AAAAAAAAAAAAHHHHH! I'll *kill* you, fat fool!"

"Now now, let us not be hasty in wishing death on the person you wronged."

"You shoved petrified wood into my feet!"

Volstagg shook his head. "I speak of the theft of the Golden Apples of Immortality! Had you not committed this foul deed, we would not be at this sorry state of affairs. And we are but the first wave. Should we fail, the entirety of Asgard will come down upon you. I couldn't help but notice that there are fewer than a dozen of you. Some of you were captured by me and my friends when you attacked on the Ida Plain. I daresay others abandoned you after Hrungnir's defeat. No doubt Thjasse imagined that his campaign 'gainst Asgard would gain him more followers amongst your kind. And perhaps it would have worked, were it not for the Lion of Asgard and his two comrades. For we are here to put a stop to this once and for all. Now then—where is Thjasse?"

"I'll die before revealing anything to you, Aesir."

Volstagg shrugged. "So be it." He turned at the sound of hoofbeats, and saw Iron Shanks cantering slowly toward him. "Ah, *now* you slow up. Cantankerous beast."

The horse walked to Volstagg and nuzzled his face.

Bursting into a grin, Volstagg said, "Ah, my fine mount. I could not stay angry with you, Iron Shanks. Come, let me retrieve my boot and—" Staring down at the stirrup dangling off the side, he saw no sign of his boot. "Od's blood, where is my boot?"

Niels laughed. "Walking with one boot is but the first of many indignities that the Housecat of Asgard will suffer this day."

"'Housecat'? Oho, very droll, giant. I daresay that, were there two of you, you would comprise one whole wit." Volstagg bent over to pick up a few more shards of petrified oak—they had proven to be useful weapons—then awkwardly mounted his steed. "Come Iron Shanks, let us rejoin Fandral and Hogun. No doubt they are struggling mightily without the Lion of Asgard to aid them against these foul creatures."

As he rode toward the castle, Niels called after him, "Pray, Volstagg, that you are long gone from Jotunheim by the time I free myself from this trap you've put me in! For I will not rest until you are crushed beneath my heel!"

"I suspect you will not rest much, then," Volstagg said with a chuckle. "On, Iron Shanks!"

In the castle, Anborn stomped through the corridors, trying to find the two Aesir who had gone to ground in the Frost Giants' home.

It was embarrassing more than anything else. He and the others had been moving quickly through Hrungnir's erstwhile keep, and all they'd found were Hrolf and Harald, unconscious on the floor of a half-destroyed dining room.

As Anborn moved into the sitting room, he wondered whether he had perhaps underestimated the Warriors Three. He checked behind the chair where they had left Frigga, bound and gagged, while they had watched Thor battle Hrungnir.

Outside, in the hall, Torvald cried, "Hey, Anborn! Somethin's goin' on inna kitchen!"

Anborn winced. He'd been hoping to avoid the kitchen, as that had always been a wretched place to go. Bad enough when that stunted idiot Kare was there, but it had grown worse since Thjasse had gotten rid of the little twerp.

Following Torvald down the corridor that led to the kitchen in the back of the keep, Anborn saw that Yngvi and Ralf also stood in the hall.

"We checked every other room, but we ain't checked the kitchen yet, an' take a look!" Torvald pointed to the end of the corridor.

A gold-maned horse and a dark-maned one stood near the entrance.

"They're in the kitchen," Anborn said.

Yngvi smiled. "That means they're trapped!"

Anborn, though, wasn't convinced. "Yngvi, Torvald, you two check it out. Ralf and I will hang back."

Outraged, Yngvi asked, "Why you hangin' back?"

"Because, you louse, those steeds could be a decoy."

"Oh, yeah, okay." Yngvi nodded. "That makes sense."

Rolling his eyes, Anborn said, "I'm grateful you approve. Now go!"

The two giants lumbered down the hall and entered the kitchen. The two horses backed away from the giants, but Anborn wasn't overly concerned with them.

Ralf pointed back the other way down the corridor. "I'm'na check out the other rooms. They coulda doubled back, bein' so tiny an' all."

Anborn nodded. "Good idea."

As Ralf moved off, Anborn watched the end of the corridor. He was tempted to snatch up the horses, but they were too small to be more than a snack.

Then he heard a resounding crash from behind him. Running toward it, he realized it had come from the dining room.

Entering, he saw that the candelabra had fallen from the ceiling and smashed Ralf on the head.

Gnashing his teeth, Anborn ran back to the kitchen. Bad enough that these Asgardians were making fools of the Frost Giants—now the castle itself was conspiring against them!

Even as he ran down the corridor, however, he heard several more noises in succession.

The clanging of metal on metal.

A cry of pain that sounded like Yngvi.

An exclamation of anger that sounded like Torvald.

The sound of a bone snapping in two.

The same sound again.

Two screams of anguish.

The sound of metal on bone.

And finally, the sound of two bodies colliding against the stone floor.

For a moment, Anborn was torn. He could go to the kitchen to see what had happened to Torvald and Yngvi. Or he could go outside and help Niels and Olav take care of Volstagg, then use the fat one as a hostage to get the other two Asgardians to surrender.

After a moment's thought, he rejected the latter notion. Just because six of his fellow giants had fallen to Hogun and Fandral didn't mean he would. Anborn considered himself to be braver and stronger and wiser than the average one of his kind, and he was quite sure he could deal with two tiny Aesir.

He stormed into the kitchen to see Torvald and Yngvi unconscious on the floor, pots and pans strewn about. There was a strange feeling of warmth in the air.

After a moment, Anborn realized that the latter was due to the giant stewpot—full of water following its use to make lunch, the wood under it was again lit. The water was steaming and roiling. Lunch hadn't been that long ago, so the water was still fairly warm and had already come back to a boil.

Anborn looked around for a sign of Fandral and Hogun, but

saw nothing. That was because they were behind the stewpot, where they were waiting for more giants to enter. As soon as they heard Anborn come in, they pressed their backs against the kitchen wall, braced all four of their feet on the stewpot, and pushed with all their considerable might.

After a few sweat-filled moments, the stewpot finally tipped over, as the pair had hoped it would.

Boiling water sloshed out of the upended stewpot and spilled throughout the kitchen.

As the hot water cascaded over the shelves and pots and pans, and over the unconscious Torvald and Yngvi, Anborn froze. He knew he should have turned to flee the kitchen, but he stood staring at the wave of scalding liquid that was coming right at him.

And then the wave hit him, and all Anborn could think of was the burning heat that seared his flesh as the water struck him.

Screaming with intense pain, Anborn finally turned and ran out of the kitchen, but the water followed him, sloshing into the hallway. Dimly, the Frost Giant noted that the horses were no longer anywhere to be found. The animals had rather sensibly galloped off when they sensed danger. Anborn was apparently not as bright as the horses. Even as he ran down the corridor, trying to get away from the boiling liquid, he realized that he'd been completely outthought and outclassed by the two tiny Aesir.

"Ho, the house!" came a loud voice, echoing from the front

door. It was Volstagg, entering through the outsized door, riding Iron Shanks.

Leaping across shelves to avoid the hot-water-covered floor, Fandral arrived at once near the door and said, "Go around back and meet us outside, Voluminous One!"

Kolr and Gulltoppr were already outside, having found their way out through one of the castle's back doors, and Fandral and Hogun used the rear entrance to the kitchen to attain egress, since the only other exit from the kitchen was covered in a considerable amount of boiling water. While it was merely painful for the giants, the smaller forms of Hogun and Fandral would have had their feet near burnt to cinders.

"I take it," Fandral said as Volstagg arrived at the rear of the keep, "that you took care of the two giants tasked with killing you?"

Volstagg chuckled. "Did you ever doubt it?"

"Every day, my friend." Fandral leavened the insult with a friendly smile as he mounted Gulltoppr. Then he noticed that Volstagg's left foot was bare. "What happened to your boot?"

"Alas, it was sacrificed in order to achieve victory. A small, if irritating, price to pay for another triumph of the Lion of Asgard over those malefactors who would dare to impede his progress in the heroic rescue of the Realm Eternal!"

Hogun climbed atop Kolr. "While you dealt with your two foes, we were able to dispatch the remaining half dozen that followed us back into the castle. But I cannot guarantee their absence for very long."

"And unfortunately," Volstagg said, "while I did question the giant who was still awake, he refused to provide me with Thjasse's location."

Fandral stared at his friend. "How was one awake to be questioned yet did not pound you into the ground?"

Grinning, Volstagg said, "I nailed his feet to the ground with petrified oak, of course! How else?"

Fandral honestly had no idea whether Volstagg was telling the truth. "How else indeed," he muttered, shaking his head and deciding that it didn't really matter.

"In any event, I doubt the other giants will be any more forthcoming than he."

Hogun stared at the ground behind the castle. "They will not need to be. Behold—tracks made by a giant's foot."

"And deep ones," Fandral added, noticing the bootprints that Hogun was staring at. "Even I, whose tracking skills pale before yours, Grim One, can see that."

"They are deep indeed—no doubt because Thjasse travelled while encumbered by a sack filled with Golden Apples."

"Then let us away, my friends," Fandral said. "Time runs short, and Asgard requires that we make haste so we may save it!"

CHAPTER ELEVEN

Thjasse's tracks led the Warriors Three through Jotunheim and toward the Asgard Mountains. The warriors were forced to bed down for the night along the way, each of the trio taking watch for two of the six hours between the making of camp and the breaking of dawn.

Hogun took the first watch, and he stood fast, keeping his eyes constantly in motion about the area. His sight was aided by the fire they needed to survive the frigid, windy Jotunheim night, lit despite the risk that its light would be seen in the darkness.

But he saw nothing throughout the two hours of his watch.

Fandral took the second watch, and he wandered the perimeter of their camp, choosing to use motion rather than proximity to the fire to keep warm. When Hogun had roused him for his turn, Fandral had been dreaming about Helga. Or perhaps it was Ella—upon waking, he could not be sure. He was sure, however, that his slumber would have been far warmer were either—or both—of them present to share his bedroll.

Fandral, too, saw nothing throughout the two hours of his watch.

Volstagg took the final watch, and he somehow managed

to stay awake for a goodly portion of it, which, by Volstagg's standards, was a quarter-hour of the two-hour time period. Fandral, however, had trouble getting back to sleep in any case, so the Dashing One kept his own eyes keen while his friend slumbered.

When dawn came, Fandral kicked Volstagg lightly in the shin of his unbooted leg. "Awaken, hearty Lion of Asgard!"

"Urf, ack, what?" Volstagg looked around quickly. "Why do you kick me so, Fandral? I am merely luring any varlets who may wish to sneak up on us into a false sense of security by pretending to be asleep. Rest assured that, though my lids covered my eyes, my other senses were fine-tuned to a razor's edge."

"The only sense of yours that is so refined is your palate."

"Alas," Hogun said, staring out at the snowy plains ahead, "the night winds have obscured Thjasse's tracks."

Fandral frowned. "Does that mean we can no longer trace him?"

Hogun stared into the distance for a moment before replying. "No, our journey from his castle to here indicated quite clearly what his destination is like to be: Surtur's Gullet."

Volstagg actually quivered at that. "The volcano near the Boiling Plain?"

"The very same," Fandral said quietly. "But why would a Frost Giant go there?"

"Most Frost Giants would not," Hogun said. "But most Frost Giants would not enact a plan as long term as that of Thjasse."

"Long term?" Fandral asked with confusion. "It has only

been a few days, and Asgard has already been brought low by his perfidy. Were it not for our fortune in gaining our supply of apples ahead of time—"

Hogun shook his head. "Asgard was only brought so low because of Loki's spell, which the Trickster cast for his own nefarious purposes. Thjasse could not have known of it. Without that enchantment of Loki's, Thjasse's theft would have taken months to have enough ill effect to matter."

Fandral nodded. "No wonder he has gone into hiding. He no doubt expected all of Asgard to go to Jotunheim to retrieve the apples, not knowing how deeply the loss is affecting all save the three of us."

"And what better place for a Frost Giant to hide," Volstagg added, "than an active volcano? It is truly the last place any would seek him out."

"Indeed," Hogun said, "though I myself have tracked him thus, I can scarce believe that a Frost Giant would take to ground there. Which means Thjasse is a foe we cannot afford to underestimate."

"He is also one we cannot afford to waste any more time finding." Fandral spoke with determination. "Let us break camp with dispatch and hie ourselves to Surtur's Gullet with all due haste!"

Disposing of the camp was a matter of only minutes, as the three had travelled across the Nine Worlds together so often that each knew which task was to be performed, and did so with ease and speed.

Off they went through the snowy plains, though snow soon gave way to grass as the temperatures rose, due both to the oncoming day and proximity to the volcano.

By midday, they had reached the base of the volcano. Looking up, the three warriors saw smoke rising from the roiling innards of Surtur's Gullet, and the red glow of lava cascading down the mountainside.

All three horses balked at going farther, as the ground had become too hot to safely traverse.

Hogun shook his head. "The heat is having an even worse effect on the horse's shoes than it would on their bare hooves. We must proceed on foot from here."

Volstagg frowned. "The horse's shoes might be an impediment, but my lack of the same will be likewise, going forward."

Fandral started, "If the Lion of Asgard wishes to withdraw from the battle and—"

"Fie upon you, Fandral, I wish no such thing! Volstagg the Voluminous would never shy away from a fight! Surely after all these centuries you know me better than *that*!"

"Surely, indeed," Fandral said with a grin.

They secured the horses to a withered oak tree that nonetheless had a stout enough trunk to keep the horses in place. Hogun watered all three horses, and Fandral gave them each feed from their bags.

And then the warriors proceeded on foot toward the great volcano.

Hogun took point, his mace out and at the ready.

Fandral followed, Fimbuldraugr drawn and prepared to strike at the foul giant.

Volstagg took up the rear, wincing and crying, "Ow! Ow! Ow!" every time he put his left foot down on the hot earth.

As they started up the incline of the mountain, they heard a voice. "I'm impressed."

It was Thjasse. He stood in the mouth of a cave partway up the volcano—one that was lofty enough to give him the high ground.

Fandral held his sword above his head. "We have come for the Golden Apples!"

Thjasse chuckled. "Have you now? I must say, I had heard stories of Hogun's ability to track, but I did not lend them credence until now."

"How do you know," Volstagg said, "that we did not learn your whereabouts from one of your subjects?"

"Because I told only Anborn where I was, and I told *him* I was hiding the apples in a cave in Skartheim. So even if you did manage to get him to betray me, his words would have done you little good."

"Very clever," Hogun said. "Though it does not speak well of your leadership abilities that you need to lie to your underlings."

"It speaks very accurately of those underlings, sad to say. Regardless, I would advise you to return to Asgard now, if you wish to save yourself the humiliation of dying on this volcano."

As if to accentuate the point, the ground rumbled. Fandral and Hogun held their ground, but Volstagg—who had most of his weight on his right foot in any case—lost his balance and fell.

Even as the Voluminous One struggled to rise from the warm rocks that made up the mountain, Fandral said, "Our charge comes from Odin himself—to return with the Golden Apples. We will not depart without them."

"Then you will not depart," Thjasse said.

Lava flowed down the volcano from above. Hogun feared it would arrive at the base of the mountain very soon, making a difficult situation worse. He wondered how the Frost Giant had endured, accustomed as he was to the frigid climes of Jotunheim.

Still, they were well to be done with this business before the lava arrived. So he leapt into battle, Fandral right beside him.

Armed only with lava that had cooled to a solid state, Thjasse kept the warriors at bay by the rather simple, yet very effective, method of throwing rocks at them.

Fandral dodged one projectile, and Hogun avoided a second.

"You'll run out of rocks eventually, Thjasse," Fandral said.

"Not before you run out of stamina, Asgardian."

Hogun immediately took a more circuitous route up the mountain, climbing up an outcropping that was hidden from Thjasse's view, and which provided a small measure of protection.

Fandral, for his part, kept to the more direct approach, charging straight up, nimbly dodging Thjasse's projectiles.

As for Volstagg, he eventually was able to get back to his feet, but moving proved difficult, as he was more or less forced by the rising temperature of the earth to move only on one foot, as the rock was becoming too hot to put his unshod left extremity down. And there were fewer warriors in the Nine Worlds less suited to hopping than the Lion of Asgard.

When Thjasse tumbled another stone down the mountain, Fandral was forced to hug the rock. He could feel the rising temperatures, and looking up, he saw the lava oozing from the volcano's mouth high above.

Out of the corner of his eye, he saw Hogun emerge from his hiding place, and Fandral knew that he had to distract Thjasse, lest the Frost Giant see Hogun coming from the side.

Fandral did a quick flip to bring himself closer, landing right at Thjasse's feet, then with another mighty jump, alighted atop the giant's shoulders and thrust Fimbuldraugr downward toward the giant's neck.

Even as he did so, Hogun leapt from the side, moving to strike Thjasse upon his massive leg with his mace.

While Thjasse was easily able to swat Fandral from his shoulder, he had been distracted long enough that Hogun's blow struck true.

Angrily, Thjasse kicked at Hogun, sending the Grim One tumbling backward across the plateau.

Fandral tumbled through the air thanks to Thjasse's swatting, but managed to gain purchase on an outcropping of the mountain itself. That, however, proved unwise, as the rock was even hotter this high up, and he was forced to let go and fall to the plateau. He landed badly, putting one of his hips seemingly out of joint. He collapsed on the ledge.

But it was more than that. As he fell, a great change came over him—tremendous fatigue and sudden pain fell over his body, seemingly out of nowhere.

At the same time, Hogun tried to clamber to his feet, but his back locked up and he was unable to move.

"The spell!" Fandral cried. "It has worn off!"

Hogun wanted desperately to curse Loki for his poor timing, but for once, he was unable to blame the Trickster. Loki had in fact warned them that the spell would wear off eventually, and that he could not determine when that would be. Had they not been delayed by Storm Giants, dwarves, and trolls, they might have been done with their mission before the previous nightfall, but the tiresome delays had timed the inevitable reversal of Loki's enchantment most inconveniently.

Unfortunately, that left Fandral and Hogun—and Volstagg, if he ever made it this far up the volcano—at the Frost Giant's mercy.

Fandral tried to get to his feet, but he found that he was too weak and injured to stand. He feared he had done significant damage to his hip.

Hogun found just the act of attempting to move to be impossible, as pain radiated from his lower back through his entire body.

For Thjasse's part, he was chuckling. "And so it ends. Obviously, Thor is still recovering from the injuries inflicted by my predecessor, or he would have been charged with the return of the apples. Neither Sif nor Balder are here, nor the Einherjar nor the Valkyries. That Odin sent the three of you, who are so easily injured, bespeaks the All-Father's desperation. Indeed, I expected far better from you Aesir."

A voice came from the bottom of the mountain. "You are the beneficiary, Thjasse, of good fortune." Volstagg had torn the sleeve off his tunic, found a flat bit of cooled lava, and used the ripped cloth to tie the lava to the bottom of his left foot so he could still walk.

"And how is that?" Thjasse said, amused at the sight of Volstagg's dishevelment.

"You see, Loki bespelled the apples so that he might, at some future date, steal them. When they were taken from Idunn, all those who feed upon them felt months' worth of ill effects of not consuming the apples in a matter of hours. Only we three were temporarily spared, with help from a second spell of Loki's."

From his prone position on the mountain, Fandral said, "But that spell appears to have worn off."

Thjasse reared his head back and laughed. "Oh, what an excellent jest! I had planned, once enough time had passed and Asgard was laid low, to take your city. Now, thanks to the Trickster, that goal has been hastened. I intend to flay Loki alive, but I must remember to thank him for his service before doing so."

As Thjasse spoke, Volstagg climbed the mountain. It was a slow, laborious process, hampered by his putting more weight on his booted right foot than on the left, unshod one. "You may have lost Fandral the Dashing and Hogun the Grim as opponents, but you still have to contend with Volstagg the Voluminous!"

"It requires little effort to 'contend' with you, fat one." Thjasse pointed at Volstagg with an accusing finger. "Fandral is known throughout the Nine Worlds as the finest swordsman in Asgard. And when Hogun spies his foe, he does not rest until that foe in vanquished. But Volstagg? He is known throughout the Nine Worlds as the finest boaster in Asgard, and when he spies a full dinner plate, he does not rest until it is empty. And you, too, have been impaired by the expiration of Loki's counterspell. What do I possibly have to fear from you?"

Grunting as he oh-so-slowly ascended the volcano, Volstagg said, "The mistake you make, Thjasse, is the reason for those tales. Yes, these last few centuries, I have been a figure of fun, known far more for my prowess in the dining hall than on the battlefield. But I am older than my fellow warriors. I was the most decorated war chieftain in Thrudheim. I'd seen more than my share of battle before most of today's warriors of Asgard were in swaddling clothes."

Volstagg paused in his speech, but not in his climbing, as the rock was particularly difficult at this point. For his part, Thjasse simply watched the Lion of Asgard, amused greatly by his struggle to ascend.

"True, I prefer to tell boastful stories and eat good food, but war is a young man's game. And unlike my fellows—or Thor, or Balder, or Heimdall, or Sif—I have a family. I would much prefer to return home to tell my children tales of my adventures than to have someone else go to my home to tell my children of how their father fell in battle."

As he grew closer, Volstagg checked to make sure that the two slivers of petrified oak that he'd brought with him from the castle were still wedged into his belt.

"But you, Thjasse, have made one of the classic blunders! You believe that the tales of my indolence and incompetence are due to the Lion of Asgard being incapable of fighting as a proper warrior of Asgard, when in fact, those tales derive from a lack of desire to engage in unnecessary bloodshed. I have had my fill of that."

Volstagg clambered onto the plateau that contained the entrance to the cave, which was barely large enough for Thjasse to stand upright in, though positively cavernous as far as the Aesir were concerned.

Volstagg stood facing Thjasse, the latter leaning forward and looking dismissively upon the former.

"But you have threatened all of Asgard with your actions! What's more, you threaten my family! And that is something I will *not* tolerate!" With that, Volstagg grabbed a sliver of petrified oak from his belt, held it up over his head, and rammed it into Thjasse's foot.

It cut through the giant's foot as easily as it had Niels's.

Thjasse cried out in even greater agony than Niels had, and Volstagg took advantage of that distraction to shove the other shard through the other foot. Both shards rooted Thjasse to the spot, just as Niels had been.

Pinwheeling his arms, Thjasse tried to maintain his balance, but he fell forward.

Volstagg backed up as Thjasse fell, positioning himself at the bottom of the arc that Thjasse's head was making, his feet still pinned to the rock.

Rearing back a single fist, Volstagg, with all his strength, punched Thjasse in the giant's jaw. The force of the impact snapped Thjasse's head and torso backward, and he crashed onto the ground at the cave entrance on his back, his knees bent while his feet remained pinned.

Though it was a reedy laugh due to the great pain he was in, Fandral nonetheless chortled and said, "Well played, old friend!"

But Volstagg was uncharacteristically unwilling to accept the praise, or even acknowledge it, instead waddling as best he could with only one properly shod foot into the cave itself.

Moments later, he came out carrying two Golden Apples in one hand, while eating a third with the other.

Hogun was too distant, so Volstagg tossed him an apple. The Grim One caught it unerringly and immediately took a bite.

Fandral was close enough that Volstagg handed him his apple, and taking it eagerly in hand, Fandral said, "I must confess to being dazzled, my old friend. I don't think I've been so surprised or impressed with your actions since you single-handedly routed those Ice Giants on the road to Fenris's lair all those centuries ago."

"As am I," Hogun said after swallowing his first bite of the restorative fruit. "You must have been struck as infirm as we, yet you climbed that mountain."

Volstagg chuckled. "Pray, Fandral, Hogun, have either of you truly *looked* at me of late? You may both be fit and trim warriors under normal circumstances, but Loki's original spell brought you low with appalling ease, as you are both unaccustomed to adjusting yourselves to account for an infirmity. I, however, have become a physically unfit warrior, and have made such adjustments for millennia now. I am quite used to fighting while not at my peak."

After taking four bites of the apple, Fandral found himself able to move his hips without pain, and he gingerly got to his feet. He also laughed with more authority at Volstagg's words. "Of course."

Hogun shook his head as his back healed enough to allow him to walk again. "That does not explain how you were able to render Thjasse insensate with but one punch."

"Look around," Volstagg said. "More to the point, feel the wretched heat. I can assure you, having just entered it to retrieve three apples, the cave is even hotter. Nothing withers a Frost Giant's resolve more than heat, and Thjasse chose this as a bolt-hole—not a defensive headquarters. He intended to remain here alone until the effects of the apples' theft became apparent."

Fandral nodded. "That explains why he was simply throwing rocks. A giant should have had a more viable strategy at his disposal."

"But he was weakened by the heat, of course," Hogun said,

rubbing his chin thoughtfully. "That also explains why he kicked at me so weakly. Well deduced, my friend."

"Naturally! After all, the Lion of Asgard is no fool! Now come, recover your strength swiftly, for the lava flows ever faster toward our position, and I would prefer to be elsewhere when it arrives. Once we retrieve the remaining apples from the cave, we may at last hie ourselves back to Asgard and save the day!"

CHAPTER TWELVE

Three days later, Asgard saw a feast unlike any it had seen in a thousand years.

Getting to that feast, however, took some time for the three warriors. Iron Shanks was the only horse strong enough to carry the Golden Apples, but he couldn't do that *and* take Volstagg, so the Lion of Asgard was forced to go on foot—and one boot. That slowed their progress considerably. But they were able to take a shortcut through the Asgard Mountains, and couldn't go much faster than a slow walk in any case, so Volstagg's inability to ride was not much of an impediment.

What *was* an impediment to Fandral and Hogun's sanity, as usual, was Volstagg's boasting. Bad enough that he exaggerated his exploits when he retold stories, he now had a story that required no embellishment whatsoever to be impressive—and yet he did so anyway! Worse, neither could legitimately complain because Volstagg's service had been so valuable.

By the time they entered the gates of the Realm Eternal, though, they were ready to complain regardless. However, by then, everyone was glad to see them. Heimdall's eyesight was failing, but even he could see their approach, and he met them at the gates, with a bleary-eyed Odin and a scared-looking Hilde trailing behind.

Immediately, Fandral gave an apple to Odin, while Hogun gave another to Heimdall. Meanwhile, Volstagg clutched Hilde to his bosom. It was impossible to say who was more grateful to see the other, father or daughter.

It wasn't until after they broke the embrace that Hilde asked, "What happened to your boot?"

"A casualty of the battle, sadly, but while I lost a boot, I gained a victory—for the boot sacrificed itself in order to bring down a mighty giant!"

"Please, Hilde," Fandral said plaintively, "do *not* get him started."

"On the contrary," Odin said, "I would very much like him to start—and finish with the tale of how the apples were restored."

Hilde practically squeaked with joy. "All-Father! You sound like yourself!"

"Of course I do," Odin said with a small smile. "Whom else would I sound like?"

"Well, the story is quite an impressive one, All-Father," Volstagg started.

But Hogun interrupted. "And it is quite a lengthy one, so perhaps we should distribute the apples before telling the tale?"

A voice came from the distance. "I will see to that!"

Idunn approached the city gates slowly, using a cane to support herself. She had been just as affected by the loss of the apples as everyone else, and she could no longer move quickly.

"I will require help from those who have already consumed the apples," Idunn said with a look at the Warriors Three and Heimdall.

"Not Heimdall," Odin said quickly. "The guardian of the Bifrost should return to it posthaste now that the full capacity of his senses has been restored."

"That is wise," Fandral said. "Word of Asgard's weakness is spreading throughout the Nine Worlds, as in addition to Thjasse's band of Frost Giants, we also encountered renegade dwarves, Storm Giants, and trolls who spoke of their ambitions to strike the Realm Eternal while it was weakened."

Turning to Heimdall, Odin said, "Assume your post."

Nodding, Heimdall said, "With pleasure, Lord Odin."

As Heimdall moved off, Idunn doled out assignments, sending each of the Warriors Three, as well as Hilde, to a different region of Asgard to distribute the apples.

Hilde insisted on being the one to give Thor and Sif their apples. However, they were her second and third stop—her first delivery was to the blacksmith, so that he and his children could recover from their illness. Hilde also assured Yngvild and Erika that the dragon had been defeated by her father, and Yngvild admitted that maybe Alaric wasn't that bad a boy after all.

Odin insisted that Loki's keep receive the apples last.

It took the better part of a full day, but eventually all of the Aesir received their share of the apples, and after another day, normality was restored.

The apples did wonders to accelerate the healing process

of both Thor and Sif, to the point that when Odin declared a feasting day, the Healer Royal pronounced them well enough to attend (as long as they didn't overdo it).

And so, three days after the Warriors Three had returned triumphantly from Surtur's Gullet with the Golden Apples, the Aesir gathered in Valholl, the great mead hall of Odin. Only the most important celebrations were held in this hall, and this celebration lasted an entire day and night.

Most of Asgard's citizenry crowded into the hall—eating, drinking, toasting, and celebrating. Dozens of tables were crammed together with benches on either side, and dozens more Aesir squeezed into them.

Only the center was left open, for dancers who came out to entertain: men and women of Vanaheim who performed an elaborate form of an art from Midgard known as belly dancing, and who were accompanied by a drummer on a doumbek.

In the rear of the Valholl was a raised table, at the center of which sat Odin, with Frigga to his right and Thor to his left. The thunder god moved gingerly, but his laughter was as strong as ever as he enjoyed the company of his dearest friends and family.

To Thor's left sat Sif—who could still walk only gingerly—and Balder. The seat on the end next to Balder remained empty. Loki had been invited, and if he chose to show up, he would be seated there. To Frigga's right sat the Warriors Three.

Throughout the feasting, people came to the All-Father's table. Some approached Thor or Sif to ask after their health.

Others queried Balder as to why he had been in Nornheim so long—usually waggling their eyebrows on the subject of the Brave One's relationship with Karnilla.

Most people, though, came to the other side of the table, eager to hear the story of how Hogun, Fandral, and Volstagg had saved the Realm Eternal.

Hogun simply ate silently and enjoyed the revelry, leaving Fandral to tell the true story of what happened and Volstagg to embellish the tale beyond all recognition.

"Naturally," Volstagg said at one point, "when Loki's counter-spell failed, it was left to me to finish the job. For while Hogun and Fandral were brought low by infirmity, I leapt into action, for the Lion of Asgard is made of sterner stuff."

Fandral leant over and stage-whispered, "In truth, Volstagg is so accustomed to being slovenly that the weakness brought upon by losing the apples' magick was of little regard."

"*If* I may continue," Volstagg said haughtily. "With one mighty leap, I bound my way up to the cave mouth and faced Thjasse, taking the petrified splinters I'd removed from Jotunheim and using them to pin his feet to the floor."

"Leap? You foul braggart," Fandral said with a hearty laugh, "you climbed. Slowly. As I recall, your ascent took several *days*."

Volstagg sniffed. "You exaggerate—my climb only took a few minutes."

"Well," Fandral said, "if any would know an exaggeration when he heard it, it would be you. And now, you *do* admit that you climbed?"

After the story ended, Frigga leant over to Volstagg. "I must commend you for the job you and Gudrun have done with Hilde. She was quite impressive on our sojourn to the Vale of Crystal, Sif had nothing but praise for her assistance in Flodbjerge, and I truly believe that Odin would have fallen to pieces without her aid."

Volstagg's haughty arguments with Fandral and his boasting pride in his own exploits fell away from his visage, replaced with a father's love. "Thank you, Frigga. Your words do this old warrior's heart proud."

"An old warrior, perhaps," Odin said, "but it is the old ones—those who survive, that is—who are the greatest."

"On that," Fandral said, "we may all agree!" And he slapped Volstagg on the back.

Thor turned to Sif and asked, "Why does your brother not feast with us?"

Sif let out a very long sigh. "Heimdall was told many times—by Odin, by myself, by Balder—that he was more than welcome at this feast, but he would not leave his post. He felt it was not adequately stood after the apples were stolen."

"Heimdall is a noble man, true, but sometimes methinks he is too duty conscious."

Sif smiled. "There is no 'methinks' about it, Thor. He's an imbecile." She sighed. "But I admire him and love him as ever I did. If nothing else, I am pleased to see him healed of his weakness. He felt so inadequate without his powerful sight."

Balder spoke up. "As did we all, milady. It was a dark day for

Asgard. I am grateful to see all of us returned to our former glory."

"Yes." Sif shook her head. "Even Lorelei."

"I did hear," Thor said, "that Amora's sister gave Thjasse the ability to change his form to that of Loki?"

"The twit." Sif slammed down her tankard. "I wish there had been some way to deny her the apples as punishment, but Idunn wouldn't hear of it. I would have enjoyed watching her suffer in ugliness for a fortnight."

Before Thor could reply to that—he had very definite feelings about Lorelei, who had seduced him via eldritch means once—Harokin, the leader of the Einherjar, came to the table to report to Thor and Odin.

"Four riders and I hied to Surtur's Gullet," Harokin said, "but while we found the cave that Volstagg described, as well as a considerable amount of blood on the ground at the cave entrance, we saw no sign of Thjasse."

With an amused, sidelong glance at Frigga's end of the table, Thor said, "Are you sure Volstagg's description was accurate?"

Harokin smiled at that. "Well, Hogun did not correct him, so I assumed it to be accurate." The smile fell. "Besides, none of the Warriors Three did bleed on the battlefield, and it had to have come from the giant, for if an Asgardian did so bleed, he would not have survived."

"Well done, Harokin," Odin said. "Please, join the feast."

Bowing, Harokin said, "With pleasure, Lord Odin."

"What think you, my son?" Odin asked.

Thor shook his head. "Thjasse may well have returned to Jotunheim. He is clever, that one, and unlike Hrungnir, he may be able to reverse his fortunes so that his humiliating defeat at our hands will not lead to his ouster. But his ranks are also thinned, and are like to thin further. I doubt we will hear much from that band of Frost Giants for many months."

"I hope you are right, my son."

"Fie!" cried Volstagg from the other side of Frigga. "The All-Father and the thunder god are far too serious! This is a celebration of a great victory!" Getting to his feet rather unsteadily, Volstagg raised his tankard of ale and bellowed, "*Attention the house!*"

Some people quieted down, but the Valholl was still quite loud.

Sif leant over to Thor. "Use the hammer."

"I beg your pardon?" Thor asked.

"*Ho, the house, quiet down, you louts!*"

Rolling her eyes, Sif said, "Volstagg will shout for *hours* otherwise. Just use your hammer."

Thor grinned. "Very well." He pulled Mjolnir from his belt, held it aloft, and summoned a bolt of lightning.

After a crack, a sizzle, and a flash of light in the center of the room (the belly dancers were on a break), suddenly the room was completely silent.

Odin and Frigga both looked angrily at Thor.

Sheepishly, the thunder god said, "'Twas Sif's notion."

Sif snorted.

"Thank you, Thor *and* Sif," Volstagg said. "All those present, raise your tankards!"

A susurrus rumbled through the Valholl as most of the crowd did as Volstagg requested.

"There are many who should be toasted this day, including Loki—"

Boos sounded from the crowd, but Volstagg shushed them.

"Now now, there is much to dislike about Loki, but give him credit. Had he not cast the spell he did, I would not have been able to vanquish the Frost Giants, with the able assistance of my two dear friends, Hogun and Fandral."

Fandral and Hogun exchanged long-suffering glances.

"Another who deserves a toast is Idunn, whose tireless work we often take for granted, but without whom, chaos would surely reign."

Ragged cheers came up the hall.

"And of course, Balder and Heimdall, who continued to defend the Realm Eternal 'gainst all comers, regardless of their physical fitness for the task. Never did they shirk their duty."

More cheers, including Thor's, saying, "Hear, hear!"

"Next, to Thor and Sif. The only way they would shirk *their* duty was if they were prevented by a previous performing of it. Thor did noble battle against Hrungnir and his enchanted armor to save Frigga, and Sif fought not one, but *two* dragons to save the town of Flodbjerge. Never were two warriors more heroic than these two have been of late!"

Again, there were cheers.

"Of course, to Odin and Frigga, the father and mother of all Asgard—indeed, all Nine Worlds, truly. Their guidance, their wisdom, and their leadership inspire us all."

The loudest cheers came for that toast, and everyone assumed it would be the last. Many partook of their drinks, at last.

"And finally," Volstagg said as the cheers and sounds of drinking abated, "I have one more, most important toast to give." He turned to face Fandral and Hogun. "Many centuries ago, in the Bilskírnir, at a feast very much like this one, a quiet boy, a callow youth, and an old braggart were brought together by Thor—and by their own boasts and foolishness. They made a wager, these three, and set out to confront the Fenris Wolf. On that day, we left Asgard three idiots and returned days later as boon companions. I have lived a long life, a storied life." Volstagg grinned. "I've told many of the stories myself, in fact."

A chuckle went throughout the hall.

"But no story is more profound than this: I have never had two greater comrades-in-arms, nor have I had two greater friends than Hogun the Grim and Fandral the Dashing. So here is to you, my friends."

Again everyone raised their tankards, but Fandral and Hogun both stood up and held up their drinks.

Hogun said, "And also to you, brave Volstagg. I had thought I would be alone for all my days after my tribe was massacred. The pair of you showed me otherwise. That is a debt I can never repay."

"All I may add," Fandral said, "is that this *must* be a momentous occasion if Volstagg is being modest!"

More laughter at that one.

"So, lest we continue to be subjected to this oddity, let us all drink our drinks and return to the way things ought to be: Volstagg telling some ridiculous story of his own aggrandizement!"

"Hear, hear!" shouted many of the revelers.

Odin then stood up. "To Fandral! To Hogun! To Volstagg!"

"Skaal!" everyone in the hall shouted, and then they all drank.

"Now then," Odin said as he sat back down, "I believe we were promised a self-aggrandizing story."

Volstagg rubbed his thick, red beard. "Well, there was the time I single-handedly took on Thrivaldi the thrice-mighty."

"*I* was the one who defeated Thrivaldi!" Fandral cried in mock outrage.

"Perhaps I could tell the tale of how I resoundingly defeated the Jinni giant."

"'Twas Thor who accomplished that," Hogun said.

Before Volstagg could say anything, Sif said, "If you claim to tell the story of how *you* saved the Korbinite vessel *Skuttlebutt* from pirates, I will run you through."

"As will I," Balder said, "if you tell the tale of how you rescued Karnilla from Utgard-Loki."

Volstagg bowed his head to Sif and Balder, and then said, "Perhaps I shall tell the tale of when Fandral, Hogun, and I did brave the concrete jungles of the Midgard city known as New

York—with our steed being a yellow metal creature known as a 'taxicab.'"

And so Volstagg told more stories as the feast went on into the night . . .

THE END

ACKNOWLEDGMENTS

The number of people who deserve thanks for this book are legion, and I hope I manage to get all of them in. I will start with the folks at Joe Books: my noble editor, Paul Taunton, as well as Robert Simpson (who first approached me with this), Adam Fortier, Stephanie Alouche, Amy Weingartner, Steffie Davis, and Rob Tokar (who shepherded the plot for this trilogy along, before handing the reins over to Paul).

Huge thanks, as always, to my amazing agent, Lucienne Diver, who kept the paperwork mills grinding and more than earned her commission.

Of course, this trilogy owes a ton to the comic books featuring the various Asgardians that Marvel has published since 1962, and while I don't have the space to thank *all* of the creators of those comics, I want to single out a few. First off, Stan Lee, Larry Lieber, Jack Kirby, and Joe Sinnott, who created this incarnation of Thor and his chums in *Journey into Mystery* #83. Secondly, and most especially, the great Walt Simonson, whose run on *Thor* from 1983 to 1987 (as well as the *Balder the Brave* miniseries), aided and abetted by Sal Buscema and John Workman Jr., is pretty much the text, chapter, and verse of "definitive." Thirdly, Bill Willingham, Neil Edwards, and Scott Hanna, who chronicled a solo adventure for Fandral, Hogun, and Volstagg in the *Warriors Three* miniseries in 2010 (as well as the trio's origin, which the prelude of this novel riffs on). In addition, I must give thanks and praise to the following excellent creators, whose work was particularly influential on this trilogy: Jason Aaron, Pierce Askegren, Joe Barney, John Buscema, Kurt Busiek, Gerry Conway, Russell Dauterman, Kelly Sue DeConnick, Tom DeFalco, Ron Frenz, Michael Jan Friedman, Gary Friedrich, Mark Gruenwald, Kathryn Immonen, Stuart Immonen, Dan Jurgens, Gil Kane, Pepe Larraz, John Lewandowski, Ralph Macchio, Doug Moench, George Pérez, Don Perlin, Keith Pollard, John Romita Jr., Valerio Schiti, Marie Severin, Ryan Stegman, Roger Stern, Roy Thomas, Charles Vess, Len Wein, and Alan Zelenetz.

While these novels are not part of the Marvel Cinematic Universe, I cannot deny the influence of the portrayals of the characters in the Marvel movies *Thor* and *Thor: The Dark World* and in the TV show *Marvel's Agents of S.H.I.E.L.D.* (nor would I wish to deny it, as they were all superb), and so I must thank actors Chris Hemsworth, Tom Hiddleston, Sir Anthony Hopkins, Rene Russo, Idris Elba, Jaimie Alexander, Elena Satine, and especially Zachary Levi, Josh Dallas, Tadanobu Asano, and the great Ray Stevenson, as well as screenwriters Shalisha Francis, Christopher Markus, Stephen McFeely, Ashley Edward Miller, Don Payne, Mark Protosevich, Robert Rodat, Zack Stentz, J. Michael Straczynski, and Christopher Yost.

Also one can't write anything about the Norse gods without

acknowledging the work of the great Snorri Sturluson, without whom we wouldn't know jack about the Aesir.

Finally, I need to give thanks to two web sites that I meant to thank in Books 1 and 2: the Marvel Comics wiki at marvel.wikia.com, and Marvel's official site at marvel.com. The former is an exhaustive source for history, characters, events, and such, and the latter has a superb archive of comics. Both were invaluable research tools in the writing of this trilogy.

Thanks to my noble first reader, the mighty GraceAnne Andreassi DeCandido (a.k.a. The Mom). And thanks to Wrenn Simms, Dale Mazur, Meredith Peruzzi, Tina Randleman, Helena Frank, and especially Robert Greenberger for general wonderfulness, as well as the various furred folks in my life, Kaylee, Louie, and the dearly departed Scooter and Elsa.

ABOUT THE AUTHOR

Keith R.A. DeCandido has a long history with Marvel characters in prose. From 1994 to 2000, Boulevard Books published more than fifty Marvel novels and short-story anthologies, for which Keith served as the editorial director. Keith also contributed on the writing side, penning short stories for the anthologies *The Ultimate Spider-Man, The Ultimate Silver Surfer, Untold Tales of Spider-Man, The Ultimate Hulk,* and *X-Men Legends,* and collaborating with José R. Nieto on the novel *Spider-Man: Venom's Wrath.* In 2005, Keith wrote another Spidey novel, this one a stand-alone book for Simon & Schuster titled *Spider Man: Down These Mean Streets.*

The Tales of Asgard trilogy isn't Keith's first foray into Norse myth, either, having written a cycle of urban fantasy stories set in Key West, Florida, that feature a young woman named Cassie Zukav, a Dís—one of the fate goddesses—who encounters many characters from the Norse pantheon (including Thor, Loki, Tyr, and Odin). Those stories can be found in the online zines *Buzzy Mag* and *Story of the Month Club*; in the anthologies *Apocalypse 13, Bad-Ass Faeries: It's Elemental, A Baker's Dozen of Magic, Out of Tune, Tales from the House Band* volumes 1 & 2, *TV Gods: Summer Programming*, and *Urban Nightmares*; and in the short-story collections *Ragnarok and Roll: Tales of Cassie Zukav*, *Weirdness Magnet* and *Without a License: The Fantastic Worlds of Keith R.A. DeCandido.*

Keith's other work includes tie-in fiction based on TV shows (*Star Trek*, *Supernatural*, *Doctor Who*, and *Sleepy Hollow*), games (*World of Warcraft*, *Dungeons & Dragons*, *StarCraft*, and *Command and Conquer*), and films (*Serenity*, *Resident Evil*, and *Disney Cars*), as well as original fiction, most notably the "Precinct" series of high fantasy police procedurals that includes five novels (*Dragon Precinct*, *Unicorn Precinct*, *Goblin Precinct*, *Gryphon Precinct*, and the forthcoming *Mermaid Precinct*) and more than a dozen short stories. Some of his other recent work includes the *Stargate SG-1* novel *Kali's Wrath*, the *Star Trek* coffee-table book *The Klingon Art of War*, the *Sleepy Hollow* novel *Children of the Revolution*, the *Heroes Reborn* novella *Save the Cheerleader, Destroy the World*, the New York City-based urban fantasy novel *A Furnace Sealed* (first in a series), and short stories published in the anthologies *X-Files: Trust No One*, *V-Wars: Night Terrors*, *With Great Power*, *The Side of Good/The Side of Evil*, and *Nights of the Living Dead* (edited by George Romero and Jonathan Maberry).

Keith is also a freelance editor, a veteran anthologist, a professional musician (currently performing with the parody band Boogie Knights, one of whose songs is called "Ragnarok"), a second-degree black belt in karate (in which he both trains and teaches), a rabid fan of the New York Yankees, and probably some other stuff that he can't remember because of lack of sleep. He lives in New York City with folks both bipedal and quadrupedal. Find out less at his hopelessly out-of-date website, DeCandido.net, which is the gateway to his online footprint.